A Grave for a Thief

Douglas Skelton has published twelve non fiction books and fifteen crime thrillers. He has been a bank clerk, tax officer, shelf stacker, meat porter, taxi driver (for two days), wine waiter (for two hours), reporter, investigator and local newspaper editor. He has been longlisted four times for the McIlvanney Prize, most recently in 2023. Douglas contributes to true crime shows on TV and radio and is a regular on the crime writing festival circuit.

Also by Douglas Skelton

A Company of Rogues

An Honourable Thief
A Thief's Justice
A Grave for a Thief

DOUGLAS SKELTON

A Grave for a Thief

CANELO

First published in the United Kingdom in 2024 by Canelo

This edition published in the United Kingdom in 2024 by

Canelo
Unit 9, 5th Floor
Cargo Works, 1–2 Hatfields
London SE1 9PG
United Kingdom

A CIP catalogue record for this book is available from the British Library.

Ebook ISBN 978 1 80436 551 9
Hardback ISBN 978 1 80436 715 5
Paperback ISBN 978 1 80436 550 2

Cover design by Henry Steadman

Cover images © Alamy

Look for more great books at www.canelo.co

Printed and bound in Great Britain by Clays Ltd, Elcograf S.p.A.

1

Prologue

The men formed from the early morning mist as though they were elemental creatures.

They were on horseback, fanned out like skirmishers ahead of battle. They didn't move. They didn't speak. They merely waited. The only sounds the snort of a horse as it pawed at the hard-packed earth, the tinkle of the brook behind them and the whistles and warbles of the birds singing to the dawn.

The woman's musket was already to her shoulder as she emerged from the farmhouse, for she knew this was no social visit. These men did not make social visits. When they showed themselves, it was far from social. A child's face, her son, peered from behind the slightly gaping doorway. The woman immediately picked out their leader, who swept his hat from his head as if paying court.

'Good morning,' he said.

'You are not welcome here,' she said, wasting no time on niceties.

'Nonetheless, here we are,' he said, returning his hat to his head. 'Where is he?'

'Where is who?'

'Come, madame, let us not play games, we are too far down the road for that. We want him and we shall have him. He is long overdue to face justice.'

'There is no justice in this place.'

The man smiled, his features growing ever clearer as he leaned forward in the saddle. His manner was relaxed, conversational. He was handsome and he could feign charm but there was an ugliness about him that she knew well.

'Not justice then. Perhaps the correct word is vengeance. Now, madame, we shall delay no further. Where is Jonas Flynt?'

Part One

London

1

Many days earlier

Blackheath

The sun was dying but clung to the sky as if unwilling to be laid to rest. Golden fingers reached out across the heath to gild the outlines of the gorse and the trees, stretching their shadows across grassland rippling under the breath of a soft breeze that came up from the river beyond Greenwich. The air here was sweet, even if the gentleman swinging gently behind Jonas Flynt was not. He had been a highwayman by the name of Bartram Allan, but though Flynt knew of him they had never met and he was unsure if being in close proximity to a lifeless body hanging in chains could be termed a formal introduction. A life on the road required many skills: a steady hand with a horse and pistol; the wisdom to know which coaches to stop and which to let pass; a keen focus on the task at hand, for a moment's thoughtlessness could provide someone with the opportunity to let off a shot. Flynt was most skilled indeed in the art of the high toby, and his mount, Horse not only in species but in name, had served him well on those dark nights. However, the life also called for a plentiful supply of luck and Bartram's ran out with a short drop into eternity. Flynt shivered against the warmth of the summer's eve. He was uncomfortable being this close to the rotting remains of the finishing of the law. That he had left his own days, or rather nights, of land piracy behind mattered nought, for there was no limitation on statute regarding past crimes and the man he was here to meet knew that all too well.

'Does being back on the heath make you long for your old ways, Serjeant?'

Flynt was startled but he covered it by quieting Horse, who had reared at the unexpected sound of Colonel Nathaniel Charters' voice. That the man could move with considerable stealth he was already well aware, that he could make a steed tread on the baked earth as though its hooves were muffled was nothing short of miraculous, but he didn't wish his former commanding officer to know that he had bested him in any way.

Flynt recovered quickly. 'I have given up such pursuits, Colonel.'

Charters eased alongside him and gave the corpse above them a study. 'Very wise, for in the end there be only two ends for such gentlemen of the road, either thus...' He jerked a thumb to the gibbet, '...or accosting a fellow who would rather part with a barrel-load of lead shot than his purse.'

As ever, Flynt understood that this meeting place had been chosen to remind him that Colonel Charters held his life in his hands.

'It is a most bleak location,' Charters observed as he gazed around. 'I can see why you and your fellow brigands would choose it for your work, although it be exceeding pleasant on a summer's eve, is it not?'

Flynt did not comment.

'It has seen much history, did you know that, Serjeant? Or were your sojourns here merely professional in nature?'

Flynt was aware of Blackheath's place in history, but he still made no effort to reply.

'They say it takes its name from being a plague pit for victims of the Black Death, but I'm unsure if that be true. The old Roman road of Watling Street ran through here and even now we may walk in the steps of kings and rebels. The second Richard, the eighth Henry, the second Charles upon his restoration all passed through. Those mutinous rascals Wat Tyler and Jack Cade pitched their tents on this very earth before losing their heads for rising against their respective betters. Death to all traitors, eh, Serjeant?'

Flynt had heard enough. 'You did not call me to this place for a lesson in history. You have a task for me, I take it.'

Charters laughed. 'So direct, Serjeant. Have we lost the art of conversation between us? Are we not old comrades? Perhaps even friends?'

'Friends?' Flynt queried. 'That is an odd view of our relationship, wouldn't you say, Colonel?'

Charters' lips twitched and his eyes sparkled with humour, but he said nothing.

'There is a term used in the borderlands of the north,' Flynt continued. 'The robber barons of Scotland and England demand tribute from those weaker than they as payment against the thieving of cattle and such. They call it blackmail, and that is the basis of our relationship. You have a charge of armed robbery and assault that you dangle above my head like a noose. You use it to force me to do your bidding and it is immaterial that I am innocent.'

'You are far from innocent, my dear Serjeant Flynt – or should I call you Captain, as we are currently upon the very ground that brought you such a field promotion, albeit honorary?'

Flynt had been termed Captain by denizens of the flash life – the rogues, the vagabonds, the procurers, the doxies, the crimpers, coiners, dippers and sharpers. It was a measure of respect, even though many highwaymen were as mean and vicious as the basest of footpads.

'I require no rank, as you well know, though you insist on applying them,' he said. 'I have done many things that bear little scrutiny, much of them at your bidding, but I did not rob that coach nor less beat the gentleman.'

7

'I have witnesses who will identify you. And you are well paid for the tasks you perform for your country.'

Flynt exhaled. They had been over this many times and it never changed. The simple truth was that Charters could have him jailed and executed and there was nothing Flynt could do about it. It was also true that he was paid well and that allowed him to walk the path of an honest man, albeit at an oblique angle.

'To the point, Colonel, if you please.'

Charters heeled his horse into motion along the track and Flynt followed, feeling no need to scan the vicinity for sign of the watchful, armed men who always trailed in the colonel's wake. Few people knew that Charters was more than he seemed. Publicly, he was a retired army officer, a hero of Flanders where he left behind an arm, but privately he commanded a small army of agents known as the Company of Rogues, drawn from the streets and the underworld to be used either as informants or as agents in defence of king and country. Flynt often considered how many of those who formed the Company, though he knew not who they were, were also coerced into the work. As spymaster Charters had enemies, and so those watchful, if unseen, armed men would be close enough to act if Flynt took it into his head to move against their employer. He had no intention of doing any such thing. He did not save the man from the blood and mud of battle in order to later kill him.

'It is such an evening that makes one feel grateful to be alive, does it not, Serjeant?' Charters said after breathing in a deep lungful of air. Flynt waited, well acquainted with the colonel's manner. He liked to skirt around each new mission, as if playing with it in his mind. 'How fare your wounds?'

Mention of them made the scars tingle. A bullet wound and various knife slashes, all received during an encounter on the frozen Thames just a few months before. 'I am fully healed, thank you.'

'God was watching over you that night, was He not? Sinner you are, but you are still one of His children.'

Flynt did not reply. It was not a deity who had dragged him from the frozen water but a man who would cheerfully kill him when the time came. That Flynt now owed that man a debt sat uneasily upon him. As for mention of God, Charters knew he followed no faith and was goading him in the hope of a reaction, for provoking Flynt into a debate, whether it be about politics, the monarchy or the existence of God, was great sport. Flynt resolutely refused to provide him with such entertainment.

'I permitted you these many months to heal, I hope you realise that,' Charters said eventually. 'But I am gratified to know that you are back to your fighting strength, as it were, for – as you have rightly surmised – I have work for you.'

At last they reached the point of the meeting, Flynt thought, but maintained his silence. They allowed their steeds to amble for a few moments.

'Do you not wish to know what that work is, Serjeant?'

'I have learned that you will tell me in your own good time, Colonel. Prompting you would be like trying to extinguish the Great Fire by blowing upon it. In the end a waste of breath and all I'd succeed in doing is fanning the flames.'

Charters' lips twitched in amusement. 'Your travails have not wounded your tongue, Serjeant. The tender ministrations of Miss St Clair have sharpened your wit.'

'Belle is a fine woman.'

'So I understand, although I have not had the pleasure myself.'

Once again, Charters was telling Flynt that even though there had been no contact for some time, he had kept a close watch on him. Belle St Clair had indeed spent a great deal of time with him as he healed, or at least as much as her owner Mother Grady would allow.

'The work, Colonel,' Flynt nudged, having no further desire to discuss his wounds or the nature of his relationship with Belle, which was complex to say the least.

9

'Ah, yes, the work. To business, quite right, Serjeant. The affairs of this great nation wait for no man, am I right? And this particular affair has waited far too long, I fear.'

'What do you wish me to do? Rob someone, cheat someone, kill someone?'

Flynt had done all three in Charters' service.

'Find someone,' Charters replied.

'Who?'

'A Mr Christopher Templeton.'

'And what interest do you have in this Mr Christopher Templeton?'

'A great deal of interest, Serjeant, a very great deal.'

'Who is he?'

'He is a lawyer.'

'And for whom does he practise?'

'He has one client and one client only.' Charters let that rest for a moment, as if waiting for Flynt to ask the name of the client. When the query was not forthcoming, he smiled. 'Really, Flynt, this lack of curiosity of yours does cause me to question whether you have the mettle to be an investigator.'

'You are free at any time to dispense with my services, Colonel.'

Charters' smile thinned. 'Perhaps not a day for which you should wish, my friend.'

Flynt sighed, weary of the threat being hung like a Damoclean blade.

'As to Templeton's client,' Charters said, 'I should think you would be very interested, for he worked for the Fellowship.'

Flynt was interested enough to bring Horse to a halt. 'Templeton is Jacobite?'

Charters allowed his mount to walk on a few paces before he wheeled it round. 'No, he is not, and neither is the Fellowship. I have learned much since you first encountered them, even though that encounter was at a distance, through Lord James Moncrieff, who, as you recall, went to his reward at Sheriffmuir.'

Flynt did recall, for he was the one who had sent the Scottish nobleman to hell on a ridge above the Scottish battlefield. Good and decent men had died that day, but Lord Moncrieff was not of their number. 'He denied being part of the Fellowship.'

Charters wiggled his head in a seesaw manner. 'Perhaps he was, perhaps he wasn't, but thanks to your pistol ball we shall never know. However, I have reason to suspect that his son is entrenched most deeply with the organisation, the current Lord James Moncrieff – dear God, I do wish these people would stop naming their offspring after themselves, it can become so very confusing.'

'Coming from Nathaniel Charters, the third of his name, that seems ironic, don't you think?'

Humour shone in the colonel's eyes. '*Touché*, Flynt. There's that tongue of yours again. I do believe you are indeed ready to get back to work.'

'So if the Fellowship is not Jacobite, what is it?'

'Their true purpose remains unclear, but what I know is that they are a decidedly shadowy group of men who wish to garner power and riches by any means necessary. If that entails destabilising a country by supporting sedition, then so be it. If it means murder, assassination, manipulation of events, providing financial support and patronage to politicians, then they will do it. I do believe there may also be criminality involved. Christopher Templeton knows many of their secrets and I would have them.'

Flynt considered pointing out that the Company of Rogues was guilty of many of the acts Charters had outlined but held his tongue. Instead he said, 'I take it you have lost this lawyer.'

Charters affected a crestfallen expression. 'Alas, it be true. I was having him watched but not everyone in the Company is as capable as you. He has vanished from his lodgings to a destination unknown.'

'What makes you believe he wishes to talk to you about the Fellowship?'

'He communicated with me some months back, anonymously, and hinted that he wished to cleanse his conscience. However, he has been slow in making such reparations, although he made contact three times, each time telling me little but enough to maintain my interest.'

'How was the contact made?'

'By letter, unsigned and hand-delivered to my home, which suggests some level of knowledge, don't you think? As you are aware, the existence of the Company is known only to very few, and my role in it to even fewer. For this lawyer to have such intelligence of my true function, not to mention where I live, was at once interesting and alarming.'

'If contact was made anonymously, how did you discover his identity?'

'I have means of investigation at my disposal other than your good self, Serjeant. My work does not rely solely on your particular abilities.'

'And yet, you lost him.'

An explosive laugh burst from Charters' lips. 'Quite so. I had a man set up surveillance over five nights, watching for another hand-delivered note. It duly came and the deliverer was followed, intercepted and the name of the person who had employed him gleaned. Templeton had been canny enough to use a further two intermediaries and the chain was followed until his identity was revealed. Our quarry remains unaware that I know of his identity, of that I am sure.'

'Then why would he vanish?'

'That's what I wish you to discover. And also to trace him, then use your considerable powers of persuasion to bring him to my embrace.' Charters reached into the cuff of his empty sleeve to produce a slip of paper, which he held out towards Flynt. 'You'll find his last known address there. I suggest that is where you begin.'

Flynt took the paper and glanced at the address. Templeton lived in Crane Court, off Fleet Street. Flynt folded the paper and would have placed it in his pocket, but Charters held out his hand for its return. He was a very careful man. Flynt passed it back and it vanished into the man's sleeve once more. He had no doubt it would later be burned.

'Why not have this other agent of yours continue?'

'Because I wish you to do it. You have encountered the Fellowship, at arm's length to be sure, and given Lord Moncrieff's involvement you have a personal stake in the game, thanks to your despatch of Moncrieff the elder.'

Lord James Moncrieff, the younger. Flynt's personal stake, as Charters put it, ran far deeper than killing the man's father. 'You are certain Moncrieff is of the Fellowship?'

'I am certain of nothing, but I harbour deep and abiding suspicions. More importantly, however, you possess a particular brand of ferocity that it may be necessary to employ before this game has run its course.' Charters pulled on the reins to guide his horse along the track again, then said over his shoulder, 'Welcome back, Serjeant. You have been missed...'

2

Flynt believed in the idiom that there was no time like the present, so even though it took him over two hours to walk Horse back to the city from Blackheath, the light fading all the way, he carried onwards from Legate to cross the bridge over the Fleet River, its stench rising like hands from hades, and then onto Fleet Street itself. The storefronts were all closed but the taverns and brothels still enjoyed a bustling trade, so the streets were thronged with gentleman and beggar mixing with cutthroat and courtesan. He dismounted on the north side of the street, close to Fetter Lane, at the narrow entranceway to Crane Court, where a lamp burned, signifying that members of the Royal Society were in late session. He led Horse through the passageway which then opened up into the courtyard itself, bound on two sides by three-storey terraced properties and, at the far end, the Christopher Wren-designed building that housed the Society. Flynt studied the illuminated windows with interest. Beyond those casements the greatest minds of the day were in congress, cogitating upon science, mathematics, medicine and philosophy. Flynt, however, was not here to consider such lofty matters.

The rooms formerly occupied by Christopher Templeton were in a house to the right of the court's entrance, the front door standing at the head of two stone steps, a lamp burning above it. A chink in the drapes of the ground floor apartments revealed some light so he dropped the reins, knowing that the mare would not move until he instructed her, and climbed to the door where he took a metal knocker in hand, rapped it twice and then waited. His gaze again drifted to the building that formed the far end of the rectangular space, from which three men had emerged and were engaged in conversation. He wondered idly what it was they would be discussing, whether it would be science or natural philosophy. Perhaps, however, they were deciding which tavern or whorehouse to visit now that their worthy matters had been exhaustively debated within and were intent on more earthly pursuits. Even learned men had itches that had to be scratched.

The door opened to reveal an elderly man, his thatch of white hair tousled, thrusting a lantern in one hand towards him to illuminate his face. The other hand was hidden behind the door holding, Flynt surmised, a weapon. London was a dangerous city, especially after dark, and precautions never went amiss. The man wore a slightly threadbare silken gown so was clearly preparing for bed. A lava cameo bearing the profile of a handsome woman hung around his neck. He saw Flynt's eyes resting upon the item and with some irritation tucked it away under the folds of his gown, as if another person seeing it was a violation of his privacy.

'Who are you, sir, and why do you knock my door at so ungodly an hour?'

In Flynt's world, the hour was not so late, but he did not argue the point. He swept off his hat in a bid to appear less threatening. Courtesy was required at all times, until the time came not to be so courteous. 'I apologise for the intrusion, sir, and the lateness of the hour, but I seek an old friend, Mr Christopher Templeton. I believe he has rooms here.'

The man's face creased in irritation. 'Templeton again? This is damnably vexatious. How many more old friends will have the impertinence to present themselves at my door?'

That others followed this trail was no surprise. 'How many such inquiries have been made, may I ask?'

'Three, including yourself, though one such intrusion was by a pair of scurvy knaves, and I'll tell you what I told them, that I have no idea where the fellow is. He rented the rooms on my top floor from me, but he was here one day and gone the next, to where I know not.'

Charters' original agent, the one who had lost Templeton, might be one, of course, but Flynt suspected that, given the lawyer's connection to the Fellowship, not all who sought the man would have his best interests at heart. The pair of scurvy knaves were perhaps the seekers of which he should be wary.

'Can you tell me anything of these other men who made inquiry?'

'I paid them little heed, sir, for they were a vexation, as you are, though the duo seemed to be brothers of a likeness so close it was difficult to tell them apart. I sent them on their way. I will not be vexed, sir, not in my own home. Now, I will bid you goodnight.'

He began to close the door but found the manoeuvre impeded by a carefully positioned boot. He looked down at it as if astonished. 'Good God, man, you would vex me further? Remove that limb, sir, on the instant.'

Flynt kept the limb where it was. 'I apologise for the intrusion, but it is of vital import that I find Christopher. We have not seen each other for many a year and I have some news of a relative that would be to his advantage.'

The man's eyes grew interested. 'A close relative, would this be?'

'Not close, but one who has remembered him fondly from his youth and has marked that remembrance in his final testament.'

The eyes took on a gleam that might even have been warm. 'A bequest, eh? Not that Templeton was short of funds as far as I could see, even though he still owed me this month's rent. I suppose any such windfall is welcome, but I am right sorry for his loss.'

He didn't sound terribly sorry for the loss but there was a trace of longing for the unpaid rent. 'Mr Templeton's departure was swift, I take it?'

'As sudden as God's wrath, which I will presently rain upon you if you do not depart from my threshold.'

He stepped back a half pace and revealed the suspected weapon to be a blunderbuss, which Flynt recognised had been manufactured by John Sibley of London, the gunsmith who had made his own brace of pistols. It was a fine-looking weapon of maple and brass, its flared barrels useless at anything other than close quarters. Unfortunately, he and the old man could not get much closer without the banns being read, so should the gentleman choose to discharge it, Flynt would have no opportunity of escape. Nonetheless, he had to press on with his inquiry.

'I regret that I cannot depart until I have some answers.'

'I cannot help you, do you not hear? Your friend gave me no notice of quitting. Whatever the reason, it was of a sudden.'

'Do you know of any other acquaintances, a friend with whom he might have shared his destination, perhaps a lady, with whom he might keep company?'

'By God, sir, you vex me sorely. Do you not see the weapon in my grasp? Think you that I am not capable of wielding it? If that is the case then I assure you I am most capable and have had occasion in the past to wield it, so I would be obliged if you would remove your appendage from my threshold and take your leave.'

He emphasised his remark by jamming the door against the toe of Flynt's boot.

'I apologise, but I would have a response to my query, then you have my pledge that I will leave you to your solitude.'

A low rasp in the man's throat signified his displeasure but he seemed to understand that an answer was required if he was to have any peace. 'Kept himself to himself, did young Templeton. He had some visitors, to be sure, but none that I knew or would wish to know.' The old man's eye drifted towards the scientists now sauntering down the lane towards them. 'Godless heathens, some of them, and damnation awaits them in the afterlife. As I said, he was quiet and fastidious, though this month somewhat tardy with his rent, and apart from exchanging the time of day if we met at this threshold or upon the stairs, I had no society with him. Now, sir, if you have no further questions, I will bid you a goodnight.'

Flynt understood he would glean no further information so removed his foot. The door slammed immediately and two bolts slid into place. He lingered for a moment on the step, reflecting on what he had been told, which was very little. The main point of interest was that others had inquired. Templeton's departure had been so swift that he had not even informed his landlord. It was possible he had become aware of the surveillance and had taken fright. It was also possible the Fellowship had somehow heard of his betrayal and had sent someone to question him. Or silence him.

'You have a fine steed, my friend.'

Flynt had been aware of the slightly stooped man who had detached himself from the trio outside the Royal Society door and who was now admiring Horse, his hat held in both hands as they rested on a long cane. He was dressed well, if slightly untidily, and his thinning grey hair was bereft of periwig. His colleagues had moved to the lane and were exiting to Fleet Street, their conversation continuing in full flow.

Flynt descended the steps. 'She has served me well.'

The newcomer inclined his head as if to study the animal's lines more thoroughly. 'She is a powerful beast. More used to open spaces than these cramped surroundings, I'll be bound.'

Flynt grinned. 'She enjoys a gallop and has the heart and stamina for it.'

The man reached out to caress Horse's flank. 'A fine beast, a fine beast,' he said, absently, and Flynt sensed that the strength of the mare was not what was on his mind. His next words confirmed it. 'Forgive me, but I overheard you inquire regarding Mr Templeton with Saint Roderick.'

Flynt's interest perked. 'Do you know Mr Templeton?'

'I do, as it happens. We often had discourse upon a variety of matters, he and I. Unlike Saint Roderick.'

'Why do you call him that?'

'You must have noticed in your brief exchange that his conversation veers to sanctimony. He likes to think he is the holiest man that ever lived. Faith, I would hazard that he views even Christ himself as something of a sinner. After all, did He not consort with fallen women?' Humour shone in the man's eyes as he glanced towards the window. Flynt followed his gaze and saw Saint Roderick glaring at them through the curtain, which was then jerked closed. 'The irony is that he was a seafarer, captained a slaver working out of Guinea. You saw his weapon?'

'I did. One of Mr Sibley's finest, I would say.'

'Perhaps, but Saint Roderick once used it to quell an on-board rebellion. Cut down the ringleader himself and has never lost a minute's sleep over it. If a charitable thought ever entered that man's head, it would die of loneliness. Not to mention a considered opinion, for the last time he even opened any book other than a navigational manual or Scripture we had a Stuart monarch – and not a female.'

The last male Stuart on the throne had been in 1688. Flynt couldn't envisage not reading anything for that length of time. 'Mr Templeton was more learned, I take it?'

'He was, most well read, for a lawyer. They can quote statute and precedent and this act or that act, but in matters of a wider nature it is my experience that they are most lacking. That said, he proffered stalwart support to me during some difficulties not such a long time ago with a damned German who was wont to claim a theory of mine as his own.'

The words 'damned German' resonated with Flynt, and he realised that the elderly man with whom he was conversing was none other than Sir Isaac Newton, who had accused Gottfried Leibniz of plagiarising his work on calculus. Flynt would have loved to have discussed the affair, which ended only after the

Royal Society published a report that came down heavily on Newton's side. As he was president of the Society, that outcome seemed to be very much as expected. However, he did not have the time.

'I must find Mr Templeton,' said Flynt.

Sir Isaac straightened. 'Ah, yes, the matter of a bequest, I heard. From a distant relative.'

'That is correct.'

The scientist tilted his head backwards slightly and gazed at Flynt as if he was a mathematical problem to be solved. 'I will tell you straight, my friend, I came to know Christopher right well. We dined together, we would share a bottle together, we discussed matters of science and literature together and during the course of such a friendship a fact emerged, a most singular fact, and it was that young Christopher was that rare thing indeed – a complete orphan. No parents living, no siblings, no aunts, no uncles. He was a man adrift on this life without the safety of a raft of blood ties. And yet, sir, here you are, claiming to carry news of a legacy from some relative who, by your testament at that door, held warm thoughts for, by my evidence, a beneficiary who was completely unaware of his or her existence. Now, my friend, would you not agree that it is a most unusual turn of events?'

Newton's mind had not blunted with age, it would seem. Whether or not it was he or Leibniz who had first unravelled the secrets of calculus, the man was no fool, so Flynt didn't trouble himself with concocting any further falsity. He had too much respect for the man's intellect.

'I regret my subterfuge, Sir Isaac, but it is necessary that I find Mr Templeton. I fear he may be in some danger.'

The scientist didn't remark upon the fact that Flynt knew who he was. Perhaps he expected him to know. 'In danger, you say? But not from you?'

'No, not from me, and on that you have my oath.'

Head still slanted back, a sharp mind calculating odds, the scientist made no comment on whether he accepted Flynt's word. 'You are some form of investigator, are you not? Come, sir, do not deny it. I have had experience of such work myself, when warden of the Royal Mint, and I recognise a man who makes his living by asking questions.' His head moved forward again as he studied Flynt more completely, his gaze resting briefly on the silver cane in Flynt's left hand. 'And I would hazard that you do more than that. There is something in your stance, your stillness, that suggests a more than passing acquaintance with physicality. I have seen such before in men of the streets.'

Flynt did not wish to go there. 'I have been engaged to find your friend, Sir Isaac, and that is all I can tell you, apart from to assure you again that I mean him no harm. Quite the opposite, in fact, for there are others who may not place a priority on his continuing good health.'

The words and tone were examined, sifted and weighed. 'And your name, sir?'

'Jonas Flynt.'

'I detect a Scotch brogue in your words.'

'I was born in Edinburgh.'

'And you are educated?'

'As well as I could be, by an aunt. We were comfortable but not wealthy.'

'And your people?'

'My mother died when I was a baby.' The truth was more complex than that, but it was not something Flynt discussed, even with one such as Sir Isaac Newton. 'My father was a mariner, but not like the saintly captain back there.'

'He lives?'

Flynt knew that the man was asking him these questions in order to discern any prevarication, all part of forming an opinion as to whether Flynt could be trusted. 'He does. He has a new family now and owns a tavern.'

'In Edinburgh?'

'It is, off the High Street.'

Newton thought about this. 'Terrible breezy there on occasion.'

'Aye, comes off the Forth and sweeps up to the Castle.'

'Indeed it does.' Sir Isaac had finally completed his computations as to Flynt's reliability. 'For whom do you perform this function, Mr Flynt?'

'I am not at liberty to say, Sir Isaac. There is an element of confidentiality that cannot be breached, even with an individual as eminent as you.'

The man preened slightly at this, for Flynt had heard he was very much aware of his position in society and defended it jealously, the plagiarism controversy being the most recent example.

'Very well, I will take you at your word, for I confess that I have been exceeding concerned regarding my young friend these recent weeks. He has been deeply troubled and no amount of urging on my part would convince him to unburden himself.'

'Troubled in what way?'

'His discourse was dulled, his reasoning distracted. Something weighed upon his conscience, I would say.'

'Did he speak of his work?'

'Only in general terms, no specifics. He knew I was disinterested in the minutiae of law and I would suggest that he had also tired of it.' He corrected himself. 'No, that is not precise. He had grown disenchanted with it, and that is the sadness of it, for a man who grows jaundiced regarding his occupation, is a man who finds life itself disappointing. I would wager, Mr Flynt, that you are a man who enjoys what he does.'

Flynt was not as certain of that but he acknowledged it with an incline of his head. 'It's a living, Sir Isaac.'

'More than that, I think. Some men are born to be what they become, others drift towards it on the tides of fortune. My sense is that you are the former.'

Flynt was uncomfortable with the direction the conversation had taken. He could be prone to self-examination and often felt he came up short, so was unwilling to take that direction now. 'Do you know of any other person in whom Mr Templeton may have confided?'

'I am aware of only one individual with whom he had any regular discourse, although I do not know her personally, but young Christopher did mention her.'

'Her?'

Sir Isaac's lips twitched, perhaps in disapproval. 'I did not condone his connection with her, you understand. I am not a fellow for the ladies. Friends have attempted to embroil me in matters romantic but I have remained a bachelor, for it is my belief that emotion is the enemy of clarity of thought and I need such precision for my work. A man cannot miss what he never had, I find. Young Christopher, however, was not of like mind and this past year or two has been engaged in what I presume to be spirited congress with a lady known as Cheshire Sal, who works from the upstairs rooms of the Cheshire Cheese Tavern. You have heard of this place?'

'In Fleet Street, correct?'

'Wine Office Court, to be precise. This lady entertains her gentlemen friends in a room on the second floor of the establishment, I understand. It was my feeling that Christopher had grown right fond of her, though whether she returned such tender feelings given her occupation I cannot say. He was neither weak-minded nor emotionally stunted, you understand, so I would not go so far as to say that she had ensnared his soul, but men do often find themselves infatuated by women who cannot, or will not, return such affections, don't you find?'

Once again, Flynt declined to comment, for he had been guilty in the past of not acknowledging strong feelings and now paid a heavy price for his failing.

He donned his hat and reached out for Horse's reins. 'I thank you, Sir Isaac. I will find this lady and speak with her.'

'I wish you luck, Mr Flynt, for I am most fond of Christopher. He is a good man, for a lawyer.'

Aye, Flynt thought, a good man who worked for the Fellowship. A contradiction there, but then, he knew himself to be a mass of contradictions. He led Horse towards the passage leading to Fleet Street but Sir Isaac placed a hand on his arm. 'I would not leave such a fine beast in the thoroughfare unattended if I were you. The punishment for horse theft may be death, but it does not deter those who perhaps see such an end as a blessed release.'

Flynt had already been turning this over in his mind. He could pay a boy to keep watch, but who was to say that the lad would not himself make away with her?

Sir Isaac had a solution. 'Leave her here, outside the Society. I have work to do and I will watch over her from my window, and will also ensure the porter is alert to her wellbeing.'

There was sense in the suggestion, so Flynt thanked him and they made towards the building at the far end.

'One thing more, Mr Flynt,' Sir Isaac said as they walked. 'From whom is Christopher in danger? Who is it that means him harm?'

Flynt considered how much to reveal and decided the less Sir Isaac knew the better. He certainly could not mention the Fellowship by name, just as he could not reveal the group for whom he worked. 'That is the issue, for I do not know. All I know is that if I don't find him first then harm may befall him.'

'How can you be certain?'

'You have told me that he acted as if he was a man with troubles. Also, the fact that he has vanished without a word to you, his good friend, suggests he is hiding from someone, don't you agree?'

Sir Isaac's nod told Flynt he had already thought of that. 'But you know not the reason behind the threat?'

'I don't,' Flynt lied, for if threat existed – and he suspected it to be real – it was because he knew too much of the Fellowship's business and they had somehow learned his loyalty was wavering.

'There is much in this world of which we know nothing, and we must discover it, must we not?'

'I think, Sir Isaac, you know more about the world and its workings than most.'

That pleased the man's ego again but he still brushed it away with a wave of a hand. 'I do not know what I may appear to the world, but to myself I seem to have been only like a boy playing on the sea-shore, and diverting myself in now and then finding a smoother pebble or a prettier shell than ordinary, whilst the great ocean of truth lay all undiscovered before me.' They had reached the front of the Society building and he took the reins from Flynt. 'I will tether her to the railings here,' Sir Isaac said, pointing to the metal posts ringing the series of steps leading to the front door. 'She will be in full illumination from the lamp and I assure you will be quite safe.'

Flynt thanked him, then took the scientist's proffered hand. 'I wish you good fortune, Mr Flynt, and that you wade into that great ocean and save young Christopher before this nebulous threat of yours washes over him.'

'I will do my best, I promise you.'

Sir Isaac held his grip for a moment longer, his gaze searching Flynt's eyes. 'I sense you are a most competent individual. If anyone can find him, you can. And I beseech you to keep me apprised on your progress. I can be found in the Society's premises and if not, the porter will know where to reach me. Good fortune, Jonas Flynt.'

3

Access to the Cheshire Cheese was gained, like Crane Court, through a narrow passage off Fleet Street leading to Wine Office Court, a location, as the name suggested, from whence licenses to sell wine were once issued. The nomenclature had been retained, if not the office. The interior of the tavern was a surprise, for with such a narrow entrance it would be expected that it be small and dingy. It was not small, with a number of rooms on the ground and floors above reached by fine-looking staircases, but like most bars it was gloomy, thanks to the ever-present fog of burning tallow and pipe smoke. As the night air was warm the large fireplace was dead, so at least the patrons were spared any billowing smoke from an unswept chimney. The room was sparsely populated, a few men either alone or in groups of two or three, tankards or glasses before them, the guttering candles on the tables bathing their faces in a shifting brown light. Flynt took a moment to study them, nerves alert for any threat, but sensing none. From somewhere beyond this small bar Flynt could hear the sound of a flute accompanying a woman singing a folk ballad about parting lovers. A ragged chorus of voices joined in with the melancholy lyrics at various intervals.

A man whose muscular frame suggested many years of manhandling ale casks and who wore his red hair long and unclasped was stationed behind the bar, both hands resting on the counter as he watched Flynt approach. Although he knew of its existence, Flynt had never before frequented this tavern, so being a stranger, and one dressed in the black of a puritan, albeit with a peacock feather in his wide-brimmed hat, he understood the man's suspicion.

In a bid to be friendly Flynt ordered a glass of the man's best brandy. The prospect of a penny or two profit seemed to dissolve, at least partly, the man's wariness.

Flynt removed his hat and laid it and his cane on the counter near at hand. 'You are the owner of this fine establishment?'

'I is,' said the man, his voice as rough as a badly cobbled street. 'Matthew Goode at your service, sir.' He set a glass filled with a generous measure of brandy on the counter and slid away with practised ease the coins Flynt had laid down. 'You ain't been in here before, has you?'

'I confess it is my first visit,' Flynt said, sipping the liquor. It wasn't the finest vintage but it was pleasing enough to his palate. He drank mostly when he had to, such as in situations like this, when he found it necessary to somehow ingratiate himself. And nothing ingratiated a person with a tavern keeper easier than buying an expensive drink.

'And what brings you here this night, sir?'

Flynt smiled, affecting a bashful air. 'It was recommended that I pay a call to a certain lady who frequents the Cheese.'

Understanding dawned on Goode's face. 'You is here looking for business?'

Flynt nodded, still maintaining the aspect of a man embarrassed by his desires. Goode leaned forward, the prospect of turning further coin banishing whatever suspicions he had retained.

'Which particular lady is it you seek? For there is a number of them what comes by here.'

'I've been given the name Cheshire Sal, for I understand she takes a room above for her services?'

'She do, and she be right popular with gentlemen such as you, her being clean and free of the flapdragon, so you has no fear of coming away poxed. Fine-looking woman, too, if a bit too proud for a whore. She don't lie with just anyone and her charges reflect as such.'

'Then she seems exactly what I'm looking for, for I'm also decided particular with whom I lie.'

'She would most assuredly be what a fine Scotch gentleman like yourself is looking for, sir, on that you has my word.' His expression changed, as if someone had recently told him that the purveying of liquor had been proscribed by law. 'But alas, she ain't here.'

'She is elsewhere tonight then? Would you know where?'

Suspicion returned and Goode reared back a little as if to better focus. 'You is right desperate for a tupping, ain't you? There is other girls what can see to your needs just as expert as Sal and without the airs and graces neither, so it would save you some coin.'

'She came highly recommended. And a fine, proud woman is what I like.'

Goode shrugged his reservations away once again, perhaps sensing that the opportunity to pocket Flynt's cash was dissipating. 'We all has our tastes but, as I says, she ain't here.'

'Will she be here later? I can wait...'

Goode's head shook. 'She ain't been here for two or three nights since. This ain't no buttocking shop, but I do lets the girls use the upstairs rooms because it's better than tupping against a wall outside. I ain't no cock bawd, you understand.'

The man would no doubt take a commission for every cull who was tupped in those rooms, so that did make him a pimp, no matter how much he protested. Flynt didn't challenge him, for he needed whatever information the man had about the woman.

'Does she fail to appear here often?'

Goode did not reply but instead served up a flagon of beer to a pot boy who had requested it. The boy seemed no taller than the jug as he tottered away holding it in both hands. Goode watched him for a moment then warned, 'Spill any of that Stitchbank, lad, and it comes out of your hide.' He turned back to Flynt. 'You asks a lot of questions for a gent what just wants to dip his wick.'

Flynt had already palmed some coins and he placed them now on the bar top. 'Then let this take the place of any further explanation of my interest.'

The coins vanished with equal dexterity as before. 'Can't say Sal not showing up here for work is a common occurrence, no. She's got a few regulars, right popular she is, and they has been asking for her.'

'Do you know where she lives?'

Goode's eyes narrowed. 'Who did you say your friend was what referred you to her?'

Flynt paused only momentarily. 'Christopher Templeton, lives not far, in Crane Court. Do you know him?'

Recognition reflected in the innkeeper's eyes. 'A legal gentleman, ain't he?'

'Aye.'

'Yes, he be one of Sal's regulars. He must have been telling a lot of gents like you about her, because you ain't the first to come here asking after her. Two brothers first off, maybe a week or two since, unpleasant-looking gents and not the type Sal would choose to lie with. And another, just this evening, in fact, stood in that very spot on which you stands.'

Given what Saint Roderick had told him about other men making inquiries, Flynt had half-expected to hear that they had been to the tavern, too. Even so, he stiffened at news of one being here so recently. He shot a glance around the room to further study the other patrons. Goode saw the move and barked out a laugh. 'He ain't here no more. He asked the same questions as you and then he left.'

Flynt turned back and dropped the affable appearance he had hitherto presented. 'What did you tell him?'

Goode's smile faltered as he detected the change in tone and stepped back a pace, his hand reaching under the bar. Flynt peeled back the fold of his coat to reveal his brace of pistols. 'If you are reaching for a weapon, friend, think again, for I will drop you where you stand.'

Goode swallowed but his movements froze. 'You ain't here for no tupping.'

'I'm not here for trouble, either, Mr Goode.' Flynt kept his voice low and even, having no desire to alarm the patrons. 'All I seek is information about the lady Sal and then I will be on my way.' He slowly eased his left hand into his pocket and produced more coins. 'And I will leave this behind.'

He carefully dropped the money onto the bar top, but just as Goode made to snatch them away, placed his hand over them.

'The information first, if you please. Now, the lady – do you know where she lodges?'

Goode shook his head.

Flynt suppressed a sigh. 'What do you know of her?'

'Why do you seek her?'

'I'm paying to ask the questions, not to answer them. Speak, man, what do you know of Cheshire Sal?'

'I already has told you. She's a whore and a choosy one at that. She don't tup just anyone. She likes 'em clean and she likes 'em with manners, like your friend Templeton. Gentlemen, she likes, which is rich for a street drab like her. She uses one of the upstairs rooms, like other girls, when she has the bunce to pay for it, or the cull has. That's where she'd meet your friend. He would wine her and dine her then tup her. Right sweet he is on her, though not sure she returns the favour.'

'And that is all you know of her?'

'That is the size and sum of it, and that's the straight God's honest. I don't ask nothing and they don't tell nothing.'

'These other men, what did you tell him?'

'Same as I'm telling you, though they didn't threaten me with no barkers, not even the brothers and they had the look of those who would. The fellow tonight was a proper gentleman, he was, paid me my due and then left.'

'Describe him.'

Goode laughed again, his initial shock at being threatened now worn off. 'Didn't pay no attention, did I? You know how many coves come and go in here in a single night?'

Flynt leaned forward. 'Try.'

Sensing the menace, Goode took a step back. 'Tall he was, like you, spoke proper well, wore decent duds, like yours. But he had manners, not like you. But what can I expects from a Scotchman?'

Flynt, used to such attitude to his homeland, let the insult slide. 'Accent?'

'I already says, spoke proper well, but he was London, I'd hazard.'

'Hair?'

'Kept his hat on, didn't he?'

'Any scars visible? Anything unique about his appearance?'

'No scars what I could see, and he was hale and hearty. There's maybe two dozen men just like him what come in here of an evening.'

'And the men you thought be brothers?'

'It were days ago, who can recall?'

Flynt tilted his head and Goode got the message. 'Ugly creatures, they were, that's all I can say. If they had spent any more time here, I would be worried about the security of my takings.'

Goode's eyes dropped to Flynt's hand as if willing it to raise. Realising there was nothing further to glean, the coins were revealed and Goode snatched them away. Flynt drained the last of the brandy from the glass as he looked at a stairway, briefly considering searching the rooms but rejecting the idea. He had already alienated the man, no point in giving him good reason to call for help. In any case, he believed he had told him everything he knew. Cheshire Sal wasn't here. Like Templeton, she had vanished. Like Templeton, others searched for her. Flynt felt instinctively that she held the key to where the man had gone. The problem was that the city teemed with women who made their living on the streets and finding one in particular would prove difficult.

Unless you knew people who navigated those same streets every day of their lives.

4

Even though Lord James Moncrieff had not expected to be asked to remain behind after the meeting, he knew the Grand Master would inquire regarding Christopher Templeton.

The meeting itself had been a fruitful one, the agenda full and wide-ranging, and the Fellowship thrived. There were representatives in the large dining room of the grand house in Piccadilly from every branch of commerce, from the British East India Company, the South Sea Company, the Hudson's Bay Company, bankers, financiers, landowners, merchants specialising in tobacco, sugar, furs, slaves, miners who dug tin and lead from the earth. Every man in that room benefitted from the work of the Fellowship, which was what it was designed to do, and every man knew exactly what kind of power the organisation wielded across the world with both government and church.

The men had shared a meal, the talk constantly of profit and power, the twin desires of any commercial enterprise, for what use was the latter if you had not the means to wield it? And the former was only a figure in a ledger unless it was put to use for the furthering of commerce. They were aided in this by the rapacity of the king's ministers, advisers and those who enjoyed his patronage, most of them from his homeland of Hanover, to which he had returned that summer, his son finally being appointed Guardian of the Realm rather than Regent, for the king had little affection for him. Moncrieff, the Grand Master and the council of the Fellowship recognised that the greed of men and women was most conducive to the furthering of their aims, and this flight of hungry Hanoverians, as someone had remarked to him, who had fallen with keen eyes and bended talons on the fruitful soil of England, were ripe for manipulation.

Moncrieff's eyes strayed to the full-length portrait staring down from the far wall of the dining room, that of the Knight Templar known only as Jerusalem Mordicant. He was a shadowy figure, to be sure, much like the brotherhood he created, and his true name was unknown, although it was known that he was born in Scotland and had made a pilgrimage to the Holy Land where he had joined the order. When the French king ordered the Templars be purged in 1307, Mordant had the foresight to escape, taking with him a considerable portion of gold and other riches. He had decamped to the land of his birth, where he set up his own order, calling it merely the Fellowship, and gave himself a title borrowed from the Templars, the Grand Master. But this fellowship was not formed to protect pilgrims to Palestine, nor to defend Christianity against those who would threaten it. Mordicant had been a Templar, but he'd had little interest in spirituality. His passion was for profit – and the power it brought – and the men of the day he gathered around him were of like mind. The men who had attended the dinner were their descendants, perhaps not by blood but certainly in spirit.

In the portrait, the knight was bareheaded, his black hair long and loose, his beard perhaps a little too clipped. He had an armoured helmet under one arm and in the other held a broadsword. His robes were white with a black Templar cross on breast and shoulder, a hint of chain mail hanging towards ankle and on his arms. They had no idea what Mordicant's features had been in reality, so it was rather fanciful. It was a commanding work but Moncrieff was not overly fond of it. It was too flamboyant for his tastes, something in which he found agreement with the Grand Master. They both preferred matters relating to the Fellowship to be *sub rosa* as much as possible, for if they were to continue to prosper then there must be little attention drawn to them. They were the men behind the men who wielded power. They were the shadows that moved in chambers where decisions were made, a whisper in the ear, a gentle nudge in whatever direction was required. That had been Mordicant's wish, for he recognised that the Templar order's mistake was not simply that it had grown too powerful but that it had become too obvious. Philip of France had owed them too much money and had regarded their treasures with avaricious eyes. In order to avoid paying them back, and in a bid to enrich himself, he had ordered them to be arrested and slaughtered. The Pope had also become jealous of the power and influence they wielded and so dissolved the order a few years later. The Fellowship influenced great men but it did so from a distance. They financed governments but through intermediaries. They profited from contracts and wars and civil improvements but at many times removed. And in doing all this they manipulated the world to suit their own pockets. That was the way of it and the way it always would be.

Which brought his attention back to the older man sitting opposite him, the present Grand Master, a man he had known all his life. He too was Scottish, for it was a principal rule that whoever sat at the head of the Fellowship table must have his roots in the country. On the face of it he was the epitome of what the Fellowship should be, no flamboyance, no ostentation. Moncrieff knew such things were anathema to the Grand Master's tastes, for he followed the strict Calvinist dictum of the Scottish kirk. He dressed plainly, outwardly lived simply, even frugally, though in private he did enjoy the finer things in life, for the meal that evening had been exquisite, the port wine they each now sipped was superb, but he had studied well Mordicant's maxim of modesty and restraint. Never boast of your accomplishments, never reveal your hand, never let anyone know how you do business. Moncrieff's father had not been invited to join the ranks of the Fellowship, because the Grand Master thought him too mercurial. Moncrieff the younger was material far more suited to the Fellowship's work. He understood the need for discretion, for subterfuge, for sometimes acting in shadow so as not to attract undue attention, for in sleight-of-hand transactions were often found the greatest rewards. He had also burrowed into the confidence of government, as adviser to Sir Robert Walpole, the First Lord of the Treasury and Chancellor of the Exchequer. Access to such an ear was personally rewarding but would also benefit the Fellowship as a whole.

Moncrieff, the point of his cane on the floor, his right hand resting on its silver wolf's head, his left idly playing with the stem of his glass as it rested on the table between them, waited for the older man to speak. He had been about to leave when he was informed the Grand Master wished a moment alone for private conversation. Some of the older members shot inquiring and even envious glances towards him as he was led back to the dining room. In the Grand Master's public life he had to show subservience, but in the rooms of this great house, and others, he could remove that mask, for here he was the superior figure. Moncrieff felt irritation grow at the lengthening silence, recognising it as mere power play.

Finally, the man laid his glass down. 'The lawyer remains at large.'

Moncrieff cleared his throat a little before he spoke. 'He does, but I will continue to make inquiry.'

'I have tasked men to find him.'

Moncrieff masked his perturbation. 'Who would they be, Grand Master?'

'The Trask brothers.'

Moncrieff knew the siblings to be effective in their own crude way, so was forced to consider how likely they were to interfere with his own arrangements.

The Grand Master let out a sigh that was almost mournful. 'As you are aware, I never met Mr Templeton, but I knew of his work and I held high hopes for him. That work on our behalf was exemplary.'

'He was perhaps granted an excess of trust.'

As the man's heavy-lidded eyes rested upon him, Moncrieff realised he had allowed a trace of criticism to lace his words. The fact was, he did believe that too much stock had been set on Templeton's skills and loyalty, even though his betrayal dovetailed his own plans.

The Grand Master's voice was heavy. 'And we are certain Templeton meant to breach that excess of trust?'

'As certain as we can be. The fact that he vanished as soon as he learned we wished to speak with him suggests it.' Moncrieff hesitated slightly before his next words, unsure if he should venture them. 'He may have fled the city.'

'It is possible.'

It is more than possible, Moncrieff thought.

'I will see that word is sent out to our friends elsewhere for a watch to be kept for him,' the Grand Master said.

The Fellowship had only a few members who knew the extent of their influence, but they had friends across the country who profited from their endeavours. Nobles, merchants, judges, politicians, even clergymen and criminals, formed an intricate intelligence network that could be tapped into whenever necessary. The Grand Master was unaware of it, but Moncrieff had done so recently, for his own reasons.

'And what of the wench?'

'She, too, continues to be elusive,' Moncrieff replied. 'She is either with Templeton, or he has her hid away somewhere.'

'The Trasks will find her.'

Moncrieff felt irritation but he kept it concealed. Setting these outsiders on the hunt was a complication he should have envisaged. His mind ticked over, looking for ways that it could hamper his own plans.

'Women,' the Grand Master sighed. 'They understand that we men are often ruled by what lies between our legs. It is a basic weakness in the male sex, and they use that warm place between their own legs against us. Mr Templeton was a loyal servant to our endeavour until he was entranced by yon strumpet and he found himself a conscience.' He studied Moncrieff for a moment. 'Do you have a conscience, my lord?'

'Not one that troubles me, I can assure you.'

'I am gratified to hear that. Having a conscience in business is rather like having two pricks. You can satisfy one but only by ignoring the other. And women, are they a weakness of yours?'

Moncrieff took a moment to answer. 'I am married, Grand Master, as you know well.'

'I do, but I ask if you have other amorous interests? Do you whore? Do have a lady in high keeping?'

'You ask me these questions, but you already know the answer.'

The Grand Master laughed. 'Aye, you're right. You remain faithful to your wife, and that is most laudable.'

'She is a fine woman.'

'She is. And for that reason I do see greatness in you, for if a man cannot be true to the woman he has not only bedded but wedded, then it shows a propensity to disloyalty. And this brotherhood of ours cannot have disloyalty, hence the task in which you and your seekers are engaged at this moment. And you seem to have it well in hand. I commend you.'

Moncrieff inclined his head slightly, wondering at the man's hypocrisy, for he had a mistress in Edinburgh. 'I thank you, Grand Master.'

He rose but the conversation was not over. 'There's another matter.'

Moncrieff remained on his feet and waited.

'Jonas Flynt,' the Grand Master said, and Moncrieff's muscles stiffened involuntarily. 'You still harbour ill feeling against this man?'

'That is a private matter, Grand Master.'

'Not when it impinges on the work of this brotherhood.'

'It does not.'

'That's my judgement to make.' The Grand Master's voice remained cool but the gaze he now directed across the room warned there could be heat to come.

Moncrieff decided to ignore the warning. 'It is a personal affair and has nothing to do with our enterprise.'

'I know of the personal nature. Your father's dalliance with Flynt's mother was ill-judged to say the least.'

'There was no such dalliance!' Moncrieff's voice rose as the irritation caused earlier boiled over and his fingers tightened on the wolf's head. 'The suggestion that one such as Flynt carries my blood in his veins is an abomination to me.'

The Grand Master seemed unperturbed by the anger directed at him. 'You know I kent your father well, James, and he often allowed his lusts to get the better of him. God knows how many such bastards breathe today because he could not keep his manhood in his breeches. That was one of the reasons he was never invited to join our brotherhood. I saw something more in you, lad, but this hatred of Flynt must not be allowed to continue. It's bad for business.'

'He killed my father.'

'I'm aware of that.'

'It cannot go unpunished.'

'You have already tried and failed. And the means you employed lacked in nuance. Hiring common street thugs to attack him? Dear God, James, has your time with us taught you nothing? Subtlety is everything, man.'

A muscle in Moncrieff's jaw tightened. 'It was clumsy, I admit, and I regret it, but I cannot allow this man to live, you must understand that. If he spreads these lies about my father...'

'He shows no indication that he wishes to acknowledge his relationship to your family.'

Moncrieff could not control his anger. 'There is no damned relationship!'

The Grand Master sat very still, his gaze down the table towards Moncrieff even. When he spoke again, his voice was low but the steely tone was clear. 'Have a care before you raise your voice to me again, your lordship.'

Moncrieff realised this time he had crossed a line he was not yet ready to cross. 'I apologise, Grand Master, but my passions rise when this falsehood is even suggested.'

The apology was accepted with an incline of the head, but the stoney look remained. 'I would consider the possibility that it is not a falsehood, and that Flynt may well be your half-brother.'

Moncrieff felt colour rise again but he kept his voice low. 'With respect, sir, he is the son of a damned tavern keeper and a penny whore!'

The Grand Master's tone saddened. 'I kent Jenny Flynt, and she was no whore. That was your father's version. The truth is he took his pleasure against her will. That he fathered a child in that single coupling speaks well for his virility, if not his morals.'

Moncrieff's anger broke again. 'That is a damned lie!'

The Grand Master glared at him. 'I shall not tell you again, sir. Curb that temper when you address me or I will have it curbed.'

Moncrieff's rage dissipated as swiftly as it rose. The man opposite appeared ineffectual and even flustered when he wished to, but it was all an act. The reality was that with a single word he was capable of destroying everything towards which Moncrieff had worked. *Was* working. The time would come for a confrontation but not yet, and not over Jonas Flynt. That situation would be resolved first.

The Grand Master maintained a stern expression for a moment, then allowed it to relax. 'However, I admit that Mr Flynt does pose something of a threat to our brotherhood. I once toyed with the notion of inviting him to join...' He held up a hand when Moncrieff began to object, '...but I see no use for him in our ranks. He's nothing but a rogue, a thief and a killer, and we have many similar individuals on whom we can call for such dirty work. We know he's part of the Company of

Rogues and though it's of little threat to us at present, this affair regarding Templeton and his contact with Colonel Charters does make me wonder if some kind of pre-emptive action is necessary. That the good colonel seems aware of our existence was evident in his conversation with you earlier this year.'

'I believe it was but a shot in the dark.'

'Perhaps so, but I am aware that secrecy is a rock and time the waters that erodes it. Murmurs can be carried upon the current. That Charters knows or suspects something is clear and Flynt is the strongest weapon in his arsenal. I believe it's time for that weapon to be spiked.'

He rose from the table and moved leisurely to where the bottle of port sat on a side table. He poured himself another glass, stared at the portrait of their founder for a moment as he sipped at the wine, then slowly turned back.

'So, my lord, what I am saying is that if you wish to remove Flynt from the equation then do so. But if it is to be done, then do it in such a way that it cannot be traced back to you and, by extension, us.'

Understanding dawned that he was being granted the Fellowship's blessing to move against Flynt. And with that real-isation came suspicion. Was there something moving under the surface of the current of which the Grand Master had spoken?

'But, for God's sake, man, remember – subtlety and nuance,' the Grand Master added. 'Remain at arm's length, further if you can. Use intermediaries, keep your distance. Use professionals, not the dregs of the street. Flynt may be a rogue but he is no ordinary rogue. He is a most capable individual. Respect that and act accordingly.'

'As you say, Grand Master.'

It took every ounce of strength to keep a thin smile from his face as he affected a shallow, but still servile, bow. It flew in the face of his true feelings towards this man to whom he was forced to defer but it was better they remained hidden, until the time was right.

As for Flynt, the matter was already in train.

5

Flynt rose early the following morning and proceeded to Wych Street, a thoroughfare which clung steadfastly to an earlier age, thanks to the land around it being untouched by the Great Fire of 1666. Stretching from the spire of St Clement Danes on the Strand to Drury Lane, it was narrow, with some buildings first erected in the time of Elizabeth still standing, the wooden jetties jutting over the heads of pedestrians acting as a sun shade. The ancient structures were each of three or four storeys, which meant that much of the street was in perpetual shadow even on the brightest of days, as it was this day, for the sun was strong and warm. Flynt walked under signboards projecting from above the doorways of shops and the workplaces of tradespeople, some signage so dangerously low that he felt the need to stoop slightly lest his hat brush the lowermost surface, before turning into a narrow entranceway announced by a handsome wooden indicator bearing the images of a mallet, chisel and plane. The passage led to a courtyard where was situated the carpentry workshop of the aptly named Wood, where Flynt knew, or rather hoped, he would find Jack Sheppard hard at work. Jack was a nimble lad, both in mind and fingers, for even at only fourteen he was easily the best foist Flynt had ever seen, despite the fact that it was a botched attempt to lift his purse that had introduced him to the lad in the first place. When he arrived those dexterous fingers were at work smoothing down a door which, given the quality of material and design, was destined for a fine house.

Owen Wood appeared from the rear of the shop and nodded his hello. He was not one for smiling, was Owen, but that didn't mean Flynt was unwelcome. 'I would have a moment with young Jack, if you can spare him.'

Owen knew that Flynt and his apprentice were acquaintances, it was he in fact who had obtained the position for the lad, so he nodded to Jack and said a few words that Flynt did not catch. Permission given, the boy set his plane to the side, wiped the shavings from his leather apron, and grinned as he walked round the bench. Flynt nodded his thanks to Owen, before leading the boy from the workshop and into the street. Jack leaned against a wall on Wych Street, his face raised to enjoy the warmth from a beam of light that had managed to traverse the roof of the building opposite. The boy was pale and slim and looked as if he needed the sun on his skin, for his lifestyle did not often lend itself to basking in daylight.

'How you been, Mr Flynt? Them wounds all healed?'

Both the boy and Belle St Clair had visited him often, bringing him food, brandy on occasion, and the tittle-tattle from the streets. Belle's proximity, on the occasions she called upon him alone, was often intoxicating enough without the brandy and he had struggled to maintain his distance. They had been intimate in the past, a business arrangement to be sure but he felt there was a connection beyond the mere exchange of silver for affections. Still, recognition that someone else resided in his heart and mind, someone who was many hundreds of miles away, had prevented him of late from any such dalliances. It was not easy, for the weakness of his flesh diluted the strength his resolve.

'They have, Jack, thank you for asking.'

'Now you is all healed and back to work?'

Flynt smiled, for the lad was sharp. 'Aye, that's the way of it.'

'And what does you need from me?'

'When did you last see Edgeworth Bess?'

Jack's eyes lit up at the name. Bess was a few years older but he was entranced by her. 'Been a while, it's true. Ain't had the bunce, see.' He lowered his voice. 'Not been on the foist these days, keeping myself on the low. Mr Wood, he's been learning me his locksmithing skills. I reckons that be a more profitable way to progress.' His expression turned to one of distaste. 'That and the work what I does for Mr Wild keeps me off the streets and out of men's pockets.'

Jonathan Wild was the Thieftaker General of London, a title he had adopted to set himself above the other thieftakers who plied their nefarious trade in the city. They caught thieves, certainly, but it was for reward and they were none too careful as to whether they had the correct culprit. Wild had built an organisation filled with rogues and cutthroats, all ostensibly working for the good of the populace but in reality only lining his pockets. They said there wasn't a major crime in the city that didn't have Wild's hands all over it.

'Does he still use you to root out information?'

Jack's face crumpled again. 'He do, now and then, and it don't sit well, not well at all. Feels like peaching but if I don't he'll see to it that it's the long walk to Tyburn and then the short drop. So I've been working hard for Mr Wood here and trying to stay on the straight and narrow as much as I can in the hope that he'll forget about me. So, no extra bunce for Bess, if you know what I mean.' A thought struck him and he chose his next words carefully. 'Why does you need her, Mr Flynt? You ain't in the mood for a tumble, is you? I thought she weren't your type. I mean, no offence, Bess is a fine-looking girl but she ain't no Miss St Clair.'

Flynt sought to assuage the lad's fears that he might have taken a fancy to the young woman. 'Bess is a beauty, Jack, but that's not why I need her. There is something in which she might be able to assist me and I need you to speak to her on my behalf.'

'Why don't you speak to her yourself?'

'Bess and I don't get along, Jack, you know that.'

The young woman had sought to profit from an incident she had witnessed which resulted in the death of four men at Flynt's hand and, though he had bought her silence with cash, Bess was almost feral in her ability to seek advantage in a situation and so he had to follow up with threats to ensure her future silence. Even though she had been drunk at the time, she seemed never to have forgotten the interlude, for whenever their paths crossed her attitude towards him was decidedly antagonistic. Or perhaps it was as simple as irritation that Jack would drop anything, including her, to do Flynt's bidding.

'What exact does you need from her, Mr Flynt?'

'Information. Ask her about a girl called Cheshire Sal.'

'She from the north then?'

'No, she works out of the Cheese off the Fleet.'

Jack understood immediately. The boy had an encyclopaedic knowledge of the city's taverns. 'What you need from her?'

'I need to find her. It's important.'

'Why is this Sal so important then?'

Flynt's blank look spoke volumes, making Jack grin. 'I got you, Mr Flynt, if I needed to know you'd tell me.'

'How soon can you see Bess?'

'She'll be sleeping last night off now so I could pay her a call at her lobkin.'

Jack was well-versed in the street slang of the criminal classes and lobkin was a term for lodging. 'Is she still in St Giles?'

'Aye, but she's moved cribs, she has. She's got a sky parlour now, an attic with a window in the ceiling, can you believe it? Pays a bit extra for a view of the heavens, but she's doing all right for herself these days. Much in demand, she is.'

If Jack held any animosity towards the men who paid for Bess's favours, it was not betrayed by his expression or tone. He either didn't care or he was realistic enough to accept the way of it. Flynt suspected the latter.

'It will take some bunce to loosen Bess's tongue, you knows what she is like.'

Flynt had anticipated such a necessity and handed the boy a small purse. Jack weighed it expertly in his hand.

'I could go sees her right away, if you wish, but you would need to square it with old Wood. I reckons he wouldn't mind, as it's you.'

'I'll speak with him for you.' He nodded towards the entrance to another narrow courtyard hidden to the side. 'You get off now, Jack, and I'll meet you at the White Lion in two hours.'

Jack pulled the strap of his leather apron over his head and handed the garment to Flynt. 'What will you do till then?'

Flynt draped the apron over his arm as he turned back towards Wood's workshop. 'I need to seek legal advice.'

–

Mr Lemuel Gribble was what some might describe as being conspicuously prosperous. Others, if they were of a charitable nature, might say that he was pleasantly plump. The less benevolent would say he was corpulent. Although his topcoat, breeches and stockings were all of the highest quality, albeit bearing stains from carelessly dropped food and drink, his expansive gut strained at the buttons of his waistcoat, threatening to send them flying should he feel the need for a sharp intake of breath. He sat at what was his usual table within Nando's on the corner of Fleet Street and Inner Temple Lane, where the aroma of coffee permeated the air. From a side room came the sound of dice being shaken in a box and a voice declaring a mark at hazard, for gambling pleasures knew no clock. A waitress scurried to deliver a tray to four men at a corner table debating a legal argument. This was a favourite place of congregation for lawyers, judges and loungers to discuss the affairs of the day and it was here that Lemuel held court. He was a lawyer by profession and a gossip by predilection and if there was anything he did not know concerning those connected to the Inner and Middle Inns, where practitioners of the legal profession were trained and gathered, then it wasn't worth knowing.

'Be this Mr Jonas Flynt approaching, or do my eyes deceive me?'

The man's voice was rich and deep, scarred by the tobacco smoke and the liquor that he imbibed to such an extent that it was said that should he ever give up that particular pleasure, at least three wine sellers within city limits would go immediately out of business.

Flynt smiled as he took off his hat and seated himself. Lemuel always made him smile, he was that kind of man. Beckoning to the serving girl, Flynt ordered himself a coffee and another for the lawyer.

'Inordinately kind of you, my friend. It has been some considerable time since these eyes have rested upon you.' Lemuel dropped his voice but not nearly enough for what he was about to say. 'I would have believed you be a blossom of the Tyburn tree but your name never appeared in the lists. You have not taken to the life of an honest man, have you?'

Even though he would rather the words had not been heard by all around, Flynt couldn't help but broaden his grin. It had been Lemuel he had consulted some years before when Old Tom, the man who tutored him in the art of picking locks, had been accused of carrying out a crack lay on a grand house in Hackney. Lemuel proffered advice concerning the evidence of a known felon who had turned queen's evidence in order to escape justice himself. The verbal ammunition the lawyer provided allowed Tom to attack the man in court. He also assisted in preparing a variety of witnesses, including Flynt himself, who would swear that on the night of the burglary, Tom was in the Black Lion tavern, supping ale and, later, tupping a lady of the night known as Drury Lane Tess in her lodgings. The jury was sufficiently impressed and found him innocent of the crime. To Lemuel's amusement, Tom later asked if that meant he could now fence the silver plate and jewellery he had taken from the house.

'I've left the flash life behind me, Lemuel.'

The lawyer affected a stricken expression. 'That is most distressing to hear, my friend, for those such as I thrive upon the activities of gentlemen such as yourself.' His sigh was theatrical. 'But no matter, for it is fortunate that I live and work in the most lawless city in the land and there is a surfeit of rogues from which to profit.'

The girl returned with the coffee. Lemuel leaned closer to her to say, 'Be this my special sweetened brew, my dear?'

She gave him a secretive little smile. 'It is, Mr Gribble. We knows what you likes well enough, even though this be on the gentleman's ordering.'

Lemuel smiled. 'Capital, my dear, capital. I am much obliged for your solicitude towards my tastes.'

As she moved on to serve another customer, Lemuel sipped at his coffee and smacked his lips in pleasure. Flynt did not comment on the exchange, as he knew that the beverage had been sweetened, as Lemuel had called it, with brandy, a special service extended to very few of Nando's patrons.

Setting the cup down again, Lemuel asked, 'So, my friend Jonas, what brings you to seek my counsel?'

'I could not simply have chanced upon you here?'

He gave Flynt a look suggesting that in the realms of like-lihood, that ranked alongside the existence of fairies and fair play in the court of law. 'You know that I am in the habit of enjoying a midmorning tightener – or indeed two – in this very coffee house and you, my friend, do not simply chance upon anyone. You came here to see me, I believe, so out with it.'

Flynt enjoyed talking with this man. In manner he reminded him of a judge he had known all too briefly. They both shared what might at first glance seem a jaded view of English law but each was dedicated to upholding it, the judge from the bench, considering evidence and handing down sentences, Lemuel constantly testing the quality of prosecutions and offering advice to the accused on how they could defend their inno-cence, or deflect their guilt, in court. Thoughts of the judge caused a moment's sadness but Flynt took some satisfaction in knowing that he had watched his murderer die.

'I seek a lawyer named Christopher Templeton.'

Lemuel's eyebrows raised. 'Aha! The mysteriously absent Mr Templeton. May I ask why you are on such a quest?'

'It is work I do.'

'You are a seeker of men now?'

'And other lost things.'

Lemuel's eyes narrowed. 'A nasty suspicion grows in my mind and I would be remiss if I did not dispel it on the instant.'

'And what is that nasty suspicion?'

'Please tell me you do not act in this matter for either of those rapscallions Wild or one of the other thieftakers who infest our city.'

'Why do you ask?'

'Whenever inquiry is made into the whereabouts of an individual, often it is those self-proclaimed guardians of the law who are the guiding force.'

'I assure you I do not act for them.'

The lawyer scrutinised Flynt's words and his face. 'But you do act for someone.'

'I do,' Flynt said, 'but I am not at liberty to reveal the identity of the principal in this matter.'

Lemuel again analysed this. 'Then I will take you at your word, Jonas Flynt, for though you be rogue, I know you to be a man of some honour, peculiar and capricious though that honour sometimes may be. But I also know you to be a man of violence when such is needed. One more query – do you mean Mr Templeton ill?'

'I do not, quite the opposite in fact.' Flynt believed he could trust this man, so added, 'He may have found himself in some considerable jeopardy.'

Understanding spread across the lawyer's face. 'Hence his sudden and quite uncharacteristic disappearance from these environs. What do you wish from me?'

'I would know a little of him. In learning more of his character I may be able to plan a way forward.'

'I knew him, of that you are aware, elsewise you would not be bearding me here at this very moment...'

'Let's say that I gambled.'

'And, from what I hear, you do that tolerably well. It is not one of my vices, however. Good food, good wine, an accommodating wench who will overlook the girth of my belly and appreciate the heft of my purse, these are my pleasures, apart from besting my fellow attorneys and confounding spurious prosecutions, of course.'

'Christopher Templeton,' Flynt urged, for another of Lemuel's pleasures was the timbre of his own voice.

The lawyer laughed. It was throaty and seemed to rumble up from his gut. 'To the business at hand, friend Flynt, quite right. He is a promising boy, well thought of, although there was a time just a few years ago when he displayed a somewhat wild side.'

'In what way?'

'You will be acquainted with the gentlemen who called themselves Mohocks, named after the wild natives of the American colonies?'

Flynt had encountered the drunken noblemen a few years before when they had run amok in the streets, attacking and stabbing people at random, and during the previous winter had dealings with an arrogant fop who had formerly been of their number. 'I had some brief experience of them, yes.'

'And I feel certain that they regretted crossing your path. Given your knowledge of them, you may also be aware that it was in this very establishment that they liked to gather, liquor themselves into a frenzy before they set off on their nocturnal depredations – or partake of the cannabis. Have you ever imbibed the substance?'

Flynt shook his head. He seldom overindulged in alcohol, let alone anything else.

49

'I tried it once,' Lemuel continued. 'Bought me it from a sea captain who sat at that very table over yonder when he found himself beached in the city for a time. He called it *bhang* and he had it from the sub-continent. Believe this or believe this not, my boy, but it rendered me quite unable to speak a single word of any sense whatsoever. I remember little of the experience to be sure, but I am informed that I became most merry indeed, though still able to perambulate. I even danced a jig, which if true is not something of which I am proud. It eventually made me decidedly fatigued and I slept most soundly, though when I woke I found my myself exceeding sharp set.' He patted his ample belly. 'Though that circumstance is one with which I am most familiar. That was how it affected me, but the Mohocks, it would seem, found that it worked them into some sort of frenzy.'

'And Templeton was one of them?'

'Most of them were students of law, as you may know. He was a touch older than the others but obviously had a great deal of energy to expel.'

'Was he charged?'

Lemuel sipped his drink. 'Indeed he was, along with some of the others. And fined, but that afforded no obstruction to his career, as you probably know. The others also found their reputations unbridled by the scandal.'

Flynt had no love for the Mohocks and the fact that Templeton had run with them did not make him look favourably upon him. 'So he has violence in him?'

Lemuel waved a beefy hand in dismissal. 'Oh, I don't think Christopher is the type to harm anyone.'

'The Mohocks left people wounded and disfigured.'

'I am aware of that, but I do not believe Christopher would have participated in that particular element of their activities. Damage to property, perhaps, but not to person. Although I do believe he is quite the swordsman. Learned his skills from John Duck in Little White's Alley, off Chancery Lane, who is a very good master of the small sword and he tutors many of the gentlemen in the Inns of Court in the noble art of self-defence.'

Flynt filed that away, thinking Mr Duck might be a useful person to speak to, and Chancery Lane was not far from Nando's.

'So, if Templeton was a Mohock, he comes from a well-to-do family?'

'He does indeed. Not nobility but certainly more than comfortable. Not that it matters in places such as this, for all a man needs here is a clean shirt and a few pennies in his purse and he can talk as loud as any nobleman.'

'He had no family, I'm told.'

Lemuel's eyes saddened. ' 'Tis true, most tragic. Mother and father both taken by enteric fever. He was but a lad, but he inherited the fortune his father had built – a draper, he was, over on Cheapside. Family friends helped raise him, kindly they were by his account, but the drapery business did not inspire him so he decided on the law as a profession. He studied well, found a place in the Inns of Court, though he did not lodge in either the Inner or Middle Temples. Had him rooms down off Fleet Street, I believe…'

'Crane Court.'

'Quite so. Built himself a decent little portfolio of clients, eschewed criminal justice for mercantile.' Lemuel shuddered. 'Can't think of anything more horrendous, to be truthful, than poring over contracts and agreements. Give me the drama, the humanity, of the criminal world.'

Charters had said he had only one client, but given the nature of that client it was understandable that Templeton would hide them behind a fictional portfolio. 'So you know little of those who sought his expertise?'

'Absolutely nothing, dear boy. I dined with him once or twice and he did not discuss his work.'

That was not surprising either. 'Would you say he was an honourable man?'

Humour twitched at Lemuel's lips. 'As honourable as any lawyer can be. He did profess regret over his involvement with the Mohocks, if that raises him in any way in your eyes. Yes, I saw the disapproval in your face, do not deny it.'

'They preyed on the weak and the innocent for no other reason than enjoyment and because they could, and effectively escaped punishment because their families had influence. I disapprove of that, most certainly.'

'Ah, my boy, which of us have unblemished histories? Have we not all done things of which we are ashamed? Even you, eh? Do not some of the crimes of which you have gone unpunished torment you in dead of night?'

Lemuel's gaze was steady but accusatory and Flynt felt some shame at his own hypocrisy.

'Christopher felt shame over what he had done, I could tell that just as I discern it in you,' said Lemuel. 'It is my belief that if amends could be made for his wrongdoings, he would have done.'

If that was true, then it could explain his desire to expose the Fellowship. 'Would he break the confidence of clients if he felt they were guilty of wrongdoing?'

'Legal professional privilege is one rule that no lawyer worth his fee should break. It is a protection for both client and attorney and is part of common law. If Christopher were to breach such an oath then he would have to be compelled by some force or other, whether external or internal.'

'His conscience, which you said was already pained?'

Lemuel sat back in his chair. 'It be true that he was subdued the last time he and I met. I put it down not so much to a troubled mind but more to his emotional state.'

'His emotional state?'

'Women, dear boy, women. They do so prick at a man's heart most severe.'

Even though Flynt already knew where this was headed, he asked, 'He was in love?'

'Love? Who can say what that is. He was most certainly in lust, for we men know what that is. Young Christopher may have been learning the art of the small sword under Mr Duck, but he was already accomplished as a swordsman in another way.'

'Was it a lady who goes by the name Cheshire Sal?'

Gribble's eyes widened a little. 'You know of her, then? A doxy, my boy, a comely one to be sure and from a good family, but still a doxy, though I gather she wielded great influence over him. And I suppose on some level he was smitten. I thought perhaps his mental unease was caused by the fact that he could not come to terms with the plain fact of her means of making a living.'

Flynt thought of his own stabs of jealousy when he thought of Belle with other men. More hypocrisy on his part, for he had no right to feel that way given his yearning for a love he lost through his own indifference. 'Did he give you any indication if she perhaps felt the same way?'

'Does anyone know what lies in a woman's heart? They can be most mysterious, can they not? We men are but open books; a pretty face, a fine body, and we are lost. But women can seek more. As I said, she influenced him and he hinted that his shame over the Mohock involvement had been prompted by her. A doxy, I said, but thanks to her upbringing a doxy with a knowledge of right and wrong. I am sure that is also something you can understand, eh?'

Flynt had not realised how well Lemuel seemed to know him. They had never discussed Flynt's life, their acquaintance had never been personal and he was not in the habit of discussing his past, or even his present. And yet, the lawyer had his measure. Again, he was reminded of the judge, who had done the same within minutes of meeting.

'You wouldn't know where I could find this Sal?'

'Sally, he called her, and Sally is how I know her.'

'You know her?'

'By sight, just as I know her brother.'

'And who would that be?'

Lemuel smiled. 'I have already mentioned the gentleman. Mr John Duck, the sword master.'

6

Sometimes it seemed to Flynt that he spent an inordinate amount of time walking down narrow alleyways to encounter the unknown. Little White's Alley itself was new to him, so he knew not what to expect. It was an indifferent offshoot of Chancery Lane, and he found it to be lined with plain and unprepossessing timber buildings with only the obvious age and condition of the wood showing they were not of recent construction. The shadows they created were a welcome respite from the heat of the sun, now almost at its zenith. He spied above a doorway a sign bearing the crudely carved image of a hand grasping a sword and the name John Duck lettered beneath.

The door was unlocked and Flynt found a cramped, bare little room with two chairs that was obviously an antechamber. A deep voice from beyond another door that lay ajar told him to come straight through. He entered a larger, longer room with looking glasses down one side, and a fine selection of blades hanging upon the opposite wall. Some were decorative, silvered or gilded and designed not so much for the fight but for the look. Others were functional; plain weapons, sturdy, intended for defence and offence. There were small swords, long swords, rapiers, sabres, cutlasses and even a claymore. A man sat in a wooden chair beneath the armoury, a fine English small sword on his lap which he cleaned with a soft cloth. He was a tall black man, his shoulders very powerful, his bare biceps bulging from a sleeveless leather tunic. When he looked up, his face betrayed surprise, for Flynt was obviously not the one he expected to see.

'You will be Mr John Duck, the fencing master?' Flynt asked.

The man's study was sharp and complete, finally resting on the silver cane in Flynt's hand. He clearly recognised it as no mere walking stick and he was correct. He spoke in a clear, articulate voice but with a hint of the back streets of the city. 'I am, sir, and who be you?'

'My name is Jonas Flynt.'

Duck rose in an easy and graceful manner. He was very tall, very erect; if he were to be placed in a room with most Londoners he would tower above them all.

'And how can I help you, sir?' His gaze fell to the cane again. 'Do you wish instruction in the sword?'

'I thank you, but no. I seek a gentleman by the name of Christopher Templeton, I understand he is a pupil of your establishment?'

Duck gave the blade he held a final wipe with the cloth, which was then dropped on the chair. 'I have many pupils,' he said, carefully.

Flynt sensed some antagonism when he mentioned the missing lawyer. 'But this one is also a friend of your sister.'

Duck's expression, already guarded, grew stiff. 'What do you know of my sister?'

It felt less than politic to mention the woman's occupation to her brother. 'Very little, but I would wish to speak with her.'

'Why?'

'As I said, I seek Mr Templeton. I believe she may be able to assist me in my task.'

Despite the warmth of the day, a frost had settled in the air between them. Duck's stance had altered slightly, as if he was preparing to either fend off an attack or mount one himself. Flynt let his hand stray to the handle of the cane.

'I mean neither of them any harm, Mr Duck.'

Duck began to move to his left. Flynt did the same, feeling it advisable that he keep some distance between them. He had no desire to cross swords with the man but had the distinct impression that such activity was inevitable.

'May I take it that I'm not the first to come asking after them?'

'You may take what you wish, Mr Flynt, but I would be obliged if you would take it elsewhere, as I have no interest in discussing my sister, or that hell hound Templeton, with you.'

It was clear there was no love lost between the fencing master and the lawyer. Was it because of his sister?

'Have you discussed them with whoever else inquired?'

Duck stopped moving and frowned. 'I am puzzled as to what portion of my statement about not entering into dialogue with you it is that you fail to comprehend.'

'But we're already in dialogue, Mr Duck, and I repeat, I mean neither Mr Templeton nor Sally any harm.'

Duck's sword rose slightly. 'I care not what your intentions are regarding him but I will thank you not to utter my sister's name. I know your type. I grew up with men like you. Gutter trash with nothing but violence in your soul, as were those others who came here asking after my Sally and that bastard, and I will send you away just as I did them, howling in pain and leaking claret.'

Flynt well believed Duck was capable of that but could not allow himself to be deterred by the threat of bodily harm. 'May I ask who these others were?'

Duck's lips tightened but he granted Flynt a reply. 'Brothers, by their look. Gutter trash like you and I sent them away.' He raised his weapon further and adopted a crouch. 'But not unbloodied, and if you have no wish to leave here in one piece then – please – continue asking your questions. It will be my pleasure to carve you, too.'

Flynt continued to ignore the threat. 'Did they give you their names?'

Duck stared at him as if baffled by the fact that he had, in fact, accepted his invitation to continue to pose questions. 'Do you not comprehend the king's English?'

Flynt was unsure if the king, being a German, understood the king's English overmuch, but he ignored the query. 'I would seek to help Mr Templeton and your sister. Knowing who these brothers are would be of assistance.'

'I am not here to assist you.'

'But I am here to assist Sally, if I can.'

Duck positioned himself side on, the sword at the ready. 'Sir, you are a man who carries a blade concealed in yonder stick. I have seen such devices before. A man who must conceal steel is a man who conceals many other things and is not to be trusted, in my opinion.'

Flynt decided to keep Tact and Diplomacy, his brace of pistols, nestling in the specially sewn pockets under his coat.

'I am not here to fight, Mr Duck…'

'Then leave and God speed.'

'I would rather we spoke like civilised men…'.

'Men are not civilised, Mr Flynt, surely you are one who understands that. The beast is not far from the surface of any man, which is why I make my living as I do. It will always rise when threatened.'

'I do not threaten,' Flynt insisted.

'Sally warned me that men like you would come and advised me to send them away. She said they may be like those brothers, brash and vulgar, or they may act like gentlemen and speak in honeyed tones. No matter what the overture, she assured me they meant her harm. So forgive me if I don't embrace your assurances to have her wellbeing in your heart. I don't know you, sir, but I know my sister, and though she may have strayed from the path of the godly, she remains my blood and I love her. I won't allow you or anyone to do her harm.'

Flynt was gratified to hear that there had been contact between the siblings, for that meant he would have knowledge of her location. The inquiry Jack was at that moment making of Bess might or might not prove fruitful so for the moment this was his best bet. If only he could convince the man that, although not himself an angel, on this occasion he walked in their shadow.

'Now, sir, final chance,' Duck said. 'Leave now, unharmed, or tarry and let God decide which of us has the better skill with the sword.'

Flynt sighed. He really did not wish to fight the man but he could see that the only way to glean whatever he knew was to engage with him. Whether he could do that without either of them drawing blood was the gamble he had to take. It was at times like this that he wished he believed in the God that Duck had mentioned. It might be a comfort to have someone watching over him.

Duck moved with an agility that might have caught Flynt by surprise if he had not earlier noted his ease of movement. One moment he was a few feet away, the next he had leaped across the divide and was striking at Flynt, who had already dodged out of the way, his hand instinctively twisting the handle of his cane and sliding the blade free. Duck came at him again, his sword lunging. Flynt parried but felt the strength behind the thrust. This man was not play-acting. This was not for show. He fully intended to wound him if he could.

He backed away, nerves primed for the next attack, which came swiftly. As a sword master, Duck would teach finesse, delicacy, even grace, but would have the ability to temper his approach depending on his adversary. This offensive was raw and powerful. Yes, he remained graceful in his movements, but the onslaught was one of strength, not subtlety. Flynt blocked a downward slash, the force of the man's strike vibrating to his shoulder. Duck followed up with a blow towards Flynt's chin with the heel of his left hand, but Flynt engineered to avoid its full force and the man's palm scraped off his cheek. So, this was to be no show match: they were engaged in a struggle under street rules, the only rule being that there were no rules. He briefly considered ending it by drawing a pistol but rejected the idea. If this man was to reveal his secrets, he had to understand that Flynt truly meant him no harm, and training a firearm upon him did not convey that message. No, he had to do his best to play a defensive game. Leave the attacking to Duck and do his best to ensure that his blade did not sneak by. If it did, he took some comfort in the hope that his greatcoat would afford some protection.

Flynt backed away, using sword in one hand and silver sheath in the other to parry each lunge. Steel clanging against steel reverberated around the room, but anyone passing in the alley would be used to such sounds and would not come to investigate. Occasionally Duck lashed out with a foot but Flynt danced away before it could connect. Only once did Duck leave himself open for attack and Flynt seized the opportunity to strike him on the temple with the hilt of his sword. He regretted the move, he'd had no intention of showing any antagonism, so at the last moment pulled the blow so that it did not land too heavily, but it was enough to make the man step back a couple of paces. The lull was momentary, for soon he advanced again, Flynt backing away, Duck constantly on the attack as they circled the room. The exertion caused Flynt to sweat and he wished he'd had the time to remove his coat, no matter what level of protection it offered. He was aware that, though his wounds had healed, he was not yet back to his former strength and the months of relative inaction had left his physical fitness somewhat lacking. But Duck was also flagging, which is what Flynt had hoped would happen. Graceful he may have been, swift he may have been, but he was still a big man and the effort he was putting behind his offensive in this close atmosphere was taking its toll. Sweat beaded his brow and sheened his flesh and his breath began to labour. The power behind his sword thrusts had diminished, while the ferocity of his expression had transformed into something akin to confusion, again just as Flynt had hoped.

Finally, he curtailed his attack, his broad chest heaving, and regarded Flynt with curiosity. 'You do not strike back, sir.

You parry, you block, you back away but you do not take the offensive.'

Flynt's own breath was faltering; he had been unsure how long he could keep up his defence so was glad of the respite. 'I told you, Mr Duck, I am not here to do anyone harm. I must find Mr Templeton and your sister may be a conduit to him. You're by now well aware that they're both in danger and time is of the essence.'

Duck lowered the sword and wiped the perspiration from his forehead with the back of his free hand. 'From those brothers?'

'Yes, very likely, and the men who pay them.'

'And who pays you?'

'I cannot tell you that, for it would breach a confidence, but you have my word that we mean to protect Mr Templeton, and Sally. I understand that my request means you must break a promise to your sister not to reveal her location but you must take my word that it is of the utmost importance that you do.'

Duck's head shook. 'I have made no such promise, for Sally has not shared her whereabouts with me.' His look was of a sudden pain, but not physical. 'She and I have drifted apart in these years, and that has caused me a great deal of anguish. You will know of her present occupation, I take it?' Flynt gave him a slight nod and the man's sadness seemed to deepen. 'There are so many ways for good people to go bad in this city. The wrong door, the wrong street, the wrong company. Sally fell victim to this city, like many others. The man you seek, Templeton, he was a pupil of mine, and right handy he proved with a blade. I liked him, trusted him, but he betrayed me. I made a request of him to seek Sally out and bring her home but he did nothing but debauch her further. I will have his heart on the point of my sword, should I see him again. She has been badly served by men, sir, and badly used. Her fall from grace has pained my wife and I, but yet she is my sister and we love her still and would bring her back into God's good grace if we can.'

'But did you not say that she had been in contact to warn you of men making inquiry?'

'A note, delivered by messenger.'

'Did you know the deliverer?'

'I did not. Some boy from the streets, anonymous, looked like any other of his kind. He merely handed the epistle to me and then left immediate after I gave him coin.'

Damn. Had the boy been known to Duck then that might have proven to be another possible route to finding the girl.

'I would make a request of you, Mr Flynt,' Duck said.

'If it is within my power then it will be my honour.'

'If you find Sally, I beg of you to bring her home. She should be with her family, not hiding alone in some hovel.'

'Are you confident that you can protect her should others come looking for her?'

'That I can and that I will. The two who were here regret crossing my path and my wife's family will be recruited to bolster defences if need be. We are all capable men, God-fearing, but able to put the fear of that same God into those who deserve it. Now, sir, will you undertake to return my sister to me?'

'I will, and right gladly.'

For the first time a smile crossed Duck's face. It was fleeting but it was a show of gratitude, as was the hand he held out. 'Then take my hand upon it and know that if you need my assistance, then you need only call.'

Flynt took the man's hand, trying not to wince when the grip tightened and he was pulled closer. 'But know this. If you be lying to me, if you do her harm, I will not rest until I see the life bleed from your eyes.'

Flynt sensed there was nothing further he could say to assure the man of his good intentions, so merely returned the pressure in his grip. They stared at each other for a moment, Duck searching Flynt's eyes for even a slight hint of duplicity and obviously seeing none for he nodded once and released his hold. Flynt understood the man's caution and believed him when he said he would hunt him down and kill him, for he sensed this man was not one to make idle threats. However, he had another question.

'The brothers, did they give their names?'

'Is that important?'

'As I said, if I know who they are it helps me gauge who it is I am up against. As you will know, it is important to understand your adversary, and if I have their names that will be a start.'

Duck accepted this, even though he had not previously. 'I did not hear any surname used but they did address each other by their Christian names, though I suspect neither of them be true Christian.'

'What were these names?'

'Their parents had some learning, perhaps, for they had drawn their sons' names from mythology, Roman legend. One was called Romulus and the other Remus.' Duck must have perceived recognition in Flynt's expression. 'I see you know of them.'

'Aye,' said Flynt. 'The Trask brothers, as vicious a pair of cutthroats as this city has ever produced, though of late they have been away from the city, I believe.' That Duck had bested them, even though they be two to his one, did not surprise him. 'I would be on my guard, Mr Duck, for they may not be willing to forget whatever hurt you gave them. They will not come at you in any honourable way, for they are more adept at backstabbing than fair combat.'

'Have no fear, I will be on my mettle.'

Flynt was glad to hear that, for with the Trask brothers in the mix, and they perhaps knowing he was on the trail, he would also have to watch his back.

–

The man sitting opposite Moncrieff could have been a lowly clerk if his reputation had not preceded him. He was of slight stature, his brown hair thin and wispy, uncovered by wig and tied back with a black ribbon. His spectacles were round, a little too large perhaps for his thin face. His clothes were clean and well maintained but unremarkable, a brown coat and brown waistcoat over a white linen shirt, black breeches and cream hose, the only adornment being dull copper buckles on his black shoes. He had been shown into his study with no introduction, but then Moncrieff's servant was used to individuals arriving at his London home at all hours of the day or night, men who often did not identify themselves. Moncrieff knew him only as Mr Lester, but he suspected that was not his true name. He had refused all forms of hospitality, neither refreshment nor sustenance, even though Moncrieff knew he had travelled far to reach the city. He suspected he had taken lodgings somewhere before attending him, for his apparel, ordinary though it may be, bore no traces of hard travel. He said little but listened carefully, his face remaining immobile, the dark eyes behind those thick lenses betraying nothing.

'Jonas Flynt is not to be taken lightly, Mr Lester,' Moncrieff said. 'He is an accomplished killer of men.'

For the first time something flickered in the man's eyes. It might have been amusement, it might have been a rise to the challenge. 'As am I,' he said in a peculiarly high-pitched voice.

'And what of the Trask brothers?'

'If they become an irritant I will remove them.'

There was a quiet confidence in Lester's manner that Moncrieff found reassuring. However, there was a further concern that required to be dispelled. 'You have come highly recommended for your efficacy, but this northern lord of yours I do not know, apart from his being acquainted to the Fellowship. Are you certain he is up to the task?'

'I wouldn't have suggested him if I wasn't.'

'It is important that my plan succeeds. It is a most complex endeavour, but Flynt is a must complex man. A simple street attack has proved unsuccessful in the past.'

Lester's tone was flat. 'I have not been involved in the past. Had I been, the outcome would have been different. It still can be. As you say, your plan is most complex.'

'Nonetheless, I wish events to proceed as I have outlined.'

'What does it matter, as long as he is dead?'

'It matters to me, Lester. I have personal reasons for not only for wishing it so but also to witness his demise. I would also prefer that there be a sheen of legality to it. However, I need you to ensure that events here in London proceed without impediment. Flynt must not know that you watch him. I have been led to believe you are most accomplished in such arts.'

Apart from a languid blink of his eyes behind the spectacles, Lester remained still. 'I have already taken note of his movements. However, professional responsibility behoves me to ask, should this contrivance of yours founder, what then?'

'Then, my dear Mr Lester, you may take more direct action...'

7

Flynt was surprised to see Bess waiting for him along with Jack in the White Lion. She sipped at an ale while he sat at her side with his arm around her shoulders in a proprietorial manner. Whether unconsciously or not, the lad was sending a signal to any cull who might fancy a tupping but Flynt knew it would avail him nought. Edgeworth Bess was fiercely independent and if she saw a means of turning a midday coin in this tavern then she would cast off that arm and do so. The purse Jack had been given was sufficient to buy the young woman's favours many times over, but his loyalty to Flynt was stronger than his priapic urges so said sum would have been passed to her in order to smooth her co-operation. So there they sat, Bess with her ale and Jack holding her as close as he could, without doubt enjoying the physical contact while also giving any randy customers that look of warning. Not that Jack could do much if that cull turned belligerent, for he was of slight build and not experienced in the art of self-defence. Flynt made a mental note to teach him some rudimentary moves, as a ready smile and a breezy nature were of limited defence in these streets. Sometimes, only violence was the answer.

Bess's disdain towards being in Flynt's company again was clear. Being a lass who preferred to get right to the point for time was coin, it was she who spoke first. 'Why's you looking for Sal?'

Flynt suppressed his own smile as he sat down. Jack knew him well and had chosen a table that afforded an uninterrupted view of the tavern and its doorways. The vacant chair was against a wall and Flynt took it.

'Nice to see you again, too, Bess,' he said, his tone amiable. 'I trust you are well?'

A twitchy sneer plucked at her left nostril. Their shared history ensured that she saw through his attempt at affability. 'Don't be giving me none of that, Jonas Flynt. I knows you, don't forget, and if you is looking for her then it ain't good for that girl's health. So I asks you again, why's you looking for Sal?'

'I take it you are acquainted with the lady?'

'I is acquainted, yes. And I ain't about to tell you her whereabouts until I knows exactly why you wants to know.'

Jack chimed in. 'Bess, Mr Flynt don't mean her no harm, does you, Mr Flynt?'

'I do not,' Flynt assured her. 'You have my word upon that.'

Bess was unimpressed by his word and remained suspicious as to his motives. 'Then what's your interest? You ain't looking for some business, because she ain't your type. We all knows in which direction your lusts take you, and it ain't girls like Sal, no matter how choosy she be about her culls. Us street girls ain't what you want. You likes them what smell sweet and sleep in feather beds. So, before I decide whether to tells you anything at all further, answer my question, Jonas high and bloody mighty Flynt, or I walks out of here and back to my bed, what is stuffed with straw, just so's you know.' She gave Jack a withering look. 'Alone.'

Jack's face fell slightly and Flynt gave him a sympathetic shrug. 'If you know Sal then you will know that she is in hiding. I wish to help her.'

'How do I know she ain't in hiding from you?'

'That's another thing on which you will have to take my word.'

A puff of her cheeks showed what she thought of that. 'Then if it ain't you she hides from, then who is it?'

'Bess, the less you know the better. Just be aware that the men hunting her are very dangerous indeed and I need to get to her before they do.'

She was not to be fobbed off. 'That's easy to say. So who is *they* then, these dangerous men?'

Flynt briefly considered obfuscation but decided against it. She needed to understand the seriousness of the situation. 'You have heard of Romulus and Remus Trask?'

Even in the dim light of the tavern he could see the tension gripping her expression. When she spoke again, her previous belligerence had been stifled. 'Why does they want her?'

'She has information they want.'

'About what exact?'

Flynt kept his voice gentle. 'Bess, believe me when I tell you it is best you do not know. Now, please tell me where she is so I can fetch her.'

'And take her where?'

Flynt had already decided on that course of action. 'Her brother. He seems a good man and I believe he can protect her.'

That seemed to satisfy her somewhat, but having recovered from news that the Trask brothers were on her friend's trail, Bess's customary antagonism began to creep in once again. 'But not before you gets to know what you wants to know from her, is I right?'

'Whether she tells me or not, I will help her.'

'You gives your word on that, too, I'll wager.'

Another slight sneer coated her words but Flynt could not blame her for her lack of trust. Bess had suffered at the hands of men, and their word meant nothing to her.

'You can trust Mr Flynt, Bess,' said Jack, his voice hardening. 'And you knows that, too, girl.'

Bess gave the lad a long look, reached out for her tankard and swallowed back a mouthful of ale, as she made a study of Flynt. 'I ain't going to tell you where she is.' She raised her voice slightly when she saw Flynt about to debate the issue. 'But here's what I will do. I'll go see her, right now, and I will has me a talk with her and if she says she will see you, then so be it.'

Flynt recognised that it was the best he could expect. 'Thank you, Bess.'

'Don't be thanking me, Jonas Flynt, for I don't wants it, not from you. Jack says I can trust you but I ain't so sure. You is a rum one and there ain't no mistake about that.'

Flynt didn't even try to object. He had been told that before.

Bess wasn't done, however. 'You say the Trasks is after her and that may be true. They is dangerous bastards, and that's for certain, but these here streets is full of dangerous men, and some of them sit in taverns in the middle of the day and pretend to be on the side of the angels. You is a gaming cove so let us put our cards on the table. We don't like each other, you and me...'

'I don't dislike you, Bess.'

'Well, I dislikes you. There's something off-kilter about you and I can't put my finger on it. You has hushed people, we all knows it, and though it may be true that most of those you snuff deserve what they gets, it's also true that you is bad luck for anyone around you. Jack here thinks you is like Moses down from the mountain and your every word is holy writ...'

Jack was uncomfortable with the direction in which this exchange was travelling. 'Bess, there ain't no need to be...'

She held up a hand to silence him. 'That's the way of it, Jack, and I sees it plain. This man has a power over you that will only be ended with the death of one of you or the other.' She looked back at Flynt and rose to her feet. 'And I prays that it is you, Jonas Flynt.'

Flynt understood that no response was required, even if he had one to make, so remained silent as she gazed upon him for a few moments before turning away from the tables and heading for the door. As she passed another table, a man's hand reached out to grip her arm but she slapped it away angrily and continued on her path. She was either not in the mood after her angry diatribe against him or she recognised that time was of the essence.

'Give her a moment, Jack, and follow her.'

The boy looked horrified. 'She won't like that, Mr Flynt.'

Guilt pierced Flynt's chest but he kept his voice flat. 'I don't care.'

Jack watched the young woman as she stepped into the sunlight beyond the tavern door. 'If she catches me…'

'Don't get caught then.' The boy's fear of angering the woman was plain. 'Jack, we have little time and I have no guarantee that Bess will bring me the result I need. You are skilled at making yourself invisible, so follow her and tell me where she goes.'

Though still doubtful, Jack rose and took a step from the table, then looked back. 'She don't mean it, Mr Flynt. What she said.'

'She meant it, lad.'

'She is wrong then.'

The girl's words bounced around his memory and he gave Jack a small, sad smile. 'No, lad, she's not.'

8

Flynt knew he should call into Wood's workshop again to convey his heartfelt apologies over keeping Jack from his employment for so long, and deliver a further promise to make financial amends for the lost time. The carpenter wouldn't accept it but Flynt would still offer. He'd do it presently, he decided, and ordered a brandy. His muscles were stiff and sore following the encounter with John Duck, and his heart was bruised by Bess's words. It was true that sometimes truth comes from the most unexpected source. The girl was sly, street-smart and, by necessity, self-interested, but that didn't mean she could not assess him with accuracy. He was a dangerous man, he had long since not only accepted that but used it to his advantage. He could defend himself with ease and kill when he had to. He might regret it afterwards but didn't hesitate when he felt it necessary. Her contention that he professed to labour on the side of the angels was also accurate, though Colonel Nathaniel Charters, like Lucifer, was more of a fallen one.

Where she was most painfully on target was when she said that he was bad luck for those close to him. He knew that to be true. He had lost friends, both those of long standing and those who might have become such. And he mourned them all, for he knew that, in some cases, if he had not been part of their lives then they might well have lived.

But he could not focus on that now. He had work to do. He drained the glass, picked up his hat and had just reached the door when a voice called to him from a table hidden deep in the shadows behind the door. 'I never thought I'd see the day when a Scotch bastard like you would fail to pull a doxy.'

The voice was familiar but Flynt's hand automatically rested on the handle of his cane as he strained in the darkness to see who sat at the table.

'No need for alarm, Jonas,' the man said, bringing his face into a beam of light from a high window. The man was handsome, his face smooth and youthful, even though he matched Flynt in years, but where Flynt kept his dark hair cropped close, his was long, blond and tied back. 'Old friends have no need of weapons drawn, do they?'

The smile that spread Flynt's lips was genuine but felt strange given his earlier brooding. 'Gabriel Cain! I took you for dead.'

Cain rose and held out his hand, which Flynt grasped tightly. 'Perhaps I am, perhaps we all are, and what we call life is merely hell, or at best purgatory. But that is a matter for the clerics to debate, not rogues like you and I. If this is life or the afterlife, then we must enjoy it while we can, eh?'

Cain settled back into the shadows and Flynt took the seat opposite, not caring if his back was exposed for he knew this man would protect it. He saw a bottle of brandy on the table and two glasses, one of which sat before Cain, half-filled. 'It's been what, four years, since I laid eyes upon you, Gabriel. Where have you been?'

'Life grew a little too heated for me in London and I took myself to parts more rural until matters cooled sufficient that I could return.'

'The law or an angry husband?'

Cain's look was reproving. 'I was too slippery for the law, Jonas, you know that.'

Flynt smiled. An inability to keep his breeches buttoned was ever his old friend's downfall. That he had never contracted a dose of the flapdragon was thanks more to good fortune than care. 'Four years,' Flynt mused. 'That husband's anger must have been prodigious.'

'Indeed it was, and he was a powerful man with equally powerful friends. I had to wait until he went to his reward before I felt it safe to return.'

'And to reacquaint yourself with his widow?'

A wistful sigh. 'Alas, she took my enforced absence as a reflection of my lack of affection for her rather than a means of self-preservation, so she has expressed little desire to enjoy any future congress. 'Tis a pity, for she is a fine-looking woman and her late lamented was as much use to her in the tup as a dog has for a side pocket, but there we have it. Anyway, there are other wives.'

'And husbands.'

Cain laughed. 'Always the way of it!'

'How long have you been back?'

'A few weeks.'

'And we only now meet?'

That brought a shamed look. 'I have felt it prudent to continue to lay low as much as possible until I sniffed the air a little. The old bastard may be gone but his friends remain. I did call at your old lodgings but you had moved.'

Flynt made a habit of moving as often as possible but leaving no forwarding address. His longest period in one place was in his current room within the Golden Cross coaching inn, where he was comfortable.

He asked, 'And the air is now sweeter?'

Cain laughed. 'As sweet as ever it is in this stinking cesspit of a city. But, by God, I missed its stench. And you, Jonas, I missed you.' He lowered his voice a little. 'Are you still active upon the heaths?'

They had both followed the highwayman life, working in tandem or singly. Flynt had preferred to work alone but he had met and liked Cain, who had proved to be a loyal, trustworthy man. For a thief.

'That life became too hot for me, too,' Flynt said, truthfully.

'We are all within a judge's fart of Tyburn, my friend. So what dark arts do you engage in now? You didn't return to the crack lay, did you?'

'When I have to, but Old Tom Schofield's death took the pleasure out of that.' Old Tom had stumbled in the street and under the hooves and wheels of a delivery wagon. 'I make a modest living turning a card and throwing a dice or two. I keep myself out of trouble when I can.'

Cain couldn't conceal his disbelief. 'You have turned square cove?'

Flynt smiled at his old friend's reaction. 'As much as a man such as I can be. But what of you?'

'This and that, my friend. A job here, a job there. Always one step ahead of the magistrates of this fair land and at least two from the hangman. But we should have a drink together.' He pushed the second glass towards Flynt and poured a measure. 'Let us sit a while, and talk over old times, eh? That is, if you have the leisure in your busy life of turning cards and throwing dice.'

He could do nought until he received word from Bess, so dropped his hat on the table. 'Nothing that can't wait.'

Cain laughed. 'It's right glad I am to see you, you Scotch bastard.'

Flynt grinned, suddenly feeling lighter of heart than he had for months. 'And I you, you cockney laggard.'

Cain raised his glass. 'To good times and bad times.'

'And those in between,' Flynt said, then sipped at the spirit.

–

Even though he was pleased to be reunited with his old friend, Flynt still ensured that he did not imbibe overmuch. Gabriel Cain, however, was chirping merry by the time they had spent an afternoon reminiscing over old times, old robberies and old acquaintances, though Flynt knew that he had a prodigious capacity for liquor. The afternoon became evening and a meal was sought in the Black Lion, Drury Lane, Flynt prevailing upon Joseph Hines to grant them leave to use the private room upstairs, where they partook of seared steaks and potatoes. Once they had eaten, Cain lit himself a pipe and puffed smoke into the air in silence, his brow creased.

'You seem pensive, Gabriel,' Flynt observed.

'No, just thinking,' Cain replied.

Flynt smiled. 'About?'

'The names of taverns in this here city. This afternoon we were at the White Lion, here we be at the Black Lion. What is the fascination with lions in the minds of tavern keepers?'

'They display a decided lack of originality, it has to be said.'

'Then there's the White Hart, the Four Swans, the Green Dragon – a mythological beast, to be sure, but still fauna. They seem obsessed with creatures.'

Flynt shrugged. 'Signage, I would suggest. The beasts make for an eye-catching sign.'

Cain considered this while billowing tobacco fumes. 'Aye, and some are so low that they might just do that, too.' He began to laugh. 'Do you remember that inn on the Hampstead road? The landlord thought we were flirting with the barmaid, who we took to be his daughter or niece...'

'And it transpired she was his wife.'

'The man was all of sixty years, if he was a day, and she was but twenty. And all we were doing was passing the time of day with the lass.'

'Well, I was, but I had the feel that you were in earnest in your wooing.'

'If yon regular customer had not tipped us the wink, I do believe that landlord would have utilised the fowling piece he kept behind the counter.'

'Aye, a hasty retreat was called for.'

Cain's mirth subsided and he fell silent again for a moment. 'I visited again, when I returned from the country.'

'You weren't going to have another crack at the lass, surely!'

'No, it was just a visit for an ale and perhaps a mutton pie. There was a new landlord, a new wife, older this time.'

'Did the man sell up then?'

'No, it seemed the lass was decided unhappy with her lot – her husband was prone to beating her – and she changed that circumstance by beating him to death with the stock of that fowling piece as he slept.' Cain paused again to inspect the bowl of his pipe then proceeded to relight it. 'Petty treason, they calls it, when a wife murders a husband. He deserved it but they hung her anyway. She was a fair-faced lass. Such a waste.'

The story cast a pall over the conversation. Flynt searched his memory to find the image of the young woman but found he could not. He recalled the incident but not her face and he wondered what that said about him. So many faces, so many stories, so many sad little deaths.

'And what of your woman, Jonas? Did you return to her?'

He knew to whom Gabriel referred, for they had been close friends and he was one of the few who knew of her existence. Nevertheless, he felt the familiar sting as he recalled her face. 'I did, just last year.'

'And?'

'And it was both painful and enlightening.'

He told Gabriel about his return to Edinburgh after fifteen years, of finding that Cassie, his stepsister and the woman he loved above all others, had in the interim married his boyhood best friend. Flynt had run away as a callow youth with a mind set to find adventure, but found only blood, death and an affinity with both. On his return, he found they had thought him fallen in some foreign field. There was a child, a boy, and Cassie had told him that he was the fruit of the marital bed but he suspected otherwise. The lad appeared older than the twelve years she had claimed and Flynt was certain he saw his own features reflected in his.

Gabriel listened to the tale without interruption, puffing on the pipe. When Flynt fell silent, Gabriel removed the stem from between his teeth and tapped the residue of the tobacco onto his plate.

'I know you well, Jonas, and I know you are not a man who finds revealing such personal details easy, and I am right honoured that you share them with me. You spoke of Cassie often, though that is something you may not realise, given your tendency to the taciturn. But here's what I say: you cannot return to the past, for it is gone and lives only in memory – and often that memory is more sun-kissed than the reality ever was. You carry this love for Cassie like a burden and allow it to weigh you down. If love exists, it should never be a burden, it should be something in which we rejoice. Accept that it has gone and move on. There are other women, other loves, and you cannot allow what was to cast a cloud over what could be.' He grinned. 'Look at me. I love freely and expansively. Tall, short, full-figured, slender, I love them all when I am with them.'

'And when you're not with them?'

'I'm looking ahead for the next one.'

'I thought you didn't believe in love. I recall you being most adamant about that.'

'I grow older and my views become less shrill. My view now is that belief in love is like belief in God: some have it, others don't, and it is not my place to dispute another man's beliefs.' He hesitated, which was something Flynt had never before witnessed. 'I will tell you something to which I have never admitted previous. I loved once, most deeply. Like you I was little more than a boy but old enough to know that my feelings for the girl were more than friendship.'

'Who was she?'

Gabriel waved a hand. 'Her name matters nothing now but she was beautiful, the daughter of a landowner in Surrey, not noble-born but squire by right of purchase. I was apprenticed to the groom of the estate, did I ever tell you that?'

Flynt shook his head. He knew Gabriel had hailed from the streets of St Giles originally, that like him had learned how to

77

fight and kill in the army, but that was the extent of it. Neither of them had spoken much of the lives of the boys they once were.

'Well, it was where I developed my love for the horses, both riding them and betting upon them. She and I, well, let us say that we discovered each other most fervently behind a haystack.'

The image of Cassie's face, her head back, neck arched, as they writhed together on his narrow bed in Edinburgh came to Flynt's mind. That was where they had discovered each other.

'I thought then that she was the great love of my life,' Gabriel said softly. 'The difference in our stations seemed not to trouble her in the slightest and we continued to discover each other with considerable abandon. That girl had a disdain for decency that appealed to my burgeoning base nature most devoutly.'

Cassie again, her smooth skin, her soft lips, her breathy voice as she said his name…

He pulled himself from the memory to ask, 'So what happened? Did her father end it?'

'He did, but not through any certainty of purpose. He introduced her to some minor but near-impoverished noble, her dowry I believe was most attractive to his family, and she decided she'd discover him too, while still avowing love of me. The greatest truth you can tell another is that you love them. It is also the greatest lie. It was but two days before that she professed adoration and then dropped me like a handful of hot manure and married the fellow. I was devastated, of course, but I soon found solace in the arms of the wife of one of the estate tenants and she became the first to whom I uttered that greatest lie. I have repeated that lie many times since. Nevertheless, I do often think about that girl, and whether she found happiness. It be true that you never forget your first.'

He stopped talking, as if he had run out words, and his eyes lost focus for a moment as he gazed at something over Flynt's shoulder. The memory of a face perhaps, or the echo of a voice. Flynt had adopted that look himself many times. He was unsure he could ever fully cast off this yearning for what was, because it had transformed into what might have been. It was the sense of loss with which he could not cope. Lost loves, lost friends, lost opportunities. And all because his need for adventure had proved greater than his need for Cassie.

Gabriel leaned forward as if sensing Flynt's thoughts. 'Let me speak plain, Jonas, as only old friends can. You did not love the woman, elsewise you would not have run off as you did. It is the *idea* of her that you love and that is the most insidious kind of torment.' Then he smiled. 'My point is this, never look back, for even the good memories can harbour pain. And there is an abundance of that in the present without inflicting further upon ourselves.'

He was roused from any further brooding on his faults by the landlord opening the door and admitting young Jack. The boy turned hesitant when he spied Cain sitting at the table. 'Sorry it took so long, Mr Flynt, but I weren't sure where you was.'

Flynt saw the question in Jack's eyes. 'All is well, Jack, you can speak freely in front of Gabriel. He is an old and trusted friend.'

The words sprang readily to his lips and surprised him. He had few real friends, and even fewer who he would trust with his life, but Gabriel Cain was such a person.

'I has that address for you, I writ it down,' said Jack, obviously still unsure. It spoke well of the boy that he remained cautious. He held out a slip of paper and Flynt glanced at the scrawl. The boy had his letters but his hand was far from perfect.

'She hides in the Rookery?'

Jack nodded, his eyes again flitting to Cain, who asked, 'Who hides in the Rookery?'

The Rookery was a ramshackle conglomeration of tenements, backyards and warren-like streets and alleyways. It was a place the lost, the lonely and the lawless used as refuge, hiding from life among the poor and the desperate.

'A lady I must find,' Flynt replied without hesitation. 'She is in some peril.'

79

Cain was suddenly less drunk than before. It was something Flynt had seen him do many times. He might spend a night on the brandy but he could snap into sobriety in an instant when the need arose.

'And you wish to save her from this peril?'

'I do.'

'Why? What is she to you?'

Flynt now hesitated. He trusted Gabriel but couldn't tell him everything. 'I've never met her, but I must find her and keep her safe, for she's perhaps the conduit to a man I seek.'

'You never change, Jonas, always there for a lady in distress, eh?' Cain's eyes narrowed. 'You are working on something?'

'I am.' Flynt hoped he wouldn't ask anything further.

Cain was silent as he processed this information. 'And the doxy you spoke with today, and sent this young cove after, she is key to finding the lady.' He wasn't asking, he was stating it as fact. Gabriel Cain was always fleet of thought. He did have another query, however. 'And who threatens her?'

Flynt again saw no reason to lie. 'The Trasks.'

An eyebrow raised. 'Good God, that brace of hellhounds should have been put down long ago. And is it safe to assume if they hunt this girl then they also seek this gentleman?'

Before Flynt could confirm that, Jack cleared his throat. 'That's another reason why I took so long, Mr Flynt. I weren't the only one what was on Bess's tail.'

'Not the Trasks?'

'No, spotted a cove as soon as I left you. Bess didn't have no notion that he was at her back and he didn't know I was at his. But he followed her from the White Lion to the Rookery.'

'Who was it?'

'Cove I knows, does some peaching when he can. I would hazard he sees a way of turning some coin. He's a cunning rogue and his peepers is ever open for anything that might be traded to his advantage.'

Flynt put it all together. 'The Trasks are none too subtle in their ways, so it's an easy thing to assume that this fellow knows

80

they are searching for Sal and perhaps knows that Bess is friendly with her. He could be keeping watch on her in case she knows where she is. I'd lay odds he's already on his way to parlay that address for coin.'

Cain stood, picked up his hat and when Flynt had not moved, gave him an impatient stare. 'So, do you intend to sit there and simply digest your meal or shall we go save this lady from whatever depredations the Trasks have in mind? I know that pair, as do you Jonas, and if they get to her first, they will not be gentle.'

'I'll be coming with you, Mr Flynt,' Jack said.

Flynt stood. 'No, you get home. This work is not for you.'

Jack was defiant. 'Bess is my girl…'

'You're a flash lad, but this may turn bloody and you are not cut out for such activity. This is what I do.' He jutted his chin towards Cain, standing at Jack's side, and amended his statement. 'This is what *we* do. We'll look out for Bess, have no worries.'

Cain rubbed Jack's mop of fair hair, an action not appreciated by the boy. 'For luck,' Cain explained.

'How does messing up my strummel bring you luck?'

Cain laughed and flipped a coin with his thumb towards Jack before making his way to the door. 'Who can say, Jack my lad? It certainly can't hurt!' He turned to watch Flynt pick up his coat and cane. 'Like old times, Jonas, eh? Lock up your valuables, your homes, your wives, prime your pistols and sharpen your blades, for Cain and Flynt are together again!'

He laughed as he descended the stairs, leaving Jack's expression puzzled. 'Is he always like this?'

Flynt positioned his hat, pulled on his coat, and threw a coin he'd fished from his pocket to the boy, who caught it with ease. 'You'll grow used to him, Jack.'

Jack nodded his gratitude for the money but gave the empty doorway a careful look. 'I ain't so sure about that, Mr Flynt. You be careful with him. What Bess said about you? I feel that about your friend there. He ain't right…'

9

The address Jack had given him was a four-storey timber tenement in the most dismal back street of the Rookery, and that
was quite a feat. The light was dying when they arrived, leaving
what sky they could see striated with reds, pinks and purples.
Flynt and Cain stood in the muck-ridden road, staring up at
the dirty windows of the rickety dwellings rising up on either
side like footpads about to pounce. The air was heavy with the
noisome aroma of human and animal waste mixed with the
rot of damp wood and smoke from cooking fires. Pedestrians
stepped around them, most taking care not to step in any of
the filth, others not caring, as if immune to the reek. Those
individuals carried about themselves a miasma of their own
thanks to unwashed clothes covering skin that was a stranger
to soap and water.

Cain grimaced slightly. 'In the name of sweet Jesus, that's
a smell I can never forget.' He took a step back to study the
building again. 'I was raised in a shithole like this. My old mum
made sure I had my letters, said she didn't want me turning
out like my father, whoever he was, because she never breathed
his name. She said she wanted me to get out of St Giles and
make something of myself but she lived there all her life, died
there before her time. I was away by then, serving queen and
country.' He fell silent but Flynt understood that it was not an
invitation for him to speak. 'She deserved better. Better than
the stinking hovel she lived and died in, better than whoever
it was that sired me, better than me, in truth. She never had a

chance in life.' Another period of reflection followed, then he said, with an element of forced levity, 'So what is our strategy?'

Flynt considered for a moment. 'I get in the room, and if the Trasks aren't there convince the girl to come with me.'

'And if the Trasks are there?'

'Kill them, then convince the girl to come with me.'

Gabriel smiled. 'Subtle as ever, Jonas.'

'Sometimes subtlety is not required, Gabriel. Sometimes all you need is Tact, Diplomacy and a steady hand.'

Flynt led the way into the gloom of the building's entranceway, flicking his coat open to thrust his silver cane into his belt.

Cain followed, shaking his head as Flynt drew both pistols. 'I never understood why you gave them names.'

'It's a foible.'

'It's not a foible, damned strange, is what it is. I often used to wonder if you spoke to them when in your private moments.' Gabriel lowered his voice as he stared into the darkness of the hallway. 'I met a fellow in the north who gave his pecker a name. Conversed with it, too.'

Flynt listened to the sounds of the building but asked, 'What name did he give it?'

'Dick.'

'Somewhat obvious, is it not?'

'Believe me, the thing was somewhat obvious. It was so big it frightened my mare.'

Voices from above were carried through the gloom. A baby cried. A dog barked. Life existed in these dismal surroundings.

'What floor?' Cain whispered.

'Top.'

Cain sighed. 'Of course it is. When is it ever not the top floor?'

Flynt smiled. It felt good to have his friend at his side again. 'Do you think the Trasks are already here?'

Flynt didn't reply immediately. His ears were alert for anything untoward. Raised voices, perhaps, boots on sagging floorboards, a woman's cries, the sound of blows. He heard nothing but that didn't mean they weren't already up there. He felt his fingers tingle and his heart beat a little faster at the prospect. He had no desire for conflict but if it was to be, then he would be prepared for it. 'They've had a sufficiency of time to reach here. What do you think?'

Cain thought about this, then reached under his coat to produce his own brace of pistols. 'I think you're right.'

Flynt paused at the foot of the stairs. The dying light reached the next landing through either a grimy window or gaps in the slats but it remained heavily shadowed. 'I need you to stay down here,' he said.

'Why?'

'Because my arrival will not be welcome, especially if Bess is still here, for the girl is no friend to me. Two of us appearing of a sudden might be perceived to be heavy-handed.'

'Heavy-handed has never concerned you before.'

'I can be subtle on occasion.'

'Let's hope this is not the wrong occasion.'

Flynt began to climb the stairs. 'Come running if you hear shooting.'

Gabriel melted back into the darkness of the ground floor, his footsteps signifying that he was moving to the rear of the passageway where there was little chance of him being seen should the Trasks appear. Flynt continued his ascent, pistols raised, every sense alert. Alleyways and stairways, he thought. How many times, he wondered, had he walked down one or scaled the other while preparing himself for whatever encounter awaited him above? He had visited the Rookery months before and it had resulted in a man's death. Previously, he'd had call to seek another in a locale indistinguishable from this Rookery across the river in Southwark. That, too, had ended with the one he sought lying dead but also himself nearly succumbing to the tender embraces of a Russian brute. That was the way of it, however. His work always brought him to hovels such as this in search of a person or an item, which more often than not ended in loss of life and violence. Such was his life. How many more times would he do similar? And which one would prove to be his undoing?

He crept along the first-floor passage, head craned upwards to detect any movement on the next flight of stairs as he attempted to reduce the thud of his boot heels on the ageing floorboards. He passed three doorways, detected voices beyond each, the crying child still wailing but now joined by a woman's soft voice attempting to soothe it. He wondered if the baby was ill, or teething, or just upset. Or hungry with no sustenance available. Behind each door men, women, children, families lived out their lives in a shared single room within a building that was broken down almost as soon as it was constructed, living side by side with the funk of effluent and sweat and the memories of meals gone by. And rats, of course. He could hear them, scurrying in corners and behind the walls. Of all creatures of the earth, those were the ones he detested, feared, the most. He shuddered as he paused halfway up the second flight of stairs to look downwards between the flimsy bannisters to the ground floor but could not see Gabriel. He would be there, though, of that he was certain. And if trouble lay ahead, he had someone at his back. It had been a long time since he'd had that luxury and it gave him pleasure.

The second floor was identical to the first, the only difference being the barking dog in one room and along with it the laughter of a child as he or she played with the animal. He smiled. Even in the grimmest of surroundings there was pleasure to be had.

He eased up the next flight, the top floor ahead, where he came to a halt. The note Jack had given him said Cheshire Sal was behind the third door, to the front. His ears cocked for sounds emanating from the room at the far end of the corridor.

If the Trasks were there he believed he would have heard something, even a woman's tears, but nothing reached his ears. He paused at each of the other two doorways to listen but no sound issued, so the tenants were not at home or the rooms were single occupancy and whoever was within had nobody to converse with, apart from their own thoughts and remembrances. And their failings. Flynt did not hold discussions with his pistols, as Gabriel had suggested, but he was well acquainted with those conversations of the mind.

He pressed his ear to the final door, detected voices, two women, one he was certain being Bess, her tone normal, conversational. Confident the Trask brothers were not there, he replaced his pistols, but in his belt, not in the special pockets sewn into his coat. What would happen next did not require firepower but some actual tact and diplomacy, though they had to be within easy reach for he felt sure the Trasks' appearance was imminent. He draped the folds of his coat over the pistol butts, slid his cane free, then rapped his knuckles on the door.

Inside, conversation stopped as if it had been cut by a knife.

Flynt waited, his ear still close to the wood, but no further conversation reached him from within. He imagined the women holding their breath as they considered whether to answer. The door's flimsy wood would be very easily broken down but he had no wish to alarm them further. He stepped back to peer over the bannister to the ground floor, saw no movement, heard no voices, then moved back, leaned in closer and raised his voice slightly, hoping it would carry no further than into the room.

'My name is Jonas Flynt, Sally. I'm here to give you aid.'

He thought he heard a few muttered words, then swift footfalls and the door jerked open to reveal an angry Bess, her eyes spitting fire, her lips thinned, her tone like a dagger blade.

'You followed me, you bastard! You let me think you was honourable but you tails me and...' She stopped, understanding bleeding into her eyes. 'No, you had Jack do it, 'cos he would do anything for you, the little bastard. He can kiss goodbye to any tupping now...'

'Jack had nothing to do with it.' Flynt brushed past her. If he waited for an invitation he would still be standing there when the cock crowed.

His tone was brusque, for he had no time to assuage Bess's rage at what she saw as a betrayal of trust. He plucked his hat off and looked to the woman lying on a cot against the far wall, a threadbare blanket wrapped around her shoulders even though the night was clement. She did not appear unwell, so it was fear that sapped the heat from her bones. Sally was an attractive woman and even in the dim light of the candle he detected the features of John Duck in hers, but whereas her brother's handsome face was unlined, hers bore the marks of the life she had led. Providing men with pleasure, and the bodily abuses that go with it, often aged a woman before her time. Bess was another example. She was Jack's senior only by a few years but she had the face of a woman fifteen years older. She also had the tongue of a grog-addled labourer.

'You are a fucking bastard, Jonas Flynt, a damned slippery weasel.'

'I apologise for the intrusion but time is of the essence...'

Bess closed the door. 'Don't trust him, Sal, he's a goddamned rogue and a cheat and he will sell you to the highest bidder sooner than I can spit.'

Flynt ignored her. 'Madame, I am come to take you to your brother, where you'll be safe.'

Sally's head shake was forlorn. 'Nowhere is safe, mister, and I can't expose my brother to the peril.'

'He's already been exposed to it and equipped himself right well, for he still breathes. He's gathering your family and friends to rally to your side when you're returned home. The Trasks won't get to you while you're in their care.'

At mention of their name, she shrank against the wall. 'They mustn't get me.'

He held out a hand. 'They won't, but we must leave this place.'

'She's quite safe here,' Bess insisted.

'No, she's not,' Flynt said, his voice firm, 'they know you're here.'

Sally's terror increased and Bess folded her arms, her face still sculpted by defiance, but she swallowed hard and shot a look over her shoulder to the door. 'How did they find her?'

'The same way I did.' She knew the truth of it so there was little point in denying it. 'You were followed, Bess.'

Guilt flashed in her glance towards Sally. 'I was right careful, honest I was, Sal.'

Flynt felt sympathy for her self-reproach but had no time to be charitable. 'Not careful enough. We're ahead of them but I'd hazard not for long, so we must leave and leave now.'

Bess was not for letting go. 'Don't listen to him, Sal, he's a liar. He just wants to know where Chris is…'

'That's true, but there's little time for such discussion. I beseech you, madame, gather what belongings you have here and let us get you to into your brother's care. I assure you that you'll be safer there than here.'

'I was proper careful,' Bess insisted, perhaps in an attempt to reassure herself. 'There weren't nobody at my back, of that I is certain.'

Flynt's gaze in her direction was stern. 'Then how came I to be here?'

He waited for an answer but his logic had silenced her. She muttered something about Jack being a sly little shit and Flynt felt brief remorse over possibly queering the lad's relationship with the girl, but he returned his attention to Sally. 'Madame, it is with deep regret that I have to say this, but at this juncture you have a choice – if you wish to live you either come with me willingly or I'll wrap you in that blanket and carry you off. One way or the other, we're leaving.'

Sally's dark eyes moved from him to Bess, as if expecting the solution to her quandary to be written upon their foreheads. Finally, she reached a decision and began to rise.

Relieved, Flynt held his hand out to assist her to her feet. She seemed weak and frail. 'When was the last time the lady ate?' he asked Bess.

'She won't eat nothing,' Bess said, one finger jerking towards bread and cheese on a table. 'I brung her food, some broth earlier, but she won't touch it. She's bad scared, she is.'

When Sally cast off the blanket, he saw how thin she was. He gripped her by both shoulders and stared into her face. 'Tell me true. Can you walk?'

A barely imperceptible nod was her answer.

'Very well,' Flynt said. 'We'll take a hackney, but we must clear the Rookery before one can be found. Bess, help the lady to dress and gather what she needs, I'll...'

He stopped when he heard the thunder of booted feet on the floorboards outside the door and he spun, pulling Tact and Diplomacy just as it crashed open to frame two men, each with a brace of pistols in their fists. They were not large men, both being short but bulky, as if they were nothing but walking muscle. Their faces were broad, their noses squashed, whether by nature or violence Flynt knew not. The eyes, though, were sharp and they swiftly overcame their surprise at seeing him.

'Look who it be, brother,' said one.

'Jonas Flynt, as I live and fart, brother,' said the other.

They were as near identical siblings as he had ever seen, but Remus was slightly taller and his voice was more nasal. He sported a deep gash to one cheek while his brother had lost the top part of an ear, both wounds still red and raw, so Flynt felt it safe to assume they had been caused by John Duck's blade. The lacerations did not undermine the men's good looks for they were far from fetching in the first place.

'Gentlemen,' he said, politely, keeping a pistol trained on each of them. 'I wish I could say it's a pleasure to see you once more, but I'm giving up lying for Lent.'

Remus smiled, revealing two rows of very small, brown teeth, some pointed as if they had been filed. 'Lent is well past.'

'I am most devout.'

Romulus narrowed his eyes. 'I didn't know you was papist, Flynt.'

'He's having sport with us, brother,' said Remus.

Romulus covered his shame at being fooled by leering towards the women. 'You here for a bit of business, Flynt?'

'He is certainly fully cocked and ready, brother,' said Remus, waving one pistol at the two pointed towards them.

Romulus raised his twin pistols a little higher. 'As are we, brother, and we is four barkers to his two. I'd say that means we has the advantage, what say you, Flynt?'

Flynt, who knew that it didn't take a Sir Isaac Newton to compute that arithmetical problem and reach a similar conclusion, wondered where the hell Gabriel was. 'It only takes one well-placed shot to rearrange matters more in my favour.'

'If you gets it off,' Remus observed. 'But there ain't no need for such unpleasantness between us gentlemen. All we wants is that whore yonder and we will be on our way, sweet as you please. You can have the other one to do with as you wish.' His eyes roamed over Bess as though they were a pair of hands. 'She looks a fine lay, she does, so I reckons you has a right bargain. That is, if you shows good sense.'

'I regret, gentlemen,' Flynt laid some heavy irony on the word, 'good sense and I are often distant acquaintances. It's a flaw in my character.'

Remus licked his lips. 'That is a crying shame, that is, ain't it, brother?'

'It be a real sin, brother.' It was Romulus's turn to smile, his discoloured teeth sporting a gap on the lower set. Flynt had seen such before, caused by a powerful blow of a sword hilt to the mouth, and he wondered if that was another indicator of how the brothers had come off the worst in their encounter with John Duck.

'That it is, that it is,' Remus said, almost sadly. 'But if that be the way of things, then so be it.'

Flynt was about to throw himself to the side when another voice joined the conversation.

'Now, now, boys, let's not be too hasty in applying finger to trigger, eh. This space is a great deal confined and the sound of gunfire would be most deafening.'

Gabriel's face appeared behind the brothers, a pistol in each hand and pressed against the back of their heads. To their credit, they displayed no fear, for they had been under guns before. They both whirled further into the room, fanning their arms so that each had one weapon trained on Cain, the other on Flynt.

Cain covered his surprise at the speed of their reaction with a grin. 'Nimble buggers, aren't they?'

Remus took a moment, then said, 'Gabriel Cain, ain't it? I heard you'd been dangled out west somewhere.'

'I also heard that, and most relieved I was to learn that it wasn't true, but as you can see I am very much alive and the only thing that has kissed this neck are the lips of some beautiful women. And my horse, once, but that's not something I like to discuss.' Cain seemed to take note of the women for the first time and he gave them a courteous nod, while maintaining his aim on each of the brothers. 'Ladies, I regret this manner of meeting, believe me it was not of my choosing.'

Bess and Sally had backed against the wall, but Bess had picked up a three-legged stool as if preparing to hurl it at the Trasks. She showed little fear, her rage being extremely evident in both stance and glare. Flynt suspected it was not directed solely at Romulus and Remus.

The four men were ranged in a tight circle, arms splayed, weapons ready. At this range, if shooting began, there was little chance of the balls missing their mark.

'Well now,' said Romulus, his only sign of nervousness being that his voice was slightly higher than before. 'Ain't we got a pretty picture here. This is what we would call an impasse, right brother?'

'That's right, brother. An impasse.'

'My goodness, d'you hear that, Jonas?' Cain seemed surprised. 'The lads here used the word "impasse".'

Flynt allowed himself a tight smile. He had seen him do this before, fill tense situations with banter until either it was resolved or some form of action could be taken. 'It's right impressed I am, Gabriel.'

'Impressed? I'm stunned. D'you think it possible – and I'm merely floating this as a theory, of course – but you think it feasible that they have perhaps… read a book?' Cain paused to mull this over. 'No, I think it more likely they heard it used by someone else. Is that the way of it, lads? You heard it from someone who actually *has* a read a book?'

Romulus sneered. 'You can mock all you wish, Cain, but you ain't so learned yourself, despite your airs and graces. You talks well, but you is from these here streets, same as us, ain't that right, brother?'

'That be the correct of it, brother. Thinks he's better than us, they both does. But Cain's just the son of a slut, gawd knows who his father is, and Flynt here is a Scotchman, and you don't gets much lower than that, does you?'

Flynt ignored the insult, recognising it for a way of hitting back, even though he carried little doubt they believed it.

'D'you notice they call each brother, Jonas?' Cain observed, his eyes dancing in a familiar way. 'Do you think it's because they're so stupid they've forgotten what the other is called?'

'Or they can't tell themselves apart,' Flynt added.

Cain wrinkled his nose. 'Nobody can be that stupid. Can they?' He looked the brothers over as he reassessed. 'Well, perhaps they can…'

Romulus spat a gob of phlegm between them. 'Gabriel Cain, you always had tongue enough for two sets of teeth.'

'Aye,' said Remus, 'are we going to jaw here all night or get to it?'

Flynt had no desire that the situation become a bloodbath, for despite the proximity there remained the risk of a stray ball hitting one of the women. He decided it was time for some reason.

'Gentlemen, let us take a moment to consider our situation. We are evenly matched now, as you can see, and a pistol exchange would result in all four of us dead or at least mortally wounded. And to what end? Who does such a bloody outcome profit?'

'We wants that there girl,' said Romulus, jerking his head in Sally's direction while maintaining his attention on both Flynt and Cain.

'And right now I have her,' said Flynt.

'Right now nobody has her, if we is being precise,' observed Remus, correctly.

'And if we are being even more precise,' Cain said, 'if we are dead that's the way it will remain.'

The brothers digested this truth for a moment.

'We can't go back to our employer and tells him we had her but she slipped through our fingers,' said Romulus.

'Then don't tell him.' Flynt would dearly love to know who had paid them but he knew they would not divulge the name. There was no honour in their business but such information was only to be used to escape the noose, or when it became more profitable.

The brothers exchanged a look, each perhaps understanding his sibling's thoughts without words being required.

'Gentlemen,' Flynt said, 'we are all professionals. There is nothing personal in this, just a job. Consider this, is this lady worth dying over? Is it not prudent to simply ascribe this to the exigencies of fate and we all walk away?'

Romulus spat again. 'Aye, but which of us walks away with the girl?'

Cain laughed. It was an easy laugh, for he was enjoying this. He always did find pleasure in extreme situations. 'As our learned friends here said, we have an impasse. So let's get to the shooting and when the smoke clears we'll see who are the last men standing.'

They fell silent, eight guns loaded, cocked and trained on four men. Eyes flicked back and forth, searching for a sign that a trigger was about to be pulled. Bess still hefted the stool but she seemed to have forgotten it. Sally had wrapped her arms over her breasts, as if hugging herself to keep warm. Flynt forced his breathing to remain even and his arms steady. Cain seemed relaxed, as was his custom, sporting a half smile that Flynt knew so well, as if he dared the brothers to make a move. The Trasks, however, began to display nervousness. Beads of sweat broke out on their brow that were not the result of the warm evening air. Romulus licked his lips, Remus's hands trembled just a little, but enough to show that his resolve might be wavering. Finally, their eyes locked and that unspoken message passed between them again.

It was Romulus who spoke. 'He what fights and runs away, eh?' he said with a wavering smile. 'Ain't no need for us all to meet Old Mr Grim over a bobtail bitch.'

He and his brother edged towards the door, their weapons still trained. Cain moved back into the hallway to allow them to pass.

'You show wisdom I never thought you to possess, lads,' he said.

'Don't need no book-learning to know a lost cause, do it?' Romulus sneered as he and his brother backed towards the top of the stairs, Flynt marking them from a position by the door. 'But we will have us a reckoning, you and us, and that is a sure bet.'

Both Cain and Flynt recognised that there was no further point in exchanging more jibes, so they watched the two men descend the stairs, weapons trained until the last possible moment. Once he was satisfied they had reached the ground floor and there was no sign of them returning, Flynt whirled back towards the room.

Cain followed. 'First impasse, then he quotes Tacitus.'

'Misquotes.'

'True, but Romulus Trask seems to have hidden depths.'

'Hidden shallows, more like. And there's more to that quote.' Flynt looked to the ladies. 'We must go. Now.'

Bess looked confused. 'But they's gone, ain't they? And who is this Taciturn cove you be talking about?'

'Tacitus. He was a Roman orator who said, "He that fights and runs away, lives to fight another day." I'm not sure if the Trasks are aware of that section but I'm unwilling to bet our lives upon it. Sally, gather what you need. Bess, help her.'

Gabriel stood sentinel by the door, his attention on the stairway. 'You believe they will lie in wait?'

Flynt joined him. 'Do you not?'

Cain's lips thinned. 'Yes.' He remained silent for a moment. 'They may split up, one to the front, one to the rear. Or they may simply ambush us on the stairs.'

Flynt nodded his assent to the latter. 'Confined space, lots of shadows making it easy to attack, less likelihood of us making our escape than if they came at us in the street or back yard.'

Cain crept to the bannister in order to peer below then stealthily returned. 'I can't see a damned thing down there, nor hear anything.'

'They are exceeding accomplished at such ambush. We won't hear them until they wish us to.'

Cain looked beyond Flynt to where Bess and Sally bustled around the room, finding clothes and thrusting what few possessions the latter had into a sack, then lowered his voice even further. 'The ladies are a liability, Jonas.'

'The ladies are why we are here.'

'I know that, but it will be difficult to defend ourselves and them if, or when, the Trasks make their move.'

'Then what do you suggest?'

'We take the fight to them. We go down there alone. Deal with them. Then we can transport the ladies to the brother.'

Flynt thought this over. The suggestion was a gamble, but there was sense in it. Confrontation was inevitable but this way they wouldn't need to worry about Bess and Sally being caught in the mêlée. 'If just one of the Tasks gets by us, they'll be vulnerable.'

'They don't want Sally dead, do they? They want the same information you seek. They won't harm her.'

'But they will harm Bess.'

'Don't you be worrying about me, Jonas bloody Flynt.'

Flynt turned and saw that Bess was holding a pistol. 'Where did you get that?'

It was Sally who responded. 'It's Christopher's. He left it with me for my protection but I fired it by accident one night when I took fright at a noise and I have nothing with which to load it.'

Flynt placed his own pistols in his belt and took this new weapon from Bess's hand in order to examine it. It was far from new but he thought it functional. 'Would you be able to wield this efficiently?' he asked Bess.

She gave him a scornful look. 'There ain't no great trick to making it bark. You cock it, point the end with the hole at what you want to hit and pull the trigger.'

'There is more to shooting at a man than that, Bess. You need to be deliberate, need to be aware that when you pull that trigger you may well take a life. That should never be easy.'

'From what I hears you finds it easy enough.' Her withering look deepened. 'Just load the damned thing, let me worry about how deliberate I is. If one of them Trasks shows his beak around that door, I'll blow it off.'

Cain shrugged, as if to say that they had little choice, so Flynt began to load the weapon, taking a ball from a leather pouch attached to his belt and a powder flask from the pocket of his coat. He poured the correct amount of powder into the muzzle before placing a patch of wadding over the barrel's end and positioned the lead shot in the centre of the bore. He then slid the ramrod from the underside of the pistol barrel and wedged it all in tightly. Once the ramrod was back in place, he lifted the frizzen, the metal hinge in the shape of a raised L, to reveal the pan. Here he placed a small amount of primer, poured from another flask in his pocket, then eased it in place with his thumb. He clicked the frizzen back in place, protecting the primer, then took Bess's wrist to place the butt of the pistol in her hand, ensuring it was aimed at the floor.

'You cock it by pulling back the hammer here then, as you say, point and fire. Don't aim it unless you mean to use it and if you have to use it, for God's sake don't try to be fancy, you've one chance to put him down and you have to take it. Don't hesitate, don't think about it, it has to be as if the weapon is part of you. As soon as he comes through the door, take aim at the centre of his body and fire. Don't think of him as a man, just tell yourself that if you don't put him down then he'll put you down, understand?'

'Whichever of those bastards comes here, he ain't no man. He comes through that door, he's dead meat.'

'And for God's sake,' Cain said, 'have a care that it's not Flynt or I.'

A little smile softened Bess's taut lips. 'We shall see.'

Still unconvinced she knew how difficult it was to intentionally take a life, Flynt merely grunted and moved back to join Cain beyond the doorway.

'She's a tough girl,' Gabriel said, 'but will she be able to handle it if the time comes?'

Flynt pursed his lips and raised an eyebrow. 'Let's do our best to ensure that she is not put to the test.' He hefted Tact and Diplomacy once again. 'Are you ready?'

Cain grinned. 'Let us pray for good fortune, eh?'

'Good fortune is what happens when preparation meets opportunity,' Flynt said.

'Are we prepared, Jonas?'

Flynt gave a final look to the women. Sally was again sitting on the cot, her sack beside her, her face drawn and terrified.

Bess stood over her, her right hand holding the pistol cradled in the left across her stomach, determination etched deeply on her face.

'As prepared as we can be,' he said, and stepped into the hallway.

Cain followed. 'Then let us once more unto the breach, dear friend...'

10

They walked a few feet apart, for two men bunched together made an easier target than one occupying his own space. No sunlight now penetrated any chinks in the woodwork or forced its way through grimy windows. The stairway was in almost complete darkness and the steps themselves groaned as if protesting about the men's combined weight, but they weren't attempting stealth. If the Trasks awaited below, and Flynt was convinced they did, then the idea was to draw them out. It was a risky strategy but they had faced such situations before and emerged relatively unscathed. They each bore scars, however, and some were not visible, for violent confrontations that result in death, like failed love affairs, can rob a man of little pieces of himself. Flynt felt the tension grow but it didn't stiffen his muscles, which was welcome. He needed to be loose, to be fluid, to be able to move freely if he was to survive what was to come.

His eyes grew accustomed to the lack of light but he could still see only a little way ahead. He stared into the darkness at the foot of the stairs, alert for any shift within the shadows, any sound hanging in the air; the rustle of fabric, the scrape of a boot heel, the rasp of hot breath, the click of a hammer being cocked. The lack of light worked in favour of both sides, for if they could not see the Trasks, then the Trasks could not see them. They reached the second floor and as they turned along the passageway he looked over his shoulder. He didn't need illumination to know that Cain would be smiling in anticipation of impending action. He had once told Flynt that the only time he felt truly alive was when facing the prospect of death; for the blood to course in his veins and his heart to beat faster he needed the thrill of violence. The rest was merely breathing, eating, shitting and tupping. Flynt understood the concept, for he felt his own blood quicken the further they descended.

They moved at a brisk pace, as though eager to face whatever lay ahead, then turned onto the final flight of steps, where as if by unspoken agreement they both became still. Cain waved one of his pistols ahead as if to say that if were to be done, it was best it be done quickly. Flynt silently agreed. It had to be now or never.

They had taken only three steps down when the first shot exploded from the shadows below. Thankfully it was poorly aimed but it buried itself in the wall less than a foot from Flynt's head. He crouched and snapped his own shot in the direction of the orange muzzle flash and was gratified to hear a groan. He and Cain, two steps above him, both ducked down below the handrail as another two pistols discharged in their direction, one bullet splintering the bannister riser close to them, sending tiny shards of rotting wood flying, but the other jerking Cain to his right, causing him to lose possession of one weapon while he let loose with his other. Flynt shot him an anxious glance but he gritted his teeth and shook his head, giving the thin trickle of dark liquid on his shoulder little more than a cursory look. The aftershock of the gunfire reverberated through the air but when it died left an even deeper silence than before. That silence was brief, for it was broken almost immediately by the dog barking again and waking the baby. Flynt hoped nobody would emerge to remonstrate with them. But then, this was the Rookery and it was more than likely they would keep away when hearing gunfire in the dark.

He considered reloading but decided against it. He had one shot left, as did one of the brothers, and the routine with powder and ball, even though in his experienced hands taking mere seconds, would distract him. He had to be ready for whatever happened next. Gabriel stretched out his hand to find the weapon he had dropped but it had tumbled down the steps into the murk. Instead, he drew a short parrying dagger with his left hand and held it ready to ward off an attack. They waited, lying flat on their backs and immobile on the stairs, legs supporting them on the uneven surface. Flynt stretched his pistol before him, swivelling it left and right, ready to fire. He had hit one of them, he knew that, because in the flickering illumination of the muzzle flashes during the brief firefight he had seen a figure slumped against a wall, one arm seemingly lifeless at his side, while the other triggered his pistol, but whether the wound was mortal he could not tell.

Someone silenced the dog and the child's cries stilled and the stairway was once again coated in a deep hush, as if the ageing timbers themselves steeled themselves for the next exchange of gunfire. The odour of burnt gunpowder floated around them. Flynt strained to hear any movement below them, perhaps a pistol being reloaded, but heard nothing. He thought he could detect harsh breathing, the wounded brother perhaps, but he was not certain. They hadn't retreated, they would have heard their footfalls, so whichever one of the Trasks remained standing, if he did remain standing, lurked within that silence, hidden by the shadows, contemplating his next move. For the time being they could only lie still but alert for whatever occurred next.

When it came, it came suddenly. Remus Trask charged out of the darkness with a bellow, both weapons raised – he had obviously reloaded – so Flynt fired quickly, saw a puff of red blossom on the man's right side but he kept pounding up the stairs, his face contorted with rage, holding his fire until he was certain of a kill shot. Flynt dropped his spent pistol, fumbled for the cane in his belt but knew in his heart that Trask could pull those triggers before he could clear the blade. Gabriel began to rise, dagger at the ready, but he would also know it was futile. One or both were going to die on this dank, dismal stairway this night.

The sound of the pistol shot above and behind them was surprisingly loud. At first it seemed that it had not hit its mark but then a look of extreme surprise filled Remus Trask's face. His forward motion was brought to a sudden halt and for a moment he was rigid, but then his features sagged as if being melted by the hot blood that streamed from under his scalp, his pistols sliding from loose fingers as he tipped backwards to vanish back into the murk, his limp body slamming against the wall at the foot of the stairs.

Flynt twisted round to where Bess stood at the stairhead, the pistol still trained on where Trask had been standing, as if she had another ball to fire.

'I did what you said, Flynt, aimed for the centre of his body.' She nodded to the shadows at the foot of the stairs. 'I still got the bastard in the head.'

He and Cain hauled themselves upright. Flynt slid his blade free and moved down to where Remus Trask lay on the floor, his head propped against the wall at an awkward angle, his eyes still bearing that look of astonishment at how death can come in a single moment. It was a look with which Flynt was familiar. Gabriel stooped to retrieve his unspent pistol and without a word, and little more than a disinterested glance at the corpse, merged with the shadows in search of Romulus.

Flynt climbed back up the stairs to Bess, who hadn't moved. When he was close enough to see her face clearly, her eyes were as impenetrable as the darkness that now shrouded the man she had killed. He reached out to ease the pistol from her fingers.

'Bess, go fetch Sally,' Flynt said, his voice gentle. 'We'll leave immediately.' With a final glance towards the foot of the stairs, she stepped away but was stopped by Flynt's voice. 'And Bess?' She turned, waited. 'Thank you for what you did.'

A curt retort must have sprung into her mind, for her mouth opened slightly, but closed as she thought better of it. Instead, she gave him a quick nod then walked along the upper corridor. Flynt listened to her footsteps as they ascended. Earlier in the tavern he had said he bore her no ill will and it was true, but neither did he have warm feelings for her. However, knowing that in a single moment, with a twitch of a finger, she had taken a man's life and in so doing had perhaps changed her own, he felt sadness.

A low whistle reached out to him from the darkness below, then Cain said, 'This one still lives.'

Flynt found him stooped over the prone figure of Romulus Trask. He was braced against the wall just as Flynt had seen in the brief flashes, his right arm resting on his lap, the hole in his shoulder oozing dark blood that trailed from the sleeve of his coat to pool on his upturned palm. Unlike his brother, however, he still breathed and his eyes raised to Flynt.

'Remus?'

Flynt kept his voice gentle. 'He's gone.'

Trask's body slumped a little and his chin dropped to his chest. Grief in one such as he was unexpected but then, Flynt reasoned, they were brothers and they had been close. Even the direst of villains can grieve a loved one's loss. Romulus had fully intended to kill him, but Flynt felt some sympathy for the anguish he now felt.

Cain was not so forgiving. 'We should finish him off, Jonas.'

Even though he knew this to be the wisest course of action, Flynt could not allow that. Killing in self-defence was one thing, but to do so when the man was no longer a threat was little more than cold-blooded murder. 'No, let him live.'

'He'll come after us. He'll come after the girl.'

Gabriel didn't mean Sally, he meant Bess, and he was correct. Trask would have heard the words exchanged after Romulus died and would know what had occurred. Still, he could not bring himself to sanction his death, but he was aware that a forceful message had to be delivered. He placed his boot on the man's right shoulder, over the wound. Trask knew what was about to happen and tried to shift away but Flynt eased his foot down, forcing blood to cascade from under his sole.

Trask screamed and wriggled violently to free himself, but Flynt maintained the pressure.

'Do you feel that, Romulus?' He leaned closer, his boot grinding into the bullet hole. 'That pain? If it as much as crosses your mind to seek redress for the death of your brother, it will be nothing compared to what I'll inflict. Mourn him. Bury him. Then leave this city, go somewhere that I will not chance upon you, for I may not be so forgiving should we meet again.' He removed his foot and leaned in closer to grip Romulus's chin between thumb and forefinger, forcing him to see the truth in his eyes. 'Do you understand me, Romulus? Do not test me on this, for you will not live to regret it.'

Romulus nodded fervently and Flynt relinquished his hold before turning away, swallowing back the bitter taste of his own bile, Trask's whimpers like dagger thrusts to his conscience.

The women approached from above and he met them halfway to assist Sally, fleetingly glancing at Bess's expression as she passed Remus's body but her mouth was set firm and her eyes bore her customary flintiness.

Cain was impassive as he watched Trask weeping and writhing, his left hand pressed at the wound as if he could somehow ease the agony.

'Let us away then, Gabriel,' said Flynt, his own sense of guilt keeping his eyes averted from the man on the floor.

'You go on, I'll stand by our friend here until you're safely away.'

Something in his tone brought Flynt to a standstill. 'Leave him be, Gabriel.'

Even in the dimness of the hallway, he could see that Cain's smile was broad and innocent. 'Of course I will.'

Flynt studied his face. 'I mean it. Give me your word.'

'My word is given, Jonas. I intend only to ensure that Romulus here does not summon sufficient strength to pursue. After all, the poor man is injured and he shouldn't be engaging in any further physical activity. We wouldn't want him to suffer further discomfort, would we?'

Cain was adept at hiding his true feelings behind a smile and a quip. He could, as he said, be merely ensuring they made their escape without further action from Romulus, but he could also have something more permanent in mind. Gabriel Cain possessed a cold-blooded streak that belied his amiable demeanour. There was no time to argue the point, so Flynt gave him a final warning look before he led the women from the building and into the night air.

If the sound of the shooting had stirred any interest in the populace there was no sign. Indeed, the narrow street was unnaturally devoid of life. Even though daylight had long faded, there should still have been movement. But that was the way of it in the Rookery. Such occurrences were not necessarily commonplace, but those who populated these streets knew well that if a disturbance, no matter how bloody, did not involve them, they should be grateful and look to their own lives. There would be no watchman come to investigate, no authority would be summoned, not immediately. Eventually, perhaps, but not now. They had the leisure to make their escape unmolested but, even so, Flynt hurried the women away.

Cain caught up with them quickly and Flynt fell back a few steps to walk level with him. Cain did not look at him and did not smile. His gaze was fixed on the two women walking ahead, Bess supporting her friend. Flynt searched his profile for any hint of what might have occurred back in that dismal hallway but detected nothing. 'Does Romulus live?'

'Although I believe allowing him to live was folly, I did him no harm, Jonas,' Cain assured him. 'He may bleed out if that wound remains unattended but if he perishes it will not be by my hand.' His attention remained on the women. 'We must find somewhere safe for Bess.'

'I have already thought of that,' Flynt said, now scrutinising the wound on his friend's shoulder. 'We have to look to that, too.'

Cain fingered the hole in his coat and adopted a dismissive smile. 'This is nothing, a nick, no more. The ball merely gave me a kiss as it passed me by. We've both had much worse and we'll have worse in the future.'

He looked over his shoulder towards the door to the tenement, a fleeting frown creasing his forehead and shadowing his eyes, before he stared ahead once again. They continued in silence, Flynt wondering what, if anything, had occurred back in that tenement.

11

John Duck and his wife were delighted to have Sally back in the fold again. Mrs Duck was a warm, motherly woman who fussed over her sister-in-law, finding a thick blanket to wrap around her, for the walk through the streets had left Sally drained of what strength she possessed and she had slumped against Bess in the hackney they had finally found. The kindly woman led her through the long room where her husband tutored his pupils while maintaining a constant flow of reassuring chatter. The fencing master remained with Flynt, Gabriel and Bess, tears shining as he watched his sister gave him a wan smile at the door leading to the private apartments at the rear before she vanished, Mrs Duck's arm around her offering both support and protection.

He stared at the doorway for a moment, then turned to Flynt and held out his hand. 'I was wrong about you, Mr Flynt. I thought you to be a villain.'

Ignoring Bess's sharp little laugh, Flynt accepted the man's grip. 'You may not be wrong, Mr Duck.'

'You bring me my sister, safe and sound. You're no villain and we'll be eternally grateful for the service you have done my family this night.'

Bess interjected, 'Don't deceive yourself, mister, for he don't do it out of the goodness of his heart. He wants what Sally knows, he does.'

'I regret that Bess speaks the truth, Mr Duck,' Flynt admitted.

Duck displayed neither surprise nor disappointment, for Flynt had already stated such that afternoon. 'Mr Templeton, correct?'

'Aye. And I would have words with her now, if I may.'

'Does it have to be at this moment?'

'Time is short, Mr Duck. We've dealt with the brothers you've already encountered, but they may not be the only ones seeking Mr Templeton. If Sally has any knowledge of his whereabouts, I must have it if I am to save him.'

Duck gave the doorway another glance. 'She is tired, undernourished. I see the terror still burns in her eyes. She needs care and attention right now.'

'I understand that, but though she's warm in the bosom of your family, she's not yet secure.'

The fencing master frowned, still unconvinced. 'Do you really believe she knows where he is?'

Flynt was truthful. 'Perhaps not. Mr Templeton may have urged her to hide herself as a precaution. But if she does know his present location, if she even has some minor indicator, then other men will come after her. You said you will gather forces here to protect her, but the best protection she can have is if I find him. After that, the enemy will have no interest in your sister.'

'I would listen to Jonas, Mr Duck,' Cain said. 'He has your sister's interests at heart…'

That brought another disdainful snort from Bess, provoking a glare from Gabriel. Duck looked at Cain as if noticing him for the first time. His eyes narrowed. 'I do not believe I know you, sir, but feel I have seen you before. Have we met previous?'

'I've not had the honour, Mr Duck, but I'm no stranger to these streets, though I have been absent from them for some time. Gabriel Cain is my name, at your, and your sister's, service.'

Duck tilted his head, as if still trying to place him. 'You assisted in finding my sister?'

'I played but a small part, Jonas here was the driving force,' Cain said, with uncharacteristic modesty. Flynt knew why – Duck had to trust Flynt, so he was playing down his not inconsiderable role in the affair. He bowed his head slightly in his friend's direction.

Duck gestured to the dried blood on his shoulder. 'You are wounded?'

'A trifle,' Cain said, glancing towards Bess. 'I've been far more wounded by a woman's tongue.'

'And with cause, I'll wager,' Bess snapped.

That drew Duck's attention to Bess. 'And you are Sally's friend?'

Bess puffed herself up. 'I is the only friend she has here, apart from you, of course, sir. You wants my advice, don't be trusting this pair. They will tell you what you wish to hear, show concern for Sally's wellbeing, but they is in this for themselves.'

'That is true, Mr Duck,' Flynt said, 'I seek this information because I'm being paid to do so. But that doesn't detract from the fact that Mr Templeton is in danger and by extension your sister.'

'From whom?'

'That's what I must find out from Mr Templeton. But the danger is very real, on that I pledge my oath.'

Duck's teeth worried at the side of his mouth as he looked from Flynt to Cain and Bess, then to the door through which his wife had taken Sally. Finally, he reached a decision with a nod.

–

Mrs Duck may have been kindly, but she was also formidable. She opposed her husband's decision to allow Flynt to speak with Sally but he assured her that it would only be for a short while. Finally she accepted it but stood on the other side of the small bed in a little room at the rear of the building and warded Flynt off with a look that rivalled cannonade for potency.

Flynt perched on the edge of the bed. Sally had been dressed in a clean nightgown and her hair had been brushed.

'I will be serving her some broth soon,' said Mrs Duck to her husband, but the words were for Flynt's benefit. 'And then she needs to rest. She is wore out, she is, the poor lamb. She don't need to be kept awake answering no questions.'

Flynt looked directly at Sally and got straight to the point. 'Sally, I've done what I promised to do, brought you to safety. Now you need to tell me where Chris is hiding.'

Despite being in her brother's care, she remained frightened. 'I don't know, honest I don't.'

Flynt knew she was lying. He could tell by the way her eyes couldn't settle on him. Yes, she was scared, but that was an evasion. He struggled to keep his voice soft. His normal course of action in such situations was to take a more direct, often physical approach, but he couldn't apply such measures here, even if he wanted to. 'Sally, he must have told you something...'

A shake of the head. 'No, he said I must hide myself 'cos there would be men who would want to use me to get to him and he had to take himself away, to think, is what he said.'

'And he gave you no clue as to where?'

'He said it best I didn't know.'

Flynt still didn't believe her. 'I must know, if I am to assist him...'

Mrs Duck's voice was firm. 'She's already told you, sir, she don't know where he is. Now leave her be.'

Flynt paid the woman no heed and added some steel to his voice. 'Chris will be killed, Sally. They will find him and they will kill him and they will not be gentle about it. And before that, they will come here and they will kill you and they will kill John and they will kill Mrs Duck.' When Mrs Duck began to object Flynt held up a hand. 'I apologise for my bluntness but that's the way of it. The Trasks are out of it now but I told you there will be others and they won't show mercy. They won't stop, believe me. The only way to prevent it is if I find Chris and take him to safety.' He returned his attention to Sally, who had listened wide-eyed, the terror having returned full strength. His conscience stirred but he had little time to tiptoe around her. 'Your brother understands this, which is why he's allowed me access to you, and I need you to understand it too.'

Her eyes dropped from him to the quilt covering her and idly picked at a thread.

'I want you out of here, sir,' said Mrs Duck. 'Leave the girl be. She don't have nothing to say, don't know what you need to know. Give her peace.'

Flynt stared at Sally, willing her to break her silence, but she did not. He felt John Duck's hand on his shoulder. 'Come, Mr Flynt, you will not get what you want this night.'

He rose and allowed the man to guide him to the door. He gave the young woman one last intense look but she hadn't moved, all she did was stare at that bed covering as though it held secrets worthy of study by the Royal Society.

John Duck closed the door gently and motioned Flynt away from it. They were almost back at the fencing school when he stopped and said, 'Let me speak with her, Mr Flynt. If she has the information you require I will get it.'

'How?'

'I'm her brother, and once we were close. I raised her when our parents died. She has become a poor creature but my sister Sally lives in that body still, of such I am certain. I will reach her, I assure you, and if she knows where Mr Templeton is then I will discover it.'

Flynt was aware that he had little choice so he nodded his agreement. 'I'd move her from that room into the centre of the apartments, if you can,' he advised. 'It's too close to the rear of the building, and that small window is a defence weakness, so if there is any attempt to gain access she is vulnerable.'

Duck saw the sense in the strategy. 'I will have her moved into my own chamber. It has no windows and one strong door.'

'That will be easier to defend. Have you others coming to assist?'

'Word has been sent. My wife's brother and his two sons will be here presently. They're strong lads, worthy lads, and I've tutored them myself in the use of blades long and short. Believe me, Mr Flynt, they're more than capable of keeping her safe.'

Flynt believed him. Despite what he had said in that room, Sally was far safer from any further attempts against her well-being than she had ever been. He told John Duck where he could be reached and rejoined Cain and Bess. He was tired and needed rest but he had another call to make before he could lay down his head.

12

Mother Grady's house was a fine establishment facing the piazza of Covent Garden. To the casual observer it was a handsome terraced dwelling, perhaps the home of some wealthy merchant or the townhouse of rural nobility. In reality it was one of London's most exclusive bordellos and behind its magnificently Grecian-columned entrance the great and the good found a safe haven in which to indulge in their vices. They could drink, they could gamble at cards, they could slake their lusts in the rooms upstairs. All for money, of course, for Mary Grady was no philanthropist. She was as hard-headed a businesswoman as Flynt had ever encountered.

Two gentlemen ascended the staircase to the chambers above as Jerome, Mother Grady's nephew and the house bully, led them across the hallway to the well-appointed, but for the moment empty, parlour. Jerome said he'd let his aunt know they were there and Bess wandered the room, her eyes wide with astonishment at such opulence. Flynt continued to watch for a sign that her conscience was pricked by what she had done but so far had seen none. That did not mean it wasn't working at her from the inside.

Cain made straight for the two decanters on a corner table and poured a hefty measure of brandy into a fine crystal goblet. When Mother Grady entered she treated Bess to a long and disdainful study before noting the glass in his hand but also regarding him with curiosity, and then to Flynt when her customary steely expression returned.

She flicked a finger at Bess. 'This is not a home for verminous bunters, Jonas Flynt,' she said, her Irish accent somehow making the insult even more cutting.

Bess flared at what she saw as defamation. 'I ain't got not no vermin about my person, you blubber-cheeked harridan, and I ain't no bunter, neither.'

Mother Grady's expertly applied eyebrows raised at the audacity of a street girl addressing her in such a fashion and Flynt dropped his head so she would not see him smile. Bess's barb was far from accurate, for though Mary Grady displayed her prosperity with a fuller figure than in her youth and had sufficient years to be the girl's mother, perhaps even her grandmother, she was far from portly of face.

'She has a tongue on her, I'll give her that,' she said and Flynt heard amusement in her voice. Mother Grady admired spirit in a girl. It was her own spirit that had ensured she survived her world. She walked around Bess, assessing her with an expert eye. 'Perhaps if she were to have a bath and a brush hauled through that tangled haystack we might make her more presentable.'

'I had me a bath last week, I'll has you know.'

'Yes, but how many had shared the water before you? What's your name, girl?'

'They calls me Edgeworth Bess.'

Mother Grady tutted, for she had no time for the custom of naming girls after their location or birthplace. She saw to it that all her girls were treated with respect and called Miss by her patrons. 'It's good to remember where you came from, I suppose. Show me your teeth.'

Bess reared back. 'You'll see my chatterers when I sinks them into your scrawny throat.'

'Mrs Grady,' Flynt said when he felt she was about to give Bess a slap. Mother Grady had a powerful arm on her and he had seen her rock a man twice her size back on his heels. 'I've not brought Bess to work. I just need a place where she can find refuge for a time.'

'I ain't staying here,' Bess said. 'I can look after myself, I can.'

'Bess, it isn't safe for you on the streets, not while Romulus Trask is out there.' He caught Cain's eyes, searching again for some revelation that he had not adhered to his wish that Trask not be further harmed. Cain sipped his brandy and revealed nothing.

Mother Grady became interested. 'The Trasks? They are after this creature?'

'Romulus only. Remus has gone to a better place, wherever that may be for his like,' explained Flynt.

The madame gave Bess a closer scrutiny and Flynt had little doubt that she was putting two and two together and coming up with a number in which one brother did not figure and that Bess was the one who had done the subtracting. 'I have little time for the Trasks,' she said. 'Nasty, brutish sods. If one is gone, then the world is a cleaner place. Well done, my girl.'

'I need Bess to be safe until I am convinced that Romulus has no desire to seek vengeance for his brother.'

Flynt continued to eye Cain, but there was no flicker in his eye, no unconscious twitch or shift in stance. His expression remained even.

'My friend here also has a wound that might require attention,' Flynt said.

Mother Grady tilted her head, one hand placed upon her waist. 'So, I am a refuge for the waifs of the street and also an infirmary? Do you take me for some kind of charity, Jonas Flynt?'

'You will, of course, be recompensed for your time and services.'

'Damn right I'll be recompensed! And I'll be adding that brandy to the bill, don't you worry.' She crossed the room to stand before Cain and examine the wound. She poked it with her forefinger and smiled when he winced. 'Tender, is it?'

'Somewhat, madame,' he replied, moving his shoulder out of reach in case she saw fit to probe again.

'It doesn't look too bad.' She tilted her head to assess him from hat to boot. 'What do they call you, lad? This lump here doesn't see fit to make proper introductions, him being a Scot and therefore a stranger to manners. And don't be giving me any street names, I'll have the one you were baptised with, and if you didn't take the water then the name your mother gave you.'

'My mother called me Gabriel and she was Meg Cain.'

Mother Grady pursed her lips as she put the names together. 'I heard tell of a Gabriel Cain a few years back, used to follow the road knight trade on the heaths, as did someone else we could mention.' A quick look was thrown in Flynt's direction. 'Would that be you?'

'It must have been another Gabriel Cain.'

'It is not such a name that it is likely to be attached to more than one cove, I'll hazard.'

Cain's smile was charming. 'An imposter then, using my name. If I were to ever meet that rascal I should remonstrate with him most ardently.'

'You had best turn to necromancy then, for I heard he was hung out west somewhere.'

'I have heard this already. A fitting end, I am sure, to befall such a foul creature, for to steal a man's purse is one thing, to take his good name leaves him much the poorer. I believe it were the Bard of Avon who wrote such words, but forgive me as I am not learned enough to recall them with exactitude. My friend Jonas has the learning and right fond he be of displaying it.'

Mother Grady's smile was genuine. She obviously liked Cain, who was now throwing Flynt an easy wink. 'What say you, Jonas? What be the precise phrasing used by old Will Shakespeare?'

Despite the grimness of the evening, Flynt felt good humour tease his lips. Gabriel always did what he could to relieve the gloom of any situation. 'I regret it does not spring readily to my mind.'

It had, but he would be damned if he would prove Gabriel correct, even if he had mangled the quotation.

'I would wager that it does.'

Belle St Clair's voice came from the open doorway and Flynt felt the smile that had been tickled by his friend burst into life when he turned and saw her. As usual, he found his breath quickening. Her dark eyes flashed towards him with humour as she walked into the room.

'Jonas, it's good to see you.'

'And you, Belle.'

They stared at one another for a brief moment but a great deal passed between them. They had been physically intimate in the past, a business transaction certainly, but since his return from Edinburgh he had curtailed such carnal visits in a belated attempt at being faithful to Cassie. However, in subsequent conversations with Belle he had come to believe that deeper feelings were harboured, though having learned the necessities of business at the hand of Mary Grady, she kept them well hid, only allowing them to break through in an occasional look, a touch, a word. She had nursed him most tenderly following his struggles on the ice with a murderer. He thought perhaps that physical intimacy had been replaced by something deeper, more lasting. Even so, he felt something more primal stirring when he looked upon her face.

And then it was replaced by a vision of Cassie. My God, they were so alike.

Belle's gaze lingered for but a moment before it shifted towards Cain and Bess.

Cain affected a bow. 'Madame, allow me to introduce myself, for as has already been established this lout has not the wit nor the manners to do so. I am Gabriel Cain.'

Flynt sighed and shrugged towards Belle, who smiled and moved across the room to extend her hand for Cain to kiss it. Flynt almost rolled his eyes. 'Anabelle St Clair,' she said.

'No offence to you, madame,' Cain said in deference to Mother Grady, 'but I can see why my friend here has such affection for this house.'

'Aye,' said Mother Grady, 'Jonas Flynt was once a regular partaker of the services on offer, Belle in particular, but now he brings me only waifs and strays.' She jerked a thumb towards Bess. 'Belle, this here bag of rags is what they call an Edgeworth Bess on the streets.'

Belle inclined her head towards Bess. 'What is your given name, dear?'

Bess hesitated for a second, as if lack of use had left cloudy her memory of the name with which she was born. Her response carried none of her customary surliness, for Belle had a way with people that others did not. 'Elizabeth Lyon,' she said, then added as if it needed explanation, 'I was birthed in Edgeworth.'

Belle smiled and it was like someone had lit a thousand candles, something she shared with Cassie. Flynt cursed himself for the memory. This was not the time. It was never the time.

'That is the way of our world, dear,' Belle said. 'We have one name that is our own, and another that is given us by those we serve. Those who cannot see beyond the colour of flesh call me Tawny Belle.'

'Not in my hearing, they don't,' said Mother Grady.

'Not everyone calls me that.' Belle's attention drifted fleetingly back to Flynt. 'For some the colour of my skin is not exotic or something to despise. There are those who only see me as a person.'

Mother Grady saw the look, glanced herself at Flynt, and then, using only her thumb and forefinger, took Bess by the sleeve of her threadbare dress. 'And you, my girl, will be Elizabeth while you are under my roof. And it's a scrub for you and right immediate.' She crooked a finger at Cain. 'We will tend to your scratch in the kitchen, Mr Cain.'

Gabriel was about to argue the point but then he too grew aware of something passing between Belle and Flynt. He took

118

her fingers again and kissed her hand lightly. 'Miss Anabelle, it be an honour to make your acquaintance.'

'And you, sir,' she said. 'Any friend of Jonas is a friend in this house.'

In the doorway, Mother Grady snorted. Cain smirked as he passed Flynt on his way out of the room. 'Jonas,' he said.

When the door closed behind them, Belle moved to an armchair but Flynt took himself to the decanters. He gestured to them in an unspoken inquiry but she declined with a wave of her hand. He poured himself a stiff brandy and drank deeply, feeling the welcome burn in his throat and gut. It had been a long day and night.

'Who is Bess, Jonas?'

'She is a young woman who needs refuge, whether she wants it or not.'

'And what is she to you?'

Her tone was casual but he sensed there was an edge to her query. 'An acquaintance.'

'A close acquaintance?'

'No,' he reassured her. 'She is friend to young Jack.'

Belle knew Jack and had met him while Flynt had convalesced from his wounds. 'A personal friend, or a business friend?'

Flynt felt a slight smile begin. 'For Jack there is a longing for the former, but he has to satisfy himself with the latter. For Bess...' He considered the girl. 'Like many women, she is difficult to read.'

'Like some men, too,' she said, but he failed to discern whether it was directed solely towards him or a general observation. 'And she requires refuge from what?'

'From men who may wish her harm.'

'There are men who always wish women harm. Can you protect us all?'

'Many do not need my protection, for they are most capable themselves.'

'Bess is not?'

He glanced to the door, as if he expected the girl to be listening. 'Probably, but I need to be sure.' He sipped the brandy again, savouring it for a moment. 'She killed a man this night.'

Belle's eyes widened. 'A cull?'

Flynt shook his head. 'A man who meant to kill either Gabriel or me, or both. She saved us. I owe her something for that.'

'Was it you who placed her in this jeopardy?'

'No, it were circumstance, but I happened to be part of it, I confess. I need her to not be alone for a time and would ask that you look after her.'

'Why me?'

'Because you were once looked after by another when you first came to this house. You have an understanding of what it is to be alone and out of your depth, and at this moment Bess wallows in deep water.'

Belle had once told him of a woman who had taken her under her wing when she first arrived in Mother Grady's house, freshly shipped over from the Indies. The woman later died but Belle always remembered her kindness and did what she could to look out for her son. However, fate has a way of mocking care.

'But she is not alone, is she?' Belle observed. 'She has you and Mr Cain.'

'We have tasks elsewhere.'

'You always do.'

The moment hung between them, as many moments had before. He knew he should say something but couldn't find the words. He cleared his throat and decided that remaining on the subject of Bess was a safer option. 'A killing burrows deep. The girl may affect a callous exterior but it is like a cancer, eating away at the soul.'

'The soul? You are not a believer, Jonas, and yet you talk of soul?'

He shrugged. 'It is as good a word as any to describe the spark that fires our life, that ignites the flame of consciousness.'

'I do believe there is a spiritual person within you after all, Jonas.' She thought this over, then said, 'I'll look after her, you know I will.'

'I'm grateful.'

They stared at each other across the room in silence for another moment. This time he sensed there was something she wished to say, something of which Mother Grady had been aware, which was why she had ushered the others out so suddenly. He waited for Belle to speak again, sipping his brandy.

Finally, her eyes dropped to her hands clasped on her lap. 'I am a free woman now, Jonas.'

If he was to hazard a guess as to what she had to say, it would not have been those words. Belle had been bought on the block and transported as a child to London to be tutored by Mother Grady. She had been lucky, for though the woman was stern, unlike some other keepers of bordellos she was not overly cruel and Belle not only learned how to pleasure both men and women but also was introduced to literature, art and music. Mother Grady allowed her to keep a portion of the fees she raised in full knowledge that one day her pupil would buy back her life and free will. Flynt also knew this, but didn't realise she had amassed sufficient funds to do so.

'You have bought your papers?' he asked.

A slight smile. 'I have been given them.'

Flynt was again surprised. 'Mother Grady did not accept your money?'

'She did not.'

He remembered a conversation he'd had with Mary Grady a few months before. He had made another attempt to buy Belle's freedom himself but she had thrown his offer back in his face.

Belle will have her freedom but not because some man wills it. She will have it because she wills it... You are like all men, you either wish to ruin us or save us and you cannot fathom that women are capable of doing both themselves.

He had ever suspected that the tough old brothel keeper harboured softer feelings towards Belle and now it was proved.

'So what will you do?'

'I will remain here,' Belle said, 'but as partner and equal to Mother Grady. She wishes to step back, to enjoy her life a little, though she'll still be present to oversee and to guide. She's told me that I deserve this.'

She will work for it and she will have it, you should have no fears on that score.

Another echo of the conversation the year before.

She will either have all this or a house of her own.

'I am right glad to hear this, Belle, I congratulate you on your good fortune.'

'Thank you, Jonas.' She paused. 'I will no longer be working, you understand, apart from a few special gentlemen.' She paused. 'I need not tell you that you are ever seen as special.'

Her gaze was steady and under it he felt himself respond not just emotionally but physically, so he turned away and laid the crystal back on the table. 'I appreciate that, and I'm glad for you, Belle. I'm sure you'll make this house even more prosperous than it already is.'

He knew the words to be hollow but there was another woman, unseen, standing between them.

Belle recognised his tone, as she had done many times that year. She sighed softly. 'You must move on, Jonas. You can never regain what you had, for, in truth, you never really had it.'

He couldn't find any words but he felt a burning in his throat that was not caused by the brandy. It grew stronger when she rose to stand directly in front of him and place her hand upon his chest. The pressure of her fingers and palm was both pleasurable and painful, as if they seared through his clothing to his flesh.

'I love you, Jonas, you must know that.' He opened his mouth to reply but she shook her head. 'No, say nothing. No platitudes, no polite gratitude, for they are empty. I say I love you and I mean it. I love you not as a friend, not as a courtesan in love with your coin. I love you because I know that you are a caring and wonderful man. I know there is another side to you. You are a killer of men, but you do not do so lightly. You will kill for a reason and when it is necessary, even if only for self-preservation, but it has affected you. You say that a killing eats away at you. How much of you is left, Jonas? You carry guilt like a yoke on a beast of burden. It weighs you down. Guilt over what you have done. The people you have killed, the people you have hurt, the people you have lost. One day that guilt will consume you completely, unless you let it go. Unless you let *her* go.' She pressed her hand against his breast more firmly. 'She has taken root in here—' She reached up with her free hand to tap a finger on his temple '—and in here. She did not do it purposely, for it was you who planted her there. I am not a free woman because Mary Grady signed a document. I am free woman because I believe it to be so, and even though I was another person's property in the eyes of the law, I always believed it to be so. You believe yourself to be a free man, but you are not. You are enslaved to the self-reproach you feel because of the people you have failed. Set yourself free, Jonas, before the contagion destroys you.'

Flynt ensured Bess was settling in as well as possible, his solicitude resulting in expletive-laden advice on what steps he could do to gratify himself, before taking his leave in the company of Cain, whose wound had been freshly cleaned and dressed by Mother Grady herself. In the piazza, where the denizens of the night milled and worked and solicited, Gabriel rotated his shoulder. 'If Mary wished to give up the bordello trade she would make an excellent field surgeon. If she were a man, of course.'

Though Belle's words remained lodged in his head, Flynt still smiled. 'It's Mary, is it? Not Mrs Grady or Mother Grady? I've never heard anyone address her as Mary.'

'What can I tell you, my friend, that you don't already know? I have a gift when it comes to the ladies.' They walked a few paces before Cain added, 'As have you, Jonas. Yon Miss Belle is a rare beauty.'

'We're friends only,' Flynt said.

'Friend or customer, I fancy she bears deeper feeling in that fine bosom.'

Flynt wondered if Cain had been listening to the conversation, but knew in his heart that he was merely someone who noticed tiny little indicators. When they brought a carriage to a halt on the heaths, he was always able to predict which way a cove was going to react. Flynt had developed the same skill, but Cain's was honed to a fine degree. It had often stood them in good stead, allowing them to avoid bloodshed. There were times, though, when that sense had deserted his friend, when the darkness that existed in his heart took over and Flynt had to hold him back from undue violence, as he had done – hoped he had done – in regard to Romulus Trask.

'You should pursue her, Jonas. Especially now that she is a lady of some enterprise and property.'

Again, Flynt was surprised that Mother Grady had revealed this. The man's ability to glean information from others was uncanny, especially if they were women.

'It would appear Mother Grady was right talkative.'

'Aye, garrulous in the extreme. Or at least, as garrulous as Mary gets, I would imagine.' They stopped. 'I am for my bed, Jonas, and will leave you here. But we will meet upon the morrow, in the Black Lion. I am invested in this quest of yours, on behalf of whoever this mysterious paymaster is for whom you undertake it. I have a suspicion the Trasks won't be the only ones seeking this lawyer, and it would be remiss of me as a friend were I to leave your back unguarded.'

Flynt was on the verge of refusing his assistance but thought better of it, for despite his misgivings over what he may or may not have done in that Rookery hallway, it felt good to have the man at his side again. He held out his hand and Cain grasped it.

'Tomorrow then, at ten of the clock, we shall have oysters and ale and we will consider the next step together, eh?'

Flynt had a report to make on his progress to Colonel Charters at that hour in the Lion. 'Make it eleven and the Shakespear's Head.'

'Eleven and the Shakespear it will be.'

Flynt nodded. 'Thank you, Gabriel.'

The charms of a Covent Garden Nun drew Cain's attention. 'Ah, keep your thanks, for what is a friend for, if not to face almost certain death in a cause he knows nothing about?'

The woman smiled as she approached, displaying teeth not yet ravaged by life. 'You want some business, friend?' She scrutinised Flynt too. 'I can takes both of you fine gentlemen, if that be your pleasure and you don't mind getting right friendly with one another.'

Cain put his arm around her. 'My dear, that is not our pleasure, and even if it were, my friend here has other affections on which he can call, have you not, Jonas?'

Despite himself, Flynt's eyes were drawn to the house in the west corner opposite the Garden, where a candle burned behind the window he knew to be Belle's. He had stood on this spot a number of times, looking to that square of light, but never proceeding further.

'So it'll just be you then, my sweet,' said the woman, her body pressed tightly against Cain's.

'Trust me, my love, I am all you will need.'

Flynt wondered at his friend's stamina. 'I thought you were for your bed, Gabriel.'

'I am for my bed. Just not alone.' He shot a meaningful glance towards Mother Grady's door. 'And neither should you be.'

'Not tonight, Gabriel.' Flynt smiled, then touched his hat to the lady. 'Goodnight to you both.'

'You're a cold one, Jonas Flynt,' Cain said as he walked away. 'Just don't let her go cold on you too…'

13

His wife's breathing was steady as James Moncrieff lay beside her staring at the canopy of their satin-covered beechwood bed, the velvet curtains tied back against the posts, for there was no cool air on this summer night that required to be baffled. He rested a hand on her hip, gently so as not to disturb her, finding the tactility comforting. They had made love that evening and it had been glorious. He always found it glorious with Katherine for he loved her deeply. If only they could manifest that love with a child, whether male or female he cared not. So far that blessing had escaped them and he feared that he had not inherited his father's fecundity.

That thought, inevitably, inexorably, caused him to consider Jonas Flynt.

He considered his feelings towards the man he had seen only once, as they both walked on the frozen waters of the Thames. He had not known it was he until later, and when told he realised that some part of him had recognised a familiarity in his features, for they both favoured their father – Flynt less so, but it was there.

The Grand Master was correct in his assessment of James Moncrieff the elder. Though publicly his son defended his name, privately he recognised that he had been something of a satyr. He had taken his pleasures as and when he saw fit, believing it to be his right. His mother knew that her husband's breeches were unfettered with such regularity that it was a wonder he did not develop callouses on his fingers. However,

Lady Moncrieff refused to discuss her late husband's infidelities, no matter how much her son pressed.

No bastards had come forward, which was yet another miracle. When he was old enough to discuss such matters, his father had revealed to him that he spurned the employ of any form of sheath as protection. He said he disliked the sensation of either linen or animal skin on his member, while the need to dip the prophylactic in water before coupling was tedious.

'I like to get on with the task in hand, James,' his father had said. 'The mood can so easily dissipate and you must strike while the iron is hot.'

It was possible, therefore, that there was a small army of bastard siblings in Edinburgh and beyond but the only one of whom Moncrieff knew was Jonas Flynt. His mother had dismissed the rumour that Flynt was his half-brother as idle chatter among those who frequented low taverns but he needed to know, so had confronted Gideon Flynt in the Edinburgh tavern he owned. As he lay in his chamber in London, Moncrieff's nostrils again twitched with the stench of the tallow candles that burned in the gloom, the odours of ale, spirits and cooking hanging in their smoke, heard the spit and crackle of the fireplace spreading its much-needed warmth against the winter night, saw in the sepia glow the unmasked curiosity and – yes – suspicion in the older Flynt's face. Behind the counter, the broad, handsome face of Gideon's second wife, Mercy, watched them as they talked. They said Gideon had smuggled her away from her owner in the Indies, her daughter too, who had subsequently married the shoemaker's son, Robert Gow. His father had hated the girl Cassie, her husband, too, for he was certain they assisted in the hiding of runaway servants. The Moncrieff family had interests in tobacco and sugar in the colonies, and also in the trade of slaves from Africa, so anyone who threatened profits was to be detested.

'Why do you wish to know of this?' Gideon Flynt had said.

'I need the truth.'

'Even if it pains you?'

'Even then.'

Gideon had taken a deep breath as he assessed him. 'I hold no enmity for you, lad. You're as innocent as my boy and his dear mother. My enmity remains with your father.'

'God rest him,' Moncrieff had said, automatically.

'I regret he'll find no rest for he won't be basking in the Almighty's good graces. He was not a good man, I think that is something you must know by now, even if you don't acknowledge it as fact.'

Moncrieff felt the need to defend his father's name. 'He was ruthless in business and in furthering the fortunes of my family. That didn't make him evil.'

'It's not his business dealings to which I refer, lad, and I think you ken that right well, otherwise you wouldn't be here asking what happened over thirty years ago.'

'There's too much blethering about that and I would know the truth of it.'

'You've asked your mother, I assume?'

'She will not discuss it, apart from to say that it is slanderous nashgab promulgated by bitter and idle men.'

A little smile tugged at the corners of the Gideon's mouth. 'Bitter I may be, but far from idle. And she kens fine what occurred that night in the parlour of your home. She saw my Jenny crying on the floor where he had left her.'

'That does not mean it was rape.'

'It was rape, lad. Jenny was a good woman, a decent woman, and she wouldn't give herself willingly to anyone other than her husband.'

'Why did she not then report it to the courts?'

'Don't be stupit, lad, you ken the answer to that. Your father was a nobleman and Jenny a seamstress and husband to a seafarer. There was no justice open to her in the courts, for your father was friend to most of the judges. Your mother threatened to have her indicted for slander if she repeated any accusations of rape. She said she would have Jenny and her sister hounded from the town. And all said while the guilty party was still buttoning himself. It was rape, lad, and my Jenny couldn't take the shame of it. Blamed herself, as women are often made to. Thought she had somehow instigated it, displayed some sign that she was open to it. But she hadn't, and I ken that fine without being present. And then she found herself with child and even though she carried it, for that child was an innocent no matter how evil the method of conception, the balance of her mind was destroyed. She was a delicate, sensitive soul was my Jenny, how she ever looked favourably on me I'll never know, but I loved her and she loved me.'

Gideon had paused then to swallow something back; lingering grief Moncrieff surmised, still lodged in the man's throat.

'In the end that love wasn't enough. She couldn't face my return from abroad and once she had delivered a fine, healthy bairn she took herself down the High Street and threw herself from the crags.'

He paused again, leaned forward and spoke in a lower voice. 'She was murdered, lad, by your father and, aye, your mother, too. They weren't there on that cliff with her but it was their hands at her back, sure as I'm sitting here.'

'I cannot believe that.'

'Believe it or believe it not, but I'm telling you God's straight truth. Your father had his way with her and though he be my boy in all other respects, Jonas is the result of it – along with my Jenny lying cold in her grave. It was only by declaring that she had slipped and fell that we were able to have her rest in the kirkyard at Greyfriars, otherwise it may have been an unmarked grave at a crossroads, maybe even with a stake through her dead heart.'

Moncrieff could make no reply to that, for he felt a twinge of guilt, even though he had not been born when this had taken place. He would not come along until the following year.

'I should've taken a pistol to your father but I didn't and that's my shame,' Gideon had continued. 'But they would've hung me for it and left Jonas with nobody but his aunt. It was left to the boy as a grown man to seek justice for his dead mother and he found it on Sheriffmuir. I'm sorry, lad, but that's the truth of it. What happened to your father *was* justice, delayed to be sure, but justice all the same...'

Lying in the dark of his chamber, his beloved wife at his side, hopeful that their lovemaking would at last bear fruit, Moncrieff turned the conversation over in his mind. Though he had denied to the Grand Master any familial connection with Jonas Flynt, he knew in his heart that it was true, but it remained a truth that he could not countenance publicly. Flynt had gunned his father down, he had known that for a fact even before Gideon had confirmed it, and for that he had to pay. He also wished to protect his father's reputation, not out of a sense of duty but because what reflected badly on one Moncrieff could taint the whole. A rotten apple quickly infects its neighbour and Moncrieff could not have any whiff of scandal, for he had plans to further his family's wealth and influence. The men of the Fellowship were certainly not angels but there was an unwritten rule that the Grand Master be relatively free of blemish. The current holder of the position was a man of probity, his only descent into sin being his mistress, but that was a minor vice and accepted. Outraging a woman and by extension causing her death was another thing entire.

Although Flynt had displayed no sign of proclaiming his blood, Moncrieff couldn't take the chance that someday he would. He was not a true Moncrieff and he could not, must not, be allowed to make any claim on the fortune, for that would open the scandal to public scrutiny, even though proofs would be impossible to produce.

Vengeance was Moncrieff's primary motivation, but Flynt posed another threat and one that the Grand Master had now come to fully understand. His gaze strayed from the bed canopy to the window, open to allow some air to circulate. He heard a carriage pass on St James' Square, the glow of its lamps briefly illuminating the glass. The man Lester was out there now, beyond those windows, those walls, beyond the somewhat noxious and unpleasant rough ground at the centre of the square, somewhere in the night of the city. The man doubted the efficacy of his plan to remove Flynt, he believed it too convoluted, but Moncrieff was adamant that it be given a chance. He felt it necessary that he be drawn beyond the city limits where Charters' influence was less potent.

His father had not been a perfect man but he was still his father. And the son would have his revenge, whether he and Flynt shared blood or not.

—

The Golden Cross faced the statue of the first King Charles astride a horse like a hero of old, although it was his steed's rear that presented itself to the coaching inn as if making some form of comment on its quality. The memorial to the old king had been erected where the cross of the village of Charing had once stood and the long-dead monarch looked down upon the pillory where malefactors were regularly punished. Flynt often wondered if the man whose arrogant belief in the God-given right to rule would enjoy the sight of the suffering of those poor souls. Perhaps not. Perhaps given his own manner of death he would have understood their misery.

A heavy sign bearing the name of the inn swung out over the footpath. When the winds were strong and swirled around the T-shaped junction, the sign creaked as though it were about to break free, but this night it hung immobile, like a dead weight on a gallows pole. The hour was late but there was life yet in the vicinity, for there were taverns and bawdy houses aplenty. Sprightly fiddle music floated through the warm air, accompanied by hoarse voices yelling the words to a song he could not quite identify. A woman's laughter rippled over and under the lyrics and Flynt guessed their nature was filthy.

He paused to let a coach thunder from the courtyard at the rear of the inn, the driver giving him a cursory glance as he passed, the flaps of the compartment down. As Gabriel had learned when he had sought him out, Flynt did tend to move around, but he had remained in this particular lodging longer than usual. He liked the old place, with its uneven floors and its warren of corridors and flights of stairs that seemed to appear from nowhere. It was within easy walking distance not only of Covent Garden and Drury Lane, where were situated the gaming halls and taverns he frequented, but also the establishment in which he lodged Horse. There was a small stable adjoining the inn's courtyard but Flynt had no desire to take further advantage of the landlord's hospitality. It was enough that John Wilkes and his wife allowed him to lodge rent-free, even though it was in gratitude for a service he had done them in dealing with a gang of natty lads who had set themselves up as an ad-hoc watchman service, demanding regular tribute if the premises were not to somehow find themselves go up in flames.

He watched the coach rattle towards Great Scotland Yard and Whitehall, enjoying the still unidentified music and savouring the night, before he turned into the archway. He seldom accessed the rambling old building by the front entrance, preferring to use the rear.

The sound of the pistol shot came from somewhere ahead of him and he threw himself to the ground to roll against the wall. The ball had narrowly missed him – he'd heard it thud into the brickwork just inches from his head – but he hadn't spotted the muzzle flash. He spun away again and while on his back, drew both Tact and Diplomacy, glad he had taken the precaution of reloading them during the journey from the Rookery. He twisted onto his belly, keeping himself flat, swivelling the weapons back and forth, but could see nobody. There had been

133

only a single shot but that didn't mean whoever it was did not have a second pistol. Or that he was alone.

He focused his attention in the direction from which he thought the shot had come, doing his best to filter out the sound of the music in order to hear any movement. He had lodged here long enough to know that the coach that had just left would be the last to visit that night, so the exterior lanterns to the rear had been extinguished and the courtyard would be deserted. He hoped neither of the Wilkes decided to investigate, as they might fall victim to the assassin. He did not want their deaths on his conscience. That space was already more than adequately filled.

He could not lie in the dust of the long archway all night so he inched to his feet, but crouched forward, keeping the wall to his right, and always throwing a cautious eye over his shoulder lest there be a rear assault. He stopped as he reached the edge of the courtyard to peer round the corner. Squares of light dropped to the ground from the inn's upper windows, but the remainder of the courtyard was in deep shadow. A door creaked and a horse whinnied as it stamped its hooves on the ground, as if it had been disturbed, so he crept towards the stable's double doors. One was ajar and he nudged it open with a pistol barrel, causing the same grate of a hinge he had heard moments before. It was black as pitch within, no candle or lantern would be left unattended, old wood and straw being incompatible with naked flames. He heard the horse stir again. He sucked in a lungful of air heavy with stale straw, horse sweat and manure, held it for a moment, then let it out slowly before easing himself through the open door, making as little noise as he could, knowing he would be silhouetted against the inn's lights but instantly dodging into the shadows and keeping low. He made out the three stalls, only one currently occupied by a large brown horse which remained agitated. Beyond them was a narrow open doorway. With no sound reaching him other than the animal's restless hooves and heavy breathing, it was possible his assailant had made his escape through that door and had vanished into the alleys and backyards beyond. Possible, but by no means certain. He had to maintain caution, so he stepped carefully across the cramped space, turning back and forward, pistols ranging around and above him, his eyes and ears alert for any sign of an attack, muscles prepared to throw himself out of harm's way.

He felt the impediment with his foot just outside the occupied stall and knew immediately what it was. He reached up to a post beside him and flipped open a lantern, found his tinderbox in his pocket and took care in setting the wick of the candle within to flame. He unhooked the lantern and knelt to study the man lying face down in the straw at his feet. Using his free hand to tug him onto his back, he saw immediately the ragged wound at the throat, the blood glistening in the glow of the flame, the mouth gaping in silent scream, the eyes wide as if still experiencing the searing agony of the blade as it sliced through flesh and gullet. He had half expected the face to be familiar but this man was unknown to him.

He sat back on his heels, frowning. Who in all damnation was this fellow? And why did he want him dead?

But more importantly, who had killed him and then vanished into the night?

14

'In the name of God, man, do you never tire of people doing their best to remove you from this earth?'

'It is an occurrence often found while I am under your orders, Colonel,' Flynt pointed out, 'so I suspect there is a correlation between the two.'

In point of fact he did grow weary with such instances, just as he was with stairways and alleyways which seldom saw sunlight. He was also less than enamoured with meeting Colonel Nathaniel Charters in this upstairs room of the Black Lion. Although the day was once again bright and warm, the daylight tried but failed to fully penetrate the grimy windows, so it was decidedly dull.

Colonel Charters kindled his pipe with the flame of a candle as he stood by the cold fireplace, his eyes brimming with amusement. 'Even so, Serjeant, for a mere gambler and thief you do appear to excite heated passions amongst those ranged against you. I have no other rogue in my company who attracts as much death and destruction. I do believe the Grim Reaper himself lives within your shadow.'

He puffed some life into his pipe, the aromatic Virginia tobacco smoke drifting towards Flynt and going some way to counteract the stench of an unemptied chamber pot reaching out from behind the screens in the corner.

Charters glanced towards the dark hearth. 'Damn me, I should've had old Hines kindle a log or two. It be decided balmy without but it's remarkably brisk in here.'

Flynt was gratified to hear that, for he had begun to consider that it was his own mood making a winter's night out of the summer morning.

Charters gripped the pipe between his teeth and rubbed his hands together. 'So who was the fellow then?'

'I had expected it to be Romulus Trask but it was someone unknown to me.'

Charters expelled smoke from the corner of his mouth. 'It was unlikely to have been friend Trask, for he was found dead in that hovel in the Rookery, alongside his brother.'

Flynt's jaw tightened. *Damn you, Gabriel.*

Charters squinted at him through the tobacco haze. 'Yet you say you left him still breathing when you spirited the girl away.'

Flynt had omitted to mention the presence of Gabriel and Bess the previous night. He seldom told Charters everything, an arrangement that was often reciprocated. 'I did.'

'And that your ball took him in the shoulder?'

'Aye, his left.' Flynt recalled his boot pressing down upon the injury and heard the man's agonised screams. 'His wound must have been deeper than I thought.'

'I don't think it was a pistol shot that did for him, Serjeant.' Charters' tone of voice was almost breezy. 'I think it was more likely to have been the fact that someone had slit the fellow's throat. Quite emphatically, I'm informed.'

In his mind's eye, Flynt saw the gaping wound on the throat of the assassin in the stable.

Charters cocked an eyebrow as he glanced at Flynt's silver cane. 'You didn't use that blade of yours on him, did you?'

'I did not.'

'Damned underhand, that device. Doesn't seem honourable.'

Flynt's voice was strained. 'My work for you demands I be underhand with considerable frequency. And you live your life in an underhand way, so I don't think I'll be lectured on honour by you, Colonel. You left the bulk of your own honour behind some time ago, both professionally and privately, perhaps with your arm in Flanders.'

Charters chuckled. No matter what Flynt said, no matter how impudent or insubordinate, he seldom pricked the man's anger. 'I cannot deny that, Serjeant.' He paced the room, leaving in his wake a trail of tobacco smoke drifting in the sunlight that managed to pierce the dusty windows. 'So it would seem you have a guardian angel, Flynt. First he put an end to Romulus Trask and then he killed this unknown assailant at the Golden Cross. Do you have any idea who this sainted protector may be? And why he wishes you to continue breathing God's good air? Or as good as it can be in this benighted city.'

Gabriel had murdered Romulus, of that Flynt was certain, and he now suspected that he had also slaughtered the would-be assassin. Why he did not reveal himself Flynt didn't understand. He couldn't share this with Charters, however.

'I have no idea, Colonel. I can think of nobody who bears me sufficient goodwill that they would do murder on my behalf. Except your good self, of course.'

This amused Charters even further. 'You think I would kill to protect you?'

'You owe me a debt. Of your life. And even though you pressed me into working for your Company, I would think that some vestige of honour still remains and you would discharge that obligation when the time came.'

'Well, Serjeant,' Charters said, pulling a chair from under the table in the centre of the room, 'let us hope that such an eventuality does not arise and my honour, tarnished though it be, is not put to the test.' He sat down, motioning to Flynt to do the same. 'Now, tell me what action you intend to take in the matter of Mr Templeton.'

Flynt remained standing. It was a minor show of defiance but under the circumstances all that was in his power. 'There is little I can do at this stage apart from awaiting word from Mr Duck as to what, if anything, he has gleaned from his sister.'

'And if he does not?'

'Then I am stymied.'

Charters removed the pipe from his teeth. 'That is unacceptable.'

'Unacceptable it may be, but that is the way of it.'

'You have been given a mission and I expect you to carry it out. You will go where you are sent and do as you are told. And you *will* go out there, find Templeton and bring him to me.'

Flynt's irritation flared again but he controlled it. 'If the girl does not, will not or cannot divulge Templeton's location then I've nowhere else to go. The man has left nothing behind, no clue as to his whereabouts. His landlord knows nothing, his friends nothing. He is hid and he is meant to stay hid.'

Charters let this rest for a moment. 'Think you that the Fellowship has him?'

'Not if it was they who despatched the Trasks, unless there is another player in this game of whom at least I am unaware.'

Charters caught the emphasis. 'You suggest that I would know of another player and would not so inform you?'

'I go where I am sent and do what I'm told.'

Charters laughed. 'By God, Flynt, I do believe I would save your life, if only to ensure we have these wonderful exchanges.' His laughter ebbed. 'Pray then that the girl is forthcoming with the information, for it is vital that we find this man. And if there are any further attempts upon your wellbeing, as I am sure there will be, then let us also pray that your mysterious protector remains alert. It is possible your assailant of last night was little more than a common ruffian on the low toby, as you denizens of the streets would call it, intent on lifting your purse but, it being you, it is far more likely that someone paid him to kill you. A name springs to mind immediate.'

'Moncrieff,' said Flynt, the man's involvement already having occurred to him.

'The very same. I thought – hoped – that my warnings earlier this year might have kept him at bay, but perhaps not. His lordship does carry deep resentment towards you. In hindsight, perhaps it was unwise to kill his father.'

Flynt saw the elder Moncrieff's face as his bullet ploughed into his chest.

'It seemed the only course of action open to me in the moment,' he said, knowing that to be a lie. At the time he had told himself it was simply an instinctive reaction to the man turning on him with a loaded pistol, but he had fully intended to take the man's life and he did. Lord James Moncrieff did not deserve to live.

Charters' expression was neutral but Flynt was aware that he suspected there was more to that incident on that hill in Scotland than he had been informed. 'Very well, but do not let this feud interfere with your work, Serjeant. Follow every lead, search every street, hovel, inn, tavern, bawdy house, employ whatever means you deem necessary but find that man and bring him to me, alive and talking.'

'And if he does not wish to come?'

Charters' gaze was even. 'Convince him...'

–

Gabriel was already in the Shakespear's Head on Covent Garden, a tankard of ale half empty and a plateful of oysters near consumed. Flynt had breakfasted on eggs and coffee, courtesy of Mrs Wilkes, so he refused his friend's offer of sharing his meal. He had never learned to appreciate the slimy sensation of the shellfish. His response must have been somewhat short for Gabriel gave him a sideways glance.

'Something irks you, Jonas,' he said.

Flynt decided to drive straight to the nub of the matter. 'Romulus Trask was found dead.'

Gabriel seemed unconcerned. 'He succumbed to his wound, did he? Well, I suppose a booted foot being applied to it would accelerate matters...'

Flynt brushed aside what he thought might be an attempt to divert blame onto him. 'It wasn't my pistol wound that took him. Someone cut his throat.'

Gabriel didn't even have the good grace to appear surprised. He held Flynt's stare. 'And you believe it was I who did this.'

'Did you?'

Something akin to sadness floated in Gabriel's eyes. 'Do you believe I did?'

Flynt's certainty in his friend's guilt began to waver. 'You gave me your word that you would not, and yet the man lies dead. You were left alone with him. What else should I believe?'

Gabriel did not reply at first. He took a sip of ale and then sat very still, as if gathering his thoughts. 'Ordinarily my word is not worth a politician's spit, I will give you that. I am liar, cheat, thief and an habitual seducer of other men's wives. I have given my word and broken it so often that much of the time I no longer trust my own thoughts. So why should anyone believe what I say?'

'So you admit it?'

'I said ordinarily, Jonas, and that is the word you must remember. On this occasion, I gave my word to you, and that makes the difference.' He paused to let this sink in, his eyes boring into Flynt's own. 'You are the only friend I have, or at least the only one I trust, and I would never breach that trust. We've been through much together. We've robbed together and we've fought together and you've saved my life, and I yours, on more occasions than I can count. The fact that you doubt me pains me deeply.'

Guilt tightened Flynt's throat and stung at his eyes. Could he have been wrong? 'Then if not you, who would have done this?'

'I cannot say. Perhaps someone who lives in that rat-infested pisshole came upon him and reached the conclusion that the contents of his purse were better spent by him. But it was not I, Jonas, and on that I once more give you my word. Whether you accept it is your decision. If you do then we'll grasp hands like the true friends we are and proceed on this quest of yours and there's no harm done. If you do not, then I will take my leave now and God be with you.'

Flynt examined his friend for sign of duplicity but, as with the night before, saw nothing. It may have been because he was most accomplished at hiding it, or because he told the truth. In the end, it was a judgement call and, even though doubts remained, Flynt came down on the latter.

He held out his hand. 'I apologise, Gabriel.'

As Gabriel accepted his hand with grace, his customary grin and insouciant manner returned. 'Apology accepted. Now, by way of recompense, I will allow you to buy an old friend who you have so grievously wounded a tankard of ale.'

Flynt agreed with a smile, waved to Melody, a serving girl of his acquaintance, pointed at Gabriel's tankard and gestured for two more. When he looked back, he saw Gabriel's expression had turned reflective.

Flynt asked, 'What?'

Gabriel took a deep breath, a slight frown forming. 'You'll recall I was somewhat tardy when the Trasks bearded you and the ladies in that room?'

'I do. Where were you?'

'I was certain that I'd heard someone moving around in the back yard so had gone to investigate. It was as black as the earl of hell's waistcoat out there and I found nothing. I put it down to rats in search of food.'

Flynt felt a shudder course through him at the thought.

'But later, while I stood guard over Romulus, I could've sworn someone was observing me. I remain unsure what it was, just this strong conviction that there were eyes upon me. I'm telling you, Jonas, it was damnably unnerving. It was like I was being watched by some phantom.'

'Did you investigate again?'

'No, I came after you once I was certain that Romulus was not in any condition to follow.' He then added with considerable emphasis, 'Though he still breathed.'

Guilt made Flynt look away, just as Melody returned with the ale. While she placed the tankard on the table with a quick smile towards Flynt and accepted some coins, Flynt recalled Gabriel's troubled look as they made away from the tenement. Was that the reason? Had he been disturbed by what he thought he had heard and felt? Was there someone lurking in the dark, just waiting for the chance to kill Romulus?

He told Gabriel about the assassination attempt as he made his way to his room and of the man whose body he found.

Gabriel observed, 'And his throat cut, you say, just as Romulus's was?'

'It was.'

'So your thinking is that it was the same person who hushed them both?'

'It seems a logical assumption.'

'It surely does, I'll grant you. So if my phantom is also this mysterious sentinel, why does he wish to protect you?'

'I don't know.'

Gabriel stared at the uneaten oysters, his hand resting beside the plate, one finger tapping. 'You continue to suspect me, don't you?'

Flynt replied, 'Whoever killed that man did seem to have my best interest at heart.'

Gabriel accepted that with a jerk of his head. 'Under the circumstances I'd suspect me too, if I didn't know for a fact that I was having a most energetic tup with that young lady in her room. But, think on this, why would I do such a thing surreptitious? Why hide in the shadows and not bask in your gratitude? I ask you, Jonas, does that sound like the Gabriel Cain you know?'

That had preyed on Flynt's mind. 'It does not. You'd want my praise and admiration.'

'Damn right I would, and I'd deserve it, too. No, Jonas, I didn't kill Romulus Trask and I didn't despatch that nameless cur in that stable and then hive myself off into the darkness. I think now that my phantom was of flesh and blood and for some reason he wishes you to live. The question is, who is this

143

anonymous and most bashful benefactor? And what precisely is his interest in you?'

Flynt did not know, but he could not shake off the feeling that the mysterious individual was no good Samaritan.

15

Flynt did not have the leisure to lounge in the tavern and remin-
isce further over old times with Gabriel, pleasurable though
that may be. Neither could he simply wait for John Duck to
come to them, so decided they would go to him. They set off
towards Lincoln's Inn Fields and thence to Chancery Lane and
into Little White's, again the shade providing welcome respite
from the glare of the sun, finding the fencing master in his
school, crossing foils with a pale, slim youth whose long black
hair was tied back with a red ribbon. Their movements were
smooth and graceful, the youth being most expert in the cut and
thrust of the light weapon. Duck's style this day differed hugely
from the blunt force he had used against Flynt, and presumably
the Trasks, for this was showman swordplay. It was polite and
delicate, each thrust, each parry, carefully placed, the body
suitably positioned for how it looked to the observer. A real
sword fight was grim and brutal, with every move designed to
put the other man down no matter what. As Flynt had learned
the day before, John Duck was proficient in both styles.

'Very stylish,' Gabriel remarked.

'Deft,' said Flynt.

'Nice footwork,' Gabriel said as the young man danced away,
then moved back to cross blades once again. 'Wouldn't last a
minute in a real fight.'

'I don't think that young man will ever find himself in such
a situation. I believe the closest he will come to it will be harsh
words with some servant.'

The lesson ended, the young man thanked John Duck with a nod and walked to the corner of the room where his coat and boots awaited him. He sat down and slipped off the soft, lightweight footwear he wore for the lesson, paying no attention as Flynt and Gabriel approached Duck, who was wiping sweat from his face with a rag lifted from another chair.

'You received my message then, Mr Flynt?'

'Where did you leave it?'

'I sent it to both the Golden Cross and to the Black Lion, as you instructed.'

He must have missed both. 'You have something for me then?'

Duck held up a finger and glanced at the young man, who had stamped into his boots and was now thrusting his arms into his coat. 'Thank you, your grace, you will return the same time seven days hence?'

The young man inclined his head in the affirmative and walked to the exit. His tread, even in his boots, was light and airy. Flynt had heard that at the French court it was fashionable for the ladies to appear as if they glided rather than walked and this young noble seemed to do just that. He barely glanced at Flynt and Gabriel, perhaps instinctively recognising them as common and therefore beneath his notice. Even his acknowledgement of his fencing master was haughty, no breath being wasted with an audible response, his head movement the merest hint of a nod requiring the least effort, and then he was gone.

Gabriel smiled. 'Talkative fellow, is he not?'

The observation seemed to require neither response nor amplification so none was given. Instead Flynt asked, 'Has Sally told you where Mr Templeton is?'

Duck was apologetic. 'She did not, I regret to say. I don't believe she knows.'

Disappointed, Flynt stifled a curse. He had been certain she would have information.

Duck picked up a roll of paper from the chair beside him. 'She did have this, though. Templeton gave it to her, telling her that should she ever be in serious trouble then she was to bring it to me.' He handed the parchment to Flynt. 'To be frank, I know not what to make of it.'

Flynt unravelled the paper to stared at a series of apparently meaningless ink marks. 'It's a cipher of some kind.'

Gabriel peered over his shoulder. 'My God, this Templeton was a cautious fellow, was he not? He even communicated with his lady love in code.'

'The man is frightened.'

'Sally said that if it became necessary I would know of someone who could make sense of it,' Duck explained.

'And do you?' Flynt asked.

Duck shrugged. 'Nobody springs immediate to mind but I have many pupils in the law. Perhaps one of them has a mind sharp enough to handle such a cipher.'

Flynt studied the lines of dashes, obliques and dots. 'May I keep this?'

Gabriel asked, 'Do you know of someone with a sharp mind who could decode it, Jonas?'

Flynt grinned. 'The sharpest mind in England...'

—

Sir Isaac Newton's office was filled with books, maps and study materials. A telescope stood in the corner and one wall bore shelves that bowed under the weight of hefty tomes and a variety of ephemera, including a wooden globe, a sextant and piles of parchment. The handsome dark oak desk was covered in papers and quills. Although the window looked out upon Crane Court, there was a sense of otherworldliness in this room, as if it were detached from the reality beyond the glass. This was a place of thought, not deed, where the mysteries of life, theology, science and – Flynt had heard rumoured – alchemy were sifted, probed and solved. The drapes, however, were somewhat incongruous in the setting, for they were a most vivid crimson. An armchair and another more workmanlike chair behind the desk were also upholstered in fabric of a similar flaming hue. Flynt mused that they wouldn't look out of place in Mother Grady's apartments.

Newton studied the sheet of paper that John Duck had given them.

'Can you decipher it, Sir Isaac?'

Newton gave Flynt a forbidding look. 'Of course I can, do you take me for a simpleton, sir? A child with his letters could solve this puzzle.'

Flynt took no offence at the man's tone, for he was known to be mercurial of temperament.

'It is a cipher of the simplest kind,' the scientist continued as he settled behind his desk and pulled a blank sheet towards him, then dipped a quill into the ink. 'And you say young Templeton penned it?'

'That's what we are told.'

Newton frowned. 'I would have thought him capable of something more complex than this. This is a fairly simple pigpen cipher, a substitution cryptograph, which replaces letters with symbols, which in turn form part of a grid. It's an ancient form of communication by subterfuge and I would say this one is based on a code said to have been used by the Knights Templar. It is derived from variations of the shape of a Maltese cross, the symbol of those gentlemen, as you can see.'

Flynt saw nothing of the sort but he kept his silence as Newton began to scribble words on the blank sheet, his eyes darting between the code to his own writing, occasionally crossing out something he believed to be in error and beginning again. It took him only a few minutes before he sat back, placed his quill in the pot, and steepled his fingers before him as he studied first Flynt then Gabriel.

'Have we met before, sir?'

'I think not, Sir Isaac,' Gabriel said, 'but I am honoured to make the acquaintance of a gentleman of such eminence.'

Newton grunted but obviously enjoyed the compliment. 'I feel I know your features.'

Gabriel's smile was easy. 'I have that sort of face.'

Newton deliberated upon this for a moment then inclined his arched fingers towards the document. 'Young Templeton was most afeared, it seems. Did he have good reason?'

'I believe he did,' Flynt said.

Newton stared at the words before him then handed the sheet to Flynt. 'Then you must read this for yourself.'

Gabriel edged closer in order to see the message. Newton's handwriting was somewhat spidery but legible, the various scores and alterations he had made in no way detracting from the sense of the missive.

> *My dear Sally,*
>
> *If you read these words then it means you have been discovered and for that I am heartily sorry. I am wracked with guilt, not just over the sin most grievous that I have committed but also the position in which I have now placed you. You know I have felt remorse concerning my occupation and it was necessary for me to take myself away in order to restore the balance of my mind. I have explained to you why I could not allow you to accompany me. It is best to be as distant from me as possible until this situation be resolved, and resolve it I shall.*
>
> *If your dear brother is the man I believe he is, he will have you in his keeping. Should events now make it necessary for you to be spirited from town, then there is one I trust implicitly who will assist you.*

Flynt read the name and sighed.

'Do you know the individual he names?' Newton asked.

'Oh, yes,' Flynt replied, 'I do indeed.'

16

Gabriel made no move to enter the doorway of Nando's Coffee House as they turned from Inner Temple Lane but continued to walk beyond it, stopping under the sign of Bernard Lintot the bookseller in Fleet Street. Flynt frowned a query at him and Gabriel smiled.

'It occurs to me that it's perhaps imprudent for us to approach this gentleman together. After all, I am stranger to him and if he does truly have the knowledge you seek then my presence could act as impediment.'

There was sense in what he said. The man Templeton had named was a fine lawyer and would be unwilling to speak with a witness present.

Gabriel continued, 'I'll linger in Mr Lintot's fine establishment, browsing the volumes, and you can find me when you have done with… what's his name?'

'Lemuel Gribble.'

'Of course, how could I forget a name like that, eh? Good fortune be with you, Jonas. Let us pray that he does indeed know that which we require.'

Though not a praying man, Flynt did hope that Lemuel could assist them. If not, as he had already told Charters, the trail was as dead as the old queen.

The lawyer appeared not to have moved since Flynt saw him the day before. He sat at the same table, wearing the same clothing, perhaps even the same tobacco ash still speckling the front of his coat. What was different this time were the empty plates, two of them bearing the smears and stains of recently-consumed meals, for Lemuel did not achieve his considerable girth through inactivity alone. Whether they had been specially cooked for him on the premises or sent over from a nearby inn, Flynt didn't know.

The lawyer's face was rosy and Flynt suspected it was not just the flush of having consumed the meat, but also the result of a surfeit of alcohol, leading Flynt to suspect his special blend of coffee had been consumed with some enthusiasm, even though it was early afternoon.

The man beamed when he saw Flynt approach. 'Ah, my good friend Jonas Flynt,' he said, his voice booming around the room but, as before, none of the other patrons took any notice. They were well used to hearing from Lemuel Gribble. 'I wondered when it was that you would appear within yonder doorway again.'

Flynt pulled up a chair and sat opposite. 'You were expecting me?'

'Of course, my dear fellow.' He drained his coffee and gave Flynt a pointed look. Flynt waved at the serving girl and indicated Lemuel's cup. She did not need to ask anything further.

'Damnably decent of you, friend Flynt,' Lemuel said, his grin a little fixed but his eyes sharp. 'I suspect you wish something of me.'

'You suspect correctly, Lemuel.'

The lawyer held up one beefy hand as the girl returned with a cup of coffee and set it on the table. Lemuel gave her a wink and they engaged in the customary conversation as to whether it was his special brew. Satisfied that it was, Lemuel patted her hand. 'Thank you, poppet.'

Flynt handed the girl a coin. 'Take what is due out of that, and for Mr Gribble's meal if unpaid, and keep whatever is left over for yourself.'

'Thank you, kindly, can I gets you anything at all?' she asked.

Flynt declined and after the girl gave them a slight curtsy, Lemuel sipped his coffee and said, 'Be you sure, my boy?'

'It's too early in the day for me,' Flynt said. 'I wouldn't want to fog my brain with spirits.'

The notion seemed to be somewhat outlandish to Lemuel, who shook his head. 'My mind unfogged is not a place I wish to visit, my friend, for the miasma conceals the ghosts of mistakes past and deeds best forgotten.'

Flynt considered what there was in Lemuel's past that he wished to hide behind a barrier of intoxication. That, however, was an investigation for another day.

Lemuel drained half the cup with such speed that Flynt doubted he even tasted it. He expressed satisfaction with a loud 'Ahhh', wiped his mouth with the back of his hand and then fixed his eyes on Flynt. 'And so to business. You have returned, I will hazard, for further information regarding young Mr Templeton.'

Flynt was grateful the man had the presence of mind to lower his voice. 'Why didn't you inform me that you had knowledge of his present location when I asked yesterday?'

'Ah, my boy, a precaution, nothing more. I had to ensure that your motives in this matter were pure.'

'And you have received such an assurance?'

'I have indeed.' He drank, though a sip only. The tang of the doctored coffee hit the mark again for he smacked his lips in appreciation. 'A fine drop of coffee this, the best in all of London if you ask my opinion.'

Flynt had no interest in the superiority of Nando's coffee, with or without Gribble's special sweetener, over the hundreds of other such establishments in the city. 'How can you be sure now I have no malevolent intent in this matter?'

'It is but a simple explanation. Mr John Duck, sword master to the gentry, has this day his beloved sister secure in his care and that of his lady wife. It is my belief that had you wished my young friend ill then you would not have taken the trouble to return his paramour to a place of safety. Young Christopher had informed me that he had left word with her that should she need him, then she should come to me.'

'Did you have knowledge of her location all along?'

'I assured you I had no such intelligence, which was why I set you upon the trail, for despite Christopher being the catalyst for her disappearance I was most concerned for the girl's wellbeing, Mr Duck being an acquaintance of mine, though I have no need for his services. A gentleman of my size has no business cavorting about a school for the intricacies of the blade.'

'What made you think I could find her?'

Lemuel laughed. It rose from his belly and vibrated upwards. 'Do not forget that I know of you, my boy, and such knowledge was sufficient to convince me that if there was anyone in this city who could find poor Sally, then he sits before me. I am most gratified to find that my faith in you was not ill-placed.'

'You knew of me, as you say, and yet you did not trust me?'

Lemuel squinted at him. 'Ah, there you have me. I will be frank with you. It is because of what I know of you that my judgement was somewhat ambivalent. In many ways you are a fine fellow, Jonas, but you and I both know that you walk a thin line between light and shade. On this occasion I had to have some reassurance that you walk with the sun on your back.'

Flynt couldn't argue with him. 'So, you will share what you know now?'

'If you will share with me why you are motivated to find him.'

'I have already done so, I am being paid to find him.'

'By whom?'

'By someone who wishes to remain hidden.'

Lemuel laid his cup down as he considered this. 'And this most circumspect of employers, what are his intentions regarding Christopher?'

Flynt responded without pause, even though he was never certain what Colonel Charters' true intentions were. 'As mine, he only has Mr Templeton's wellbeing at heart.'

Lemuel was brandy-soaked but he was no fool. 'Why?'

It was clear to Flynt that time was passing and there would be no further advancement without revealing at least something.

He placed his forearms on the tabletop and leaned in, dropping his voice as low as he could without actually adopting a whisper. Lemuel tilted forward slightly to meet him. 'Mr Templeton has performed legal services in the past for a group of individuals who are dangerous in the extreme. His liaison with Miss Duck has given him cause to reassess his priorities and he's severed connection with those individuals, who are now of the opinion that he may reveal some of their secrets.'

'To whom?'

Flynt knew he was on dangerous ground. 'To anyone.'

Lemuel pursed his lips. 'Anyone, eh? And they will kill to keep what they have hidden from this anyone?'

'I believe they will. They're ruthless, Lemuel, and they will not baulk at murder if it suits their purpose.'

Although Lemuel appeared to ponder upon this, Flynt had the impression that he had known it all along. 'I will ask you a question, friend Flynt, and I beg of you to respond with truth. Are you aware of a gentleman by the name of Colonel Nathaniel Charters?'

Lemuel was a canny attorney who had been part of the London establishment for many years and so, the law and government being bound to one another, it was not beyond the realms of possibility that he had heard a whisper here, a murmur there, and had put them together to reach a shout. Even so, mention of the name caused something within Flynt to lurch. Lemuel watched him intently, his mind still sharp despite the liquor. Flynt considered a lie but rejected the idea. This was a time for truth, or at least some form of it.

'He was my commanding officer in Flanders,' Flynt said carefully.

'Then I will make an assumption that it is he who has engaged you on this inquiry and further, that he is the "anyone" this group of individuals of whom you speak worries would learn more of their activities.'

He paused for a response but Flynt believed he had already said enough, and perhaps too much. He also was increasingly aware that Lemuel already knew the answer to many of these questions. He grew weary of the exchange and some irritation scratched at his voice. 'Lemuel, will you tell me where Mr Templeton is or not?'

The lawyer smiled. 'I think you tire of our verbal fencing.'

'I think if you don't answer my question in a straightforward manner with no further prevarication or interrogation concerning my motives then this conversation will be at an end.'

A sly look spread across Lemuel's features. 'You will not do that, for you and I both know that I am key to you completing this mission of yours.'

Flynt considered whether this was all preamble to a demand for some financial incentive, or if it was just Lemuel making sport of him, toying with him for his own pleasure. He pondered whether he was in some way related to Charters.

'I will answer that in this way,' Flynt said. 'You are key to whether Christopher Templeton lives or dies, and if you are the friend to him that you claim then you will assist me. Now, Lemuel, no more delay, where is he?'

Lemuel threw back what was left of his special brew, then once again wiped the excess from his lips with the back of his hand. Flynt understood his hesitation but was impatient. 'Damn it, Lemuel, tell me!'

The vehemence in his voice seemed to startle the lawyer. He looked around them, to ensure nobody was listening, then laid his cup down. This time it was his turn to lean forward. 'I apologise. I believe you do have Christopher's best interests at heart, even if you are merely hired to do so. There is a village in the north, Gallowmire, have you heard of it?' He saw by Flynt's expression he had not. 'Of course, you will not. It is a small place, exceeding remote. A man on a fast horse could ride through it without even noticing.'

'And Mr Templeton is there?'

'He is. I was left a house by a maiden aunt and I have allowed him to conceal himself within it for the time being. The Millhouse, it be called.'

'It's a mill?'

Lemuel's head shook. 'No, the mill be a way down the river, but the house was once owned by the miller and retained the name. Miller's House it were for generations but since has been shortened to Millhouse.'

'Have you heard from him since he left London?'

'A letter arrived only this day, informing me that he is safe ensconced and all seems well.'

Flynt did a swift calculation. For a letter to arrive in London from the north, if the post boy was swift, it meant it was despatched two or three days before. So given that the Trasks didn't know where he was the previous night, he would still be alive and well. Unless there were others on the scent.

'You've told nobody else this?'

'I have not.'

'I have your word on that, Lemuel?'

'You do, and right solemnly.'

'And nobody else has made inquiry of Mr Templeton with you?'

'There was, but I revealed nothing.'

Flynt stiffened. 'A man alone or two brothers?'

'The former.'

'When was this?'

'Two days since.'

'Why did you not tell me this before?'

'You did not ask me before. I am a lawyer and I answer only that which I am asked, and even then I may choose equivocation above candour.'

Flynt had already experienced that. 'Did this person give you a name?'

'He did but I suspect it was not a true one. John Smith, he said.'

'A common enough name, to be sure.'

'I have met many John Smiths in my profession and I can discern by its delivery if it be true or not. It did not fall from his tongue as though it were a name he had uttered since he could first speak.'

Lemuel was well used to dealing with charlatans and liars of all stripes, so Flynt believed him when he said that the name given was what Jack would call a queer chant. 'What did this gentleman look like?'

'He was about your height and build, fair of face and complexion, carried with him an easy manner. I suspect him to be most charming when he has a mind to be, but with me he was courteous but businesslike.'

Flynt blinked as he recognised the description. His next words were strained. 'How was he dressed?'

Lemuel detected the tension that had stolen over the conversation and spoke slowly, as if studying his words before he uttered, 'Dark clothes, like your own. Boots, coat, waistcoat, white shirt.'

'Bewigged?'

'No.'

'Hair colour?'

'Flaxen, carried long but tied with a ribbon...'

17

He found Gabriel in Mr Lintot's shop, leafing through a book of John Donne poems. The rotund proprietor himself was at a table, a pile of volumes before him as he put quill to ledger to note their titles. He gave Flynt a nod when he entered, for he was a regular customer, his aunt's kindling of a love of reading in the child still burning within the man.

When he saw him, Gabriel flicked back a few pages of the tome he held. 'Listen to this, Jonas, Mr Donne on a broken heart.' He began to read.

> 'Yet nothing can to nothing fall,
> Nor any place be empty quite;
> Therefore I think my breast hath all
> Those pieces still, though they be not unite;
> And now, as broken glasses show
> A hundred lesser faces, so
> My rags of heart can like, wish, and adore,
> But after one such love, can love no more.'

He laid the book down on another table and gave Flynt an oblique look, his tone mischievous. 'Do those words resonate at all, Jonas?'

They did, and well Flynt knew them, but he was in no mood to discuss matters of the heart, broken or otherwise. What Lemuel had told him of the man who had made inquiry regarding Templeton had disturbed him. It was possible, of course, that it was another blond-haired individual in dark clothing but Flynt suspected that to be unlikely and, notwith-standing Gabriel's earlier impassioned assertion of the bonds of friendship, his suspicion of his motives had been revived. It had seemed fortunate at the time that Gabriel had reappeared when he did, for he had proved most useful the night before, but it occurred to Flynt, and it had niggled him since he had heard of Romulus Trask's death, that the resurfacing was not so much propitious as engineered. He didn't know with any certainty that Gabriel was playing a duplicitous game but the odds did appear stacked in its favour. However, Flynt maintained an impassive mien, even though he still reeled from the shock of it. It saddened him, hurt him, but he was best to have knowledge of it, for that way he could strive to protect those rags of his heart.

Sensing that no comment on the verse would be forth-coming, Gabriel set the book down. 'Did that fellow possess the knowledge we require?'

Flynt touched the brim of his hat to Mr Lintot, still scratching at the paper, and turned to the door. 'He did not.'

Gabriel followed him onto Fleet Street, where carriages and chairmen and courtesans mingled with those citizens who would utilise their various services. There was noise and stench and life and at that moment all three were just what Flynt needed. He needed to have such activity around him for his mind was filled with thoughts of betrayal. His pace was brisk as he strode towards Temple Bar.

Gabriel quickened his own pace to keep up. 'What did the fellow say?'

Despite his need to appear normal, Flynt's voice was edgy. 'He has no inkling of where Templeton is, simple as that.'

'Damn, I felt sure he would. Why would Templeton say in his note that he did?'

'I have no idea.'

Gabriel slowed, touching Flynt on the arm. 'In that case we must return and further question the girl.'

Flynt continued moving. 'She knows nothing, I feel it. Templeton has been most clever. He has told nobody of his hiding place because if nobody knows, nobody can peach.'

Gabriel's eyes narrowed in thought. 'Then what is our next step?'

'For me the game is over. I have nowhere else to go.'

'Giving up? That doesn't sound like the Jonas Flynt I know.'

Flynt halted with such suddenness that Gabriel had carried on a pace or two before he realised. Flynt knew rage was colouring his voice but he couldn't help it. 'I'm at the end of a blind alley with no doorways. The man has vanished and he's done it right expertly. All I can do now is inform the person who hired me that my involvement is at an end.'

Gabriel soaked in the barely concealed anger. He let Flynt's words hang between them for a moment before he thinned his lips in acceptance. 'Aye, I see the sense of it. There's no finding someone who doesn't want to be found and has taken precautions to ensure such.'

Flynt began walking again.

Gabriel moved with him. 'You will see your employer immediate?'

'I will.'

'How will he take it?'

'He will not be pleased. He's not a man who brooks failure.'

They were now walking under Mr Wren's ornate arched gateway of Portland stone spanning the roadway where once stood the old gates, the bars, delineating the western jurisdiction of the ancient city. Beyond the baroque edifice, with its walkways running parallel on either side of the wider arch utilised by street traffic, they entered the Strand.

'You will speak with him alone, I take it,' Gabriel said.

'He's most jealous of his privacy.'

Gabriel accepted that. 'Then here I'll leave you, old friend, for there are matters to which I too must attend. We'll meet later, a meal perhaps, say at eight of the clock in the Black Lion?'

'Aye,' said Flynt, coming to a standstill again as Gabriel held out his hand. Flynt grasped it and Gabriel's other hand clasped him by the arm.

'It's right glad I am that we're together again, Jonas. Old friends are like fine wine and faithful spouses, we must savour them for they are all too rare. Do you agree?'

Flynt was aware that his faltering trust was becoming overly apparent, so contrived as warm a smile as he could. 'And you would know about the faithful wives, Gabriel.'

That provoked the grin that had charmed women and men across England. Flynt saw it now as a cover for something else, yet he knew not what, so for the present he resolved to continue displaying another face to this old friend.

'Until tonight then,' Gabriel said. 'Good fortune with this mysterious employer of yours, and I pray he'll understand the folly of further pursuit.'

'Whether he understands or not, I'm done with it.'

They parted, Flynt continuing along the Strand where he knew he would find a messenger, Gabriel cutting up towards Covent Garden. Flynt looked back to watch him go, and when his figure vanished behind a stream of vehicles, the anger evaporated until only sadness remained.

-

Flynt had the messenger take his own coded missive to an address in Whitehall from whence it would then be passed along to Colonel Charters. It would take time, he knew, so he found himself with some much-needed leisure to enjoy a walk in St James', where he had suggested they rendezvous. He seldom came to the park, though he enjoyed it when he did, it being an oasis of peace in the rough and tumble of city life and a salve to his troubled mind. Looking at it now he found it hard to believe that it had once been wetlands soaked by the River Tyburn, until over a hundred years before the land was drained on orders of King James who had it utilised to house a variety of exotic animals. Now only cattle grazed on the grass and Flynt stood in the shade of a tall tree watching milkmaids approach to drive them to be milked. These women paid a fee to pasture the beasts on the royal parkland and every morning the milk was sold to eager Londoners at the park's Lactarian. The more fashionable in society partook of a syllabub, a meld of milk and wine, which Flynt had tried once but, like oysters, he found the mixture's taste unpleasant. He could drink wine and he could drink milk but not the two together. It was served to him by a lady who told him that her family had been trading in the Lactarian for almost a hundred years, the licence for which was passed on through the female line, from mother to daughter. It was honest work and Flynt wondered, not for the first time, if he should be seeking a profession that did not require him to walk alleys, climb stairways and forever carry loaded pistols about his person. Returning to a life on the road and the high toby that he had shared for a time with Gabriel was out of the question. He also no longer had appetite for the crack lay, though he could still gain access to any property thanks to the skills taught him by old Tom. Honest work didn't appeal. He couldn't envisage himself as a shop assistant or a clerk. He gambled excessively well and made more than a decent living gaming, so much so that there were those who thought his expertise at the tables either verged on the supernatural or he was amazingly adroit at sharp practice. He could, he knew, live tolerably well on the back of his skills. But luck, like love, could be fickle. It could kiss you one day and then desert you the next.

He recognised these musings as nothing but fantasy, for he knew in his heart that the only time he would be free of those alleys and stairways was when he was dead. Colonel Charters held his life in his hands and he wouldn't relinquish that hold until it suited his purpose.

As if he had somehow sensed his thoughts, Charters manifested himself with his customary stealth and for a moment stood in silence at Flynt's side to watch the women prodding the cows together. It was a peaceful, pastoral scene and the sunshine slanting through the trees and greening the grass suggested a peace that Flynt himself did not feel.

Charters spoke at last. 'Contemplating the mysteries of life, Serjeant?'

'There is no mystery to life, Colonel. We live, we die, that is all.'

'Ah, but death, surely that is the greatest mystery of all?'

Flynt shot Charters a quick glance, not for the first time wondering whether the man really had added the reading of minds to his list of accomplishments. 'Not one I am keen to investigate.'

'None of us are, Serjeant.' Charters began to walk leisurely along the pathway, his long cane tapping on the pathway, expecting – knowing – Flynt would follow. 'And what of our mystery, you have news, I gather?'

Flynt quietly told him what he had learned, omitting again any mention of Gabriel's involvement, pausing only when a gentleman and his lady approached. Charters bowed politely to them as they passed, surreptitiously ensuring they were well out of earshot before he said, 'So, Mr Templeton has gone furth of the city. A fine word of your countrymen, Flynt. Furth. Has a texture to it, has it not? Nevertheless, though his decision to do so is an understandable reaction to his predicament, he must surely be aware that the Fellowship's reach extends beyond the boundaries of London.' He took another few paces. 'We will have to show him that ours extends just as far.'

'I take it that means I am heading to the north.'

'It does indeed.'

Flynt had expected that and, in fact, welcomed it. He needed to get away from London for a period. He had been considering it before Charters had set him upon this mission, and the business regarding Gabriel had only strengthened the desire. 'I'll leave at first light.'

Charters nodded his agreement. 'Sound idea. You will require funds, I assume?'

'Naturally.' Flynt had money but he never admitted that to Charters.

'I will have an adequacy delivered to your lodgings by morning. Make haste, Flynt, and given recent events I need not remind you to maintain a weather eye on your flank. There always appears to be someone who wishes you ill, but in this year past it has become something of an epidemic.'

'You are concerned for my wellbeing, Colonel?'

'A good commander is forever concerned for the wellbeing of his troops.' He smiled. 'Even the surly ones.'

18

The meal with Gabriel was difficult. They dined again in the same upstairs room in the Black Lion where Flynt often met with Charters, the music from the tavern below drifting towards them on the rise of voices and the clatter of ale pots and plates. The stench of piss from earlier had thankfully dissipated, or at least was successfully countered by the fragranced candles guttering around the room. He knew Gabriel well enough to be aware that he would have intuited something amiss, for the man's empathetic skills rivalled Flynt's at gaming, but this night they had either failed him or he chose not to remark upon it, instead keeping up an endless stream of reminiscences of their time on the road and tales of his amorous adventures. Flynt listened and smiled and laughed and contributed a story and a quip or two, but all the while he wondered what game his old friend was playing.

At around ten of the clock Flynt made his apologies, telling Gabriel that the day's labours had left him fatigued, which was no lie. He also knew he had a long journey ahead of him and he needed a decent night's sleep. He had already warned the retired military officer who owned the stables where he lodged Horse that he would require her to be bridled and saddled by cock crow. Mrs Wilkes was also aware that he would be absent for some days, although not his destination.

Gabriel seemingly accepted the early termination of the evening's conviviality with a comment about them both growing old and that in years past they would have carried on all night. At their parting, he suggested that they meet in the morning to discuss if there was any way forward regarding finding Templeton, irrespective of what Flynt may have told his employer.

'I believe we can't leave the matter there, Jonas,' he said. 'There has to be a way of finding this fellow. After all, people don't simply vanish into thin air. He is a lawyer, not a magician. There must be a trace of him and damn it, we'll find it, you and I.'

Flynt agreed, the deception on his part not stirring his conscience a whit.

In the tavern downstairs he saw Bess talking to a soldier in the blue coat with red facing of the recently formed regiment of artillery, who was no doubt negotiating a price for her favours. She spotted Flynt looking at her, said a word to the artillery man, giving him a reassuring caress of the arm, and moved to face him. She was considerably more pristine than previous, and her dress was of more recent vintage than her usual garb.

'Before you says anything, Jonas Flynt, I ain't staying in that place no longer. I don't care what you think, but I am my own girl and that's all there is to it. That Mother Grady, she's a right tyrant, she is, and she forced me into that bath and rubbed me down herself. You ask me, I think she enjoyed it.'

Flynt knew Mary Grady would merely be ensuring that Bess was properly clean before she took up space in one of her beds. Anyway, knowing that Romulus Trask was dead did mean that Bess no longer faced any peril from that quarter.

Nevertheless, Trask was not the only reason Flynt had lodged her in Mother Grady's house. 'That has to be your decision, Bess, but Mother Grady and Miss Belle would have taken care of you.'

'I don't need no taking care of and not by the likes of them, what looks down their noses at ordinary street girls like me, even though we all be the same on our backs, which is what our station is. So I'll thank you not to preach me no sermon.'

He saw fire in her eyes but no shadow of guilt, no sign of self-recrimination. 'It was not my intention…'

She flapped her lips to recreate the sound of a fart to let him know what she thought of his intentions, then caught him glancing down at the dress. 'Yes, I took this with me. They gives me it, they did, for they had burned my other one without even as much as a by-your-leave, so I calculate that this is mine by right, fair exchange being no robbery.'

She glared at him, as if daring him to debate the point, but he merely shrugged and smiled. 'You must do as you please, Bess. The danger has now passed and you are free to follow your life as you see fit.' He tipped his hat and stepped around her to make for the door, then paused again. 'And when you see young Jack, I would be grateful if you would inform him that I will be leaving the city on the morrow for the north and may be gone for some time.'

She sneered. 'Stay away forever for all I cares. You ain't good for that lad. One day you'll be the death of him.'

A promise that he would never purposely see the boy in harm's way took life in his mind but died before it reached his tongue. She would never accept it. Instead he said, 'You care for him, don't you?'

He saw something then that he never thought he would. It was a brief look in her eye, the merest flash, but it revealed the young woman underneath the rock-hard exterior. In that moment he realised that there had once been hopes and dreams in that breast, but they had been eroded by the winds and tides of life to leave the sharp edges. The look was gone as soon as it appeared but Flynt knew she bore tender feelings for Jack, even though her voice was as cutting as usual. 'He's a God-rotting pest, is what he is. Panting after me like a little dog. But he has the bunce occasional for a fumble, not that he lasts long, bless him. He'll learn though.'

'I feel certain that you'll be the one to teach him, Bess.'

As he made for the door he could feel her eyes burning into him. She was a formidable young woman but he was gratified that there was even a tiny spark of affection for Jack. She had killed a man only the night before and yet appeared to be entirely unaffected by it. He'd told Belle that murder has a way of festering in the soul, but Elizabeth Lyon seemed to have some form of immunity. He wished he possessed such resistance.

He genuinely was tired so he had chairmen carry him to Charing Cross. Sitting back in the sedan, he rested as much as he could given the fact that the mode of transport often meant being jostled. Thankfully, the journey was as smooth as the expert chairmen could engineer and they deposited him at the coaching inn quickly. No music floated from across the way and as he turned into the archway, his hands rested on his pistols lest there be another attempt at ambush. There was no attack, but in the light of the courtyard lanterns he saw two familiar figures. The largest of them touched the other on the shoulder and pointed in his direction.

'Jonas Flynt,' said Jonathan Wild, as ever impeccably dressed and sporting the sword that he believed was a mark of his self-appointed rank.

'To what do I owe the pleasure, Mr Wild?' Flynt said, nodding to the Thieftaker General's companion. Blueskin Blake's broad face, his chin heavily shadowed with a beard that no amount of scraping could clear, did not return the acknowledgment but stared back with his customary mix of distrust and dislike. A fine way for a man to be with someone whose life he once saved, Flynt thought, even though he done so only upon Wild's order.

'You are well, I trust?' Wild said, his voice still bearing echoes of his Wolverhampton roots.

'Quite well, thank you,' Flynt replied.

'Your wounds have healed fully?'

'They have.'

'Right glad I am to hear that. There was a moment, back in the winter, when we thought you were lost to the world.'

Flynt felt the icy waters gripping him, numbing the pain of the knife slashes but dragging him down into the depths. Had it not been for Blueskin, they would have. 'For a moment, so did I.'

'You had some excitement in this very locale just recent, too, I hear.'

Word travelled fast in the city's underworld and Wild had an intelligence service to match Charters'. With all these mouths passing on gossip and occurrences, there was no need for news-papers in the flash world, for it would spread through the streets faster than any press could roll it out.

Flynt asked, 'Do you know the name of the man who tried to kill me?'

'I do. Peter Simms, a killer of minimal prowess.'

'His prowess was most certainly minimal last night.' Flynt didn't recognise the name. 'I've never met this fellow so had no argument with him.'

'He was a sword, pistol and fist for hire, but I would wager he would be no match for you, for he worked mostly the lower end of the market. However, it is my understanding that someone got to him before you did.'

Wild's intelligence was most precise and Flynt had no reason to argue against it.

'Do you know who?'

'That is the reason I be here this night. I bring you warning of the man who it was that slit Simms' whistle. Have you heard of the Wraith?'

'I have not.'

'He is very much as his appellation suggests. He comes, he goes, and nobody knows who he really is.'

'He is also a sword for hire?'

'That he is, and he is the best. I do not believe he has operated in London before this but I have heard of his work from other parts of the country and, they say, the continent. Most skilled he be at the hushing game.' He paused to stare beyond Flynt to the street, as if expecting this apparition to manifest himself. 'They say he has spilled more claret than a drunken nobleman.'

'Who has hired him?'

'I hear many things but the names of those who avail themselves of his services is never something that is bruited. The Wraith ensures that his anonymity is secure by using intermediaries for his transactions and that also protects those who pay him. I do know his services are not cheaply bought and that he promises the principal complete satisfaction. All I can say for reasonable certain is that he is walking these streets.' His gaze drifted again to the street. 'He may even be watching us at this very moment. Somewhere out there, in the night. Seeing but not being seen.' In the brief silence that followed Flynt understood that Wild himself was concerned. That, in itself, was concerning. 'You have irked someone most grievously, my friend. Do you know who?'

Flynt glanced at Blueskin, who remained stoic. 'There's a list.'

A chuckle eased Wild's tension. 'I thought as much.'

'There is something that puzzles me, however. If this Wraith is indeed out for my blood...'

'You may take that as gospel. As you know, my information is seldom wrong.'

'Very well, why did he not finish me last night when he had the chance? Why kill this Simms fellow and leave me drawing breath?'

Flynt didn't mention that Romulus Trask had also been killed in a similar fashion. Wild would know of the deaths in the Rookery but hopefully wouldn't link them. That was a complication to be avoided.

'From what I understand, the Wraith is exceeding precise in what he does and does not like others of his kind, those lesser qualified shall we say, interfering in his affairs,' Wild explained. 'Reports tell me that there is a feline side to his nature. Have you seen a cat with a mouse? He often plays with it, allows it to believe it can evade him, then he pounces. It is a game to him, all sport. I would hazard that is what he is doing here. He plays with you and Simms was finished off because he dared to come between him and his prey.'

Flynt wondered if Wild himself had utilised this man's services in the past.

'And you have no idea as to his identity?'

'Nobody has, from what I understand. Just this name, the Wraith, in which he revels, it seems. Nonetheless, I felt it my duty to warn you of his attentions.' He touched the brim of his hat and stepped under the archway, then halted and added, 'I have great respect for you, Jonas, and you did me a service in the affair regarding Justice Fremont. I will not forget that. I look upon you as a friend and, in faith, I would be dismayed should harm befall you.'

Flynt had identified a rogue in his organisation who was working to his own agenda rather than that of Jonathan Wild, who was not a man who encouraged such free enterprise among his associates. He preferred his followers to obey his every command, much as Blueskin had done that night on the icy water.

Blueskin waited until his master was sufficient distance away before he leaned towards Flynt. 'For what it's worth, Jonas Flynt, I hope this here Wraith does for you good and proper. You is a rum one, but Mr Wild, he don't see it clear. But I does. If this phantom do exist, then you is in the shit deep and this time I will not be the one what drags you out. On that you can have my oath.'

He gave Flynt a rare smile, which did not serve to make his features more becoming, and swaggered after his superior. Blake was unaccountably loyal to the Thieftaker General and one day his devotion would prove misplaced. Flynt watched them both turn onto the street and vanish from sight. He took a deep breath and scanned the shadows around him, feeling unease ripple in his stomach.

Moncrieff did not much care for the man before him but his business interests often dictated that he deal with many individuals for whom he did not care. The gentleman's corpulence was not the issue, for there were a number in his circle whose fondness for food but lack of appetite for any physical pursuits led to an abundance of girth. However, he found slovenly appearance distasteful and drunkenness even more so. Ash speckled the front of the lawyer's suit along with what appeared to be the residue of meals gone by, suggesting to Moncrieff that a lack of care went into both the smoking of the pipe and the shovelling of sustenance, perhaps caused by a superfluity of liquor. Once again, he felt irritation rise. It was his belief that a man who could not function without overindulgence in any vice – gambling, drinking, women – was not a man to be fully trusted. They did, however, have their uses.

Lemuel Gribble was admitted even though Moncrieff was preparing to retire, Lady Katherine having already done so in order to leave him to deal with correspondence. The man had somewhat laboriously lowered himself into a chair on the opposite side of his desk and Moncrieff regarded him while toying with a blunt silver blade he used to slice the seals on this correspondence. He held it in both hands as though he were testing its weight before throwing. Not that he would ever do anything as common as throw a knife. He hired people to perform such functions.

'I take it by the fact that you have arrived at my home at such a late hour that you bear news?'

As a member of the legal profession, Gribble was well used to sharp words so he didn't react to the slight barb in Moncrieff's timbre. Instead, he cast an avaricious eye towards a table carrying an array of wines and spirits. He even licked his lips. Moncrieff was not oblivious to the rules of polite society and so rose from his chair.

'Forgive me, my friend,' he said, feeling neither need for forgiveness nor any form of friendship. 'I neglect my manners.

Would you care for something to wet your thrapple, as we say in my homeland?' His hand rested on a rather dull bottle filled with an amber fluid. 'Can I tempt you to sample the aqua vitae of my country? The highlanders call it *uisge beatha*.'

Moncrieff did not speak Gaelic but he could at least pronounce the Scottish name for the drink. Gribble, however, struggled with it. '*Oosh… Ooshkay bee…*'

Moncrieff allowed himself a smile. 'It is much easier to simply say whisky.'

Another lick of the lips, causing a wave of revulsion to ripple through Moncrieff. 'I have never tried it, my lord, though I have heard it be most potent.'

Moncrieff poured a liberal measure into a crystal goblet and carried it to the lawyer, who accepted it eagerly with profuse thanks. To his credit he didn't empty the vessel immediately but sniffed at the liquid before taking a first tentative taste. However, by the time Moncrieff had returned to his chair on the other side of the desk, half of the measure was gone and Gribble was wiping his mouth with the back of his hand.

'Most pleasing, my lord, I thank you for introducing me to it.'

Moncrieff waved the gratitude away with one hand. 'You are welcome. Now, Mr Gribble, the hour is late and I would be gratified if you would deliver your report. I trust my plan proceeds as we hoped?'

'Like a Swiss timepiece.'

'Flynt has taken the bait then?'

'He has, sir, swallowed it whole and did not even taste it.'

Somewhat like that whisky, Moncrieff thought.

Gribble this time took a sip of the spirit. 'It would not surprise me if he has not already set off for Gallowmire.'

Moncrieff sat back in his chair. Gribble's allusion to the art of the clockmakers of Switzerland was fitting, for the plan was ticking along nicely. 'And he suspects nothing?'

'I sensed no mistrust of me in his demeanour.' Another mouthful of whisky was gulped. 'I added a conceit of my own.

A cipher, which I prevailed upon Templeton to leave with the whore. I thought it added something, I hope you are pleased.'

Moncrieff permitted himself a thin smile. 'Well done, Mr Gribble.'

'You are satisfied with my work?'

Gribble's role had been pivotal in the plan's success so he felt no compunction in bestowing praise. 'More than satisfied, your contribution has been exemplary and I am extremely pleased.'

The lawyer preened and swallowed another mouthful of the whisky, the hand darting upwards to wipe his lips as before. It, too, seemed like a mechanical movement, as though there were cogs and wheels linking the drinking arm with the hand. How often had the man done that over the years, Moncrieff mused, and if the hand that cleared the residue were licked by a dog, would the creature grow intoxicated?

'I am delighted to have been of service, my lord,' said Gribble, 'and if I can assist you in any further matter then I would be honoured if you were to call upon me.'

'I will, Mr Gribble, I will. One can never have too many legal minds to consult when conducting business. Especially one with your unique connections.'

It was Gribble's past history with Templeton that had drawn him at first, but the man became even more important when he discovered his previous connection to Flynt. For his plan to work, the information had to be steered to him by someone he trusted, at least as much as he trusted anyone. It was Gribble himself who added the whore to the mix as a means of seemingly testing Flynt's resolve. Moncrieff suspected it might over-complicate matters but allowed it to proceed, ultimately recognising that there was a slim chance of the Trasks besting Flynt and thus queering the rest of the plan. And if they did emerge victorious, and Flynt fell victim to them, the only disbenefit would be that he himself would not be present to witness it. Gribble, of course, had no idea what lay ahead of Flynt in Gallowmire. Beyond this point in the affair he need know nothing.

The lawyer emptied the glass and cast a hopeful eye towards the bottle but Moncrieff had no intention of refilling. He had spent sufficient time in this man's company and now wished him to leave. To that end, he rose, walked around the desk and took the empty goblet from his grasp.

'I thank you again, Mr Gribble.'

Drunken sot he may be, but he recognised that the interview was at an end. He pushed himself to his feet and extended his hand. Moncrieff did not welcome physical contact with anyone other than his dear wife but he often had to shake hands with those who saw themselves as his equal, or with whom he had to engender some level of fidelity. In this case, he had no intention of allowing Gribble any ideas above his station as a functionary and he cared nothing for his loyalty so ignored the hand and gestured towards the door. Gribble was taken aback by the snub but he recovered quickly.

'I trust you will consider my name favourably for any service I might perform for your friends,' he said, hope managing to overcome the slight.

Moncrieff's jaw tightened. Templeton had been most indiscreet in telling Gribble about the Fellowship, but then if he had not been, he might not have been able to put this plan into motion. Despite his earlier praise, he had no intention of allowing Gribble anywhere near his, or the Fellowship's, business. The lawyer's involvement was a one-time-only affair, as he would soon discover.

Nevertheless he managed another smile and said, 'Of course, my dear fellow. You will, without a doubt, hear from me very soon.'

He opened the door and gestured to the footman stationed outside to show the man to the door. Gribble's smile was askew as he followed the servant across the hallway, his step hindered by the fact that one of his legs seemed bent inward, the result of a childhood injury he had explained on their first meeting. When he finally reached the door he realised that some obsequiousness would still be required so turned again and bowed towards Moncrieff. It was not an easy manoeuvre for him to make, thanks to his deformity and the fact that he was suffering from the effects of intoxication, but his expertise with both conditions allowed him to achieve it without any mishap. Moncrieff knew nothing of the disappointments in life that had caused the man to seek solace in wines and spirits but of one thing he was certain, he would soon be free of them.

He told the footman that would be all for the night and turned back into his study to find Lester seated in the chair Gribble had recently vacated. Moncrieff knew the man had been waiting in the side room but had made no sound as he entered.

He returned to his own chair. 'You heard what was said?'

Lester inclined his head.

'Matters proceed smoothly this far, at least,' Moncrieff said. 'As I told you, dealing with a man such as Jonas Flynt requires subtlety of Machiavellian proportions. Now we have to see if he takes the bait.'

Lester spoke quietly. 'I took the liberty of taking action that may help focus his mind.'

Moncrieff contained his sharp anger. 'What sort of action?'

'Further pressure. The instillation of fear and even suspicion can be very potent.'

'Suspicion of what?'

Lester did not reply straight away. He stared at Moncrieff through his spectacles, his expression as bland as ever. 'He does not work alone as you thought.'

'The boy, Sheppard…'

'No, he has another at his side. A man named Gabriel Cain. He and Flynt seem to be old friends.'

His sudden anger subsided. 'You know this man?'

Another pause. 'Our paths have crossed.'

'And he assists Flynt?'

'He does. I felt you would wish them separated.'

'It would be for the best.'

'Then, as I said, I have taken steps to drive a wedge between them.'

'What steps?'

Lester's expression changed slightly. It was little more than a slight hardening of the eyes but Moncrieff understood that he did not like being questioned. Moncrieff didn't care and held the gaze.

'Lord Moncrieff, it is not my practice to explain myself,' Lester said, 'but I will tell you this and this only. I had a man make an attempt on Flynt's life…'

Moncrieff cut in, 'I told you that using common street bullies would not succeed!'

Lester's manner remained calm. 'It was not intended to, it was merely a means of driving that wedge, as was the removal of the man Trask. That, and some information I leaked into the city's underworld should, if successful, make Flynt suspect Cain and separate himself from him.'

Moncrieff considered this. He would dearly love to know what information the man referred to but felt no further amplification of his methods would be forthcoming. Instead, he nodded his assent. 'Very well, you are most experienced in this line of work and therefore I will make no further inquiry.'

Lester once again inclined his head, whether in thanks or merely acknowledgement Moncrieff could not tell.

'I presume you wish the lawyer dealt with immediately?'

'I do.'

Lester was already at the door. 'The city is a dangerous place for a man alone.'

'We shall know on the morrow if Flynt leaves for the north,' Moncrieff said. 'If he does, it will be in the hands of your friend Lord Gallowmire, although we shall also make all haste there to ensure it.'

Lester turned back. 'Gallowmire will perform his function admirably.'

'How can you be so certain?'

A rare smile. 'Because he enjoys it...'

Part Two

Gallowmire

19

The journey from London had been uneventful, even pleasant thanks to the continuation of the temperate weather. To call the route north a road would be to give it ideas far above its station, for it was little more than ground that was slightly less rough than that which bounded it on either side, and in winter it would have been a rutted mass of mud and filth where a carriage could very easily become bogged down. Flynt had ridden it more than once in that condition and even Horse had found it heavy going, and she was as sure-footed as any of her species could be. On this trip, even though the sun had baked the trail hard, he still made sure that he walked her behind him for long periods to ensure he did not overstretch her strength. She was a game girl who would forever give him her all but he would never risk overburdening her. In any case, he didn't feel time was of the essence, Templeton believed himself safe and there was no evidence to suggest that any other searchers knew of his location, so Flynt was at liberty to take his leisure during the journey.

He slept in inns when he came upon them, barns or haylofts when he did not and under the stars when he had to. After the turbulence that was London both night and day, he welcomed the silence of the English countryside as well as the solitude, just he and Horse and the occasional exchange of pleasant-ries with a fellow traveller. It gave him the breathing space, both literally and figuratively, to consider events, in particular the motives of Gabriel Cain, a matter on which he pondered at length but reached no clear conclusions. His old friend's reappearance in the city could simply have been circumstance, and had certainly been fortuitous, given the assistance he had subsequently offered in dealing with the Trasks, but that chance meeting in the tavern could also have been a contrivance. Consideration had to be given to the individual described by Lemuel Gribble who had been making inquiry regarding Templeton. It was most certainly within the realms of possibility that there were other fair-haired men in London who wore the black of the puritan, but was it likely that two such similar coves would have expressed such an interest in the missing lawyer? If Gabriel was indeed Gribble's previous interlocutor, then that could mean he was working for the Fellowship. Such was not outwith the realms of possibility, for though Gabriel's company was entertaining and he was most sturdy in a fight, he would always pursue coin and had little compunction about from whom he would accept it. Thoughts of such a betrayal stabbed at Flynt's chest. There were few people in this life he trusted but until that night in the Rookery, when he suspected him of silencing Romulus Trask, he would have said that he'd had more faith in Gabriel than in any other man. Yes, he made himself free with other men's wives, but Flynt tended to see this more as a reflection of his own fear of committing to one person than a comment on the virtue of the ladies in question. Those already wed were simpler to keep at arm's length, at least figuratively, than single ladies who might expect some manner of promise before clergy.

So Gabriel could be working for the Fellowship, but the possibility that he could be the individual Wild had called the Wraith was somewhat confusing. If so, why would he be inter-ested in Templeton if his target was Flynt? Gabriel had claimed to have heard someone moving in the Rookery, but it could have been a fabrication to cover the fact that he himself had slit Trask's throat. Later, he made it look as if he was headed for a night of abandon with the Covent Garden Nun but had he in fact followed Flynt to Charing Cross, where he despatched the man Simms and vanished into the night?

And yet… and yet…

Doubt there was and Flynt was uncomfortable with that. Like most people, he preferred certainty. He had doubt enough over his own failings.

Flynt's mind was in turmoil as he considered all this. Gabriel's possible, perhaps probable, betrayal was hurtful but the idea of the Wraith, whoever he be, had deeply unsettled him. Charters had observed that many individuals had been intent on removing him from this earth and he had always emerged as the last man standing. Most of the attempts had been made by brutish louts who preferred ambush, such as the man in the Golden Cross's stable, but this mysterious individual seemed unlike those others, at least according to legend. There was an intelligence working, cunning and underhand though it may be. The notion that he would remove anyone standing between him and his target spoke of ruthless determination, which was something Flynt understood. Toying with his victim, however, suggested a distemper of the mind, and that was what was so disturbing. Flynt's mother's mind had been unbalanced, thanks to her abuses at the hands of Moncrieff's dead father, and that instability had led her to take her own life while he was in swaddling. Gideon had told him that Moncrieff the elder had been a cancer on the world and it had been right that Flynt had cut it out. He had never known his mother, knew only what Gideon and the aunt who had raised him had said of her, but it was possible that he had inherited both the delicacy of her nature and the callous heart of his real father. He knew that within him, there were two sides in constant tumult.

But whether he lay on a cot in a roadside inn, on a bed of hay or on the hard ground, he knew he could not dwell on such matters. As Gabriel had once said, an excess of introspection tends to lead a man into corners of his mind that are not meant to be explored. We do what we do because it is what we do, he had opined. But that memory brought his mind back again to Gabriel and the Fellowship. Gabriel and the Wraith.

Could they really be one and the same? Or was it all a confluence of fortune, the chance convergence of unrelated incidents, brought together by a mind grown too used to perfidy? Round and round the thoughts would go, twisting and coiling in his mind like the ouroboros symbol, the serpent eating itself, until Flynt knew not where they began or ended.

He did find some peace of mind when he'd been accompanied for a little way by a post carrier. They had met in an inn where the midlands gave way to the north country and the man had struck up a conversation with him as they shared a table, each dining on a meal of bread, cheese and ale. Despite the warm day, the fire was roaring, for pork was roasting, the skewer powered by a turnspit dog running in a wooden wheel set into the breast of the fireplace, far away from the heat of the flame so as not to make the animal too uncomfortable. A chain ran from the wheel to the spit to turn the meat and ensure it browned evenly. Fat spat from the flesh and hissed on the hot stonework of the fireplace, the metal clanked and the wheel rumbled as the dog performed its function. The animal was small, its hair light brown, its front legs slightly crooked but its body was strong. It would have been bred specially for the work, but Flynt still hoped that it was not maltreated. He had seen canines undertake such labour many times and each time had had studied the animal for signs of abuse, but this one seemed happy and healthy. The old man had noted his scrutiny and commented upon it.

'Old Spinner there is in fine fettle, lad, don't thee worry about that,' he'd said. 'That's a decided apt name for that creature, given his occupation, don't thee agree? Our friend the innkeeper may have many faults but he loves that creature as if he was family, on that you have my oath. He even takes him to church with him. Can't say if t'dog gives voice during hymns as I'm not from these parts.' He held out a hand. 'The name's Addison Severs, postal carrier t'gentry and all else beside.'

Flynt shook the hand. Severs was much older than others of his occupation that he had met previously. His hair was thick and white, his face weathered by many days and nights riding from north to south. The old man swiftly proved himself to be most garrulous and though Flynt himself leaned towards the taciturn, after a few days of his own garbled thoughts for company, he welcomed the man's chatter.

'Addison, being son of Adam,' he'd explained concerning his name. 'My old sire, he'd be Adam, me not being descended from nobody hailing from biblical times, y'understand, don't let this white mane fool you, lad. And thy name, sir, what would it be that they call thee?'

Jonas told him and the man sucked at the pipe that seemed forever protruding from between his lips or held in his hand as though it were part of him. 'Another biblical antecedent, is Jonas. Some call him Jonah, did thee know that? Does thee know thy holy book, lad?'

'Well enough,' Jonas said.

Addison gave him a sideways glance as he popped a final bit of cheese into his mouth. 'There's them that know it well and them that know it well enough and well enough be good enough for me, not being much of a one for prayer. He was swallowed whole by a sea creature, tha namesake were. Got vomited out after three days and three nights. Seems he wasn't such a tasty morsel, was Jonah.' He chewed on the cheese and grimaced. 'Something he shares with this here cheese, I'd say, and I don't care who hears it.'

The last few words were for the benefit of the innkeeper, who merely laughed, obviously knowing Addison well. The mail carrier seemed a most relaxed individual. The others who followed his profession, and Flynt had encountered a few in his travels, had been most energetic, if not galloping their horse to the next change station then at least keeping it at a steady canter. When he and Addison set out together, agreeing that as they were both heading north they could spend some time in each other's company, this man seemed satisfied to walk his animal rather than force it to exert itself. Flynt could not tell if this was due to Addison's own lethargy or concern for his mount's wellbeing. No matter, he enjoyed sharing the road with him and as dusk began to gather, they made camp beside a brook. As darkness grew around them and the song of nature stilled, they discussed the continuing fair weather, the condition of the roads, and the state of the kingdom. Or rather, the man seemed to hold an almost unbroken monologue.

'I'll tell thee this, and I don't care who hears it,' he said, his pipe clamped tight between his teeth as he stared into the small fire they had built in order to cook a rabbit he had shot. 'I don't have much of a notion for yon king down by London way. I don't care if he's from Germany or the moon, I don't hold with him. He don't give as much as a Dutchman's damn for this here land, does he? I hear he's left us, gone back to Hanover. Now, I ask thee, is that any way for the king to be, that no sooner has he set his backside – and a right ample backside it is, I hear tell – on't throne then he's off back from whence he came? It's not right. It's not being proper, is it? And I hear his grasp of the king's English isn't too tight, neither. Does tha think that right, Jonas lad?'

Flynt didn't believe a response was required so he merely smiled in acknowledgement.

'And be it true that he has two mistresses? That seems down-right unchristian to me. Two mistresses. One is bad enough but two seems greedy. Keeping them happy and a wife, I'm surprised that t'fellow has such an ample backside. To my mind his manhood should be worn down to a nubbin by now.'

A much-needed laugh vibrated in Flynt's chest. It felt good to listen to this man.

Addison smiled for a moment as he considered the state of King George's member, then inquired, 'I neglected to ask thee, lad, much as I enjoy having thy company at least until the morrow, where thee be headed on these fine summer days and nights?'

Flynt saw no reason to lie. His suspicious nature had already considered and rejected the possibility that Addison was not as he seemed. Being alert was one thing, but the notion of the Wraith could not have him seeing phantoms everywhere. 'A village by the name of Gallowmire, a little way north of here.'

That silenced Addison. He took his pipe from his mouth and set himself to staring at the flames for a few moments. Flynt sensed a change in the man's mood. Mention of the village had for some reason made the man uneasy.

'Have you heard of it?'

Something that could have been a sigh dropped from his lips. 'Aye, lad, I know yon place. What business would thee be having there?'

'I seek a friend, who is staying there for a while.'

Addison ruminated further. 'This here friend of thine, does his blood hail from't village original?'

'No,' Flynt said, 'he's simply visiting.'

Another pause for thought. 'Has tha been there previous, lad?'

'No, I've never had the pleasure.'

Addison's laugh was short but devoid of mirth. 'Pleasure? Nay, there's damned little pleasure to be had in that place. If I was thee, I would be turning yon fine-looking beast back in opposite direction, and be leaving Gallowmire well to my back.'

'It's not welcoming to strangers?'

'Strangers are viewed with suspicion no matter where tha goes, whether it be north, south, east or west.'

'But it's worse in Gallowmire?'

Addison plucked a burning twig from the edge of the fire, then set the flame to the bowl of his pipe, puffing some life back into the tobacco. When it was sufficiently lively, he threw the twig back. 'Their view of strangers be worse than most, I reckon.'

'Why is that?'

The man looked across the flames at Flynt for the first time. 'It's a bad place, lad. I carry all life in my bag. Birth, death, marriage, news of good fortune, news of bad fortune, but I say this, and I don't care who hears it, there is only that last in Gallowmire.'

Flynt edged forward. 'But why say that, man? You must have reason.'

The hesitancy with which the man now spoke was at odds with his earlier conversation, suggesting that on this subject at least he did care who heard his words. 'I have doubtless said too much, lad. Tha has business and thy friend to consider so I expect thee cannot go back, but I would urge this – Gallowmire is a cursed place and thee would be well advised to steer clear of it. If there be a little piece of hell on earth, then that piece goes by't name Gallowmire.'

They had parted at first light, Addison to the north-east, Flynt north-west. The man had grasped Flynt's hand before they went their separate ways and stared into his eyes as if he were attempting to communicate another warning but made no further verbal comment regarding Gallowmire. He would be wise enough to know that he could not divert Flynt from his path. In fact, no sooner had he delivered his damning condemnation the night before, he announced it was time for sleep, wrapped himself in his greatcoat and turned away. Sleep had eluded Flynt for a time as he examined Addison's words. What could be so wrong at Gallowmire that would provoke such dire counsel? And if it were such a dreadful place, did Lemuel know and, if so, why would he allow his friend to seek refuge there?

When sleep came it was filled with dreams of a village he had never seen where all was grey, populated by dead-eyed men and women, their bodies gnarled and suppurating, the sky under which they dragged themselves black and threatening, the land around them blighted, the vegetation twisted. Among the faces he saw Gabriel, smiling and gesturing to him to come closer, but in his hand he held a dagger, dripping red. Moncrieff also appeared, standing on the edges of the scene, leaning on a wolf's head cane that came to life under his hand and snapped and snarled at those who came too close. Then there was another figure, forever in shadow, but moving to and fro, his tread deliberate, sure and steady, as he watched and waited.

20

An arsehole is a useful thing, Gideon had once told his son, but sometimes they walk and talk. Flynt had met more than his share of such men, he believed, but he had not expected to meet one within minutes of setting foot in the village of Gallowmire, though perhaps he should have. After all, Charters had once said he attracted trouble like flies to dung. That was the way of it, but as he saw the look in the eye of the walking muscle and waited for that look to transform into action, he reflected upon Addison's warning.

'Gallowmire is a cursed place,' he'd said, 'and thee would be well advised to steer clear of it.'

When Flynt approached the village around midday, he saw nothing particularly cursed about it, at least not from his vantage point on a slight hill. Smoke from cooking fires curled from the roofs of the dwellings, most constructed of timber, a few older wattle and daub, a few of stone and brick. A river was spanned by a wooden bridge devoid of parapets, at that moment being crossed by a cart pulled by a single horse. He reached into his saddlebag and found his spyglass. The cart was led by a woman, with a child and a black and white dog riding up front. He swung the glass towards what appeared to be an inn, judging by the sign hanging over the door, where he saw three men dressed in black seated at a table set outside to allow patrons to take their ease in the afternoon sun. He then picked out a wooden construction in the centre of a patch of grass opposite the tavern and his lips thinned.

A gallows.

It wasn't the three-legged design of Tyburn but a single upright carrying a crossbeam spar. He saw no rope looped around it but its purpose was sufficient to cast a pall across the sunlight. He examined the road through the village. It appeared sturdy enough but the dry weather would have solidified the mud that would clog it when the rains fell. The most substantial building he could discern was the church, Norman in design, its square steeple topped by a single bell open to the elements. Around it was ranged a small graveyard peppered with memorials of stone, wood and slate, itself enclosed within a low wall of dry-stone construction. Low moorland hills crowded around the outer reaches of the settlement, as if trying to prevent it from growing – or going – further. The heather was beginning to turn purple, the land punctuated by white dots that were sheep, and green pockets of trees.

He slipped his glass back from whence it came and nudged Horse into motion, walking her down the hill and over the bridge, her hooves clipping on the old wood. The cart had come to a halt outside the inn where the woman was in conversation with the three men. Flynt and Horse ambled around the green sward, giving the gallows a cursory glance. Now that he was closer he could see where the hemp had scraped at the timber. He recalled Addison Severs' words about this being a little piece of hell on earth. How much of a hell could it be that it required a permanent execution site?

The woman's raised voice reached him as he neared the inn. A man who would make a plough horse feel undersized had her gripped by the arm and was propelling her back towards her cart, which Flynt could now see bore baskets of vegetables and piles of recently shorn wool. The woman protested at being so manhandled and the innkeeper, a squat man with the build of a labourer, had appeared in the doorway. The large man had seen him and waved a finger in his direction. Flynt urged Horse forward again until he was in earshot.

'Don't thee get thyself involved in this,' the big man warned the innkeeper, his voice deep and threatening, 'it's no business o' thine.'

The two other men had moved to the rear of the cart where one hauled at the baskets and tipped out the contents while his friend ground them into the dusty earth with his heel. The woman twisted in the big man's grip and spat something at them in a tongue that Flynt didn't recognise, but he knew by the tone that whatever she said was far from complimentary regarding their parentage or manhood or perhaps both at the same time. He sighed inwardly. Wherever he went he found arseholes that walked and talked.

'There's no need for this, Joshua Cooper,' said the innkeeper, and Flynt heard the sound of the Scottish borderlands in his words.

'His lordship's orders, they be, and you know it,' said Cooper.

'Please, Andrew, do not interfere,' the woman said.

The innkeeper seemed inclined to do just that but a glare from the big fellow made him reconsider and he backed away a couple of paces. One of the other men glanced over his shoulder and saw Flynt leaning on his saddle, watching the scene. 'Josh,' he said.

Cooper turned to squint against the sun, which was at Flynt's back.

'Good afternoon, gentlemen,' he said, amiably, touching the brim of his hat towards the woman. 'Madame.'

The men exchanged looks and the one named Cooper seemed even more annoyed. 'And who be thee, stranger?'

Flynt smiled. 'Just a traveller, heading north.'

The man let the woman go and she rushed to stand at her cart, where the child, a boy he now saw, watched from the seat, his face pale, his eyes wide, his arm around the dog which was up on its paws, its eyes fixed on the big man, a low growl vibrating. Flynt sensed that should the boy remove his arm, that dog would launch himself.

'Stand easy, Samson,' the woman said, and the dog immediately obeyed, sitting back down at the boy's feet. His gaze never left Cooper, though. One word from the woman, perhaps even the boy, was all it would take.

Cooper's eyes narrowed a little and he gave his companions another meaningful look. 'What's thy business in Gallowmire?'

Flynt had no intention of making his reason for being in the village common knowledge. 'As I said, just passing through.'

'Then pass through and God speed.'

Flynt swung one leg over Horse's back and dismounted. 'I would patronise yonder inn, for the road is long and I have a thirst and hunger upon me that requires attention.'

'Then get yourself within and leave us to our business.'

Flynt led Horse to a hitching post and tied her off, pausing to stretch his back, the hours of riding and sleeping on hard ground having taken their toll. He considered removing Tact and Diplomacy from where they nestled in his saddlebag but decided against it. Instead he slid his cane from under a leather strap stitched into the saddle and glanced back at the men, each of whom watched his every move intently. He looked at the woman, who stood her ground, her dark eyes flitting from Cooper to Flynt and back again. Her skin was of a darker tinge than Flynt would expect to see in this small northern rural setting, her black hair tucked under a scarf of bright colours, but there was a careworn look to her eyes accentuated by the shadowed flesh beneath them.

'Thee seems right hesitant to enter, traveller,' said Cooper. 'Has thy thirst and hunger deserted you of a sudden?'

'Not at all,' Flynt said.

'Then I would advise thee to leave us be and do it now.'

Flynt nodded, touched his hat to the woman once again and took a step towards the inn door, where he saw the innkeeper watching him carefully, now drying his hands on a rag that had been draped over his shoulder, but the action seemed only to be a means to keep his hands occupied. He caught Flynt's eye and gave him a warning shake of the head, somehow sensing his intention to make this his affair. Flynt gave him an almost imperceptible shrug, as if matters were out of his control, and paused again.

'It's just...' He turned to face the big man once more. 'It's just I do wonder why this lady is being so manhandled and why it takes three of you to do so?'

'I already told thee, this here does not concern thee, stranger. This be village business.'

Flynt smiled. 'I merely make an observation, friend.'

Cooper studied him, taking in his hat, coat, boots and the silver cane and something in what he saw made his eyes narrow. 'Then tha should keep thy observation to thyself,' Joshua said. 'Or better yet, mount up and be on thy way.'

Flynt held up his hands as if in supplication, his cane gripped between his right thumb and forefinger. 'No need for unpleasantness, friend.' He half-turned, then swivelled back. 'But I would really like to know.'

A wicked little smile crossed Cooper's lips. 'Would thee now? Would thee really?'

'I really would.'

Cooper adjusted his stance in a way that told Flynt he was preparing for attack, then made a show of scrutinising him again. 'Scotch, be thee?'

'Scottish,' Flynt amended.

Cooper sneered and shot the innkeeper a meaningful glance. 'Just come up from London, by any chance?'

Something in the way he asked the question put Flynt even further on his guard. 'No, Manchester.'

'You live down there, eh?'

'From time to time, but I return home now.'

'You be travelling out of thy way to reach here.'

'I'm in no hurry to be home, so I thought I would see more of your fair county.'

Cooper took this in, then spat at the ground, as if cleaning out his mouth. 'I don't like t'Scotch much.'

'I feel sure my fellow countrymen are in mourning.'

Cooper's lips thinned. 'I give thee fair warning again, Scotchman, and I'm not one to repeat myself, but tha really don't want to be inserting thyself into this affair.'

'You're right, friend, I don't wish to insert myself. And yet, here I am, inserting myself.'

He hoped the man would not ask why, because he did not have a satisfactory answer. Sometimes he did things simply because he had to.

Cooper had braced himself. 'Then thee should be aware that I am constable here, appointed by his lordship hisself, and by thy actions, thee is interfering in true process of law.'

'True process, eh?' Flynt said, a slight laugh rippling his words. 'And is it true process in these parts that allows destruction of property and the abuse of women by a witless, hulking brute?'

Through gritted teeth, Cooper said, 'Did thee just call me a witless, hulking brute?'

'I did. I feared calling you a bulging sack of pus might offend.'

Cooper soaked that in for a moment before launching himself with an enraged roar, but Flynt had long anticipated such a move and easily stepped to the side. The big man blundered beyond him a couple of steps but whirled quickly and came at him again. This time Flynt stood his ground and met the onslaught, jabbing his right fist sharply into Cooper's face. The force of the blow and the man's own impetus caused blood to erupt and he rocked back, both hands darting to his nose. Pain jagged from Flynt's knuckles and he considered drawing his blade from its silver sheath but decided no weapons were required, so he merely swung his booted foot with considerable force between the man's legs. Air squealed through Cooper's gritted teeth as he sank to his knees, his hands now clasping the fresh injury. He was a big man, though, and the street fighter in

Flynt was well aware that he would have to put him down. He clenched his hands together, his gloved fingers laced around his cane to give the blow additional solidity, and swung both arms like a club against the man's jaw. Cooper's face snapped to one side, a spray of blood bursting from his mouth, then his body twisted slowly in the air as he pitched to the ground.

Flynt heard the woman curse and he whirled on his heels to see one of the others had gripped her from behind, but she jerked her head back sharply to connect with his nose. There was an audible crunch and he let out a high-pitched howl. She spun and followed up with a right-handed swing that sent him crashing into the side of the cart. His companion had at first been caught by surprise at the suddenness of the violence but he realised some action was required on his part so lunged forward.

'Samson, bring down,' the woman shouted, and the dog immediately flew from the cart to barrel into the man, knocking him from his feet. The dog stood over him, legs splayed on either side of his torso, his lips curled back to reveal sharp white teeth as if daring the man to make a further move, his low snarl rumbling in his throat, his hair razored on his back. The man chose to remain still, which Flynt thought was a wise decision.

'I'd be making myself scarce if I were you, stranger.'

The innkeeper had emerged once more from the shadow of his doorway and again Flynt detected the Scottish burr. 'You're a borderer, correct?'

'Aye, but been in this place for more than twenty years. I'd recommend you not remain a moment longer though. Joshua there is a bad loser and he has the support of his lordship.'

The woman interjected, 'His lordship is as bad as Joshua Cooper, worse, for it is he who has corrupted him.'

The innkeeper glanced around as if fearful that the woman's words would be overheard, but for the first time Flynt realised there was nobody else in view. No one had emerged from their homes, no one walked the narrow dirt street. For all intents and purposes, this village may have been deserted.

'That may be the case, Masilda lass, but he is still the might in this land and Joshua there works for him.' He jabbed a thumb towards Flynt. 'And you, my friend, laid hands upon him and they will take that ill. You too, my dear. Both had best leave now and don't look back. There is only one way this will end and it will not be pretty.'

'I must sell my goods,' the woman insisted.

The innkeeper's look was pained. 'Nobody will buy them, lass, for the word has been given and that word is law. Nobody dares.'

Flynt frowned. 'Word given by whom? This lord of the manor of whom you speak?'

The innkeeper glanced towards the man still being guarded by Samson. 'The who or the why matters little, my friend. What matters is that by your actions this day you have put yourself in harm's way. Go now, and may God speed you, for you'll need His aid, I fear.' He gave the woman Masilda a meaningful look. 'Both of you.'

Flynt was about to say that he had business to attend to in the village but the third man was listening while keeping a wary eye on the dog standing over him, so he kept his own counsel. He merely accepted the innkeeper's urging with a compliant nod and said, 'Madame, I think we should take our leave.'

She stared at him for a moment as if intending to argue the point, but in the end she reached the same conclusion. Without even looking, she said, 'Samson, leave.'

The dog immediately leaped away from the man and back onto the cart where he was once again folded in the boy's embrace. His mother took the reins of the horse and wheeled the cart round. Flynt climbed into his saddle as the innkeeper moved to tend to the recumbent, though now stirring, Joshua Cooper. Flynt followed the woman as she walked towards the bridge.

She stopped midway across and looked back at him. 'I don't need your company, sir, though I do thank you for your assistance.'

'It would be remiss of me if I failed to ensure that you are not further molested.'

'They are in no condition to come after me.'

'Perhaps, but I would be happier if you would allow me to see you home.'

She still did not move, but rather studied him as if trying to fathom his motives. 'Why did you involve yourself in this, sir?'

'It seemed like the thing to do.'

Her narrowed eyes pierced him. 'You will not get anything from me. Not my coin nor my body.'

He began to say that he required neither but she jerked the horse's bridle and the cart began to move again. The boy looked back and gave Flynt a weak smile. That was something, at least, he thought as he followed. As they left the bridge, Flynt had Horse pick up her pace to bring him alongside the cart. He had intended to seek directions to the Millhouse at the inn but that avenue seemed closed to him for now, so this woman was his only available conduit.

'My name is Jonas Flynt and I heard the innkeeper call you Masilda. That isn't a local name, is it? I detect an accent in your speech.'

She said nothing for a few paces, then spoke reluctantly. 'I am Romani.'

'And what brought you here?'

She gave him a quick glance. 'You make many inquiries, sir.'

'I have an inquiring mind. So what brought you to this place?'

She ignored the question. 'What brings you to Gallowmire?'

Understanding that she meant to tell him nothing of herself, he replied, 'I seek a friend who has taken up residence here.'

She glanced at him this time. 'Who is your friend?'

'His name is Templeton, and he lives in the Millhouse.'

She brought her horse to a halt once again. 'The Millhouse,' she repeated.

Something in her tone made him wish he hadn't mentioned it. 'Aye. There is something amiss with that?'

Her eyes flicked over him, taking in his boots, black coat and hat. She saw something that spawned fresh suspicion. 'That property is owned by Lord Gallowmire. Your friend is his guest?'

Gribble had said that he had inherited it. 'It was my understanding that it was once the property of an elderly lady, now deceased, and is now in the possession of a nephew in London.'

'There was no elderly woman there, just an old man, though he did die, and the property has been in the ownership of the Gallowmires since I came here.'

'How long has that been?'

She fell silent again. His reason for being in the village had not assuaged her suspicions. He already knew there was friction between her and the lord of the manor so the fact that the man he claimed as friend lodged in a property owned by the nobleman had not gone down well. He could not backtrack on that now.

'I can assure you that I have no knowledge of Lord Gallowmire,' he said. 'I am here only to find my friend and return him to London.'

She jerked the horse into motion again. 'Then let me detain you no further.'

He continued to follow. 'There are many people who seem to either suggest that I avoid this place altogether or, now that I am here, to move on. Why is that?'

'Ask your friend in the Millhouse, perhaps he will enlighten you if he is close to his lordship.'

'As far as I am aware he has no connection with anyone in Gallowmire.'

'Then why is he here?'

Flynt was beginning to wonder about that himself, Gribble's lie over the Millhouse grating at his mind. 'In truth, he is in hiding from troubles in the city, troubles with which I can assist him.'

She began to walk again up the hill. 'Then assist him and leave me be.'

His curiosity had been kindled by the altercation in the village square, now it was aflame. There was something amiss in this place and he needed to know what it was. 'Masilda...'

'I did not give you leave to call me by name, sir. Go to your friend. If he is as innocent as you say, if you are as innocent as you say, then take him from this place and never think of Gallowmire again. You will be much the better for it.'

She pulled the horse and cart ahead of him and he reined Horse in to watch her go, the boy craning backwards to look at him as they crested the hill, his eyes still wide but filled now with curiosity more than fear. The cart vanished from his sight and he looked back along the track towards the village. The area outside the inn was deserted now, so the men had either moved on or had repaired within for a commiseratory ale. She had made it plain that he was not welcome, even the innkeeper had stated it. The actions of Cooper and his men seemed to confirm it. Addison had been correct in his assessment that there was something badly wrong in Gallowmire, but he was here now and he had to fulfil his mission. The problem was, he still did not know the location of the Millhouse.

He would have to return to his original plan, but with added stealth.

21

It was late afternoon before the innkeeper appeared in the small courtyard behind his establishment. It had taken Flynt some time to follow a circuitous route back to the village and then find his way to the rear of the inn without being witnessed. He stood beside Horse within a stable only large enough for two animals but which was at that moment empty. He took the liberty of feeding her some oats from a sack hanging on a nail, then leaned against the doorpost, ensuring he was hidden in the shadow of the lowering sun and keeping watch on the rear door, always alert for voices or footsteps. He was aware he had made an error in inserting himself in the situation earlier but it was an error he could not have avoided. Common sense told him he should have carried on into the inn and left the locals to their drama but had he done so, he knew it would have eaten at him.

The rear door of the inn opened and the man for whom he waited emerged with a bucket of dirty water, which he threw onto the ground. When Flynt stepped from the shadows of the stable door he was startled at first but then he nodded, as if he had expected to see him. He shot a glance over his shoulder before pulling the door shut behind him and holding two fingers to his lips. With another glance at the closed door, he crossed the courtyard to join him.

'I saw trouble in your eyes the first I clapped my own upon you,' he said in a near whisper.

Flynt matched the timbre of his voice to his. 'I don't seek trouble,' said Flynt.

The innkeeper gestured for him to move further into the gloom of the stable interior, taking note of Horse munching on oats. 'But it finds you, I'll wager, and right often, too. I've seen your kind before, here and at home, and you are always trouble.'

At home, he had said. The man still thought of Scotland as home. Flynt envied that connection, for though he had family in Edinburgh, he did not think of it as home and neither did he think of London in that way. Flynt was a man out of place wherever he went, never settled, never content.

'I see you make yourself free with my horse feed. You're a thief as well as a fool.' There was a smile in the man's tone which took the edge from the accusation.

'I'm many things, thief and fool being two of them. But I'll pay for the oats.'

The innkeeper waved the suggestion away as if it were an irritant. 'Take it as payment for the entertainment you provided this afternoon, foolhardy though it was. I'll repeat again what I said then, leave this village, don't come back.'

'I seek only directions, friend,' Flynt said, aware that his accent had reverted to a broader Scots than he used in the south. Being with a countryman always caused this.

'You already know the way out of Gallowmire, and that's all you need know.'

'I must call at the Millhouse first.'

The innkeeper took a step back and gave Flynt a long look, like Masilda taking fresh note of his apparel. 'Why?'

'I must speak to the man lodging there.'

'You know this man?'

His lesson learned following Masilda's reaction, Flynt decided that some element of truth was required. In any case, even in the dim light, this man's gaze penetrated deep and would recognise any extreme prevarication. 'I've never met him, but I must convince him to return to London with me.'

The intention of returning to London seemed to give the man some grim satisfaction. 'Then do that and do it right speedily, for you're no safe here, lad.' He stepped to the doorway and pointed to the archway that led to the village main street. 'You'll find the Millhouse maybe a mile upstream to the north, first past the old mill. It sits on a parcel of ground all its own. You can't go by without seeing it.'

'Thank you.' Flynt paused, knowing he should be on his way but his curiosity proving stronger. 'What ails this place, friend? It seems like any other village, yet there's a darkness hanging over it. A stranger on the road urged me not to come and within minutes of my arrival you, yon brute Cooper and the woman all exhorted me to leave. What's happened here to make this place so inhospitable?'

The innkeeper glanced towards the inn and placed a hand lIghtly upon Flynt's shoulder as if to propel him forward. 'I wouldn't be concerning yourself with it. Just take your man and go, while you can.'

Flynt stood his ground. 'I would know what malady has infected this place, and why such focus was placed upon that woman and her child.'

The man sighed, but a smile played upon his lips. 'By God, you're a thrawn bugger, but it's a characteristic of our people, is it no?' He thrust out his hand. 'My name's Andrew Drummond.'

Flynt took the proffered hand. 'Jonas Flynt.'

There was a slight pause and a flicker of recognition when he heard the name but the man's handshake was firm. 'Aye,' said Drummond. 'I should have kent.'

'You've heard my name before?'

'Aye, it's a wee village and things are said and things are heard. It was mentioned by Joshua just yesterday.'

'In what context?'

'They've been waiting for your arrival.'

Flynt glanced to the tavern door, as if he could see through it to the men beyond. He had been expected. That could not be good news. 'They knew of my coming? Did they say why they awaited me?'

'I only heard the name. I think it was their task to merely report your arrival, not engage with you.'

'Report to whom?'

'Their employer, Lord Gallowmire, young Lord Gallowmire as I still call him, though his father has been gone these five years, God rest his soul, for he was a good man.'

'Your tone suggests that the son is not.'

The man grimaced. 'He's no. He's rapacious where his father was gracious, vicious where his father was merciful. He's a handsome bugger but yon fair features hide an ugly heart. Old Lord Gallowmire was blind to his son's cruelty and while he drew breath it was tempered, but since he's inherited the title and the estates it's been allowed full expression.'

'And there's bad blood between this lord and the lass Masilda?'

'Aye, he wants what she has.'

Flynt asked, 'He has designs on her?'

'Aye, very likely, because he has his lusts, to be sure, and he's no respecter of the marital bed, though she be widowed, but that's not all he hungers for. He wants her land, and not only hers, for in the land there's power and in power there's coin, and he desires both.'

'He's laird, does he no have enough?'

Another sigh from Drummond, another pointed glance at the door leading to the tavern. It was obvious that he wished Flynt to leave but he had recognised his stubborn nature and knew he would not do so until his questions were answered.

'For someone like Philip Fitzgerald there's never enough. Not land, not power, not fear and not blood. The Fitzgeralds have been lairds of Gallowmire since the Normans first came across the channel with the Conqueror and right powerful they were. They owned all here, they built a keep, they built the church, they were the law. Mostly, I'm told by folk here, they were fair and just. Back when old Bess was on the throne, they took to improvements. They built a manor house around the old keep, they imported brick to shore up the old steadings in the village here. But all that cost them dear and they were as near penniless as noble families can get, so land was sold or, in Masilda's case, gifted. Her husband's family worked that tract for centuries and served the Fitzgeralds for generations. His grandfather was given it freehold by the old Lord's father as recognition for loyal service and it passed to William Chilcott's father and then to him. And when poor William went to his reward, God rest him, to Masilda. That didn't sit well with some people here, for she's no Gallowmire born, which is suspicious enough for some, but…' He sighed and shook his head '…she's gypsy and that's deemed unforgivable. His lordship has used her race against her in order to turn people's faces against her. But still she'll no leave, so more direct measures are bound to be taken sooner or later. His lordship's no averse to such moves.'

'He's done similar previous?'

Drummond grew restive. 'Lad, in the name of God, every moment you tarry brings you a moment closer to discovery, can you no see that? Leave now, fulfil your purpose and get yourself away from here.'

Flynt saw the wisdom of the advice but also sensed that somewhere within the background to this village and its troubles might lie the answer to why Gribble had lied to him and why his arrival was anticipated. He repeated his question, his voice falling heavily upon the words. 'He has done similar previous?'

Drummond took a breath. 'Since he's taken over the title he and his agents, like Cooper there, have snatched back many tracts that had been lost.'

'Snatched?'

The innkeeper's face seemed frozen. 'Aye, snatched. Some took coin to relinquish possession, others held out. Men have died, good men. Some by what they called accident, others not.'

'There's been murder done?'

'Some would see it as such, but they call it justice. Crimes were committed, at least on legal documents, and due process followed. For generations the lords of Gallowmire wielded the power of *furca et fossa*, are you familiar with the term?'

'Gallows and pit, granted by the crown to loyal vassals.'

'Aye, and the young lord likes to think he still has such rights. The pit was a deep hole that still lies beneath their great hall and the gallows were right here in the village. My first fifteen years here the gallow pole was never used, but in these few years past it feels as if the damn thing has never stopped swinging. He has built himself an army, small to be sure, but an army all the same. His riders, he calls them, and he kits them out in the black, just as you. I confess when I saw you first I thought you were a new recruit, until you stepped in over Masilda.'

That explained why she had regarded his outfit with suspicion when he mentioned a friend in the Millhouse. 'And this army is made of local men?'

'Some, but others from further afield. Scum, the bulk of them, or just lads who need the coin. Joshua Cooper, the fellow you tangled with, he's local. He was always an unpleasant lad and he's grown even more so under Gallowmire's influence. There's a darkness here, lad, you're right, and Philip Fitzgerald is the heart of it, and now you've been drawn into it. I don't ken why they knew you were coming, I don't ken your intent here, apart from what you have told me, and I don't want to ken.'

'Damn it, man, if it's so hellish here, why do you stay? Why no return north?'

The innkeeper looked away. 'Sometimes there is no going home.'

The strange drift of the man's focus told Flynt that something back in those borderlands prevented him from returning, then his eyes sharpened again as he thrust whatever memory that had risen back into the depths. 'I've made this my home. I've put down roots. They say it's always darkest before the dawn and I can only hope that's true. Life here can't continue in this way.'

'Have you no alerted the authorities?'

'We have, but the Fitzgeralds have friends of power and influence. And all that's occurred here has been twisted to appear lawful. In this land, money cleaves to money and power to power, I feel certain you must know this, and those of us who grieve over what's happened have neither coin nor sway and therefore no voice.'

'And what of the kirk? Has the minister got nothing to say about the treatment of his flock?'

'He did, and right vocal he was too. Too vocal, for he met with one of those accidents of which I made mention. He fell from the bell tower one night, though why he was up there at that hour was never explained. That bell hasn't pealed since under his lordship's order, for he will not suffer its sound. It disturbs him, he claims, and he has not seen fit to seek a new divine.'

Flynt's thoughts turned again to the woman. 'Masilda is in considerable peril, is she not?'

The innkeeper's lips flattened. 'She is. It's only a matter of time, I fear.'

'What will they do?'

'I've heard talk of declaring her witch.'

Flynt was horrified. 'Surely we're beyond such things. Have we no progressed from those dark times of last century? We're entering an age of science and reason and superstition should have no place in it.'

Drummond's laugh was short and bitter. 'This is Gallow-mire, lad, it's beyond nothing. Witchcraft is still a crime on the statutes, even in London and Edinburgh. As I said, Masilda is gypsy and to some that's witch enough. And she has cures, salves and such, that they can twist to being works of the devil.'

'Then she must be assisted.'

Drummond's look grew pained. 'There are decent people here, people who see what occurs and deplore it, but there's fear, and fear can paralyse. We've urged Masilda to leave but like you she's gey thrawn.' For the first time a small smile twitched at his lips. 'Aye, she's thrawn enough to hail from our homeland. She'll no go and they'll hang her, as certain as day follows night, and no just because his lordship wants her acres. There are women here who resent her for her beauty and the way their husbands look at her as she passes. It's the laird who will pass sentence but it's those wives who have already judged her.'

22

He stole away from the inn, avoiding the road by leading Horse by the reins across rough ground until he cleared the fringes of the village just as the sun began to sink beyond the dales surrounding it. It was still light, however, and so he needed to take care over being seen. The news that his arrival was not entirely unexpected weighed heavily upon him. It had been his intention to merely knock on the front door to gain entry but an increased degree of circumspection was now required. He found a copse of mature oak and wych elm where he climbed down from Horse and let her pull at the undergrowth as he sat with his back against a rounded rock out of sight and waited for nightfall. To pass the time he inspected Tact and Diplomacy, ensured that all was well with their load, for something told him he might need them before this visit was over. That done, he slid the sword from its sheath and wiped the blade with a rag taken from the pocket of his greatcoat, then leaned back to watch the heavens transform from day to night. The canopy of blue and white gave way to streaks of red and gold and, finally, pinpoints of stars pricked through the black velvet, but no moon shone, which suited his purposes.

He left Horse tethered in the woods and walked back along the track towards the river, then followed it downstream. His night vision was well honed so he found the Millhouse with no difficulty. He halted a little way off, his senses alert for movement or sound that was foreign to nature. Candlelight guttering in a downstairs window suggested Templeton was still awake, but the lamp burning above the front door told

Flynt that another means of entry would have to be found. He squatted in the shadows, ears straining for any sound, eyes searching for any sight of watchers in the dark. A movement within drew his attention back to the window and he saw a man peering out, his face illuminated by the candle glowing on the sill. He knew not the man's likeness but he had to assume it was Templeton. His further reconnoitre revealed no watchers in the dark. That didn't mean they weren't there, though.

He moved again, remaining cautious, head down, the brim of his hat obscuring his face, taking a meandering route closer to the river's edge, ever careful not to dislodge a loose stone and send it cascading. He followed the tinkling water to the rear of the house where he circumnavigated a small courtyard until he was satisfied that it was clear before moving to the door. He slowly rotated the heavy metal ring, holding his breath lest it creak, but it was locked fast. His fingers found the keyhole and he smiled again as he fished his dub from his pocket and inserted it. The door was solid but the lock was old and easily sprung by the lockpick, which had been gifted him by Old Tom before he died. He drew a pistol before easing the door open. He stepped inside, finding himself in a small room used as a pantry, a door opposite lying open. Here he stopped to gather his bearings and listen for voices. The house was silent but the need for caution remained, for he didn't know whether or not Templeton was alone. There had been no watchers without, but that didn't mean there were none within. Ahead was a hallway leading to the front, a sliver of candle glow slicing the darkness from a slightly gaping door to the right. He crept along the narrow space, his back to the wall, pistol held before him. A staircase rose to his left and he peered up it but the floor above was in darkness. He put one eye to the crack between the door hinges and the frame but the sight-line was extremely limited. There was nothing else for it but to make an entrance and hope that the shock of it would defuse any potential powder keg before it went off. He withdrew his second pistol and stepped back. A deep breath. Eased it out. Another deep breath. Another corridor, he thought. Another deep breath. Another door. Another long, easy exhalation. Another room. Such was his life.

Then he moved.

The door swung back smoothly when he toed it open and stepped in, both pistols ranging around the room, but there was only one person present, sitting at a desk and scribbling at paper with a quill, a man of around Flynt's own age, tall and thin, his brown hair hanging loose. He shot to his feet and was about to cry out in shock but Flynt silenced him with a finger to his lips. He glanced at the window, which was uncovered by a drape, so remained by the door where he could not be seen by anyone watching.

Keeping his voice to a whisper, he asked, 'Is there anyone else in the house?'

The man he presumed to be Templeton shook his head, the expression on his thin face displaying relief when Flynt hid his pistols under his coat.

'My name is Jonas Flynt. You are Christopher Templeton, correct?'

The man nodded, swallowed, then said in a voice still coarsened by surprise, 'You should not have come here, sir.'

'I have little time to explain fully but I would have you accompany me back to London.'

Templeton's head shake was emphatic. 'That is out of the question, I am not safe there.'

'You are not safe here.'

A faint gleam reflected in the man's eye as he took a step away from the desk. 'I don't know you, sir, but I will not be leaving this place of safety with you for there are people who…'

'Colonel Charters sent me,' Flynt said, abruptly.

The man didn't react. 'I care not who sent you, sir.'

Flynt paused, sensing something amiss. 'Whose house is this?'

'It belongs to my Lord Gallowmire.'

Flynt kept his face impassive, the sense of disquiet growing. 'And who sent you here?'

The man continued to approach the window. 'You should leave…'

'Was it Romulus Trask?'

'Yes, it was he…'

Flynt drew a pistol. 'You're not Christopher Templeton.'

The man froze, one hand stretching out towards the window. 'Of course I am.'

'Then who is Romulus Trask?'

'A friend, from London, he…'

Flynt aimed the weapon directly at his face. 'Where is Christopher Templeton?'

The man's mouth opened and closed. He licked his lips, edged a little more to the window.

Flynt said, 'Friend, you take one more step and it will be your last.' The man obeyed, his eyes fixed on the pistol. 'I ask you again and for the final time, where is Christopher Templeton?'

He swallowed. 'His lordship has him in keeping.'

'Lord Gallowmire?'

A nod, another swallow, another lick of the lips.

'What interest does he have in Mr Templeton?'

'I know not. I was told to sit here and wait.'

'Wait for what?'

The man wasn't willing to answer so Flynt took a step closer, still careful not to be seen through the window. 'Do not make me repeat my question.'

'For you.'

Flynt expected the answer but even so, it vexed him. The phrase wheels within wheels came to his mind as his memory shot back to when a woman of his acquaintance, who also had knowledge of the Fellowship and its ways, had once explained that any circumstance in which they were involved was like the interior of a timepiece.

The dial is merely the public face of the clock. The maker needs you to know only what he believes you must know, that is the time of day, and so will have you look at the face alone where all is straightforward. One hand marks the minutes and in turn moves the hour hand. But to understand how it all works you must look below the surface. There are cogs and ratchets and little wheels... so tiny it is a wonder the clockmaker can operate them at all, and they all work in harmony while at the same time working against each other. One may turn this way, another that, but together they make the timepiece tick.

There were indeed wheels turning and Flynt had no clear picture yet of who the clockmaker was, or who was turning the key to put them in motion. What was clear now was this entire machination was a lure, and he was the prey.

He backed out of the room, his pistol still trained, and confidence seeped back into the eyes of the bogus Templeton. He darted swiftly to the window and raised the candle, shouting 'He is here! He is here!'

Flynt didn't trigger the weapon, for the man was unarmed, but he did fire off a stream of invective. He spun and ran towards the back door, voices and footsteps already approaching the front. He twisted and fired a shot into the wood, heard muffled curses but the door remained closed. *That should hold them for a few moments*, he believed, and laid hands on the door handle. He stood a better chance outside, in the darkness.

He opened the door to find the man Cooper, his fist already bunched and raised at shoulder height. Flynt had only time to register the wide grin on his face before the heavy blow to his chin spun him backwards and sent him tumbling. Jagged pain shot through his skull accompanied by flickering shafts of bright light but he knew he could not allow himself to be incapacitated. He recovered quickly, his hand reaching for his second pistol, but Cooper picked him up as though he were no weight at all and tossed him against the wall with such force that the impact vented the air from his lungs. He managed to free the weapon, but it was knocked from his grasp by one beefy paw while strong fingers threaded through his hair to slam his head against the stonework. His vision burned with a light that fractured and gyrated, accompanied by a harpy-like screech that filled his head. Cooper's strong hands cracked his head against the brick again. He pushed back at Cooper but his strength was waning. The next time he was slammed against the wall consciousness began to slip.

As he drifted into a warm, welcome blackness, he heard a voice say, 'That's enough, Joshua. We must leave something for the hangman…'

23

Drifting through mists.

Voices floating around him, but no words could be discerned.

The ticking of a clock he couldn't see.

Wheels within wheels, Jonas.

Shadows appearing, vanishing, looming.

The gaunt shape of a gallows, noose already hung.

Leave something for the hangman.

Falling. Dropping. Landing heavily.

Open your eyes, Jonas.

A boot crashing into his ribs. Once. Twice. Three times.

Fight back, Jonas.

A laugh. A face swimming from the mists. Cooper.

Ain't so high and mighty now, eh?

A punch. Powerful. Pain lancing, reactivating other agonies, some new, some old.

Think thee right clever, don't thee, up from London, dealing with dog boobies and clod hoppers.

Hands gripping the lapels of his coat. Raising him.

That's what city folk call us, ain't it? That's what thee thought.

Falling again. Head striking hard stone.

Nothing but ignorant savages up north. Well, what does thee think now?

A laugh. Cruel, guttural. Footsteps climbing wooden stairs. A door slamming. Heavy. Echoing.

Darkness again, the ache of his body subsiding as the mists enfolded him once more.

Sunlight.

On his eyes.

He opened them, blinked against it, moved to a sitting position against a cold wall, wincing as pain burned throughout his entire body. Inside his head a blacksmith was banging an anvil, the heat of his forge drying his mouth. Flynt licked his lips but there was no moisture to dampen them. He tried to rise but found he couldn't. He was too exhausted, in too much pain.

He decided to rest a moment, gather his strength, take his bearings. He still wore his greatcoat, which was something. He recalled the power of the beating he'd taken and was grateful that the thick material would have protected him somewhat. He still ached, though. His hat lay beside him but not his weapons. That would have been too much to ask for. The sunlight streamed from a small window high up a bare stone wall. He swivelled his head, gingerly to be sure, in order to survey his surroundings, his sight gradually becoming accustomed to the darkness beyond the sun's rays. It wasn't a large room but it made up for its size with austerity. There was nothing in it. Not a chair, not a table, nothing adorned the rough-hewn walls. A wooden staircase led up to a door near the heavily beamed ceiling. Straw littered the earthen floor and a stench rose from it. Human waste. Decay. He felt his nostrils recoil, unused as they were to the odour after being on the road.

'Makes you believe you be back in London, my friend.'

The voice came from the corner of the room, deep in shadow. Its owner shifted a little to allow himself to be seen, then hauled himself to his feet and crossed the floor to kneel at Flynt's side. The man was thin and dirty, his hair unkempt, his beard growing, his black coat speckled with dirt, his white shirt smeared with blood, his breeches and what had once been white hose grimy. He had no shoes.

The man noted that Flynt had observed this. 'A man with no shoes is at a disadvantage.'

Flynt gazed at his own feet and saw he was also bootless.

The man held out his hand. 'As we are sharing accommodation, I should introduce myself. Christopher Templeton, at your service. Or what little service I can offer.'

Flynt accepted the outstretched hand, that slight movement sending new waves of agony washing through him. Between his travails upon the ice in the winter and now Cooper's tender ministrations, he was unsure how much more his body could take. Perhaps this life was truly not for him.

'Jonas Flynt,' he said, letting his hand fall away.

'And what brings you to this godforsaken place, Mr Flynt?'

A small laugh tickled Flynt's throat. 'I came to rescue you.'

Templeton laughed. It was a brittle sound, betraying his own anxiety. 'I see that is working well for you, my friend. Why, may I ask, did you come for me?'

There was no reason to lie. 'Colonel Charters sent me.'

Templeton didn't seem surprised. 'Ah,' was all he said as he settled down beside Flynt. 'I appear to be in safe hands, then.'

Despite himself, Flynt laughed, but it caused another ripple of agony, so the levity was strangled by a groan.

'Friend Cooper does seem to have a most fervent need to inflict pain upon you, Mr Flynt.'

Flynt concentrated on evening his breath. 'I have that effect on some people.'

'I apologise for being the cause of your discomfort. I regret many things, but that is the most recent.'

'What else do you regret?'

'Mostly my stupidity. I should have placed myself in the hands of your employer when I had the opportunity.'

'Why did you not?'

'I was ill-advised by a man I thought friend.'

'Lemuel Gribble.'

Templeton was again unsurprised. 'I thought you would know of him. Otherwise how would you come to be here? He was the only one who knew of my location.'

'Is Gribble of the Fellowship?'

'I think not. He is an aspirant only. I regret that my own indecision, my own flux of reason, prevented me from seeing that.'

A movement in the far corner startled Flynt. He peered into the gloom, saw a brown shape with a long tail skittering across the straw. Then he saw another. No, three. He shuddered. Rats. There had to be rats.

Flynt shifted into a more comfortable position, ignoring the stabbing pain from his bruises, his eyes fixed on the creatures scrambling in the corner. 'Tell me what occurred in London, what brought you here.'

Templeton sighed, apparently unconcerned by the presence of the vermin. 'Does it matter at this remove?' He waved a hand around him. 'Now?'

'What else can we do?'

Templeton shrugged. 'I see your point. What do you know of me?'

'That you were the lawyer for the Fellowship—'

'One of them.'

'—that you became dissatisfied with the work you did. A crisis of conscience and you contacted Colonel Charters. A crisis caused perhaps by love?'

Templeton sighed. 'Sally, yes. Is she safe?'

'She is with her brother and his family. I believe she is as safe as she can be.'

That pleased him. 'I am right glad of that. She is an innocent in this. And yes, it was my love of her that caused me to examine my life and work. She is a good person, Mr Flynt...'

'Jonas, please.'

'Jonas. I know she be whore, but that matters nothing. It is her soul that matters...'

Flynt thought fleetingly of Belle but forced his concentration back to Templeton. And the scampering rats. 'So you contacted Charters, intending to inform him of the Fellowship's affairs.'

'Those of which I know, yes, for they are wise enough not to place all their secrets into one legal basket. I had heard him mentioned in the course of my work, people do talk when a lawyer is present, and I made it my business to discover what I could. But my interrogations were too clumsy, and the Fellowship heard of them. I took fright and had to flee.'

'But you didn't take Sally?'

'Until my present situation that was another regret. I had hoped they would focus on me and leave her alone. I reasoned that if they found me and she was with me it would not go well with her. I believed she had a better chance of melting into the city without me.'

'And you discussed all of this with Gribble?'

Templeton's voice saddened. 'I thought him friend. I was most candid, as a client should be with his lawyer. He arranged accommodation in the village, told me that it was an old family home.'

'He was playing a double game, I fear.' On us both, Flynt thought.

Sadness lowered Templeton's voice. 'I did not factor in his own greed and ambition. He must have contacted the Fellowship and bartered my life for his own gain. What I fail to comprehend is why go through this charade of sending me, why not take me in town? I was arrested by Lord Gallowmire's men almost immediate on arrival and placed in these delightful accommodations.'

One of the rats nosed towards them. Flynt swore he could hear its claws scraping at the earth. He struggled to keep his voice steady. 'Is Gallowmire of the Fellowship?'

'He is what they might call an associate. He is too deranged for them to embrace him fully.'

'Then why involve him at all?'

'I know not. I confess to being mystified as to why I remain breathing. The Fellowship is not known for its mercy toward those who betray its trust, or even consider to do so, as in my case.'

A theory began to shape in Flynt's mind. Wheels within wheels, he thought. 'Did you mention a Lord James Moncrieff to Gribble?'

'I did, for he is most exalted within the ranks, second only to the Grand Master.'

The Grand Master. Good God, these people were exceeding self-reverential. But that didn't mean they were not dangerous.

The rat was now only a few feet away and Flynt felt the skin upon his bones creep at the thought of it touching him. It was a fear that stretched back to his days on the battlefields of Flanders. The horrors he saw there perpetrated on the bodies of the dead and the dying by these loathsome creatures with their dark eyes and sharp teeth haunted him still. Templeton saw him gaze towards the animal, perhaps sensed him flinching, so he stamped hard on the ground to make it retreat. Flynt breathed a thanks.

'I have grown used to them this past month or so, though I confess I have lost all track of time,' Templeton said.

'You have been here near two weeks,' Flynt told him.

Templeton was shocked. 'Is that all? Time passes slowly when you are alone in such surroundings.' The lawyer glanced around, drew his knees up to his chest and wrapped his arms around them as if hugging them. When he spoke again his voice was hoarse. 'What will they do to us, Mr Flynt?'

Flynt didn't reply, but words he had heard while semi-insensate rang in his ears.

Leave something for the hangman...

24

It was around an hour later that the door above swung open and Cooper hove into view carrying a bucket in one hand and bread in the other that Flynt recognised as maslin, which he'd sampled in London thanks to the Golden Cross's cook, who hailed from the north. Despite his situation he could already taste the rustic wheat and rye mix. Cooper was flanked by a tall, slim man, like Templeton of around Flynt's age, who smiled down at them as he made a leisurely descent. A smile should be welcoming, but this one was not.

As Cooper stepped from the stairs, a rat scurried past and he kicked it out of the way. He smiled as it squealed. Flynt had no love of the creatures but he had even less for Cooper.

'Don't you be trying nothing untoward, Jonas Flynt,' he said, his tone and expression more a dare than a warning. 'Elsewise I'd have to punish thee some more.'

Flynt hadn't the strength to try anything untoward. All he wanted was what he hoped was the water in that bucket and some of the bread. Cooper maintained his attention on Flynt as he set the bucket down and threw the bread onto the floor. Templeton snatched it up and tore chunks from it greedily, then his manners intervened and he reached into the bucket to produce a wooden goblet. He handed it to Flynt, who swallowed the water gratefully. Surprisingly, it was fresh and cool. He'd expected it to have been drawn from a muddy hoof-print. Templeton then gave him a fistful of the bread.

The second man had reached them, his smile still set in place, Flynt's silver cane held carelessly in his left hand. 'Mr Flynt, it is a great pleasure to meet you. I have heard so much about you and your exploits. They tell me you are most redoubtable. I am Philip Fitzgerald, Lord Gallowmire.'

His features were finely honed thanks to generations of careful breeding, his cheekbones sharp, his jaw firm, his auburn hair unadorned by wig but tied back with a green ribbon. Up close the smile seemed even less pleasant and when Flynt looked into the man's blue eyes he saw nothing but darkness.

Flynt struggled further into a sitting position but Cooper placed a foot on his chest in order to prevent movement. Fitzgerald laid a hand on his arm, shook his head and the impediment was removed, allowing Flynt to haul himself more erect against the wall. 'I can assure you the pleasure of meeting is entirely one-sided.'

Cooper swore at him and kicked him again, but this time on the leg. It hurt but it was nothing compared to the burning of his chest.

'Gently, Joshua, gently,' said Fitzgerald. 'I remind you again that we cannot have him rendered incapable of reaching the gallows.'

Despite his agony, Flynt felt a coldness steal over him and he struggled to keep his voice conversational, not wishing to allow these men see his fear. He bit a chunk of bread free and forced himself to chew and then swallow. It wasn't easy. 'And for what exactly am I being hanged?'

Fitzgerald smiled that unpleasant smile. 'Word reaches me from London that you are more demon than man, so that should be sufficient. But I recognise that a firmer reason is required, so you will be executed for murder.'

Gribble had sent such word, perhaps. On behalf of the Fellowship. 'Ah, committing such an act seems to have slipped my mind. Who did I murder, pray tell?'

'A number of people, if the intelligence I have received is correct, and I feel certain that it is. The source is unimpeachable.'

Though he was not proud of such acts, Flynt didn't characterise any killings he had committed as murder, he considered them something like self-defence, but did not argue the point. 'Very well, who have I murdered within this jurisdiction and on what evidence am I charged?'

'We'll get to that presently.' He held a hand out to Cooper, who reached behind him to produce one of Flynt's own pistols. Fitzgerald examined it, then hefted it with a practised movement. 'A fine weapon, nicely balanced. Handmade for you special, I take it?' He didn't wait for a response. 'Its partner is also exquisite. I had a mind to add them to my collection but instead made present of them to Joshua here. You are a gutter ruffian, Mr Flynt, but you have taste, I will grant you that. Cooper here is most taken with that horse of yours – yes, we found it in Hopkins Copse, where you left it last evening. I feel sure he will put it to sterling use after your death.'

The coldness gnawed at Flynt as he watched Fitzgerald study the pistol. 'Those weapons and that horse are too good for an oaf like Cooper.'

That brought him a kick to the face from Cooper. The blow was misjudged and skimmed Flynt's cheek but it was painful all the same, sending a prismatic explosion through his brain. The coppery tang of blood filled his mouth and his flesh ruptured above the bone.

'I really would not antagonise Joshua further, my friend,' said Fitzgerald. 'He bears a grudge for your cruel treatment of him during that little skirmish in the village.' He gave Cooper a stern look. 'A skirmish that really should not have occurred.'

Cooper's head slumped in shame. 'I apologise again, your lordship. We didn't know who he were.'

'A little thought might not have gone amiss, Joshua. After all, how many strangers from the south pass through our charming little hamlet?'

Cooper's voice grew defensive. 'He is a Scotchman, my lord, we had no way of knowing for certain where he come from. He said he were hailing from Manchester.'

Fitzgerald's nod was solemn. 'True, my information lacked that one detail regarding nationality.' He glanced at Templeton, then again at the pistol. Flynt knew where this was heading and there was nothing he could do about it. 'And so to you, my dear Christopher.'

Templeton, tearing at a chunk of bread, froze as if captured in aspic. There had been fear in his eyes before but now there was absolute terror. Like Flynt, he had guessed what was coming.

'You made a grave error of judgement when you betrayed the Fellowship in London. A very grave error.' That smile flickered in Flynt's direction before he swung Flynt's pistol. The report was deafeningly loud and Templeton bucked against the wall, a fountain of red spewing from his chest. Flynt attempted to rise but Cooper's foot thrust him back none too gently. Templeton still lived, a groan underpinning each gasping breath.

Fitzgerald studied the pistol, his forehead puckered by a slight frown. 'The recoil was greater than I expected. I had aimed for the gut – a more painful wound, as I'm sure you are aware. I thought perchance I had struck the heart but it would appear not, which I find most gratifying.' He handed the spent pistol back to Cooper then leaned over Templeton to stare into his eyes. 'There is something fascinating in seeing a man gaze into eternity, is there not, Mr Flynt? I'm sure you have experienced this many times.'

Flynt had watched men die. Some had deserved it. Others had not. Unlike Fitzgerald, he had taken no pleasure from the sight.

'You see the life fade away, like an ember dying in the grate.' Fitzgerald's breath quickened a little and he shuddered. 'It is a most pleasurable experience, I find.'

Templeton's hand reached out to grasp Fitzgerald's coat. It wasn't an attack, it was more like a spasm, but Fitzgerald prised the hand free, then twisted the handle of Flynt's cane and thrust the blade into the lawyer's throat. A gurgling breath, a spray of blood from between his lips, a portion of half-chewed bread sliding from his lips, a final convulsion and then Templeton was finally still. Again Flynt attempted to rise but Cooper pressed him tightly against the wall.

'You bastard,' Flynt snarled. 'That wasn't necessary.'

'Not only was it necessary, but it was overdue.' Fitzgerald tutted in disgust as he caught sight of a smear of blood on his coat. 'Damnation, I do like this coat. Blood is so difficult to clean, don't you find?'

'It stains more than cloth.'

Fitzgerald shrugged. 'If you allow it.'

Cooper left Flynt to poke Templeton with his foot. The body slid over to land on its side. 'He's a dead 'un, your lordship.'

Fitzgerald affected sorrow. 'I fear he has fallen victim to this man's murderous nature, Joshua. So sad.'

A moment's silence followed as Fitzgerald bowed his head in some solemnity, as though in prayer. Cooper looked from Templeton's body to his master, then to Flynt, his mind working out what had occurred. He smiled as he reached a conclusion.

'Shall I have him removed, your lordship?'

'No, leave him where he lies. Mr Flynt will enjoy our hospitality for another night yet and he will require company. The rats also deserve a little sweetmeat.'

His eyes narrowed when he detected a reaction from Flynt. His smile returned. 'Joshua, do me the service of catching one of those creatures.'

Cooper seemed not to fully comprehend the order. 'Your lordship?'

'Catch me a rat, Cooper.'

The big man was far from enthusiastic as he slumped across the room to the corner. Fitzgerald took a pair of riding gloves from the pocket of his coat and pulled them on, a smile of anticipation curving his lips. Flynt couldn't help but watch as Cooper scrambled in and out of the shadows, his big arms outstretched, until he managed to snatch up one of the creatures. It struggled in his hands as he carried it back at arm's length. Fitzgerald took it from him and twisted it in his hands so he could inspect its face, clearly not as squeamish as Cooper, or as repelled as Flynt.

'Intelligent beasts, the *Rattus*,' he said. 'One can discern such by simply looking into the eyes. Just as I see the extinguishment of death, I can also see the working of the mind. The windows to the soul, it is said, but I know not by whom originally, though it was most certainly a wise man. The observant among us can see right through into the very being of man – or rat in this case.' He suddenly thrust the animal towards Flynt, who recoiled. This pleased Fitzgerald and Flynt regretted his reflexive action. The nobleman held the rat directly in front of Flynt's face.

'Look at him, Mr Flynt. Like us all, capable of the most frightful acts, but yet remains one of God's creatures. Do you believe that animals carry the spark of the divine? There are many who don't, who believe that only humans possess it, but I have made some study of such matters, in my own way, and I remain unconvinced that it exists at all.'

Flynt craned his face away from the rat as it wriggled in Fitzgerald's grasp, its mouth opening and closing, exposing its sharp little teeth. Too close, he thought, too close…

'I see you don't accept my premise, Mr Flynt. Or is it that you don't believe in the Lord, our saviour?'

Flynt swallowed, forced himself to look Fitzgerald in the eye. 'I wouldn't accept anything you say if you told me that the sun shone by day.'

Fitzgerald laughed. 'Oh dear, does that mean we can't be friends? Never mind, I will assume that you are not a God-fearing man, but then, neither am I.' He edged the rat even closer and Flynt tried to slide away. 'Look at it, Flynt, imagine those teeth ripping at your flesh, that tongue lapping your blood, those claws tearing at you.'

Flynt closed his eyes against the image, but he still saw it. The bodies with gaping wounds created not just by sword, pistol or cannon. And the brown and black bodies seething in craters…

'I see you don't have to imagine it,' Fitzgerald said. 'You have witnessed it for yourself. I envy you.'

He took the rat away and Flynt forced himself not to sigh with relief. Fitzgerald placed it beside Templeton's body. 'Let us see if it is hungry.'

The rat, however, merely ran away into the gloom. Fitzgerald was disappointed. 'That's a shame. Perhaps he and his friends will return when he is hungry, or when friend Templeton here is sufficiently... gamey, shall we say. You'll be able to witness the feast, Flynt.' He again stared at Templeton's body. 'You are wondering why I killed him perhaps?'

'I think it is in your nature to kill,' Flynt said, glad that the rat was nowhere near but his voice still hoarse and shaken.

'Perhaps. But I said he had committed a grave error and now that error put him in his grave, I believe,' he said as he straightened. 'I do so dislike disloyalty, don't you? And when it is discovered it has to be dealt with, what say you to that, Mr Flynt?'

'I say you are a candidate for Bedlam.'

The suggestion that he was insane perturbed Fitzgerald not at all. 'That has been said before, my friend. My own dear mother even thought such up until her dying day, which I admit was not soon enough for my liking.'

'I am surprised you didn't stoop to matricide. You seem capable of all else.'

Fitzgerald laughed. 'Oh, but I did. I'm sure you will understand that it's not something I would wish to be bruited abroad, for the sanctimonious and decrepit hag was well regarded, but I feel I put her out of her misery. Or more to the point, I put her out of *my* misery. The old *pater familias* loved me, of course, for I was the only fruit those withered loins managed to produce, but Mama never really took to me. I think it began when she chanced upon me as a child with a litter of kittens. She really did not appreciate what I was doing with them in the name of scientific research. Searching for the divine, you see. I was a most inquisitive child, and my curiosity killed those particular cats.' He frowned as though he could not fathom his mother's reaction. 'She never understood her son at all, and that made her most unhappy, so it was a blessing, I believe, to creep into her chamber one night, place that pillow over her face and hold her down. She writhed and kicked but I was full grown by that time and she was decided frail so was no match for me. I would have preferred something more exploratory but that might have raised an eyebrow or two.' He paused, his smile wistful as if he recalled the scene. 'She was my first. My first human being, that is. You always remember your first, eh Mr Flynt, and wish to recreate the delicious sensation of taking a life, but really it is never the same after that. There is something deeply satisfying in your first kill, a thrill that is so exquisitely pleasurable that nothing ever really comes close, don't you find?'

Flynt recalled the man's little shudder as he stared at Templeton's body. 'So I am to hang for Templeton's murder?'

'Well done, you have a keen understanding of the situation.'

Flynt flicked a glance at Cooper. Again, Fitzgerald caught it and tutted. 'Please, Flynt, don't be so naive. Cooper, what did you see?'

'I saw Flynt murder the man Templeton, your lordship.'

'And where did you witness this foul act?'

Cooper grinned. 'In Millhouse. Flynt here burst in and did murder him.'

'You see, Flynt, Cooper will swear to whatever truth I instruct him. So, here then is your murder and there lies your victim. That fact that he was destined for death in any case matters not at all.'

'And why would I wish to kill Templeton?'

'Ah, the true why of it all will be taken to your grave, I'm afraid, and will become one of the many mysteries of life. Justice has no interest in the why, only the who and the what and the how.'

Flynt interjected, 'The execution is to be summary then? There will be no trial?'

Fitzgerald's amusement increased. 'Of course there will be a trial, my dear fellow, we are not savages. All legalities will be observed.'

'And no shortage of witnesses to testify that I am the murderer, I presume.'

'Indeed not. It be known that you were seeking this poor fellow in London and many fine men will swear that you made inquiry in the village as to this poor man's location and, as you have just heard, Cooper was witness to the deed.'

'Perjured evidence.'

'Evidence is evidence and it will be accepted, of that I can assure you. The jury will properly consider their verdict, the judge will pass sentence, and then we'll hang you, right and proper. We have a grave ready dug and awaiting you, up there on the high ground, away from the good folk of my village.'

'You really are quite mad, aren't you?'

Fitzgerald was not insulted. 'One man's madness is another man's alternative perception of reality. Or morality.' He pushed himself to his feet, catching sight of the blood on his lapel again. He sighed. 'That really is most maddeningly inconvenient.'

'Why are you doing this? What do you gain?'

He stopped picking at the drying stain and grinned at Flynt. That smile was most irritating. 'Why? Grace and favour, my good sir.'

'The grace and favour of the Fellowship?'

'Yes, and the man who will one day take his place at the head of the table.'

'James Moncrieff,' Flynt guessed.

'I know not why he does detest you so grievously, but he does, and it is my good fortune that I am in a position to rid him of you. We'll have the trial on the morrow, for that is when his lordship arrives from London. He has a fervent desire to see you die, and due course of law will be complete before the following sunset. Justice is swift and sure here in Gallowmire and there is nothing your friends in London can do to stop it.'

'So the judge is already here?'

'Oh yes. He's an old family friend, overly fond of wine and easily suggestible, which is not good news for you if you harboured any lingering hopes of judicial deliverance. In the meantime, please enjoy my hospitality, basic though it may be. This was once called locally the pit, basically a dungeon, and for many a generation it lay sealed. I had it reopened.' He looked around as if surveying it for the first time. 'I know not what I will utilise it for, but I feel sure I will think of something.'

'With men like you, whatever you think of, it will be deranged.'

Fitzgerald's gaze was unwavering as he stared into Flynt's eyes, his half smile playing again.

'You do not show it but you are afeared, Mr Flynt. What lies before you fills you with dread. I see it there, in your eyes, and...' he sniffed around Flynt's face '...I smell it about you. Terror, my friend, has an odour of its very own.' He stepped back, closed his eyes as if savouring the moment. 'It is most intoxicating. I shall inhale it once again, when you stand with the hemp about your neck. It shall be most invigorating.'

'Breathe it in now, you mad bastard, because you will never see me dangle. It will be my pleasure to kill you, my Lord Gallowmire.'

Fitzgerald laughed as he and Cooper crossed the room to the foot of the stairs.

'Laugh all you wish and do it now,' Flynt called after them as they ascended, 'for though you have created your own little hell in this place, know this – you said I was more demon than man and that may be true, so believe me when I say that perdition is most jealous of those who would purloin its station and you will feel its rage. Hell's fury is coming, you demented bastard, and I will be its deliverer.'

Fitzgerald's laughter heightened as he reached the top of the stairs. It only stopped when cut off by Cooper slamming the heavy door closed, leaving Flynt in the pit with a dead man and the unseen rats, their claws scratching in the darkness.

25

Lester was far from an ideal travelling companion, Moncrieff was unsurprised to learn. The man had turned taciturnity into an art form and seemed constantly on edge. As they rode north or ate at hostelries he often had the opportunity to study his expression, which never seemed to change. He seldom smiled, he never laughed, or displayed anger or exasperation. Moncrieff had heard of, but not himself seen, a device created two centuries before by the mechanician to the Holy Roman Emperor Charles V, it being the figure of a monk which walked in a square, moved its arms, eyes and mouth in a most miraculous fashion. An automaton, it was called, and that seemed a most fitting description of his travelling companion. He took sustenance, he communicated on occasion, he pissed and defecated and slept. And yet, he seemed no more human than that clockwork contrivance, volunteering nothing of himself but that which was required for the work in hand. His only curiosity regarded what needed to be done and not the motivations behind it, his easy acceptance of its somewhat complex nature proof that he cared only for the coin. Whether he agreed or not, Moncrieff had wanted matters handled this way and so it was done.

On reflection, 'on edge' was too strong a description for his demeanour. Lester wasn't nervous, for Moncrieff suspected that like the automaton he did not have a nerve in his body. He was not on edge, merely forever watchful. Katherine had urged him to take servants with him, for the byways of rural England could be hazardous, but he had declined. Lester was being paid handsomely for the service he had provided thus far – finding and making arrangements with this lord of Gallowmire and seeing to the swift disposal of the lawyer Gribble being just part of it. There was a promise of further funds ahead so he was confident that this generally silent, bespectacled man would afford protection sufficient against any threat of banditry on the road. His reputation was as a most formidable and resolute man with sword and pistol. In any case, what they were heading north to witness was not something of which he wished his servants to be a part. He thought himself a decent master to his staff, both in London and in the Edinburgh house, and ensured that his private life was as separate from his life with the Fellowship as possible. He had dispensed with those few slaves his father had imported from the Indies because something about the notion of owning human beings was distasteful to him, though he knew not why. He had not given them their emancipation, for he was still a businessman and though human they were property after all, but he had sold a few and shipped the remainder back to the plantations where they belonged. His father, he suspected, was most broad in his sexual tastes and he often wondered how many mixed blood bastards he might have spawned. They, at least, would have no claim on the family fortune.

That thought, as it often did, brought him back to Jonas Flynt and the reason he and Lester travelled to this northern county. Lester had lived well to his reputation for discretion, for he had kept a weather eye on Flynt and had ensured, through means by which he never fully explained, that further pressure had been placed upon him to exit the city. He had even witnessed the man ride out from that low establishment in which he lodged. Alone, he had noted, so it would seem that whatever Lester had done, he had succeeded in severing the bond with that fellow Cain.

Lester had been most unforthcoming about that man. That he knew him was obvious to Moncrieff but apart from stating that their paths had crossed in the past, an expression that carried a myriad of explanations, he would amplify no further. Moncrieff detected no hatred towards the man, nor any warmth, but then, Lester was not the type to display any such emotions. Like nerves, it was doubtful he possessed such sensibilities. Which was all to the good, for once this Flynt matter had been dealt with Moncrieff had further work for him. It was his intention that the Fellowship's influence, and by extension his own, would continue to grow and the skills of a man like Lester would be invaluable.

—

The day's passing was marked only by the progress of the sun beaming through the window. It must have been south facing for he was able to watch the beam of light slant across the floor until it faded and died. He had hooked the remainder of the bread, picked off the blood that had crusted upon it, and eaten it, all the while Templeton's dead gaze upon him. He couldn't decide if it was an accusing one or not. The water he had also drunk, stretching the supply out as far as he could, but the bucket had not been overfull in the first place.

He didn't sleep. He couldn't, not with the rats still about their business. He kept the empty bucket to hand in case he needed to wield it in defence of himself or the dead man. He was resolved not to allow them to feast on flesh, whether dead or otherwise.

He pulled himself unsteadily to his feet, the heat from his bruises oozing throughout his body, and forced his unwilling muscles to pace the room, watchful, of course, for his verminous companions. Cooper had delivered quite a beating, and he promised himself he would repay that agony somehow. He emptied his bladder in a corner, the bucket ready to swing at any curious creatures.

His threat to Fitzgerald had been bluster, of course. Even though he had done his best to hide it, he had been furious over

Templeton's murder but also unnerved by the man's divination of the deep and abiding terror he experienced over both the presence of the rats and the prospect of being hanged. He had to lash out and the only way he could do so was verbally. He had no allies, no one to come to his aid, even if he could alert them. The only way in or out of this pit was by that door, the strength of which he tested after laboriously climbing the steps. It was of solid oak and he wouldn't be able to force it, nor was there any room at the stairhead to hide and incapacitate anyone who entered. The only option now was to wait until he was to be transported to the village, maintain a sharp eye and grasp any opportunity to escape, no matter how slim. He might be shot or succumb to a blade thrust in the process but that was infinitely preferable to providing further delectation for the mad nobleman. Flynt had met many dangerous people, even some who were mentally unbalanced, but there was something disconcertingly unique about that man. He recalled the slight shudder as he looked down at Templeton's body, as if he had experienced a sexual thrill. Poor Templeton had thought he was eluding the Fellowship by coming here but really he was nothing more than bait.

And Flynt himself was the prey, he knew that now.

It was still dark when they came for him. Despite his intent to remain wakeful, he had dozed and the sound of footsteps on the wooden stairs aroused him. When his eyes snapped open he found the face of a rat perched on his chest staring at him, its whiskers twitching. He cried out, brushed it away and leaped to his feet. Cooper's laugh greeted his actions.

'Not such a brave man, are thee?' he said, two men at his back also smiling. 'Freeten'd of such a creature.'

Flynt raised the bucket to use as a club but Cooper's arm snapped up and aimed one of his own pistols at him. 'Do it, Jonas Flynt. Please. I be fair itching for a reason to fire this here fine piece.'

Flynt lowered the bucket and Cooper sneered his disappointment at being deprived of an excuse to kill him. He threw Flynt's boots at his feet.

'Put them on and be quick about it.'

Flynt stifled a groan as he did as he was told. One of Cooper's men then pinned his arms behind him while the other bound his wrists with rope. They pushed him forward and he had no option but to go.

'Where do you take me?' he asked as they began to climb the stairs.

'To the village. We has a place there we use as gaol and courthouse,' Cooper replied as he followed him. 'It's small but thee won't be there for long.'

Moncrieff must have arrived then, Flynt thought, as he noted a hitch in Cooper's step behind him. 'You have hurt yourself? Nothing trivial I hope.'

Cooper's look was sour. 'I was throwed by a horse.'

The look told Flynt that he would not discuss it further so he didn't waste his breath. The door out of the dungeon led to a cramped, dismal corridor with a doorway at its end that in turn opened onto the courtyard where a man waited holding five horses, his own among them, he was pleased to see. She acknowledged him with a jerk of her head and a stamp of a forefoot. With his arms pinioned behind him he had to be assisted into the saddle, Cooper watching him with his pistol still levelled before he climbed onto another and took hold of Horse's reins. 'I thought thee would enjoy one final ride on your blasted mare.'

'That's very thoughtful of you,' Flynt said, realising with grim satisfaction that it was Horse who had thrown the man. She didn't welcome riders other than himself.

'Aye,' Cooper said, giving Horse a vengeful look. 'When thee is gone, we'll see who is master.'

Retaining his grip of the reins, he thrust Flynt's pistol into his belt before heeling his own mount into motion. Three men clustered around them, the two who had been with Cooper in the pit both armed with pistols, and the one who had held the horses sporting a musket which he handled gingerly as though he were unfamiliar. He was a young man and he was nervous, so it was to be hoped that the weapon did not discharge accidentally. Flynt glared at Cooper's broad back trotting out of the courtyard ahead of him, the night air nipping at the open wound on his cheek, every breath sending splinters of pain stabbing through his chest. They emerged from an archway onto a rough track, the river gurgling somewhere in the darkness, the solid blackness of the moorland hills rising beyond it towards a silky sky still peppered with stars. Dark boughs of trees loomed and somewhere within them an owl hooted. A sinuous breeze fingered the reeds and grass, making them sigh as though in pleasure. The peaceful, bucolic nature of the surroundings was quite at odds with reality and a mix of rage and anxiety surged along with the pain through Flynt's body.

As they left the manor house behind them, he forced his breathing to settle into a rhythm and, even though he had to maintain a tight grip on Horse's sides with his knees, he tried to relax, hoping that the agony would ease. He concentrated on the rhythmic clip of the hooves on hard ground as a means of bringing focus. Anger and panic and pain were his enemies; he had to think clearly, and master the tenderness of flesh and bone, if he was to seize any means of deliverance. He could not submit meekly to the fate mapped out for him. Vigilance was all that was required and, when the opportunity arose, some intrepidity. With glances that he strove to appear more casual than furtive, he examined the faces of the men surrounding him. Like Cooper, they were country folk, he believed, and he wondered how accurate their aim would be should he manage to somehow slip away. It was possible that they would miss him and hit Horse, and that was a risk he could not countenance, although should Gallowmire have his way then she would be given to Cooper who he suspected would not gently use animals, especially now she had ejected him from her back. Perhaps being shot was kinder for her, but he still could not bring himself to place her in such peril. If he saw a means of escape he would seize it on foot. A headlong gallop through the night across an unfamiliar landscape while his hands were tethered was not something he relished.

'Gentlemen, I would be obliged if you would afford that man his liberty and be after placing him in my care.'

The voice that floated from the darkness ahead was familiar, even though the Irish accent was alien to the owner. He had often used such vocal trickery like a mask when they worked the Heaths around London in order to disguise his identity. On hearing it, there was, at first, the thrill of anticipation of deliverance, closely followed by suspicion. Gabriel Cain, Flynt thought. How the hell did he know to follow him north?

The men came to a halt and pistols were drawn as Cooper strained to see in the night. Good luck with that, Flynt thought, Gabriel was most adept at contriving to remain hidden when he had the need. Like a wraith.

Flynt subdued his concerns over Gabriel's motivations. This was an opportunity for escape and he must grasp it readily, and deal with whatever was to come later.

'We be on legal business,' Cooper said, sounding as officious as he could to overcome the concern that rippled in his throat. 'Show thyself, stranger, and let us see thee.'

'I think not, for you are a somewhat large fellow and, in truth, you scare me half to death.'

Gabriel's voice had moved slightly to the right. Flynt hid a smile, sensing nervousness rising from the men as they adjusted their aim. Gabriel's night vision was highly developed, it had to be in order to adequately work the heaths, and the suspicion that he might see them without himself being seen clearly made his captors ever more skittish. Flynt tensed in order to throw himself from the line of fire at the first available opportunity.

'Who be thee?' Cooper asked.

'I am the night,' Gabriel said, his voice now shifting to the left. 'I am fear.'

Flynt almost laughed out loud, recognising that Gabriel was using theatricality to unsettle the men and also to give him time to study them for weakness.

Cooper eased the hammer of Flynt's pistol back. 'Then come closer, Sir Night Fear, and I will show thee how we deal with such as thee here.'

Gabriel's chuckle was low, but now behind them. He was on foot, for only that way could he move so soundlessly. 'Stars, hide your fires; Let not light see my black and deep desires. If I must die, I will encounter darkness as a bride, and hug it in mine arms.'

The men on either side of Flynt whirled their horses to follow the sound, their pistols wavering in trembling hands as they shot edgy glances towards one another. Flynt craned over his shoulder to the young fellow bearing the musket, who was now clutching it to his chest as if it was a shield and pulling his mount back in order to put distance between himself and this phantom. Flynt did his best to keep Horse steady but she had sensed the brittle nature of the atmosphere and was restless, ready for flight, but not until he gave her the command. He turned his attention to Cooper, who had twisted in his saddle. Even in the gloom, the man's expression was taut and he swallowed hard, he too being thoroughly intimidated by Gabriel's ploy. Whatever was going to occur, it would occur soon, and Flynt tensed himself in preparation.

'Pretty words, stranger, but thee be coward,' Cooper said, perhaps trying to goad Gabriel into revealing himself, but Flynt knew that would not happen until the moment was propitious. 'Thee hides thyself like a craven thief. Come, show thyself like a man and we shall send thee to hug that bride.'

Another low laugh, but now coming from Flynt's right. 'I am over here, friend.'

They twisted in their saddles to this new direction, the musket holder raising the weapon to shoulder height, the barrel quivering like a leaf in a breeze. His face was a mass of twitches as his terror crawled and nipped at his muscles. The guards' focus was completely on the disembodied voice that seemed to float around them so none of them paid Flynt the slightest of heed, and even Cooper had relinquished his grip of Horse's reins to draw Flynt's second pistol. Seeing Tact and Diplomacy in someone else's possession made Flynt even more furious than before.

'And now I am here.'

Gabriel had quickly moved ahead of them once again. The musket holder whirled his horse, levelled the weapon and, whether consciously or unconsciously, jerked the trigger. There was very little risk of him hitting anything on purpose but the subsequent explosion of sound was deafening and startled the animals. Even Horse edged slightly to the right, bumping into the flank of the young man's mount. He discarded the musket then hauled the reins to the side and spurred it into motion. The last thing Flynt saw of him was his pale face glancing back as he pounded into the darkness.

Cooper's horse had reared up onto its hind legs, a frightened whinny slicing through the air. Both pistols flew from his grip as he slid from the animal's back to land heavily. Flynt, seeing his moment, summoned every ounce of strength he had to launch himself from the saddle and cannon into the man nearest him. They both tumbled to the ground but Flynt rolled, ignoring the screaming pain, and righted himself quickly to kick him in the face then saw the third guard had steadied his horse, wheeled it round and raised his pistol. At that range he couldn't miss, but Flynt's body resisted any further movement. There was a shot from the darkness and the man was plucked him from the saddle.

Cooper, though clearly groggy from his fall, reached for the pistol nearest him on the grass nearby. He found it, positioned himself on his knees and aimed at Flynt, but Gabriel, only his eyes visible between hat brim and the scarf he had wrapped around his jaw, loomed from the dark and struck a blow to the back of his head with his pistol butt. Cooper merely swayed a little and began to rise so Gabriel hit him again, with considerably increased force, and this time he pitched forward like a felled tree. Gabriel swung the muzzle towards the fellow Flynt had kicked, who was stretching a hand towards his own weapon.

'Choose wisely, friend,' Gabriel said.

The man withdrew his hand.

'Correct choice,' Gabriel said and moved to Flynt's side, his knife ready to saw at the bonds, but his weapon still trained on the man in case he changed his mind. 'Making friends again, I see, Jonas,' he whispered, his Irish accent dropped.

Flynt wrenched his wrists free and rubbed the raw flesh. He matched his tone to Gabriel's. 'How in hell's name did you find me here?'

Gabriel shook his head as if to say *not now*, his expression hardening as he noted the gash on his cheek that had been left by Cooper's boot. A groan from Cooper made him glance in his direction. He straightened and raised his voice, the shades of blarney returning. 'What do you think, Mr Flynt? Should I be after ridding the world of these two?'

Flynt was sorely tempted to give his assent, especially with regard to Cooper, but he shook his head and held out his hand. 'Leave them be, but your blade, if you please.'

Gabriel helped Flynt to his feet before handing it to him. Flynt scanned around him for Horse but she was more used to the sound of gunfire than the country animals so had wandered only a few paces where she calmly plucked at the grass. He allowed her to enjoy this moment of leisure and took a brief moment to gather himself before he limped slowly to stand over Cooper, aware that Gabriel watched his every move intently. The big fellow was stirring and his eyes were open, but showing a lack of focus. Flynt stooped to retrieve Tact and Diplomacy, then lowered himself to one knee and rested the tip of the blade on the man's throat. The prick of the cold steel on his flesh seemed to sharpen Cooper's faculties with remarkable swiftness.

'I know not why, Cooper, but I'm going to let you live,' Flynt said. 'But here's what I wish you to do in return. Run to your master and tell him that I regret I cannot entertain him further this day, but also tell him this – I've no stomach for further friction between us. Tell him I've returned to London and that, as far as I am concerned, this business is done. Enough blood has been spilled over an affair of which I understand little and care even less. Does *thee* understand that, Joshua?'

Cooper swallowed and nodded. Flynt removed the knife from his throat and rested it below his eye. 'However, I owe you for the considerable bruises and, perhaps, damage to a rib or two.'

He flicked the blade with his wrist once, then back again, carving a V-shaped wound on Cooper's cheek and jaw. The man screamed at the searing agony and lurched away, blood streaming through the fingers he held to the lacerations.

The thrill of the action now completely dissipated, the ache of his contusions had returned with a vengeance. His leg where Cooper had kicked him was tender, his torso throbbed, the gash on his own cheek smarted. A brace of nicks on the face was a small price to pay for the punishment he had received. Flynt left Cooper writhing and hobbled to Horse, gathered her reins, then paused for a moment to summon his strength. When he felt ready to mount, his rise to the saddle was less a leap than it was a drag but the animal didn't complain at this unaccustomed lack of grace. Gabriel backed away, his pistol ever at the ready, but neither Cooper, still cursing bitterly over the kiss of the cold steel, nor his companion, who had not moved since Gabriel's warning, had appetite for further engagement. Flynt followed Gabriel to where he had tethered his horse to a tree a few yards away and kept watch for signs of pursuit.

'It's a mistake to let them live, Jonas,' Gabriel said softly.

'To finish them off would be murder.'

'An enemy allowed to live is one you will face again, you know that.'

As Flynt returned to Gabriel his knife, he saw Trask lying wounded in the Rookery passageway and Gabriel standing over him. He was too tired and too damaged to pursue that line of thought yet, though, so he whispered, 'What was all this "be after" nonsense? I've known many an Irishman but never heard one say that.'

Gabriel leaped nimbly into his saddle, then pulled away his mask to reveal his broad smile. 'Ah, those fellows will never be after knowing the difference.' He glanced back into the darkness. 'So are we really returning to London?'

Flynt shook his head and spurred Horse into motion, still wary of further attack. When sufficient distance had been placed between them and he was satisfied that there would be none, he said, 'I suspect his master will not believe I have gone, but it was worth the attempt.'

'So who is his master?'

'Lord Gallowmire, who owns most of the land here.'

'And you have antagonised this nobleman exactly how?'

'I was lured here in order to be made guilty of murder.'

'And who did you murder?' Flynt gave him a sideways glance and compressed his lips, forcing a laugh from Gabriel. 'Very well, let me rephrase. Who do they say you have murdered?'

'Christopher Templeton.'

That brought Gabriel reining his horse to a halt, his surprise genuine. 'The man you came here to find was already dead?'

Flynt stopped a little further on. 'No, he was alive when I arrived.'

'But you did not kill him?'

'I did not. I was here to help him.'

'So who did the deed?'

'Lord Gallowmire, before my eyes. He is both mad and bad.'

Gabriel urged his horse in motion again as he comprehended this news. 'Not an attractive combination in a fellow. Very well, let me try to wrap my faculties around this. You say you were lured here, so does that mean that it was always the intent that Templeton would die and you be implicated?'

'I believe so.'

'But why drag you to this godforsaken spot to do it?'

'I think because they believed I have too many friends in London to make such a charge viable.'

Gabriel was silent again. 'And do you have friends in London who could prevent it?'

Flynt let that hang between them before he replied, 'There is one, perhaps, who could.'

'And would he?'

'I don't know,' Flynt replied, truthfully, as ever being never truly certain of Charters' loyalties.

Silence again, broken only by the sound of their horses' hooves.

'But why not just have you killed in London, why all this?'

'There are those who have tried the more direct approach and failed.' Flynt was tempted again to mention again the murders of both Simms in the Golden Cross stable and Romulus Trask but he needed to see clearly Gabriel's face when he raised them and even though the first line of dawn was beginning to stretch over the moorland, it was too dark to do so. 'As for this plot, I believe my death had to at least bear the semblance of legality. And who would question the word of the lord of the manor?'

Gabriel rubbed the back of his neck with his hand. 'I don't know, Jonas, it all seems convoluted to me.'

With the excitement of the action fading, Flynt could feel weariness take hold, but he had questions of his own. 'Why did you follow me, Gabriel?'

'When I learned you had left London without informing me, I knew you were off on some wild adventure and sooner or later would find yourself in trouble. And I was proved correct, was I not? However, the question is why did you go off without as much as a fare-thee-well?'

'I thought this was something I must do alone.' Flynt pressed on with his inquiry quickly. 'How did you know I had come to Gallowmire?'

'You are not the only bloodhound, you know. I can also follow a trail. I spoke to that wench, Bess, who told me you were heading north.'

Damn it, he should have held his tongue. He should have known Bess would not have held hers.

'North is a big place,' he said. 'How did you narrow it down to this particular location? You did not arrive here by chance.'

'No,' Gabriel replied, 'I followed the trail. That you left the city very quickly after speaking with Gribble suggested to me that he had indeed imparted some specific information. He and I had a conversation.'

'And he told you where I was?'

'It took some persuasion, but yes.'

It was Flynt's turn to stop. 'How badly did you persuade him?'

'I didn't kill him, if that is what concerns you. I did threaten it, for he was reluctant to enlighten me. But enlighten me he did, and here I am. And not a moment too soon, I would suggest.'

Flynt began moving again, hoping that Gabriel spoke the truth about Gribble still drawing breath, for he intended to talk with him on his return to London, in order to discover why he had sent him on this road. However, Gabriel had further news.

'Gribble is dead, though.'

They came to standstill once again as Flynt gave Gabriel a searching look.

'The attack in the street had the appearance of a low toby lay,' Gabriel explained. 'He was stabbed and his purse taken.'

'You suspect it was not robbery?'

Gabriel's face creased with doubt. 'Until now I would have said it was his bad luck, London being London, but given what you have told me I tend to think it was not mere chance. This is the man who had you go through some kind of test before he gave you the information you required, that information now appearing to be merely a means to trap a prey, in this case you. As soon as you took that bait, he was murdered.'

'But not by your hand?'

Gabriel sighed. 'No, Jonas, not by my hand. It would be my guess that Gribble was also a mere player in this comedy and the playwright is your true enemy.'

'That man is Lord James Moncrieff.'

'And why does he hold you in such low regard?'

He wasn't going there. 'People like you and I make enemies. But how did you know to come rescue me?'

'Gallowmire is not large. I spoke with the innkeeper, a countryman of yours, and he told me you had come by looking for a certain house...'

'The Millhouse.'

'Yes. But that was deserted, though I did find some blood in a hallway. Yours I take it?'

'I regret to say it would be.'

'Further inquiries revealed that you had been taken to the manor house. As I said, Gallowmire is not large and things are seen and spoken about, even if in whispers. I must say, the people to whom I spoke were most nervous when it comes to this lord of yours, though I now understand why. I kept watch on it until I saw you being escorted away and the rest you know.'

Flynt was grateful that Gabriel had appeared but the doubts and suspicions over his true motives still niggled. He was too weary to make sense of it yet, nor to question him further.

'Now, in the name of all that's holy,' Gabriel said, 'will you tell me where we are headed, for this constant stopping and starting is upsetting my horse. Those fellows will not sit still back there. I'll wager that even now they are on their way to report to that mad and bad nobleman of yours.'

Gabriel was right. The night's activity had taken its toll and he was in no condition for another skirmish. He needed to rest and he needed to sleep. He needed somewhere safe, even if only comparatively.

'There is perhaps somewhere we can try,' he said. 'But we may not receive a warm welcome.'

26

Before he'd left the innkeeper, Flynt had asked exactly where Masilda's farm was, explaining that when he headed back south he would attempt to convince her she should leave with him. Oak Beck Farm was across the bridge, over the hill and down river about a mile, the entrance marked by an ancient oak tree beside a stream, both of which gave the farm its name, Drummond had said, but Flynt didn't want to risk passing through the village again so they had to navigate a longer way round and find a point at which the River Galwes was shallow enough to ford. The sky had lightened when they finally came upon the tall oak, streaks of colour darting through the clouds as the sun climbed the hills. By that time, Flynt slumped low over the saddle. Gabriel did not remark upon it, but as their horses splashed through the stream he reached out to steady him. Flynt nodded his thanks and straightened, noting the concern on his friend's face, causing his confusion to deepen.

They climbed up a slight rise to the farmyard, bound on one side by a sturdy, but small, limestone steading with a gorse and heather thatch and on the other a medium-sized timber and clay-walled barn. It was in fine repair and judging by its shape, Flynt suspected it was of cruck construction, with strong curved timbers supporting the roof. He had seen them before in parts of England.

Gabriel seemed prepared to step down but Flynt waved his hand to tell him to remain in the saddle. He recalled Masilda's reaction when he had used her name without permission so thought it likely she would not take kindly to them dismounting without first being invited. His decision proved wise, for when the farmhouse door opened and she appeared, a musket of some considerable vintage aimed directly at them, her face was as stoney as the walls of her home. Samson was at her heels and eyeing them with the kind of wariness only a dog can accomplish. He didn't snarl, he didn't bark, but Flynt could tell he was primed to defend his mistress.

'Well,' Gabriel muttered appreciatively when he saw the woman, 'now I know why you wished to come here.'

Flynt raised a hand to tell Gabriel to hold back as he gently nudged Horse forward.

'That is far enough,' the woman said, the weapon unwavering.

'I mean you no harm, madame,' said Flynt, aware that exhaustion rasped his voice. 'We met before, in Gallowmire and...'

'I remember you, Jonas Flynt, by name. I thought I made it clear I did not require your assistance.'

'You did, but I regret it's your assistance I require.' He freed his right leg from the stirrup and waved his hand towards the ground. 'May I step down?'

'You may not.'

There was some satisfaction in knowing that he had judged her correctly, but pain vibrated through his body as he settled back in his saddle. If he did not find somewhere to rest soon he was in danger of falling from Horse's back.

'There are men searching for you,' she said.

Flynt involuntarily cast his eyes around him. 'They have been here?'

'They have, early this morning.'

'Fitzgerald's men?'

'Who else would be so bold as to come onto my property without my permission and demand to search my home and my barn?'

'And you allowed them to do so?'

'I had nothing to hide and they were too many, even though I had this...' She twitched the musket slightly.

'They didn't attempt to molest you or harm the boy?'

A slight smirk. 'They were perfect gentlemen, or as perfect as they are able, but I kept them under my gun all the same. They looked for you and some Irishman.'

Her eyes flicked to Gabriel behind Flynt and he took this as his cue to whisk off his hat and affect a bow. 'Gabriel Cain at your service, madame.'

'You do not speak the Irish.'

He laughed and adopted the sound of the land across the Irish Sea. 'Ah, it comes and it goes, darling. Like life and love and laughter.'

Flynt thought Fitzgerald's men having been here already was a stroke of good fortune. Finding no trace of them, the chances were they would not return. At least, not immediately.

Gabriel had another thought, though. 'They could have left someone to keep watch, Jonas.'

They both scanned the hillside behind the steading then twisted to examine the road beyond the oak tree. 'We're here now,' Jonas said, 'the damage may well be done. We'll have to risk it.'

'You'll risk nothing, either of you, for you will not be remaining. In any case, fear not, for they have left nobody to keep watch. They scour the countryside for you and all men are needed for that. But leave you will and now, if you please.'

She emphasised her instruction by raising the musket a little.

'We're on the same side, Masilda,' said Flynt.

'I am on my own side, and I remind you that I have still not given you permission to be so familiar.'

Gabriel spurred his horse come forward a few steps. 'Madame, I can assure you that we are both friends to you.'

'I have no friends in this place. None that would admit it, at least.'

'There is a saying in Latin,' Gabriel said. '*Amicus meus, inimicus inimici mei*. Roughly translated it means that we are a

249

friend if we are the enemy of your enemy. We share a common foe in Lord Gallowmire. Jonas here has suffered at the hands of he and his men, hence the reason why we need some shelter, if only for a few hours.'

The musket lowered but not enough to make it less perilous should she decide to discharge it. 'Why did they abuse him?'

'They didn't like my manners,' said Flynt, feeling himself wilt. Once again, Gabriel put out a hand to steady him.

'For pity's sake, madame, have you no charity?' Gabriel pleaded. 'A stranger in need should be cared for, should he not? It is mere hospitality we require, a few hours and then we shall be about our business.'

This appeal to her sense of hospitality hit home, for she lowered the weapon further. 'If they seek you they will come back.'

'They will come here anyway, sooner or later, whether they seek us or not. You know that,' said Flynt. 'At least with us present you will have weapons behind you that will serve you better than that old musket, along with men who know how to use them. And when I have rested, it is my intention to cause them such harm elsewhere that they will have more to concern them than you and Philip Fitzgerald's desire for this land of yours.'

She frowned. 'What do you know of that?'

Jagged pain lacerated the deep breath he took. 'Sufficient to state once more that we are on the same side.'

She thought this over, her eyes reaching past them as if she was looking for more men to ride in. The weapon remained level as she asked, 'Who was it that gave you the wound on your face?'

'Your friend, Joshua Cooper.'

'Was it in payment for the assistance you gave me?'

'Partly, but also because, as I have already explained, he and his master have taken me into a severe dislike.'

Her lips compressed. Finally, she allowed the muzzle of the weapon to droop. Flynt could not discern if she realised there was some security in numbers or if Gabriel's appeal to her hospitality was the deciding factor. Whichever it was, he was relieved. Even so, she didn't invite them to dismount immediately, but instead stared at them, her brow furrowed as she reached a final decision.

Then, eventually, a curt nod, as if she resisted the very idea of it. 'You may rest in the barn. I will bring you food and you can draw water from the stream.' She waved a hand towards Gabriel. 'You seem healthy, so you can fetch it. You will find a bucket in the barn.'

Gabriel gave her an exaggerated bow. 'I thank you kindly, madame.'

She studied him, her face stern, and seemed to take his measure immediately. 'I warn you that nobody enters my chamber unless I invite them. I have knives and I will use them if either of you intend to attempt any familiarity.'

Gabriel seemed hurt. 'Madame, I can assure you that we would do nothing to compromise your good name or, indeed, your virtue.'

'My virtue was taken long ago and my good name means little, but I am most skilful with a blade and I can slice you like a ham.'

Gabriel smiled. 'Partial though I am to ham, I am in no hurry to be served as breakfast. You are safe with us.'

Her head bobbed again and she turned away. Gabriel watched her go, his smile broad. 'My God, Jonas, she is a fine-looking, spirited wench, however did you meet her?'

'We shared an encounter with Cooper, the large gentleman you incapacitated.'

With a final look at the woman as she snapped her fingers at Samson to follow her, Gabriel took Horse's reins and wheeled his own steed towards the barn. 'Well, by the warm reception we have received, I would say that you certainly charmed her.'

'Charm is not my responsibility,' said Flynt. 'I leave that to you.'

27

The barn was indeed a cruck construction, with three massive, dark oaken supports vaulting the roof, giving it a cathedral-like appearance. It didn't smell like a cathedral, though, unless it was one that housed animals, for they shared the space that morning with two cows, the horse that Masilda had been leading the day before and their associated effluence.

Gabriel sniffed. 'Charming,' he observed, 'but I've slept in worse.'

He wandered around the interior to inspect the clay and wooden walls as Flynt hefted the saddles from their mounts, feeling the strain drag on his bruised ribs. When he looked back, Gabriel was kneeling down to stroke two cats that had emerged from the shadows. 'We have protectors, Jonas. These girls will keep the dreaded rats from your person.'

Gabriel was the only person to whom he had ever revealed that particular revulsion and even though he knew the cats were there to keep the vermin down, he still felt a chill. He'd had a sufficiency of the creatures for this trip.

Gabriel inspected the underside of one of the felines. 'I correct myself, this girl and boy. And I'm thinking they are more than friends, for the girl appears pregnant to me.' He straightened and smiled. 'The place looks to be wind and water-tight, not that there seems to be any threat of inclement weather that I can detect. We'll be fine and cosy here for a time.'

Flynt grunted as he stooped to lift a sack of oats but Gabriel got to it first. 'I'll do that, you get yourself settled. That hay there looks clean and fresh.'

Flynt was grateful. 'We'll give Masilda some coin for the feed,' he said as he limped to the pile of hay to the right of the door.

Gabriel began to tip the feed into a trough. 'We can't stay here, Jonas, it's not safe for the woman, or us, come to that.'

Flynt lowered himself onto the freshly cut hay, grateful to be horizontal. 'I know. We have a few hours grace, no more than a day, but then we will move on.'

'Away from this place, I hope, back to London.'

'You can, if you wish, but I have business here.'

Gabriel dropped the sack and led the horses to the trough. 'Your business here ended when Templeton was murdered.'

'I have new business.'

Gabriel faced him again. 'You seek vengeance?'

'I seek justice for Templeton.'

'What happened to him was not your doing, Jonas. He was a dead man as soon as he left London.' Gabriel found the bucket the woman had mentioned and moved to the door. 'You rest, Jonas. We can discuss this after you have slept. I'll fetch some water.'

As he willed his muscles to relax, and to take his mind from the pain, Flynt considered whether his old friend was in fact his friend and not the man they called the Wraith. He freely admitted to himself that he had been disturbed by the notion that he was being stalked by someone who did such things for a living, but he found it difficult to accept that the Gabriel Cain he knew, capable though he was of violence – just as Flynt himself was – could be a killer for hire who could calmly cut the throats of Romulus Trask and Simms. And if he was this phantom, then why rescue him? Could that be part of the Wraith's game-playing?

He sighed, flinching at the ache even that movement caused. He was still no closer to a decision over whether to trust Gabriel. He desperately wanted to do so but something held him back.

He lay back in the hay, his eyes closed, lulled by the whistling and warbling of the birds in the morning sunshine, the horses padding softly on the earth as they nosed at the oats and the occasional movement of the cows in their stalls at the far end. The sounds were redolent of a peaceful existence and he basked in this moment of calm. As he lay, his eyes closed, he considered his present situation. Gabriel had said his business in this country was done and all reason told him that was indeed the case. A wise man would have returned to London at the first opportunity and left this place in his dust.

Flynt had been accused of many things, but wisdom was seldom one of them.

Gabriel had described his decision to remain as revenge, and there was truth in that, but something within him could not simply walk away and leave Masilda, Drummond and what good people remained in this place at the mercy of a man like Lord Gallowmire.

His gaze wandered towards the open barn door, the sunlight catching the slow dance of dust motes, and he wondered what had delayed Gabriel, for a trip to the stream and back should have taken only minutes. He drew himself somewhat laboriously upright and staggered the few steps to lean on the door. My God, his strength was waning. He saw Gabriel at the farmhouse door, the bucket at his feet, and a burst of exasperation filled Flynt's mind. The man's lusts had taken possession of his faculties, for he was convinced that Masilda's threat of bodily harm at the first sign of predatory behaviour was far from idle. However, his suspicions evaporated when she emerged from the house with a cloth over her shoulder and an iron pot in her hands from which steam rose. Her son followed, Samson at his heels. Gabriel's offer of carrying the pot was clearly rebuffed for she strode ahead of him, frowning when she saw him standing in the barn doorway.

'You should be resting,' she said as she approached. 'Is that not why you are here?'

Flynt didn't wish to admit he was observing Gabriel. 'I was taking the air.'

'There is air in this barn and you can take it lying down,' she said, a flick of her fingers acting as an instruction to return inside. He did as he was told, slumping heavily into his position on the bed of hay once more.

'The air in here is far from fragrant,' he said.

'It's a barn,' she said, 'you cannot expect it to be perfumed. I have boiled water to clean your wound.' She knelt by his side, set the pot down then dipped the rag into it and wrung it out two-handed. Her son watched them from the door, his face blank, Samson faithfully at his side.

'What's the boy's name?' Flynt asked.

'His name need not concern you as you will not be here long enough to strike up an acquaintance,' she replied, her tone matter-of-fact rather than terse. She gripped his chin with her hand and tilted his head towards her in order to examine his cheek, which she assessed with a clinical eye. 'That wound will require cleaning. Who can say what foulness the likes of Cooper has on his boots.'

'I said it would be fine, Jonas, but the lady insisted,' Gabriel said as he poured some of the water from his bucket into a trough for the horses.

'The filth must be cleaned from it, or it will fester,' she said over her shoulder. 'You people have no conception what evil lurks in such a wound.'

Flynt allowed her to dab at the dried blood on his cheek as Gabriel settled himself against one of the oak beams that stretched up and over their heads, one leg straight out, the other bent, his elbows resting on the knee as he watched them with an amused expression. Flynt wondered what he found so damned entertaining, then winced a little as Masilda cleaned the gash.

She tutted. 'Such a way to be over a little cut. I believe you are not as brave as you would like to think, Mr Jonas Flynt.'

'None of us are, madame,' he said, wincing again.

She grunted her assent. 'Men are such curious creatures. You believe you are fearless and strong and you show it off by employing violence, but you are none so fearless and strong. All are but little boys who need succour. You should try being a woman for a day, we would see how strong you were then.' She reached into the pocket of her smock and produced a little box. 'This is a healing salve used by my parents and their parents and their parents before them to heal such wounds.'

She scooped two fingerfuls of the ointment from the box but he pulled his head away. 'What is in this concoction?'

She smiled, the first time she had broken the stern nature of her features. 'You are best not to know, but it is quite safe and most effective.'

Recalling Drummond's statement that she was a healer, he allowed her to gently smooth the lotion onto the wound. At first it was soothing but then heat began to build and he jerked as if he had been stung, making her laugh.

'I omitted to mention that it was also extremely painful on first application. That is good, that means it is working, and the discomfort will soon ease, I assure you.'

He winced again.

'Such a little boy,' she said, working the unguent into his skin and, true to her word, the burning sensation receded. He shifted his position and the gingerness with which he moved caused a slight puckering between her eyes. 'You will let me examine these other wounds.'

'Bruises, only.'

'Cooper's boot again?'

He nodded and her serious aspect returned. 'Take off your coat and shirt, let me see.'

'Thank you, but they are nothing and you have already done enough.'

The amused expression was back again. 'You are ashamed to show me your body, perhaps? I have seen men's bodies before and I am sure yours is nothing exceptional.'

That provoked a snort from Gabriel. Flynt shot a glare in his direction. 'I am glad we are affording you some measure of entertainment, Gabriel.'

'I take my diversion where I can, Jonas,' said Gabriel. 'And there being no playhouse, alehouse or whorehouse, this little comedy will have to suffice.'

Masilda began to pull at Flynt's coat. 'Off with these clothes, Mr Jonas Flynt, and let me see.'

He continued to hesitate. 'Madame, I...'

She sat back on her heels and cocked her head in a mix of curiosity and levity that had thus far been absent in their brief acquaintance. Just as men were but little boys seeking solace, in that moment he saw the girl that lived within the woman. 'You have no need to be bashful. Come, remove them and let me see what damage there is. After all, if you brave men are to protect me I will require you to be fit and healthy.' There was a somewhat sarcastic emphasis placed on the words *brave men* and *protect*. Nevertheless, Flynt knew that she was not to be denied, so began to peel off his coat, small but involuntary moans escaping his lips as he moved. She helped ease the coat and his shirt from him, then bade him to lie back while she inspected his torso.

'Would you two like me to grant you some privacy?' Gabriel asked.

'You are not helping, sir,' she said as she bent to study Flynt's ribs. She reached out to gently touch his flesh. Her fingers were cool but a shock still jolted him. 'That oaf Cooper did not hold back, I fear, but I do not think anything is broken. You were lucky you wore such a thick coat in the summertime.'

He did not tell her that men like he and Gabriel had such apparel to facilitate the concealment of weapons.

Her fingers moved to the scars on his chest and shoulder. 'You have been wounded before, I see.'

'I have.'

She brushed the evidence of the bullet hole on his shoulder with her fingernails, then moved to the vestiges of the knife wounds on his chest. 'You are lucky to be alive.'

'They were not as deep as they appear,' he lied, knowing he was indeed fortunate to still draw breath. If the pistol shot and the blade had not taken him, then being immersed in icy water surely would have, if Blueskin Blake had not hauled him free.

She recognised the lie for what it was but made no further comment. 'I will apply the salve to the contusions on the ribs. It will relieve the pain.' Once again, her eyes danced as she mocked him. 'Do you wish something to bite on to control the pain?'

'I'll persevere,' he replied, already bracing himself.

She bent to her task and he willed himself not to flinch as the ointment, at first cool, began to burn. To take his mind from it, he asked, 'Why do you stay here, madame?'

'That is none of your business.'

Flynt glanced at her son, who had not moved, the sun slanting through the open doorway. He looked at Gabriel and gave his head a little jerk towards the lad. Gabriel took a moment then understood and raised himself. Samson, who had been sitting on his haunches, eyed him warily as he approached.

'Stand easy, Samson,' Masilda said.

Gabriel held his hand out to allow Samson to sniff it. 'You're a good lad, Samson. Why don't you and your young master show me this fine farm of yours. With your permission, madame.'

Masilda paused in her application of the salve for a moment but nodded her assent.

'It would help if I knew this fine young man's name.'

Flynt detected defiance in her eyes but she relented with an exhalation. 'He is named for his father, William. Will, he prefers.'

Gabriel smiled in acknowledgement and ruffled the boy's hair. Samson, sensing no threat, allowed his tail to wag. Gabriel gave Flynt a wink as he led the boy and the dog into the sunlight.

'I was born on a farm just like this, Will. Well, perhaps not as fine as this one, but it was home all the same...'

Flynt listened to Gabriel's voice, keeping up a monologue as it receded. The woman had bent to her task again, easing the ointment onto his bruises. He was becoming more used to the sensation now. 'What age is Will?'

She clearly contemplated refusing to reply, but then said, 'He is ten.'

'Does he not speak?'

'When he has something to say,' she said.

'Most boys his age have much to say.'

'You have a son?'

He thought of a boy in an Edinburgh apartment, of the features that mirrored his own. And Cassie watching them, fearful that the boy would sense the truth of his birth.

'No,' he lied. 'I merely state a general principle.'

She took a breath. 'Will has said little since his father died.'

'What took him?'

She hesitated to reply but eventually said, 'The White Plague, you may have heard it called.'

Flynt knew of it. 'You did not contract this consumption, or the boy?'

A slight shake of the head. 'We were spared, thanks to God. William knew sufficient of the malady to protect us, even taking himself to this barn for some time.' She smiled when he unwittingly glanced around him, as though the cause of the fever still lurked. 'You need not fear, it is long gone from this place.'

'There was no cure?'

'No. They said that the disease is related to the King's Evil...'

'Scrofula.'

She nodded. 'It was considered to take him to London for the royal cure, but Queen Anne died. I do not think this king would be willing to do what is necessary.'

It was believed the laying of a monarch's hands on the sufferer could perform a miracle. The late queen had permitted the ceremony a few years before she died. Flynt did not believe in such nonsense but he supposed sufferers needed some hope for a condition for which there was no remedy.

'Will was deeply affected by the loss of his father?'

'William loved his son and his son loved him. He still mourns his loss, even after these two years.'

Flynt winced as she touched a tender spot. She apologised. There was indeed a first time for everything.

'You must know that to remain here is perilous in the extreme,' he said.

Her tone regained its caustic edge. 'But I have you two brave men here now.'

'We will do what we can while we are here...'

'Which will not be for long,' she said.

He agreed. 'Which will not be for long, but you must see that it would be better for you if you left this place, at least for now.'

She straightened. 'I have said this need not concern you, sir.'

Flynt decided he had to be blunt. 'They will kill you, one way or the other. Either judicially or otherwise.'

Her expression was grim but remained determined. 'Yes, either an accident will befall me, for there have been many, or they will brand me witch and hang me.'

'You know this?'

'I know this.'

'And yet you remain.'

She took her hands away from his body and busied herself with wiping her hands on a cloth. 'I will say this but once. This is my home, Will's and mine, but more than that, it was my husband's home, man and boy, and his father and his father's father. I will not allow that monster to take it from us. From them.'

She was a resolute woman, he already knew that, but he couldn't let this lie. 'You have the boy to consider. You would leave him motherless, too? Or dead himself?'

'They will not harm a child.'

'They will. Children are harmed every day up and down this land. They hang boys younger than Will for the theft of a kerchief. They die of hunger and disease through poverty or in service of a king who cares not a fig for them, or because some politician or general demands it. Fitzgerald will not allow your Will to survive, believe me. Insanity such as his makes for a most focused mind and right now that mind is focused on garnering as much power as he can. I have little acquaintance with the man but I know he will baulk at nothing in this desire.'

She placed the box back in her pocket. 'Let the salve do its work for an hour or two before washing off the crust.'

'Madame...' he began.

She cut him off. 'I will not leave, Mr Flynt.' She stood to gaze through the doorway. At first he thought she was searching for her son and Gabriel but she seemed fixed on something else. 'Did you notice the small hill behind the house, Mr Flynt?'

Both he and Gabriel had cast an experienced eye over the surrounding land as they approached, for they had to know the lay of it. 'I did.'

'My husband lies there, along with his father and mother and his grandfather. He is part of this land now, much more so than that creature Fitzgerald. If I lose it, I lose the last of him, can you understand that?' She turned to face him again. 'Have you never loved someone so much that you cannot bear the thought of losing that one last connection to them in this world? Or have you never called anywhere home?'

Flynt had no wish to explore either question at this time. 'Are you prepared to kill to protect this farm then? For it may come to that. You may have to take a life, perhaps more than one. Do you think you can do that?'

Her eyes were hard. 'I pray to God that he gives me the strength to do whatever is necessary.'

He gave her a small smile. 'Then, madame, let us hope your God is in a listening mood...'

It wasn't a large room, but it was reasonably comfortable for a manor house in the wilds of the English north. Moncrieff had surveyed the building as he and Lester had ridden along a tree-lined approach. It wasn't exactly a palace but neither was it a hovel, he thought. In fact, it was far grander than he had expected it to be. The more recent portions, perhaps Elizabethan, had been constructed out of gritstone around a Norman keep, with two projecting wings on either side. When they arrived they had been shown through the double front doors into a great hall which acted as a somewhat grand vestibule. Light arced downwards from a large, arched window high up on the far wall above the oaken staircase, the mullion splitting it in two and the transom creating a large cross on the bare, lime-washed floorboards, like the stairway fashioned from oak. The large room was designed to show off the wealth of the family and yet it was sparsely furnished, the only item of note being the long table at the far end of the hall. Despite the warmth of the day, and the sun beaming through the window above, this room had a chill about it that made Moncrieff shiver.

They had been led through it by a servant into the parlour which, even though the handsome fireplace was cold, presented a warmer aspect thanks to the fine pieces of furniture, the rush matting covering the floorboards and the fact that the dark panelling had been painted with landscapes.

Moncrieff was glad to have finally arrived, for it had been a long and tedious journey, made even more tedious by Lester's lack of anything resembling companionability. The offer of port by Lord Gallowmire, who had greeted them warmly when they entered, was even more welcome, as was the prospect of food, which the nobleman had demanded be brought to them. The feeling that the Flynt issue was about to be resolved contributed to the lifting of his mood.

His good humour was short-lived, for his host had ill tidings to relay.

Moncrieff was by the large fireplace, feeling the need to remain standing after being bounced upon a saddle for hours, the glass of indifferent port in his hand as he glared at the man, who had the decency to at least make an attempt at contrition. However, that did not lessen his rage. His eye flicked from Fitzgerald to Lester, standing by the door. Moncrieff's anger was also directed at him, for it was he who had recommended this northern lord, but if Lester withered at all under his eye then it was well hid.

He returned his attention to Lord Gallowmire, but though his anger had kindled, he kept his voice low. A raised voice was an example of an excess of passion and it was better that such rage be channelled rather than expelled into the air. 'What do you mean, you do not have him? You did not snare him?'

'Oh, we snared him,' Fitzgerald said with an airy wave of his free hand as he settled in a wing-backed chair by the fireplace. 'The plan worked to perfection.'

'Aside from the small detail that you lost him.'

Fitzgerald, sipping his port, settled back and crossed his legs, any self-reproach now absent. 'Let us say, mislaid him. We will find him again. I have men scouring the countryside and the road south for him now.'

Moncrieff laid his glass on the high mantlepiece and willed his tightened jaw to relax. 'You assured me that as soon as he set foot in your village he would be arrested.'

'And he was and will be again, I assure you.'

Moncrieff turned back to face him. 'You also assured me that by the time I arrived we would be within hours of seeing an end to this matter, yet here I am but he is not, so forgive me if I am not assured by your assurances.'

Fitzgerald stared at the glass in his hand for a moment before he raised his head and narrowed his eyes. 'Have a care with your tone, my Lord Moncrieff. I am not accustomed to being spoken to in such a way in my own home. Allow me to remind you that you are not yet Grand Master.'

Moncrieff's eyes again strayed to Lester, but the man was as inscrutable as ever. He took a deep breath, reined in his anger but it strained at the bit. 'How did he evade you?'

'He was tethered and in the process of being transported from the dungeon here to the village to prepare for trial and ultimate execution, but the escort was ambushed.'

'Ambushed? By whom?'

'An individual bearing the accent of a bogtrotter, I am told. One of my men was rendered insensate, one was murdered, another fled.' A tremulous smile tickled his lips. 'We have that one and he will not live to regret his cowardice.'

Moncrieff mentally flicked through the men of Flynt's acquaintance but could identify no Irishmen. 'Who was this man who assisted in Flynt's escape?'

'We know not. He was masked and dressed in dark clothing, is all the description that we have.'

Moncrieff addressed Lester directly. 'What do you think?'

Lester did not reply immediately. He blinked once, twice, three times, as if he was drawing strength to form a sound. When the single word came, it was uttered in that strangled near falsetto of his, as if the strain of talking was too much for his throat. 'Cain.'

'I thought he had left him behind in London.'

'He did. Obviously Cain followed him here.'

'Why?'

Lester shrugged as if to say they would have to ask Cain that.

Fitzgerald asked, 'Who is Cain?'

'A complication,' said Moncrieff.

'One that perhaps you should have foreseen? And informed me of his existence?'

Moncrieff glared into the man's mocking eyes but ignored the impudence. 'You were not present when this man assisted Flynt to escape?'

'I was not, but he was amply guarded.'

'Obviously that was not the case.'

'We had no reason to believe that this fellow Flynt had an accomplice, for when he was seen in the village earlier he was alone. And had we been informed in advance that the man was a God-rotting Scot, then he would have been taken immediate.' Fitzgerald jerked his head in Lester's direction. 'That, along with forewarning of an accomplice, was intelligence that would have proved decided helpful had it been relayed.'

Lester didn't react to the barb aimed at him and Moncrieff wondered at how often men who were much lauded for their efficiency could stumble over a tiny detail. 'May I remind you, Lord Gallowmire, that I am also a God-rotting Scot.'

'My apologies,' Fitzgerald said, his smile far from penitent, 'but I feel sure you are aware that there are Scots and there are Scots. You are of quality, while this fellow Flynt is nothing but a gutter wastrel with a decent gunsmith.' For the first time something that resembled genuine self-reproach vanquished the self-satisfied smile in Fitzgerald's expression and tone. 'I regret that I have failed you in this instance, my lord, but we will find him, of that you can be certain, and bring him to the justice you demand. My dear friend Judge Black is fully apprised and has taken statements from witnesses. He sleeps above now, comforted by my best brandy. In the meantime, please accept the hospitality of my hall. You will be most comfortable, I can assure you.'

Moncrieff did not respond but stared through the window across the moorland. Flynt was not on his way back to London, he would stake his fortune on it. He was out there, somewhere, and he would soon make that fact known.

This fellow Cain was a complication that he had not – could not have – foreseen. Who in hell's damnation was he, and what was he to Flynt?

28

Masilda completed her ministration and then left Flynt alone, telling him she had work to do, and some time later Gabriel reappeared.

'That is the quietest boy I have ever met. Didn't say a word as we walked around the farmyard. Even I found it difficult to keep up the one-sided conversation and I am seldom lost for something to say, as you know, old friend.'

Being called old friend made Flynt frown inwardly but he let it pass. 'He misses his father. Boys need their fathers.'

As he had lain in solitude, the conversation with Masilda had turned his mind to his own life, his loves, his failures. And a young boy only a few years senior to Will, perhaps still mourning the loss of the man who had raised him, unaware that his real father lived.

'I was never certain who my father was,' Gabriel said, 'so I find it difficult to miss him.'

'Why did you tell him you were raised on a farm?'

Gabriel laughed. 'I was born in the gutter, you know that well, Jonas, mother a whore, father unknown, but it seemed advantageous to claim some kind of common ground with the lad. Unfortunately, I think he soon divined my fabrication when I could not tell a goose from a gander.'

'He corrected you? He spoke?'

'By look and incline of the head only he relayed his feelings.' He dropped into his previous position against the beam. 'Did you convince the lady it was advisable to vacate this place?'

'The lady was not for convincing.'

Gabriel set his head against the wood and closed his eyes. 'I sensed she wouldn't be. Fine-looking woman but I believe her to be most tenacious in her convictions.'

'We can't let them take her land, Gabriel. They will murder her in order to obtain it.'

Gabriel's eyes opened again and he gave Flynt a long, cool look. 'I have gone along with you thus far because you needed rest. But this is not our fight, Jonas. We should have galloped at speed back to London. We are rogues, you and I, and have little time for crusades.'

'Even rogues have occasion to stand up for what is right.'

That brought a short but bitter laugh. 'That was ever your weakness, Jonas. A damsel in distress, the oppressed to be defended.' Gabriel waved an accusatory finger in his direction. 'There is a streak of altruism running through you that can be most disconcerting in a rogue; a sense of justice, of honour, that's forever in conflict with your sense of larceny. Such attributes make for uneasy bedfellows and that explains your temperament, always at odds with yourself. Decide which you are, sinner or saint, Jonas, and you'll be a happier man for it. There's no profit in such lack of equanimity.'

'And which are you, Gabriel? Saint or sinner?'

The smile he returned was mischievous. 'You know the answer to that, my friend. I sin most enthusiastically.'

Flynt delayed asking his next question, but he knew it had to posed sooner or later. 'In your travels have you heard of the one they call the Wraith?'

Gabriel betrayed no surprise at hearing the name, nor displayed any outward unease. 'I have heard it whispered there is a killer of men who rejoices in such an alias. Why do you ask?'

Flynt watched him carefully. 'It is rumoured that he's in London for the first time.'

Gabriel's tone was conversational. 'Let me preface this by saying that I believe he is some kind of phantasm dreamed up to explain a multitude of sins, many different swords for hire amalgamated into one, but if he does exist then, if the stories be true, some poor soul is not long for this earth, for the legend tells us that he is devilish efficient in the spilling of claret.'

'It would appear that the poor soul in question is me.'

Gabriel's gaze was as even as his voice. 'You have a penchant for irritating people you really shouldn't, Jonas, but my understanding is this Wraith fellow's services do not come cheap. Who harbours such an abundance of hatred for you that they'd lay out a small fortune?'

Flynt had no wish to enter into an explanation of his relationship with James Moncrieff. There might have been a day when he would have revealed that facet of his family history to Gabriel, but it was not this one. 'As you say, I irritate people I shouldn't, and the list is long. Have you heard a whisper as to who the Wraith may be?'

Gabriel leaned over to the side and propped himself up on his forearm. 'Assuming he exists, he ensures his true identity is well hid and keeps himself to the shadows, which would be understandable given his occupation. It's always possible that I've met him, or at least one of the men whose work has been attributed to him, without even being aware it was he. I've often thought that if our paths ever did cross – and let me say I hope that day never comes – that I would be disappointed.'

'In what manner disappointed?'

Gabriel smiled. 'Well, the reputation is so fearsome that the mind conjures up an image of someone of equal ferocity, but it's more likely that he would be an unremarkable man, perhaps even insipid in appearance. After all, how better to walk unnoticed than to be a man who nobody notices?' A thought struck him. 'Is this why you exited the city so swiftly, Jonas? Has this intimation that this Wraith has you in his sights got you afeared?'

'I came to fetch Templeton.'

And a fine job you did of that, he told himself.

'Well, let me say that if you were in any way intimidated by the prospect, I couldn't blame you, my friend,' Gabriel continued. 'This fellow would be a powerful nemesis to have on your trail and right glad I am to be here to guard your flank.' He paused, then emphasised, 'If he exists, of course.'

Flynt had studied Gabriel intently as he spoke but failed to detect any sign of equivocation. 'Why did you follow me north, Gabriel? You spoke of profit and there is none here for you.'

Gabriel's laugh seemed unforced. 'That's for damn sure.'

'Then why come?'

The laugh died as Gabriel realised there was more behind Flynt's questioning. 'I told you, you are my friend and I do not have many.' He straightened again. 'Now, perhaps you should tell me what spawns this interrogatory?'

The conversation had been heading this way from the beginning, Flynt realised. The question was going to have to be asked. He struggled to pull himself upright, labouring to maintain a casualness to his movements and wishing he had his cane to assist him, but that remained in Gallowmire's possession.

'I will be straight with you, Gabriel,' he said.

'I wish you would, because I detect a shadow behind your words.'

Flynt regarded him steadily, ready to reach for the pistols resting on top of his coat at his side. 'Are you the Wraith?'

A silence sprung up between them that was almost corporeal. He fathomed nothing from Gabriel's eyes as they regarded each other across the barn, but a tension was building. Flynt allowed his right hand to edge slightly closer to the pistols.

Then amusement twinkled in Gabriel's eyes and laughter barked from his throat. 'Good God, Jonas? You think I am he?' He set his head back and laughed again. 'How many opportunities have I had to kill you since we met again? If I was this individual you would be cold and I would have taken my fee and be off to the next kill.'

Gabriel had vocalised thoughts that had already occurred to Flynt, but there was another aspect to the Wraith's method of operation that had to be raised. 'I am informed he likes to play with his victims first, like a cat does its prey, and he cannot countenance any rivalry. Simms made an attempt in that stable and someone cut his throat.'

Gabriel's face betrayed nothing.

'Romulus Trask was also murdered in similar fashion, as you recall,' Flynt added.

'And you will recall I heard something in that building, so perhaps whoever despatched this Simms fellow also sent poor Romulus into the void, but in the name of heaven, you cannot seriously believe that I would wish you harm? We have history, Jonas. I have saved your life more than once and you have done similar for me. And to think I am this Wraith of the imagination is ludicrous. I'd be insulted if it wasn't so damnable amusing.'

Gabriel was very convincing and Flynt did feel a little ridiculous now that he had given voice to his suspicion. But there was one other thing that had coloured his mind regarding his old friend, and now that he had stepped upon this path he felt he should continue.

'Why were you asking Lemuel Gribble about Templeton?'

'I told you, to discover where you had gone.'

'No, someone answering your description inquired about him before you and I renewed our acquaintance.'

That made Gabriel's smile slip a little and in that moment Flynt knew for certain it had been he. Nevertheless, Gabriel made a wan attempt at deflection. 'Men of my appearance are relatively commonplace.'

'Relatively,' Flynt repeated, then waited. Gabriel, his levity replaced by something more sombre, pushed himself to his feet, turned away and stretched, his arms spread, his head rotating on his neck to ease away the kinks. Like Flynt's own change of position, it was clearly only a means of playing for time while he considered his reply. He dropped his arms and turned back to face Flynt.

'I assume a denial would not be accepted?'

'It was you, Gabriel. I would now know why you were looking for him.'

Gabriel exhaled deeply and stepped to the open doorway. He placed one hand on the door and stared out onto the yard for a moment, then raised his face to catch the sun, the dust motes flirting with his features like fairy lovers. Flynt kept his silence, knowing that Gabriel would speak when he was ready.

'Our meeting in that tavern was not coincidental,' Gabriel said eventually, his voice low.

'I suspected not.'

Gabriel probed at something in the dirt with the toe of his boot. 'I'd been in London for some little time previous and had sought you out, that much is true. But I was not in pursuit of a lady.'

'What were you doing?'

Whatever it was at which he worried with his foot was proving stubbornly impossible to move. 'I was working.'

'Doing what? Knowing you, nothing legal.'

A slight laugh then. 'Believe it or not, it was on the side of the angels. For once.' He stopped his excavation and reconsidered his words. 'At least, I think it was. With this particular gentleman sometimes it is hard to tell the difference.'

A suspicion rose in Flynt's mind for, scant though it was, this description of the work and the employer seemed very familiar. However, he maintained his silence.

Gabriel gave him a sideways glance. 'I believe you know him. Colonel Nathaniel Charters.'

'I served with him,' Flynt confirmed, his words cautious.

'You saved his life, as I recall. Hauled him from the mud of Malplaquet, you once told me, minus an arm.'

'The arm he still retained, but not for long,' Flynt corrected. 'It was an army surgeon who relieved him of it.'

'Aye, I remember now. But I suspect there is a further connection, eh, Jonas?' Flynt remained tight-lipped and Gabriel smiled. 'Ah yes, we don't discuss the Company of Rogues, do we? Not even with old friends. And old Nathaniel ensures that one doesn't know another. But there's no need for subterfuge between us, Jonas. Not now.'

Flynt still could not bring himself to confirm his connection to the Company and Charters, but neither could he deny it. 'What service did you perform for him?'

Gabriel did not answer directly and for a second his attention seemed to be refocused on the work with his foot. 'I grew weary of life away from the city, Jonas. I'm a London lad, born and bred, and whenever I am away I long to return. But I wish to God I had stayed away, for no sooner had I given up my nomadic existence around England, and even into your homeland, than Charters pounced upon me. By God, he seems at times to be omniscient, does he not?'

Flynt nodded, for Charters' intelligence network stretched into every stratum of London life. 'What service did you perform, Gabriel?'

Gabriel hesitated again. 'It was a watching brief.'

Flynt had already guessed the direction of this conversation but still he asked, 'Upon whom?'

Gabriel took a breath before saying, 'Christopher Templeton.'

'And you lost him?'

Gabriel resumed digging at the dirt. 'There were others tasked with following him, protecting him if need be, but it was on my watch that he slipped away.'

'How did he engineer that?'

For the first time in Flynt's recollection, Gabriel's smile was bashful. 'I regret I fell asleep on the job. I'd spent a particularly energetic afternoon with a lady of my acquaintance whose husband is in the west country on business and, well, I'm not as young as I once was and my satiation had sapped me of my usual vigour. If you had told me when we were working together that I could find myself in the arms of Morpheus while seated on a hard wooden bench and sipping ale in a tavern, I would have scoffed, but that was the way of it. There was a woman singing nearby, too, and her notes were as flat as paper, so sleeping through that was difficult but I managed it, by God.'

'Was this in the Cheddar Cheese?'

'Aye, Templeton was upstairs dancing the blanket hornpipe with the Duck girl. He slipped away while I slept.'

'Do you think he knew you were on his tail?'

'At the time I thought that it was mere circumstance, but given he fled immediate after, and his inamorata also, I would hazard that he had become aware.'

'You were working solo?'

'I believe that to be the case. I had suggested to Charters that this was a two-man job but, as I have already noted, he guards the identities of his agents as a suspicious father does his daughter's virtue. No two of us know the other and I am not in the city long enough to garner apprentices such as your lad Sheppard. Anyway, I was overly confident that Templeton had no notion that he had watchers. Such arrogance, like pride, comes before a fall, eh?'

That Gabriel was convinced Flynt was one of the Company was clear, so he saw no reason to deny it. 'Charters was displeased, I assume.'

'Incandescent, I believe would be the word. He placed great stock on what Templeton could reveal regarding the Fellowship, so in an attempt to retrieve my pride from the mire into which it had become embroiled I set out to track him down.'

'Did Charters know of this?'

'I did this of my own volition, for despite his hold over me I yet have free will. During my days of following him I knew that, in addition to his frequent enjoyment of sexual congress with the Duck girl, he was also friendly with the lawyer Gribble.'

'I believe it was more than mere lust. He loved her, truly.'

Gabriel shrugged that away, his views on the existence of love not the point of the conversation. 'Nevertheless, I made inquiry of Gribble but the man told me nothing. I sensed he knew far more than he said and so kept a close eye on him. That was when I saw you, Jonas, and followed you to the studio of the fencing master. I knew you then to be on the same trail as I, so resolved it would profit us both if I contrived that meeting in the tavern.'

'How did you know that I didn't mean Templeton ill, that I didn't work for the Fellowship?'

Gabriel gave him a smirk. 'I know you, Jonas. You would never ally yourself with such a body. It wasn't until later, on piecing together some things you said, that I realised you and I were, in fact, unwitting colleagues once again.'

'Does Charters know you have followed me?'

'It was he who sent me. I didn't interrogate Gribble, for he was dead in the street before I could do so. I'm sorry for lying to you, but I believe now there should be no secrets between us. When the good colonel heard of his death he decided it was best to break his own rule and have me assist you.'

'So he knows of our past association?'

Gabriel laughed. 'What think you? I told you, the man is omniscient.'

Flynt felt some relief as he listened to Gabriel's explanation, for he had been uncomfortable in suspecting him. 'And what is it he holds over you to ensure you do his bidding?'

Gabriel again grew sheepish, obviously ashamed. 'Ah, are you familiar with Mr Isaac Watts' Divine Songs for Children?' When Flynt shook his head, he continued, 'Of course, you were never one for matters of faith, were you? There is a line which reads "and how does the little busy bee improve each shining hour". God knows that I have little of which to be proud in my life, including letting Templeton slip through my fingers, but the incident that Charters uses against me is far from my shining hour.'

'What did you do, Gabriel?'

Gabriel seemed reluctant to discuss it but would know that he had to. 'It was a high toby lay I performed solo a few years ago, on the heath of Hampstead. A private coach, a damned duchess and her young coxcomb of a fancy piece who decided to display his manhood by coming at me with a sword. I should have had you at my side, Jonas, for you were always one to temper my more violent tendencies.'

Flynt felt his flesh prickle. 'What did you do?'

'I didn't put a ball in him but I did beat him down with the butt of my pistol. Damn me if the fellow's skull didn't cave. He lived but it was a close-run thing, I believe. Anyway, Charters tells me that I could be identified by the woman, and all it would take would be for me to be paraded before her, and the theft of her jewels alone would set me upon the Tyburn trail, never mind the assault on the young buck.'

Flynt was unsure how he felt on hearing this. He should be furious but he merely wanted to laugh. That Charters had used the same robbery to blackmail both himself and Gabriel into working for his Company of Rogues was an astonishing display of hubris. He actually felt like applauding it.

Gabriel moved away from the door. 'So, how did that devil Charters inveigle you into the ranks? Or are you motivated by patriotism?'

Finally, the laugh that had been building within Flynt erupted.

29

Andrew Drummond was ill at ease as he glared at Flynt.

'I'd heard you'd gone back to London, lad,' he said. 'I'd hoped it to be true.'

'My business here is not yet complete,' Flynt said.

'That friend of yours staying in the Millhouse is dead and you killed him, they say. If that be true then I'd say you have completed your business.'

'Consider the source of that news. I didn't kill him. It was Fitzgerald. And I think you know that.'

Drummond's jaw tightened as he switched his attention from Flynt to Gabriel, who was scratching at the rough cloth of his borrowed shirt. It had once belonged to William Chilcott and its fit was unflattering, for the man was broader of shoulder and chest than Gabriel so the fabric hung upon him as if it were he who had suffered from consumption. At nightfall, Flynt had despatched him to fetch the innkeeper, reasoning that his features had not been revealed during his encounter with Cooper and his men, so he wouldn't be recognised as long as he used his own accent. His clothes might be familiar, especially his soft linen shirt, so Masilda had provided the shirt, a pair of baggy work breeches and some worn, very old, calf-length boots. Even so, he told him to avoid any interaction with locals and gave him directions as to how best he could approach the inn from the rear.

Drummond jutted his chin in Gabriel's direction. 'If you are so innocent why did you send this one to abduct me at point of pistol?'

Flynt gave Gabriel an inquiring, slightly exasperated, look and when his friend caught it, he stopped clawing at himself. 'He was unwilling to accompany me and you said it was important that you speak with him.' His expression bordered on the innocent. 'I wouldn't have discharged it.'

Drummond's growl suggested he was far from convinced and Flynt shook his head slightly in Gabriel's direction before addressing the innkeeper again. 'I remain in the vicinity, does that not suggest innocence? Had I been guilty of murder I would have put as much distance between me and this place as I could.'

'Why do you remain?'

'My mission was to return Templeton to London, as I said, and Fitzgerald has prevented that. I feel responsible for the man's death.'

'An eye for an eye, is that the way of it, lad?'

'Aye.'

Drummond looked to Gabriel once more. 'And he is friend to you?'

'Aye.' It felt good to say that and experience no suspicious qualms.

'And you two friends intend to confront Lord Gallowmire?'

'We do,' Flynt said, ignoring Gabriel's soft clearing of his throat. 'But we can't do it alone.'

Drummond turned towards Masilda, who stood by the barn door, a lantern in her hand. Will was presumably in bed with Samson guarding him. Flynt wagered that dog would give his life for the boy and his mother.

'Are you in accord with this, Masilda?' Drummond asked.

'I neither support nor oppose, Andrew,' she said.

'And yet you give them shelter?'

'Your countryman was hurt and needed tending,' she said, 'the other one was simply there.'

Gabriel grinned at being called the other one. Flynt had noted a thawing of her attitude towards them as the day progressed and she had even brought them a meal of roast mutton and what she called a dripping pudding made of batter she said had been cooked under the meat. That hot meal and whatever secret ingredient the painful salve contained seemed to work its magic, for his aches were considerably lessened and his strength had returned. It could merely have been her sense of hospitality overcoming her resistance to their presence but he thought otherwise. Masilda Chilcott may have been thrawn, as Drummond had put it, but she was wise enough to understand that she needed assistance and at this juncture Gabriel and he were all she had. Flynt intended to do what he could to change that, however.

Drummond turned back to Flynt. 'And what is it you wish me to do?'

'You must rally those villagers who you believe might be willing to stand up for themselves.'

The innkeeper's small laugh was bitter. 'They are but simple country folk.'

'It is simple country folk who win battles.'

'Aye, but they receive training, so have some facility with weapons. These are farmers, labourers, weavers, sheep herders. The closest they have come to wielding a blade is swinging a scythe.'

'From what I saw of Fitzgerald's men, they are not much more experienced.'

Gabriel chimed in. 'One of them took such fright last night that he took off like the devil was on his tail. I do believe he may have reached London by now.'

'They are still more dextrous at the taking of lives than the people here,' Drummond insisted.

'But there are those who wish to see this reign of Fitzgerald's brought to an end, correct?' Flynt insisted. 'You told me complaints had been made in the past.'

'Aye, and if you recall I said they did no good at all. I also told you there was fear here. Some who complained have left the village forever, and not necessarily of their own free will. Remember, most of them were born here and their ancestors lie in the earth of the kirkyard. I told you there have been deaths. One man the week after he raised the issue, when a cart horse bolted and ran over him.'

'A common enough occurrence,' Flynt said, thinking of Old Tom.

'Aye, I ken that's true, but nobody saw it happen save Cooper. They did see his broken body, though, and there was little left of his face. The minister of the kirk I've already told you about. It was his death that took all the fight out of them, for if Philip Fitzgerald would murder a man of God, he would murder anyone.'

'Will they allow me to speak with them?'

'You'll do nought but waste your time.'

'Will you let me try? Can you gather them in secret? Masilda tells me there's a place up on the moors, a shelter provided by rocks used by fleeing rebels centuries ago. Do you know of it?'

'William showed me it, years ago,' Masilda explained. 'His family knew of this place, but few others. I can show you, Andrew.'

Drummond sighed as he addressed her. 'You're happy with this?'

She shrugged. 'Fitzgerald will come for me sooner rather than later, you know this. I have nothing to lose.'

'You trust these men?'

She looked at Flynt. 'He appears to be the enemy of my enemy, our enemy, and that makes him friend,' she said, referring to Gabriel's words to her earlier that day, then jerked her lantern in his direction. 'Even the other one.'

Gabriel gave her a slight bow.

Flynt asked, 'Can you bring men to me, Andrew?'

Masilda's judgement went some way to satisfy Drummond, for he pursed his lips and faced Flynt again. 'All I can promise is that I'll try, but these are a frightened and beaten people, Mr Flynt, it'll take more than words to rally them.'

Flynt had already taken that into consideration. 'How many men does Fitzgerald have at his command?'

Drummond stared into the darkness above Flynt's head as he performed a swift calculation. 'Perhaps around a dozen who would be stalwart in their service, a few others he could call upon if he had to.'

Gabriel's eyebrow raised slightly at the numbers but Flynt ignored him as he led Drummond back to the door. 'You should return now before your absence is noted.'

'You're no safe here, friend,' Drummond said, his concern genuine. 'It's only a matter of time before they return.'

'I know. We'll depart for this refuge on the moors immediately.'

Drummond stopped in the barn's threshold and looked into the night, as if searching for Fitzgerald's men, then turned back. 'I don't doubt your sincerity in this, but you are only two men and a lass – meaning no insult, Masilda, for I know you're most formidable, but I refer more to the lack of numbers than any reflection on your sex.'

'I take no insult from it, Andrew,' she said. 'That is why you must help these men, if you can.'

'Andrew,' said Flynt, resting a hand on the man's shoulder, 'speak to your friends and neighbours, but I need to urge caution. Communicate only with those you trust fully. In the meantime, Gabriel and I shall see what we can do to further signify that the tide can turn in their favour.'

Drummond nodded once, pulled a woollen cap on his head and moved to where he had tethered his horse, his path lit by Masilda and her lamp.

Flynt watched them go then turned back to find Gabriel pulling off the shirt. 'I do believe something other than me lives in this garment. Fleas I am used to but I fear whatever feasts upon me is excessively voracious.'

He inspected his body but found no bite marks although there was a slight flushing of the flesh where he had been scratching.

'Your soft southern skin is unused to such rough material is all,' said Flynt. 'Silken shirts have made you weak, Gabriel.'

'I swear I could feel something moving over me all the while I had that damned thing on.' He threw the dead man's shirt aside and another thought struck him. 'D'you think that it might carry the vestiges of his affliction?'

Flynt smiled. 'I never knew you to be such weakling, Gabriel.' He picked the shirt up from the ground before Masilda could see it had been so casually disposed of. 'This has been freshly boiled, and I doubt that whatever virulence made the poor man consumptive would survive both the passage of time and cleansing by hot water.'

Gabriel reached for his own shirt hanging from a nail in the upright oak beam behind him. 'That fellow is right, you know that, do you not? Those men sent to find us will soon realise that we're not on our way south and will return. We are but two, three if you include the woman, and they're at least four times our number.'

'You're under no obligation to stay.'

'Only the obligation of friendship. Even if I am merely "the other one".'

Flynt smiled. 'Having an attack of honour, Gabriel? That could be dangerous. Soon you might begin believing in love and then what will happen?'

Gabriel grunted. 'Let's not run away with ourselves. I'll stay for now, but the second I determine with certainty that this crusade is a lost cause, then I will render you insensate and drag you from this place. I've no desire to see you on the end of a rope and even less inclination to the sharing of such a position with you.'

'Understood.'

His own shirt now donned, Gabriel pulled off the baggy breeches and reached for his own. 'But let me make this clear, if I have not done so already, just so that I can say I told you so in the event that we do both face our maker. Involving ourselves in the problems facing these people is at best folly, at worst suicidal. I know you are a gambler and have enjoyed considerable luck, but have you considered that this could be a dice throw too far?'

Flynt thrust his pistols into his belt and led Horse from her stall. 'Perhaps, but let's see if we can reduce the odds against us, just a little, eh? And in doing so, bring a little of the fear to his lordship.'

Gabriel was seated and hauling his boots up his leg. 'How do you propose to do that?'

'When last I saw him I promised to bring hell's fury.' He smiled. 'Fire and brimstone, Gabriel, fire and brimstone...'

The dinner had been extremely fine, Moncrieff thought. Fitzgerald kept a fine table and served venison cooked in bacon grease, seasoned with onion, nutmeg and cloves, then marinaded in white wine before roasted on a spit. There were other additions to the recipe, all outlined by Fitzgerald as if he had performed the work himself, but Moncrieff barely listened. He cleared his plate, however, for it had been many days since he had dined so well. Fitzgerald peppered his cooking narrative with boasts of how he had saved the family estate from near-ruin. He didn't go into great detail but from what hints he dropped Moncrieff was left in no doubt that the means by which he achieved it would be far from appetising to some people. For his part, Moncrieff cared little, for the end often justified those means.

Lester maintained his customary silence throughout. He ate his fill but refused any form of wine or ale. Moncrieff had noted that temperance on the journey.

Fitzgerald was in full flow about the laziness of what he called the peasant when he was interrupted by the sound of raised voices and running feet. He frowned and rose, saying, 'Excuse me.'

He strode to the door and jerked it open, where a burly man with a bruised face was in the process of crossing the wide hallway. 'Cooper, what in all damnation is this hullabaloo?'

A chink in the drapes caught Moncrieff's eye, for beyond it he saw a glow.

'I was coming to fetch thee, my lord. There's been an occurrence down at big barn.'

'What sort of occurrence?'

Moncrieff recalled seeing a large timber stable as he and Lester had approached the hall, so he crossed the room and peeled the curtain open slightly with the back of his fingers to stare at the orange flare of something ablaze.

'Someone has put flame to it, my lord. They let beasts free and left two of our men unconscious, then set the whole thing afire. We can't save it, my lord.'

Fitzgerald's good humour vanished. 'Damn it! Who would do such a thing?'

Moncrieff let the curtain drop back into place and turned. 'I think you know who, Lord Fitzgerald.'

'Flynt? He is headed back to London with his tail between his legs.'

'No. He's still here. And this is his way of letting you know.'

'Damn the man! I'll have his head on a pike for this.'

Moncrieff allowed himself a tight little smile. 'Or he will have yours…'

Despite the smile, something uncoiled in his gut, as if everything was unravelling and there was nothing he could do to stop it.

30

The rocks appeared to have been thrown there by some giant in prehistory playing a game of bowls. They were strewn across the moorland, huge and in the main smooth, although a few had cracked and split open over the centuries. Somehow, whether by an accident of nature or design of Man, some of them had clustered together to form a rough shelter. At one time wooden beams had been stretched across them as protection against the elements but they had long since rotted away, although the gouges carved out of the rock revealed where they had once rested.

Gabriel dropped his saddle and the bedding Masilda had loaned them onto the ground. The horses stood just beyond the opening to the refuge, untethered because both men knew they would not stray.

'It's a charmless place now but I imagine this would be grim in the dead of winter,' he said, looking around him.

'I like it,' said Flynt.

Gabriel pursed his lips. 'That's the Calvinist in you, Jonas Flynt. You're not happy unless you're suffering.'

Flynt laughed. It felt good to laugh, but also to be doing something. Until this point he had been simply reacting to events, now he was glad to take a bolder approach.

'And rebels hid themselves here, you say?' Gabriel asked. 'I have never heard tell of such a rebellion.'

'Over two hundred years ago the people of the north opposed the levy of the king's new tax.'

Gabriel tutted. 'Kings and taxes, they cleave together like shit on a shoe. Which king would that be then?'

'One of the Henrys, I believe.' Flynt had learned the story from Masilda, who in turn had been told it by her husband. 'He needed coin to defend Brittany against France.'

'Brittany is part of France.'

'Not at that time, that came later. The people up here took exception to putting their hands in their purse further and stated same in a forceful manner, which resulted in the death of a nobleman sent by the king to remonstrate with them. Whichever Henry it was sent a strong force north to punish them but they had fled. Their leader, a man named John a Chambre, was caught however and hanged. Some of those who fled hid for a period here.'

'There were further executions?'

Flynt shook his head. 'The rebellion, such as it was, evaporated. Their new leader proved useless…'

Gabriel laughed. 'A useless general? Who has ever heard of such a thing?'

'…but the king didn't press for further vengeance. Those who rose and were involved in the killing of his emissary, which may have been accidental, were pardoned.'

'And the tax?'

'Never collected. Henry found funds elsewhere for his war in France.'

'No bloody repercussions? That be most unlike any monarch I've heard of.'

Flynt had to agree. The reprisals against those Jacobites who had followed the Earl of Mar the previous year saw near forty men executed in Lancashire and two nobles lost their heads in London. It might have been more but two escaped, one with some small assistance from Flynt. Over a thousand men were transported for their part in the rising. Such was what was termed a muted response to rebellion.

Gabriel had thrown himself down on the blankets he had spread on the ground. 'Speaking of rebellion, think you the villagers will rally?'

'I'll do my damndest to ensure it.'

'You realise that what you propose might be seen as treason? And if unsuccessful it won't merely be a hanging, it'll be drawing and quartering too?'

'I have considered this, which is why I would urge you to leave here now and go home.'

Gabriel fished a pipe from the pocket of his coat but made no attempt to light it. He poked his thumb in the bowl thoughtfully. 'I confess I'm no longer sure where home is for me. Our friend Charters has made London untenable. I failed to settle in one place for very long when I travelled.' He put the pipe stem between his lips and blew through it. 'So, for now at least, this be home. Such as it is.'

Although he had not expected Gabriel to take the opportunity to leave, Flynt still felt the warmth of friendship burn in his throat and eyes.

Gabriel folded his hands behind his head and used them as a pillow. 'I trust you do not contemplate further adventures this night, Jonas, for I am weary.'

'No, not tonight. You sleep and I'll take first watch but we'll strike out again at first light.'

'And our aim?'

'We sent Lord Gallowmire a message tonight. Come morning, we'll deliver the postscript...'

–

Long nights on the heaths had taught them how to materialise from darkness with alarming suddenness, although in this case it was from the early morning mist. In such undertakings, shock and awe were equally as important as Tact and Diplomacy. They had positioned themselves in the centre of the track and awaited someone to happen along. If it were an innocent local then they would be allowed to pass and hope that the sight of them might help bolster the resistance Flynt desired. If that local was in the thrall of Fitzgerald then that would help contribute to the unease that they intended to create with their actions. But what they wanted was one or two of Fitzgerald's riders.

A man's voice giving a fine rendition of the song 'The Merchant's Son of York and the Beggar Wench of Hull' accompanied by the squeak of a wheel drifted from the grey blanket ahead. The singer, pushing a wheelbarrow filled with rocks, emerged and the song was cut short mid fa-la-la when he saw them.

The man set his barrow down and regarded them with a suspicious eye. 'Nah then,' he said in friendly greeting but there was a wariness in his tone and countenance, which was understandable.

Gabriel tipped his hat and said, 'A fine morning, friend.'

The man made a show of looking at the sky. 'Aye, a fine morn be there, beyond this here murk, though can't see nowt of it at moment.' He resumed his study of them. 'Thee'll be the lads that be giving his lordship a pain in his arse, am I right?'

'We do what we can, friend,' said Gabriel.

The old man stared at Flynt. 'I saw thee in village other day. Thee gave that bastard Cooper a right thumping.'

'He received further that night,' said Flynt.

The man nodded his satisfaction. 'Aye, heard similar I did. If anybody deserves it, it be that lump.' He paused for a moment. 'Heard tell that thee did murder the incomer in't Millhouse.'

'I did him no harm. It was Lord Gallowmire who pulled the trigger.'

This didn't surprise the man. 'Aye, 'appen that be the way of it, right enough. His lordship is good for nowt but causing mayhem. We all knows it.'

'And yet you do nothing about it.'

The man accepted what seemed like a rebuke with weary equanimity. 'Folks here 'ear all and see all but have learned to say nowt if they know what's good for them.'

Drummond had said something similar before but it carried weight from this man for some reason.

The man rested his foot on the lip of his barrow. 'His lordship lost hisself a fine barn last night, I hear tell.'

'Very dry weather we've had,' said Gabriel. 'Wood and straw can tinder spontaneous.'

The man pondered this. 'Aye, 'appen that could be way of it, though I doubts it meself. His lordship would be in a right strop.'

'He wasn't best pleased.'

Fitzgerald had been incandescent with rage. As the flames leaped into the night sky, as if attempting to reach the stars, from the darkness they had watched him rant and rave at his men, issuing orders to have the blaze extinguished without actually lifting a bucket himself.

The old man looked to Flynt again. 'Thee'll be set on further mischief, am I right?' Not waiting for an answer, he twisted to stare into the mist behind him. 'This be t'road to Hall, so thee's in right place. But then, 'appen thee knows that. There'll be some of his men along presently, I should expect.' He turned back and stooped to heft his barrow. ' 'Appen I'll be on me way now. These rocks are needed for a dyke up ahead and I'm only one who knows how to fit them proper and right.'

The man's hearing was sharp, for Flynt now heard the faint sound of two horses approaching. The barrow trundled quickly between them. 'God be with thee both, lads,' he said.

'And with you, friend,' Gabriel said, giving Flynt a smile.

The man didn't look back as he merged with the mist and the faint squeak of his barrow wheel was first muffled then died altogether.

The two riders didn't see them until it was too late. As they came upon Flynt and Gabriel on horseback blocking their passage, surprise splashed across their faces. One overcame it more swiftly than the other and reached for a pistol carried in a holster attached to his saddle but Gabriel put a ball in his shoulder before he could touch it. Flynt was glad that his insistence that none of these men be killed had been adhered to, for he regretted the death of that guard when Gabriel freed him, even though it couldn't be helped.

As his friend slumped in the saddle, his hand pressed to the blood streaming through his coat, the second rider visibly paled and his darting eyes conveyed the panic of one who contemplated the wisdom of retreat.

'Don't bolt,' Flynt warned. 'I guarantee that you won't travel far before we bring you down. Now, what are your names?'

There was a brief delay, as if he contemplated defiance, but it was gone in the blink of an eye. 'I be Benjamin, he be Thomas.'

Flynt inclined his head in greeting. 'Well, Benjamin, you know who we are, I assume?'

At first he seemed unwilling to answer but then he nodded. 'You'll be Jonas Flynt and your friend there will be Gabriel Cain.'

Gabriel would be surprised that they knew his name but he kept his counsel, Flynt was glad to note, for it was ever wise to never let the enemy know that which they need not know. Exactly how they were aware of Gabriel's identity puzzled him but was something to be explored at a later juncture.

Benjamin swallowed hard. 'Do you mean to kill us?'

'That depends on you, Benjamin,' Flynt said. 'I would much rather use you and your injured colleague here as messengers.'

'Their dead bodies would be message sufficient, Jonas,' Gabriel said, with a grim little smile.

Flynt made a show of considering this. 'Perhaps, but we can show mercy, can we not?'

'And what mercy did the likes of them show the poor souls they have no doubt murdered upon the orders of their master?'

'We have murdered no one,' Thomas said through teeth gritted with pain.

Gabriel dismissed that with a shrug. 'That's what a murderer would say.' Keeping his unspent pistol trained on the two men, he leaned back a little to slide the other into his belt and then drew his dagger. 'Come, Jonas, I say we put them down like the rabid dogs they are and send their heads back to Fitzgerald in a sack.'

Again, Flynt seemed to study upon this suggestion. Finally, he addressed the men. 'I confess, that would relay the message to your master just as easily as a verbal communication. What think you, friends? Should we do as he says and separate your heads from your bodies?'

Both men shook those heads with such vehemence that Flynt was sure he could feel the draught across the divide.

'Tell us what you wish us to say to his lordship and we'll do it,' said Benjamin.

Flynt feigned further consideration, then said, 'It is a most disagreeable pursuit, decapitation, and messy in the extreme.' He addressed Gabriel, who he could see was struggling to maintain his stern facade. 'All that blood before breakfast, Gabriel, not the most appetising of sights. No, let us simply use them as messengers.' Gabriel shrugged and hid his knife away once more as Flynt spurred Horse a little closer. 'Return to the hall and find your master. Tell him that his days here are numbered and he would be best advised to either take himself into exile or to confess his crimes and seek the mercy of the courts, for if he does not then let him know this: I am here and here I will remain until I see him dead upon the ground. I once promised him that hell's fury would be visited upon him and I would be its deliverer. Tell him that day of judgement is coming, and right soon.'

Moncrieff had grown ever more unsettled as he saw what he had thought was a carefully prepared plan fall apart.

The smoke from the barn still permeated the morning air as he listened to Fitzgerald fume further. The two men, one wounded, had ridden into the courtyard at the rear of Gallow-mire Hall just after they had breakfasted and informed them of their encounter with Flynt and that fellow Cain – Good God, Moncrieff wondered, who was that man and why was he so damnably loyal to that rogue? Fitzgerald strutted around the courtyard, his language colourful, the two men still astride their mounts and watching him, their fear evident. The complexion of the one with the pistol ball in his shoulder was decidedly pale and by his posture in danger of plummeting from his horse.

'Lord Gallowmire,' Moncrieff said. 'Might I suggest that you have this man attended to?'

Fitzgerald seemed not to understand at first, then his eyes flicked to the man slumped on the saddle. It was clear that, so enfolded in his own rage was he, he had not even considered the man's condition. For Moncrieff that was another black mark. He believed a good master should always take care of those who serve him, for such solicitude, even if only for show, buys a loyalty that mere coin can never do.

'Of course,' Fitzgerald said, finally. 'Take Thomas to Mrs Matson, she will see to him.'

Moncrieff struggled to conceal his exasperation. 'The man has a ball lodged in his flesh. He needs a surgeon, or at least an apothecary.'

'My estate manager's wife is well versed in tending to wounds, I assure you,' Fitzgerald said, his hand waving the men away. 'Thomas will be well taken care of.'

The men wheeled away but Moncrieff could not let it rest. 'That is not a mere wound, it requires proper attention.'

'Sir, do not presume to lecture me on what is proper when it comes to my affairs,' Fitzgerald said, his voice low, his gaze icy. 'I will not have it, do I make myself clear?'

Moncrieff felt the warm air between them chill and he glanced towards Lester, watching from a few feet away. He had become increasingly aware that Fitzgerald was unstable and, given he had bought and paid for Lester's services, by rights he should expect him to intercede should the nobleman take any action against him. However, he could not be certain that Lester would do so. After all, he and this northern lord had history. How much history Moncrieff could not hazard and whether it bought the man's loyalty he could not say, for beyond his claim that he cared only for coin, Lester's reasoning was opaque. Nevertheless, he could not allow this popinjay to speak to him with such disrespect.

'Then let me make myself clear, Lord Gallowmire,' he said, holding the man's gaze. 'The groundwork for this enterprise was laid most carefully, and all fared well in London, but as soon as Flynt comes to this godforsaken corner of the north it has become a farrago of mistakes and incompetence. As for being lectured, by God, you will listen to whatever I feel is pertinent, do you understand?'

'You forget, sir, you are not in London now...'

'No, you forget, sir, to whom you speak. You are of the Fellowship,' he paused for emphasis then added, 'for now.' He paused again to make his meaning clear, then continued, 'But I am highly placed on its council. Our ranks are most jealously regarded and a member can be expelled far swifter than he is admitted.'

Fitzgerald's rage was evident as he glared at Moncrieff, who stood his ground, knowing well that he could not let this man best him in any way. His authority had to be made clear.

The lord of Gallowmire was in no mind to back down, though. 'You are correct, Lord Moncrieff, that you look down upon me from the lofty heights of the Fellowship council, but I say again, this is not London. This is my domain.' Heat crept back into his voice. 'This land, these stones, the trees, the fells, the sheep, the cows, the *people*, they are mine, do you understand? *MINE!* And this rogue, this Flynt, who you sent to me has not only disrupted the peace that I have striven so hard to establish but has demeaned me in the eyes of my men, and that I cannot have. The blood of Plantagenet kings runs in my veins, and that supersedes your council position and your Scottish nobility.'

Moncrieff ensured his own voice was outwardly calm, for matching the man's passion was not the way to counteract it, but he maintained an authoritative tone. 'Then bring Flynt to heel but do it right swift, for the longer it takes, the further he demeans you. In the meantime, have your estate manager's woman tend to that man by all means if you have confidence in her skills. But remember he received that wound in your service, man, so show him that you value his sacrifice. Look after your staff, Lord Gallowmire, and they will look after you.' He recalled the look in the men's eyes as Fitzgerald had fumed. 'Fear only goes so far. Loyalty goes further.'

Fitzgerald displayed an intention to continue the argument but then decided against it. 'Very well,' he said, his voice tense, 'but mark this, my Lord Moncrieff, this Flynt of yours has thrown down a gauntlet and I will pick it up. We shall see how far fear goes.'

He didn't wait for a response from Moncrieff but made a clicking sound with his tongue, whirled and strode across the courtyard, his every step a physical exhibition of his rage. Moncrieff watched him go, then faced Lester.

'You have performed services for this gentleman in the past, you told me?'

Lester inclined his head in the affirmative.

'And you did not think to inform me that he was lunatic?'

'You not only required a man of some influence in a remote portion of the kingdom but also one who was willing to commit murder, for let us be clear, that was your plan, my lord. Such men are rare, even among the nobility. I would have thought, given that criteria, it would be a foregone conclusion that he be somehow mentally suspect.'

Hearing it stated so baldly, Moncrieff understood that in his own single-minded determination to have both revenge upon Flynt for the death of his father and also to remove a potential blemish on his family's name he had allowed himself to become embroiled in this shambles. Nevertheless he felt Lester should share a portion of the blame.

'Then allow me to be equally as blunt, sir. You commit murder for a living, does that mean you are mentally suspect?'

Lester blinked and Moncrieff wondered if finally he had penetrated that chill exterior to find a sore spot. However, the man permitted himself a slim smile. 'We are all mentally suspect in some way, are we not? Lord Gallowmire's affliction, I suspect, is one with which he was born. Yours is generated by your hate.'

'And what contributes to yours, Mr Lester?'

Again Lester paused. 'I have already stated it. I do what I do for coin, nothing more. The taking of a man's life means nothing more to me than the stepping on of an insect does you. If that be a form of madness, then I embrace it.'

Moncrieff cast his eyes in the direction Fitzgerald had taken. Even though the man was no longer visible his distemper of the mind seemed to linger in this sun-filled courtyard. This had been folly, Moncrieff saw that now. He had permitted his hatred to overcome his reason and now left himself open to failure. He should have had Lester simply make a direct attack on Flynt in London. Lester was most competent and there was every chance he would have succeeded where others had failed and would perchance have made it appear an accident. And if he had not succeeded, then so be it. There were always other Lesters. What was clear now was that he had to somehow distance himself from the events in this place, for whatever was about to transpire was not something with which he should be associated.

'We shall leave here within the hour and return to London,' he said, turning back to the entranceway to the hall.

Lester remained silent and didn't move. Moncrieff stopped closer to him. 'Did you hear me?'

Lester's eyes swivelled towards him in a languid fashion behind his spectacles. 'I heard.'

'Then let us be about it.'

Lester remained still. 'I cannot.'

'Cannot or will not?'

'It is a little of both, I would admit.'

Moncrieff was stunned and curious. 'But why, man? This entire affair has proved to be a disaster, I accept that, and that man is plainly deranged.'

'Nonetheless, I will remain here.'

'This is some form of loyalty to Fitzgerald, is that it? Where is the profit in that?'

'It has nothing to do with Lord Gallowmire.'

'Then may I remind you that I have purchased your services and that you are required to accompany me back to London.'

'You have purchased my services, it is true, and that is exactly why I must remain. I have been engaged to perform a function, and that was to see this man Flynt dead. I must fulfil that contract.'

'Then I rescind that contract and present you with a fresh one, to see me safely back to the city.'

Lester's face remained impassive, his eyes reflecting neither sorrow nor defiance over the stance he had taken. 'It doesn't work in that manner, Lord Moncrieff. I have a reputation in my field, a good one. Part of that reputation is that when I set out to take a man down, he is taken down. If I were to walk away from this enterprise now, that reputation would be diminished, and there are others who would capitalise upon that.'

In the name of God, professional pride among cutthroats, Moncrieff thought. Who would have believed it? He would have laughed if this were not so serious. 'And I can assure you Flynt will be taken down, and by you, but not here.'

'This is where Flynt is and so it is where I must be. As you say, I recommended Lord Gallowmire for this task and I feel some measure of responsibility to ensure that it is carried to its conclusion.'

'That man is going to do something desperate, I can feel it, and I cannot be a part of it. I must return to London forthwith.'

Those calm eyes rested upon Moncrieff's face. 'If he does something desperate, Lord Moncrieff, then he will do so upon your challenge, let us not forget that. It is right that you accept your responsibility in regard to whatever occurs from here on. You are already a part of it, as am I.'

Moncrieff felt his face blanch as he fully understood the enormity of what he had caused. Fitzgerald had said that Flynt had thrown down the gauntlet and he now realised that he himself had done the same. His mind raced, trying to find the words that might deflect Lester from this course, for he needed the man's protection on the roads, there being a plethora of bandits lurking in the wild stretches between Gallowmire and London, but could think of nothing that would convince him to sacrifice his professional pride. More worryingly for his own peace of mind, neither could he justify his part in what was to come.

31

The villagers didn't arrive at the refuge en masse but individually. Flynt suspected that was at the instigation of Andrew Drummond and berated himself for not thinking of it. There was only half a dozen of them, not including Masilda, but had the four men and two women travelled in a group and were spotted, that might have raised eyebrows. Drummond declined to make introductions, explaining that it was best that Flynt did not know their names.

The guttering of the candles that Masilda had supplied cut deep lines in their faces as they gathered among the rocks. They regarded Flynt and Gabriel with curiosity but there was reserve evident too. Flynt recognised the old dyke builder who had passed them on the road that morning and they exchanged a very brief nod of acknowledgment but that was all.

Masilda lingered at the rear, young Will standing silently next to her with Samson as usual at his side. She caught Flynt's eye and jerked her head as if to tell him to get on with it. He glanced at Gabriel, lounging with his shoulder against one of the rocks, his arms folded as though he was simply taking the air.

'I think it's time, Jonas,' he said. 'You invited them here, now you must entertain them.'

Flynt took a deep breath, stepped before the assembly and cleared his throat. Nerves danced in his gut, for he was unused to public speaking. He was one who preferred to keep to the shadows, not to stand before a group of men and women to deliver a speech. But it was a task that had fallen to him and he would see it through.

'I think you will all know of me by now,' he said.

'Aye, that we do, lad,' said the dyke builder.

'Thee ist murderer who will bring further tribulation upon us,' said a woman's voice from the rear.

Drummond swirled immediately. 'Hush, Martha, the man is no murderer.'

Though Flynt knew that not to be quite true, he didn't contradict the innkeeper. 'I didn't kill Christopher Templeton,' he said.

He heard someone ask in a whisper who Christopher Templeton was to be told, 'Incomer in Millhouse.'

'He was murdered by Lord Gallowmire,' Flynt said. 'I understand he was not the first to die by that man's hand, or at least on his order.'

A murmur of agreement ran round the group but the woman Drummond had called Martha was not convinced. 'Thee will bring further tribulation upon us.'

'No, it is my intention to end it.'

The dyke builder spoke again. 'And how exactly will thee do that, lad?'

Flynt looked him steadily in the eye. 'I will deliver him to justice.'

The old man laughed. 'Others have tried and haven't achieved owt. His lordship still sits in hall watching his fortune grow and the rope burns on't gallows pole remain fresh. Justice sides with those that have coin.'

Flynt was aware of that so decided to be more direct. 'There is another form of justice. Natural justice.'

One of the other men piped up, 'You mean you will kill him?'

'If I have to.'

'So you *are* murderer then?' Martha again.

'It is not murder to put down a mad dog,' Masilda said from the back. 'It's a service.'

Martha's disdain was evident. 'We won't be listening to owt from such as thee, Masilda Chilcott.'

'That's enough, Martha,' Drummond snapped. 'Masilda is under threat too, more so than any of us as Fitzgerald has his eyes on her land.'

Martha was unstung by Drummond's sharpness. 'Her husband's land thee means, Andrew Drummond. And his lordship has his eye on more'n Will Chilcott's farm, from what we hear. He wants his hands on summat more flesh and blood and dare say he's already had his pleasure, too.'

Masilda bridled, her hand reaching to grasp Will's as if the action could prevent him from hearing this. 'What is that supposed to mean, Martha Harland?'

The man beside Martha, Flynt presumed her husband, tried to quiet her but she waved his restraining hand from her arm.

'Nah then, Martha,' said the woman on her other side. 'This lass has done nowt wrong from what I can see and there's the lad to consider. He don't need to hear such things.'

'I won't be silenced,' Martha insisted. 'We all know that this one here has used her charms to bewitch men before, poor William Chilcott being one of them. We've heard that his lordship wants that ground and yet still she bides. Now, I ask thee all, why would that be? Nowt has been done to move her on…'

There were assenting murmurs from one or two of the women present, while others shook their heads.

'Cooper and his friends prevented her from bringing in her vegetables to sell and her wool for weaving,' said Drummond. 'I saw it myself.'

'Aye, and Cooper and them other two came off worst,' the dyke builder said. 'This lad here stepped in and Masilda settled with one and her dog there did t'other.' He grinned at Flynt. 'Did my old heart right good to see that lad Cooper getting his lumps.'

Flynt had to steer this away from the woman's bile. 'And he will get more if we have anything to do with it,' he said, indicating Gabriel, to whom faces turned as if seeing him for the first time.

He pushed himself off the rock and gave them a slight bow. 'Gabriel Cain, at your service.' He winked at Masilda. 'Although some know me as the other one.'

Despite her anger, something like a smile twinkled in Masilda's eye.

Martha grunted her disapproval and Flynt diverted them again. 'There is much we can do and will do. We are both competent men...'

'Both killers, tha means,' Martha sneered.

Drummond's patience broke. 'In the name of God, Martha, will you let the man speak. We wish to hear what he has to say even if you don't.'

'I has me a right to speak my mind, Andrew Drummond, more so than any outsiders, I reckon. This may be a man's world but it's us lasses who have to support you men and clean up the mess you leave behind. So I will speak my piece, thank thee very much.'

She pushed her way forward to give Flynt a defiant stare. Now that she was closer he could see she was large woman, a strong woman, her build suggesting she was well acquainted with manual labour. Her face was broad and even in the shadows cast by the candles he noted the deliberation in her eye. She had something to say and she was going to say it.

'So, Mr Jonas Flynt, I know nowt about thee but what I've heard and what I've heard doesn't impress. Old Ralph here told us what occurred on't road to the hall this morn and the message you sent to Fitzgerald. Now, I have no love for that man, as all here can testify, but it be my belief that you and this one have as much violence in your hearts as he.'

When she said 'this one', she jerked a thumb towards Gabriel, whose eyebrow twitched as he no doubt considered if it was a promotion from 'the other one'. Now Flynt knew the old man's name, Ralph, and that he had hid himself in the mist to overhear their conversation. And she was Martha. So much, he thought, for Drummond's intention to maintain anonymity.

'Nah then,' she said, folding her arms, 'what I wonder is this – what would it profit ordinary folks like us to throw our lot in with one set of violent men against another? What do we know of such things? We are ordinary folk in Gallowmire, God-fearing folk. Pistols and swords and pikes aren't for the likes of us.'

Before he could answer, Masilda stepped forward. 'So you would stand by and let Fitzgerald commit his outrages? You watch as one by one your neighbours, people you have known for years, lose what little they have? And their lives?'

Martha didn't even trouble herself with facing her. 'I told thee, Masilda Chilcott, I won't be hearing from the likes of thee. Thee aren't Gallowmire born, not even England, so have no say here.'

Anger flashed in Masilda's eyes. 'I may not have been born here but I have made it my home. I buried my husband in Gallowmire earth and I sweat and toil upon it same as you, so I believe I have a right to speak.'

That made Martha twist round. 'Right? What does a godless creature like thee know of right, or wrong?'

'Godless creature?'

'Aye, godless creature I says and godless creature I means.'

'Martha, in the name of God…' Drummond said.

'I have a mind and I speak it. William Chilcott was a healthy lad until he took up with this gypsy, nowt wrong with him, never a day's illness, and then he sickened and died and she took possession of his land. I'm not the only one that thinks it, neither, tha knows. She bewitched him and then killed him, sure as I stand here.'

Masilda launched herself with taloned fingers but was prevented by Gabriel, who in a swift, fluid motion intercepted her with an arm around her waist. Samson took a few steps forward, the hair of his back hackling, his teeth bared in a growl.

'Stay, Samson,' Masilda said, still struggling energetically against Gabriel's grip. The dog did as he was told but his eyes never left them.

'Some assistance here, gentlemen,' Gabriel pleaded, strain evident in his voice, 'for I fear this she wolf may prove too much for me.'

Drummond and Ralph moved to help drag Masilda further away from Martha. Her eyes, though, carried so much virulence that Flynt would not have been surprised if somewhere a preacher was already practising his funereal expression.

'Please, ladies,' he said, 'fighting amongst yourselves is exactly what Fitzgerald would wish. If there is one thing that undermines a cause it is disunity. Strength in numbers only comes when those numbers act as one.'

Masilda's ire had not concerned Martha one bit. 'Thee hasn't been hearing me, lad. I know what thee wishes. Thee wishes us to fight but, as I said, what fight there was within us is gone.'

Flynt knew now that if he could win this woman over then the others were more likely to follow. 'Then tell me this, do you believe that you and your neighbours are on the losing end of injustice?'

'Injustice is the lot of poor folks like us. We come into this world with nowt and we go out the same way. What can we do against such as his lordship with his coin and his power and his friends?'

'It was folk like you, ordinary folk, who 250 years ago recognised an injustice, and they stood up against it and they won.' He gave Masilda a meaningful glance. 'They put their differences aside to protest what they saw as an unfair tax and their concerns were noted. The tax was never applied. It can be done. When good people with right on their side come together there is nothing they can't accomplish.'

Eyes turned to Old Ralph, who had let Masilda go, knowing that her moment of violence had passed. The man gathered his thoughts for a moment. 'Aye, 'appen that were true, and blood-less it were, relative speaking, but there were another rising hundred years after that weren't so peaceful. The northern lords brought the ordinary folk out against old Queen Bess in support of your Scottish queen Mary, lad, and that didn't end so prettily for them what were put to death.'

Muttered agreement met the man's brief history lesson and Flynt sensed he was failing to win them over. He couldn't blame them, for what Martha had said was true. They were not fighters, they were workers. Untrained, untested, unwilling. It was different for him and Gabriel, this was their life, but it was not theirs. However, he had to make one last attempt.

'Then let me say this,' he said. 'It is my intention to continue on my course of action. The chances are that I will fail, but I will fail on my feet and not on my knees. And when you gaze upon my dead body, you'll remember what decision you have taken this night and reflect on the fact that, had you found the courage to stand, then you might have changed the course of events. Sometimes that's what it takes, for good people to stand rather than hide, to say to power, as those good folk who hid among these very stones did centuries ago, that they will take no more. This is your home, your land. You have lived on it, worked it. Those who have gone before are buried within it. Fathers, mothers, brothers, sisters, children, wives.' He found Masilda, now back with Will. 'Husbands. They've become one with the land and Fitzgerald wants to tell you that he owns them and everything on it. Do not allow that. Stand against him. Men like him are only strong as long as they believe you are weak. Show him that you are not. Show him that the people of Gallowmire say enough is enough. Tell him that his reign ends here.'

A silence followed his speech. Behind the villagers, Masilda nodded what he thought was approval. He looked at Gabriel, who gave him an appreciative wink. None of the villagers seemed willing to speak first, even Martha was silent, though her expression revealed no sign of his words having reached her. Drummond was also mute as he scanned the faces of his neighbours.

Finally, it was Ralph who spoke. 'A right pretty speech, lad. A bit awkward but I reckons thee doesn't take to such with ease. But I reckon that if thee desired a decision right now then thee is bound to suffer disappointment. Tha knows there be very real fear here and it will take more than words to overcome that.'

Flynt made to speak but Ralph held up his hand. 'Nah then, lad, thee has said enough, so best leave it be. We'll go back t'village and we'll study upon your words. 'Appen when time comes, if time comes, we'll either be there or we won't.'

There were nods and vocal assent and the villagers began to turn away, occasional glances being directed back at Flynt.

'Let me add this,' Masilda said, and heads turned to her, apart from Martha's. 'I am Romani, it is true, and my people have been reviled by such as you for generations. We have been declared thieves and whores and murderers and some of us have been these things, it is true, for we are but people after all. But because we are Romani that makes our sins worse than you English. We have been burned out, chased out, forced out. We have been spat upon, beaten, hanged. This Jonas Flynt, he says it is time to say enough and I agree. I say enough. No more. I care not what you think of me, Martha Harland, for such has been said before and worse. No matter what you or Fitzgerald think or do, I will go nowhere, I will not run. I am here. Here I stay.'

Nobody made any attempt to reply, not even Martha Harland. They stood in an awkward silence for a few moments, then began to file from the enclosure. Martha passed Masilda and her son without a glance, Samson monitoring her every move. Drummond moved to Flynt's side and together watched them disperse into the darkness beyond the range of the candles.

'That woman seemed most determined to oppose us,' Gabriel said. 'Can she be trusted?'

Drummond considered his words for a moment. 'Martha is vocal but she's solid. She'll tell Fitzgerald nothing.'

'I can follow and ensure that she doesn't,' Gabriel offered, and Drummond looked shocked.

'No,' Flynt said. 'Andrew here knows these people and if he says she can be trusted then so be it.' Drummond gave him a grateful look. 'What do you think of the others? Will they rise?'

Again the innkeeper reflected on his reply. 'I wouldn't depend on it. I told you from the start it was unlikely. You heard them tonight, these people are not fighters. I'll say this again: leave this place, get away now while you can.'

'And you heard the lady,' Flynt said. 'Here she stays. And so do I.'

Drummond looked from Jonas to Masilda, who had cradled Will before her, both arms across his chest. The boy stared back at them, his face blank. Jonas wondered if he understood what all this meant. He had to, he was not an infant, and yet he listened and soaked it in.

Drummond's head shake was sorrowful. 'Then I fear there may be new graves dug in this earth before very long...'

32

Moncrieff had no wish to accompany Fitzgerald and his men that morning but the man threw his own challenge back in his face. He had entered his chamber unannounced and before any protest could be made of such a breach of hospitality, he informed him of his plan. Moncrieff had listened with mounting horror but Fitzgerald regarded him with scorn.

'You instructed me to ensure that Flynt is returned to my custody forthwith, my lord,' he had said, his mouth in a tight line, the emphasis on the words 'my lord' weighted heavily with disrespect. 'This will bring him to us.'

'This is a most drastic step you take,' Moncrieff had protested. 'A pretence of such magnitude would…'

Lord Gallowmire's smile was crooked, raising only one side of his mouth. 'What makes you believe it be pretence, sir?'

'You would surely not…'

'I assure you that I do not make empty threats, but I do make promises. If Flynt does not bring himself forward then I will do as I say. Remember, this course of action has been formulated in response to your own order and therefore I would think you would wish to be present.'

Moncrieff felt something within him break as that truth hit home once again but he reasoned that perhaps if he were present he might somehow contrive to prevent this lunatic from carrying out the dire act he had outlined.

And so they had set out when the sun had not yet lightened the sky, a line of twelve dark-clad men, Fitzgerald at their head, Lester beside Moncrieff, as silent as ever. They rode at a steady pace through an early morning mist that hung like a winding sheet around the countryside, stifling the clip of the horses' hooves on ground made solid by many weeks of heat. The air gradually lightened as they travelled and he was able to make out the dark trunks and boughs of trees close to the trail but nothing more, though he knew the mist would soon lift. He fancied he already saw it begin to swirl a little as if the beams of sunlight forcing their way through had stirred them up.

An aged oak loomed ahead of them and two men cut themselves free of the company to trot into the mist. The remainder splashed across a brook to where the land rose gradually towards the slowly forming outlines of a small farmhouse and a barn. Fitzgerald motioned for his men to fan out on either side of him but did not order them to dismount. He sat easily in his saddle, his reins held in one gloved hand, the other resting in his thigh.

And so they waited, the mist continuing to thin and evaporate as the sun grew in strength. Birds sang. Behind them the brook bubbled over rocks. A trickle of smoke rose from the farmhouse chimney. One of the horses stirred a little, prancing out of line with a whinny, and the rider guided it back into place with a tug of the reins and a hoarse word.

And still they waited.

What on earth was the man waiting for, Moncrieff wondered? But Fitzgerald remained motionless as if posing for a portrait on horseback, his eyes on the door.

And then the door opened and a woman appeared. She was tall and slim, her dark hair loose about her shoulders, her complexion either naturally dark or the result of exposure to the elements. She levelled an aged firearm at them, a black and white dog emerging from the house behind, its stance betraying tension. The face of a young boy peered through the slightly open door, his eyes wide. Knowing what was about to occur, guilt again pierced Moncrieff's chest. What on earth was he doing here? He should have taken his chances on the road south, to hell with Lester and his professional pride.

The woman risked a glance behind her and said something Moncrieff could not hear and the boy ducked back, closing the door. She returned her attention swiftly to the riders lined up like phantoms in the mist.

'Good morning,' Fitzgerald said, sweeping his hat off like a gallant, but to Moncrieff it was all artifice, for he knew of his dark intentions.

'You are not welcome here,' the woman said, wasting no time on niceties, her voice carrying an accent that was not native to this land.

'Nonetheless, here we are,' he said, returning his hat to his head. 'Where is he?'

'Where is who?'

'Come, madame, let us not play games, we are too far down the road for that. We want him and we shall have him. He is long overdue to face justice.'

'There is no justice in this place.'

Fitzgerald smiled. 'Not justice then. Perhaps the correct word is vengeance. Now, madame, we shall delay no further. Where is Jonas Flynt?'

'Who?'

'Please, my dear woman, don't be coy with us. He has taken refuge somewhere on my land and given he came to your assistance recently I believe it safe to assume that refuge is here.'

'This is not your land.'

Fitzgerald chuckled. 'Yet. It is not my land *yet*.'

'It will never be yours as long as I draw breath.'

'On that point we agree. Now, where is Jonas Flynt?'

'If you speak of he who interfered in my conversation with your man Cooper then I have not seen him since.'

'I don't believe that.'

'I care not what you believe. Your men have already searched my farm and they found nothing.'

Moncrieff knew Fitzgerald had not expected to find Flynt here and so was unsurprised when he accepted her word easily. 'Very well,' he said. 'To other business then.'

'What other business?'

'You have already touched upon it, my dear. The current ownership, for want of a better term, of this land. It is by rights mine.'

'It was given to my husband's family by...'

Fitzgerald cut her off. 'Yes, yes, I know, but I simply do not accept that the transaction was legal.'

'Then have the law attend to it.'

This provoked a tut from him. 'I could do that very thing and I would win the suit, but I find such formalities so very tedious. I much prefer a more direct approach.'

The woman's smile was grim as she kept her barrel aimed directly at Fitzgerald. 'So the day has come then?'

'It has. I confess it has taken me longer than I had planned but I have been devilish busy of late.'

'You may well speak of the devil, Philip Fitzgerald. They say the devil is the dark one but I know him to be reddish of hair and fair of flesh and to sport manners that belie his true nature.'

Fitzgerald shrugged away any suggestion that he carried satanic blood in his veins. Moncrieff could feign faith better than most men, even though he suspected it to be mere poppy-cock first generated by churches to control minds, but even he sensed something more than mere instability of reason in Fitzgerald. If there was evil in this world, he sat at its side this day.

'Nonetheless,' Fitzgerald said, 'I have come to claim what I am due.'

'The only thing you are due from me is the content of this musket.'

He laughed. 'Ah, Masilda my dear, there is the reason I have not made my move until now. Spirit. A fine wildcat spirit, you have. But wildcats are dangerous and must be caught and dealt with.'

'Come closer, I will show you my claws,' she said, pulling the stock of the weapon tighter to her shoulder.

Still smiling, Fitzgerald made a show of a deep sigh then waved a languid hand. 'Gentlemen,' he said.

The men, apart from Fitzgerald himself, Moncrieff and Lester, all drew pistols and pointed them directly at the woman.

She seemed unimpressed. 'That matters little, for I suspect you will kill me anyway. Whether I succumb to a pistol ball or the gallows pole it makes no difference. But you may rest assured that I will drop you from that saddle before I go.'

'You may take me, you may not. I have seven pistols aimed at you and it requires only one to find its mark. That said, you are destined neither for pistol ball nor gallows pole.'

'Then for what am I destined?'

'Would it interest you to know that my man Cooper has expressed an interest in you?'

Her eyes ranged along the line of horsemen. 'I see him not.'

'Ah yes, how remiss of me. Joshua, be so good as to reveal yourself, will you?'

The door opened and Cooper emerged armed with a brace of pistols along with another man carrying the boy in one arm, his other brandishing a firearm which he aimed at the woman. The boy struggled but was held fast. Cooper aimed a pistol at the dog, which had whirled and was clearly preparing to leap.

'Keep thy cur down, lass, or I swear I will end him,' the man promised.

'Shoot the damn creature anyway, Cooper,' Fitzgerald ordered.

When the man made to comply, the woman emitted a low whistle and said, 'Fly, Samson. Go to the hill.'

The dog was already in motion, darting to the left, so Cooper's ball buried itself in the ground with a puff of dust. He bellowed and followed the animal as it sped around the side of the house, but before he could fire his second weapon, the dog had vanished into the mist. Cooper swung his pistol towards Masilda, who had trained the barrel of her musket on him.

'Let's not be foolish, Masilda,' Fitzgerald said, as if bored by the proceedings. 'You may take down poor Joshua but we will still have the boy.'

'You came here for me, leave my son be.'

'I don't recall saying I was here for you. Cooper is the one who wants you. I confess I had entertained thoughts of lying with you myself, for you have a certain exotic appeal, but in the end it is most unbecoming for a man of my bloodstock to soil himself with a filthy gypsy. I am here solely for the boy.'

She seemed taken aback and took her eyes from Cooper to look over her shoulder at Fitzgerald. 'What do you wish with my son?'

For the first time Moncrieff heard fear tremble in her words.

'My intentions with regard to the whelp need not concern you. Now, put up your weapon and we shall proceed with our business with no further ado. I grow weary of this.'

Her resolve returned and she ignored his order, keeping her musket aimed directly at Cooper. Moncrieff could not help but admire her, for she had courage. How many men, when faced with such odds, would continue their defiance? He glanced at Fitzgerald's face, but it betrayed nothing, no anger, no weariness. He was calm, his tone measured, as if he knew there was only one way this interlude would end. Unfortunately, Moncrieff also knew where all this was destined to lead and it did not bode well for this woman and her son. He swallowed back his revulsion, wishing he could think of something to do.

'Very well,' Fitzgerald said, his voice remaining conversational. 'Cooper, be so good as to put a ball in the boy's head.'

Cooper smiled, but before he could move the woman took a step closer to him. 'Move that pistol, Joshua, and it will be the last you ever make.'

Fitzgerald sighed again. 'Masilda, my dear, this is becoming dreary in the extreme. You have to see that your situation is hopeless.'

There was a long moment of silence, during which the woman must have weighed up her options. Yes, she could take

Cooper if he edged his pistol any further in her son's direction. But if she did, she would be dead and Fitzgerald would still have the boy. Moncrieff contemplated what he would do if he was in her position and when she reluctantly lowered her weapon he knew it was that. But then, he did not yet have a son to protect. Perhaps if he had, he would think differently.

Cooper moved swiftly to take the musket from her and jerked his head to his companion to take the boy to Fitzgerald. The lad struggled but, Moncrieff realised, had not made a sound throughout, leading him to believe that he was mute. The woman stretched out a hand towards him as he passed but a back-handed slap from Cooper sent her sprawling into the dirt.

'I suspect Cooper is not a gentle lover, madame,' Fitzgerald said. 'I regret that what lies ahead of you will not be comfortable.'

The blow had been powerful and painful but her eyes remained fiery as she looked up at him. 'I will endure it.'

'Endure it, perhaps. Survive it, perhaps not.'

Moncrieff could maintain his silence no longer. He leaned closer to Fitzgerald. 'Good God, man, is this necessary?'

Fitzgerald's cold eyes swivelled towards him. 'Inevitable, I would say. My man Cooper has coveted this gypsy whore since she was brought here by her husband. She would die either way. He might as well take his pleasures first.'

Fitzgerald watched as the boy was handed to one of the men and draped unceremoniously across his saddle. The lad's exertions to break free were rewarded with a heavy blow to the back of the head and the boy was still. Moncrieff winced. The woman Masilda leaped to her feet and darted towards the horses but Cooper was upon her with a few easy strides and brought her down with the butt of his pistol between her shoulders. Moncrieff winced again. With a cry of agony and frustration, she pitched forward on her hands and knees.

'I would comply, if I were you,' said Fitzgerald. 'It will be so much easier.' He turned his attention to Cooper. 'When you have had your fill of her, attend to me in Gallowmire. We end this charade with the man Flynt today.' He aimed a finger at the man who had carried the boy. 'You remain here, too.'

He wheeled his horse and led his men back towards the brook. Moncrieff edged his horse closer to the woman who remained on all fours, watching them carry her son away, her face taut with the effort not to plead for mercy, but her eyes betraying her anguish, he suspected not for her plight but for whatever his lordship had in mind for the boy.

'I regret this affair, madame,' he said.

She turned her eyes on him and hatred kindled. She spat at the ground beneath his horse's hooves. 'To damnation with you and your regrets, sir. You ride with that devil so you are as bad as he.'

Moncrieff could think of nothing to say in his defence, for there was no defence. What she said was true. He turned his horse's head to find Lester watching him. As he drew level with him, Lester said quietly, 'You set this in motion, my lord. You cannot stop it now.'

The woman's curses made him look back to see Cooper forcing her to the farmhouse. She writhed in his hands and clawed at his face, causing him to curse then deliver a powerful blow to her face. She fell limp and he half carried, half dragged her the rest of the way, telling his companion to stay where he was. Moncrieff felt bile rise and he looked away again. Lester, as ever, was unmoved.

'Then she is correct,' Moncrieff said, his voice strained. 'I am heading for damnation...'

33

Flynt watched from a distance as the lone rider approached.

He had found an ideal vantage point among the rocks to survey the moorland surrounding them. Those who had rebelled centuries before had chosen their refuge well, for there was an uninterrupted view and it would be impossible during daylight hours for anyone to approach without being detected. He had studied the man on horseback through his spyglass but he was not yet close enough to make an identification. He glanced down to the enclosure, saw that Gabriel was stretched on his blanket, his head on his saddle, his hat over his eyes. He was the very picture of leisure, with his feet crossed at the ankles and his fingers threaded together on his chest. His slumber would be light, but Flynt decided to let him bide there until he could ascertain if the rider was friend or foe. He settled against the rocks, the aches from his beating little more than a memory now, thanks to whatever was in that concoction of Masilda's. However, there was still a little power left in them and he was grateful to have some leisure.

As he watched the figure make his way across the fells, Flynt thought of the situation in which he had found himself and whether he could have done anything to avoid it, apart from following Gabriel's advice to flee this land – an opinion that he had again shared following the gathering the previous night. His life had a way of leading him into such situations whether he wished them to or not. Certainly, had he not chosen to travel the path of the highwayman he might not have given Colonel Charters the opportunity to hold a baseless charge over his head, a charge he now knew was also being held, with some merit, over Gabriel's. Flynt had not yet decided what he would do in that regard. Men and women were condemned on spurious evidence of crimes they did not commit with some regularity, for any laws that were created by man could easily be subverted by man, so the fact that he was innocent of the assault mattered not a whit. Lord Gallowmire was an example of this. From all reports he had danced free of any repercussion for his crimes thanks to his position and influence. And so he would continue. Unless he was stopped.

It occurred to him that had he not dragged Charters from the mud and blood of Malplaquet he might also have avoided this current situation, for then he would not have drawn the man's attention and therefore would not have been recruited to the Company of Rogues. However, such speculation was pointless for, as a saying of his homeland would have it, what's for you, won't go by you. Call it fate, call it destiny, call it the will of a God in which he didn't believe, this was the way it was and he had to deal with it the only way he knew how.

He squinted through the spyglass again and saw it was Andrew Drummond who approached, and at a fair pace, too. Whatever had brought him here in broad daylight, it was important.

Unease caused his flesh to tingle. Something had occurred. And whatever it was, it couldn't be good.

Drummond's expression when he drew level confirmed his fears.

'You'd better come with me,' he said. 'It's Masilda...'

–

The first thing they saw as they crossed the stream to approach Oak Beck Farm was the door lying ajar. Nothing stirred. No smoke floated from the chimney. Flynt scanned the hill beyond the farmhouse to where the stones marking the graves of the Chilcott family stood and saw no movement.

'Perhaps she isn't here,' Drummond said with more hope than conviction.

It was possible, Flynt thought, but something told him it was not the case. She was here, he was convinced of that, but given what Drummond had told them, she might not be alive.

He drew a pistol and Gabriel did the same, then wheeled his horse towards the barn. Drummond reached under his coat and came out with a third.

The innkeeper saw his quizzical expression. 'It's time I did something. I can no longer allow things to simply occur. After today's events, I have to take a stand. I can only pray I am not alone.'

Flynt gave him a brief nod of thanks and nudged Horse ahead, alert for any sign of ambush. Gabriel had pulled the barn door open without dismounting and peered inside. He shook his head and headed back to rejoin them.

'Masilda!' Flynt called out. 'It's Jonas and Gabriel, we're with Andrew Drummond.'

There was no response, just the song of birds and that gave them no clue. If any Fitzgerald men lurked then they were in no hurry to make their move. Flynt swung down from the saddle and moved to the farmhouse door, drawing his second pistol. He halted, listened for sound from within, heard nothing. He pushed it open further with the toe of his boot, peered inside. The small room beyond was in shadow, a square of sunlight falling through the window to land on the stove, which appeared dead. A bench sat before it and a crude table with two chairs sat in the centre of the room. A large wooden cupboard that had perhaps been handed down for generations took up the other wall. He moved his position slightly to peep round the door, his eyes resting on a curtained area opposite. That would be where Masilda and Will slept, he presumed, and if she was here that was where he would find her. He already knew where the boy was. He stepped inside.

He motioned Gabriel and Drummond to keep watch and stepped across the threshold before again coming to a standstill on the earth floor. Still no sound greeted him, the only movement a slight flutter of the curtain ahead, the result of a window allowing in the summer breeze. He moved forward again, fearful of what he might find beyond that makeshift doorway. He held his breath, counted to three, then, using the barrel of one pistol to flick the fabric aside, stepped into the bedchamber, ready to bring down any of Fitzgerald's men he found there.

It was Cooper he saw, but he was beyond shooting. He lay on his back on the bed, his mouth open as if screaming, his eyes wide but seeing nothing, his body peppered with puncture wounds, a blade buried in a throat that oozed blood like a crimson neckerchief.

'What do you find, Jonas?' Gabriel's voice, yelling from the farmyard. Flynt took a final look around the room, then one more at Cooper's body, feeling no sadness at the man's passing, and walked back out to the sunlight.

'Masilda's not here,' he said.

A horse approaching the farmhouse from the rear made them all whirl, pistols at the ready. Drummond's hand trembled and he was obviously fearful but he didn't run, which was heartening. The horse walked into view and relief flooded through Flynt's body.

'I'm here,' Masilda said from the saddle. 'I had to catch this beast, for it had bolted.' She paused, her eyes filling with tears but she held them back, her face tight. 'They took Will.'

'We know.'

That was what Drummond had come to tell them, that Fitzgerald had arrived in the village with the boy held captive and two strangers forming part of his company. He had left immediately for Masilda's farm but had seen one of the riders standing guard so had ridden to fetch Flynt and Gabriel.

'Cooper?' Flynt had no need to say anything further.

Masilda's lips thinned. 'He entered my bedchamber uninvited. I saw to it that he will not do so again.'

Gabriel raised an eyebrow at Flynt but it was plain he understood what had happened. Drummond, though, was perplexed.

'I killed him, Andrew,' Masilda explained. 'There is another of Fitzgerald's brutes out back, who I shot with this.' She held up her musket. 'I was not so accurate as I was with my blade so wounded him only as he fled. Samson it was who brought him down and finished him off.'

They all looked at the dog now standing between her and them, his muzzle still stained with blood. Flynt took note not to irritate the animal in the future.

'I caught this horse because mine is a cart horse and not saddle trained,' Masilda continued. 'Fitzgerald's men all have fine steeds. That devil has my son and I will get him back.'

She spurred the horse into motion and whistled for Samson to follow. Flynt gave the interior of the house a final look and climbed back into the saddle, as if expecting Cooper to rise from the dead.

Drummond looked ill at ease. 'What about the dead men?'

'Let them lie,' Flynt said, his voice flat. 'They're not going anywhere and they are beyond caring.' He jerked the reins a little to turn Horse to follow Masilda, who was crossing the brook. 'We must look to the living.'

34

Masilda had to be dissuaded from galloping into Gallowmire to wrest her son from the clutches of Fitzgerald. Flynt saw in her the same determination he'd often seen in Cassie in Edinburgh. If her son, *their* son, was thus threatened she would move heaven and earth to save him. Flynt fully intended to do the same but knew caution had to be employed, and he said so, backed by Gabriel. Masilda dismissed them both but Drummond's words finally made her see sense.

'We must listen to these men, Masilda,' he said. 'You are spirited, to be sure, and God knows you are motivated, but this isn't something in which you are expert. Jonas and Gabriel, well, this is what they do, am I right?'

Neither of them denied their expertise in such matters, nor did they admit it, but Masilda reluctantly agreed to wait until they had assessed the situation in the village. Nevertheless, she remained edgy, her feet in constant motion, her grip on the stock of the musket tight, her expression fluctuating from diverted to intense.

Drummond showed them where they could tether the horses away from the road among a stand of trees and Masilda bade Samson to stay where he was, assuring them the dog would alert them if anyone should come by. The innkeeper led them on foot across the moorland to a point from which they could survey the village entire without being seen. They lay flat upon the heather and looked down on the scene below, Flynt studying through his spyglass the men moving through the village. They were all clad in the dark coats and hats that marked those in Fitzgerald's service but he could see no sign of their employer. Villagers stood sullenly by their doors, but few did anything to prevent the men from accessing their homes and those who did were pushed out of the way. He picked out Old Ralph, his pipe clenched between his teeth, exchanging words with a Fitzgerald man. The old man's stance was stiff, his hands at his side but his fingers clenching and unclenching as if he wished he held a weapon. Words were exchanged, and by the look of Ralph's expression they were far from pleasant. The exchange came to an abrupt end when the black rider drew a pistol and whipped the barrel across Ralph's face. The pipe flew from his lips as Ralph lurched backwards, only to be grabbed one-handed by his attacker and the pistol thrust against his temple. Martha Harland and her husband rushed from their own doorway a little way along the street and pulled Ralph free. The rider's smile was triumphant as he entered Ralph's home, leaving the three villagers staring after him. Ralph wiped a trickle of blood from where the pistol blow had broken his skin, then looked about him. He stooped and picked up the broken pieces of his pipe and stared at them as if in mourning.

'I don't see Will,' Masilda said.

'Neither do I,' Flynt said. 'I wonder if…'

He stopped abruptly when a face he recognised appeared in the company of a smaller, bespectacled man. Gabriel must have noted a change in his demeanour or expression. 'What do you see, Jonas?'

Flynt handed him the glass. 'In the doorway of the inn, two men. The taller of the two is Lord James Moncrieff, the other is stranger to me.'

Gabriel focused on the doorway, a sibilant breath escaping between his teeth. 'I know him.'

'Who is he? He has the look of a clerk or a bookkeeper.'

Gabriel maintained his scrutiny. 'He is neither clerk nor bookkeeper. His names are legion so who can say which one he uses this day.' He lowered the spyglass. 'He's a killer of men and a right efficient one at that.' He stared down the hill. 'Jonas, that wraith we discussed? If he be flesh, then there he stands.'

Flynt was aware of a querying glance from Drummond but didn't enlighten him as he took the glass in his hand and studied upon the man once again. Could such an unassuming little man really be the Wraith? When Gabriel had said he thought it would be such an individual, did he have this particular one in mind?

His deliberations were set aside when Fitzgerald appeared behind Moncrieff, his hands resting on the shoulders of Will Chilcott. Masilda saw them and snatched the glass from Flynt's grasp. She hissed something in her own tongue and began to rise but Gabriel hauled her back down.

'Stay hid, in the name of Christ,' he said.

Her head whipped round towards him. 'That is my son...'

'They'll cut you down before you reach him,' Flynt said. 'We must remain concealed until we formulate a plan of action.'

'Then formulate speedily, for my patience wears thin.' She peered through the eyepiece once more and frowned as Fitzgerald guided the boy across the green. 'What is he doing?'

A horse and cart waited under the gallows pole and Flynt could hazard a guess as to what Fitzgerald was about. When Masilda shifted her focus and tensed even further, he knew she had also made the leap. She lowered the glass again. 'He can't...' she said, her voice hoarse with terror.

Drummond, his eyesight not as keen as Flynt's, took the glass from her. 'Good God,' he said. 'The man is evil.'

One of Fitzgerald's men hefted Will onto the rear of the cart then climbed up beside him and draped a noose around the boy's neck. Fitzgerald wandered into the centre of the green and rested his clenched fists on his hips. He strutted in a circle for a few moments until he was certain that all eyes were upon him, and only then came to a halt.

'I want Jonas Flynt!'

His voice was faint but they could make out his words. Flynt took the glass from Drummond and swung it across the faces of the villagers. Before they had been surly but now, as they looked at the boy standing on the cart under the shadow of the pole, he believed he saw something else. Ralph, blood drying upon his cheek, leaned over to Martha at his side, murmured something and she nodded.

'I want him here and I want him now.' Fitzgerald pointed dramatically towards Will. 'That will be the price paid if my wishes are not met. The boy will die unless that hell spawn Jonas Flynt either comes to me willingly or is brought to me unwillingly but alive.'

He walked in a further circle.

'I know some of you are aware of where he cowers.'

He looked beyond the village, even shielded his eyes as he gazed at the hill on which they lay with the sun behind them.

He raised his voice even further. 'He may even be watching me at this very moment, and if he is, let me assure him that I will do as I say. The boy's life is forfeit unless you present yourself. A life for a life, Flynt. Yours for his. Let's see what kind of man you are.'

He made a show of removing a timepiece from his waistcoat.

'You have precisely one hour.' He raised one finger of his free hand. 'One. Hour. Your life for his, Flynt. Only you can save this poor lad.'

Flynt focused the glass on Fitzgerald's smiling face. The man was enjoying this. He breathed out harshly and resumed his study of the villagers. Yes, there was something more there than fear and resentment. There was fury.

Fitzgerald strode back to the inn, passing Moncrieff and the other man without a glance or a word. Flynt fixed on them, noting the sharp lines in his half-brother's face as he stared across the green to the boy on the cart. He thought he saw a slight shake of the head before he followed Fitzgerald inside, the other man's gaze lingering on the gallows pole, then sweeping around him before he, too, turned to vanish into the gloom beyond the inn's door.

'Jonas.'

The plea from Masilda in that single word was clear and when he looked at her he saw the tears brimming in her eyes.

'We must do something,' she said.

'I know,' he said.

He didn't know what else to say, so crawled away from the brow of the hill and, when it was safe to do so, rose to his feet. Gabriel caught up with him.

'I know what you're thinking, Jonas.'

Flynt glanced over his shoulder to ensure Masilda and Drummond were far enough behind not to overhear. 'I don't know what I'm thinking, so I fail to see how you can.'

'Because I know you and I know you intend going into that village. I assure you that sacrificing yourself will not change things. Don't do it.'

Flynt knew that it was fruitless to deny that was what he was thinking. 'I can't let the boy die for me.'

'Fitzgerald may simply be manoeuvring.'

'This is no manoeuvre. The man is mad. He will do this.'

'If he is mad then he will do it anyway.'

Flynt had already considered that. 'You would have me stand by and allow him to hang the lad? Is that it?'

'Damn it, Jonas, don't you see? This cause is lost. It depended upon the people finding the will to defend their own interests and they are manifestly unwilling to do that.'

Flynt wasn't as certain about that. 'We have Masilda and Drummond.'

'A man who could not even hold his pistol without trembling and a woman are not enough.'

'Need I remind you that woman proved herself well enough this morning.'

Gabriel ceded that point. 'You know I make no comment upon her gender, for I have known women to be most proficient at the slaying of men, but it is still not enough. We're

323

outmanned and outgunned and you submitting yourself meekly to the rope is nothing but folly.'

Flynt put a little more heat in his words. 'Then what would you have me do, Gabriel?'

Another snatched glimpse of Masilda revealed that she watched them most intently. Their conversation had been hushed but perhaps not sufficiently. Gabriel also glanced behind him, saw the woman's expression, and turned away, a flash of guilt crossing his own face. Masilda quickened her pace, as if she wished to contribute to the debate but Flynt waved her back. Thankfully, she did so.

He maintained his silence for a few paces and when he spoke he lowered his voice even further. 'Jonas, this is not our fight. You and I are thieves. We gamble. We wench. Well, I do, but you also did once. Thievery, gaming and women. That is our life. Not this, not fighting for lost causes.'

'A cause is only lost when you stop fighting for it. But you must look to yourself, Gabriel, for this never was your fight.'

'Nor yours.'

'Moncrieff made it mine when he had me lured here. Fitzgerald made it mine when he murdered Templeton and then involved the boy. I cannot desert the lad. I cannot desert the mother. I've done that before and won't do it again.'

'You didn't desert Cassie and her son, Jonas. They had their life and you had yours and neither the twain would mix. You know that. Throwing your life away this day will not benefit them or anyone else.'

Flynt sighed. 'This may well be my last day upon this earth, but it needn't be yours. Go now, back to London, or take to the road. You've proved to be a good friend and a stalwart companion but it's time to part.'

They had reached the horses now, where Samson lay in the shade of the trees, his tongue dangling from his mouth, but his eyes alert. Masilda stared directly at Gabriel as she and Drummond caught up with them. 'Well? Will you help me save my son?'

Her words were demanding but her tone was not. Her eyes implored Gabriel and he held her gaze for a moment before his eyes narrowed and he exhaled long and hard as he looked back up the hill as if he could see over it to Gallowmire. Flynt knew he was torn between friendship and common sense and didn't know which way he hoped his friend would go. Finally, Gabriel rubbed the back of his neck with his hand. 'Damn you, Jonas Flynt, I do believe I've spent too much time in your company because I think I've been infected by your altruism.'

Tears formed in Masilda's eyes and she reached out to Gabriel's arm. The touch was gentle, fleeting, but it was a way of showing an appreciation she could not vocalise. Gabriel looked at where her hand had rested so briefly and smiled.

'I think we'll need a miracle,' he said. 'Or at least a plan.'

All eyes turned to Flynt.

–

Fitzgerald seemed most relaxed while seated in a shaft of light that beamed through the inn's open door, sipping a glass of wine and occasionally glancing at the timepiece he had laid on the table before him beside a silver cane. Apart from the men moving outside and the occasional lacklustre protest from locals, the only sound was the tick of that watch marking the passage of time. The innkeeper had been nowhere to be seen so he had helped himself to the best bottle in the house, declaring it to be far from vintage but adequate. Moncrieff had declined to partake, and had taken a seat as far from him as possible, although that wasn't far enough, for the inn was cramped and dull, the sun barely penetrating the interior so illumination was provided by rushlights dipped in grease, which gave off a powerful stench. The floor was of hard-packed earth and Moncrieff was sure he could still smell the bullock blood that had been mixed with it to help it harden. The heavily beamed ceiling was low and the smoke from the rushlights gathered between the handful of small, poorly constructed tables and chairs, with a rough-hewn plank set upon trestles acting as a bar. Lester sat alone in a shadowy corner, as still as death, his face as impassive as ever. The man Moncrieff had been introduced to as Justice Black took up another table, a bottle of brandy before him. He was small and overweight, his face bloated with too much liquor, but he was obviously unhappy with the turn of events. His hand shook as he lifted cup to lip in an attempt to wash away his role in the affair.

The events earlier on that small farm and Fitzgerald's threat to kill the child churned Moncrieff's gut. He had been complicit in, and had ordered, the deaths of men before, for the work of the Fellowship required an extreme degree of ruthlessness. He had been happy to have the lawyer Gribble murdered to ensure his silence. Templeton had a price to pay for having broken his compact with his employer. He had sent men to dispose of Flynt. But in all those cases there had been a considerable remove between word and deed. That morning, as those men had dragged the woman away, and the boy was carted off over the saddle, the bile had risen in his throat. He had not intended this. He had no desire to see the mother and child being so abused. He thought of his wife, Katherine, back in London, and their joint desire for a family. He berated himself for not being more forceful in his protestations and, taking his own timepiece from his fob pocket to see that only a few minutes remained of Fitzgerald's time limit, he resolved to correct that failure.

Fitzgerald languished in the wooden chair, his left hand resting beside the glass, his other unseen under the table, presumably draped over his lap, his languid gaze towards the sunlight framed by the doorway. His attention drifted towards Moncrieff as he stood over him.

'You will put an end to this madness now.'

Fitzgerald's eyes seemed amused. 'Madness, my lord? I merely carry out your wishes...'

Moncrieff again felt guilt lance his chest but he ignored it. 'I did not wish innocents to be harmed.'

'Innocents. Now, there is a concept. Is anyone truly innocent?'

'The boy...'

'Ah! The boy. The son of a gypsy, so will there not be generations of guilt coursing through his blood? And what of the notion of original sin? And so I ask again, is anyone truly innocent? I know you are not, my Lord Moncrieff, and I am sufficiently self-aware to know that I am not. Justice Black has been party to many a dark deed in the name of law and order, or rather in name of his purse, have you not, your honour?'

The judge's head dropped to study the table and he raised his cup once more but made no reply.

Fitzgerald laughed. 'And Mr Lester over there, he carries more sin on his conscience than all of us together, although I remain unsure if he actually possesses such a thing as conscience.'

Lester must have heard him but remained motionless, his face and upper half of his torso shadowed. Lester was not Moncrieff's concern at this moment, though.

'Do you have a conscience?'

Fitzgerald raised the glass to his lips. 'Conscience is for clergy and women. Men must do what must be done, surely you above all understand that? After all, and I repeat, this was of your making.'

Moncrieff's anger bubbled over. He'd berated himself for his error in judgement, he didn't need this obviously deranged individual to continually remind him of it. He placed both hands on the tabletop to lean closer to Fitzgerald's smirk. 'I wanted Flynt dead, not women and children. Had you been able to retain a grip of the man it would be him on that cart and not an innocent lad.'

Fitzgerald shrugged. 'There's that word innocent again...'

'Free the boy.' Rage seethed over Moncrieff's words.

Fitzgerald placed the glass carefully back on the table. 'Matters have proceeded too far now. If you have lost your appetite for the game then so be it, but I have not. Flynt has shamed me and I will see him dangle. The boy is the means towards that end.'

'How do you know he will come?'

A quick glance at the watch face. 'He will come.'

'There are but minutes left on your ultimatum, how can you be certain?'

'Are you not certain? You know him better than I, do you not? Do you not believe he will come?' Moncrieff had not the first clue as to whether Flynt would sacrifice himself. Fitzgerald, giving him close study, smiled. 'I see you do not understand your adversary, Lord Moncrieff. But I do. I understand him decided well. He will come.'

'How can you have such surety? He may not even know of your threat.'

'He knows. The innkeeper is not present and he is a coun-tryman of his. Those Scotch vermin stick together like shit to a boot. Drummond will have gone for him as soon as he saw us with the boy.'

'Then you have no need for the charade out there. Flynt can be taken immediate upon showing himself. I am ordering you to free the lad immediately.'

Those mocking eyes rose again. 'That I cannot do.'

'Cannot or will not?'

A shrug. 'The distinction is immaterial. I will see this through, for a man must be deliberate and resolute in his actions or he will have nothing.'

Moncrieff's jaw tightened as he straightened. 'Then I will issue the order.'

Fitzgerald's right hand appeared with a small pistol aimed squarely at Moncrieff's chest. 'If you take one step towards that door I will not hesitate to put a ball in you.'

Moncrieff was at a loss for words. He had never before been presented with the business end of a pistol and he felt alarm tingle his flesh. His voice, when found, was strained by the combined effects of fear and outrage. 'You would threaten me?'

'I believe I stated previous that I do not threaten. I make promises, and I promise you most solemnly that I will not hesitate. I am exceeding deliberate and I am decided resolute, you see. Now, if you please, resume your seat and allow me to proceed with my business as I see fit. One way or the other this will all be resolved in a few minutes.'

'Do you expect me to simply sit back and...'

Fitzgerald's calm evaporated. 'Damn you, sir, I care not whether you sit or stand or float in the blasted air, but say nothing further for I will hear no more about it.'

Moncrieff bristled but he understood now that there was nothing further he could say that would deflect this creature from his path. He didn't return to his table, but took instead a seat beside Lester. He glared across the room at Fitzgerald, who paid him no further attention. The pistol was hid again and he poured himself another glass of wine as if he were in his own salon having recently enjoyed a fine meal.

'We must stop him,' Moncrieff muttered to Lester.

Lester took his time to respond. 'He is not my concern.'

'This cannot be allowed.'

Lester's tone was sharp, 'I have one priority here, and that is Jonas Flynt.'

'The boy...'

'The boy is nothing to me. Only the contract matters. And I will see it completed, one way or the other.'

'But...'

'Damn it all, sir, do not persist in this! I have stated my position clear and I will stand by it. Jonas Flynt dies, either by Gallowmire's hand or mine.'

Fitzgerald's eyes had turned towards them, and he raised his glass in a grim toast. Their voices, though hushed, had carried in that small, noxious, dingy little room.

And in that very moment, in that small, noxious, dingy little room in a forgotten little village on the way to nowhere, Lord

James Moncrieff knew that before this day was out he would either kill his first man, or be dead himself.

And then he heard a man's voice call from the street that a rider approached.

35

Flynt eyed the black-clad men lined up on either side of the village's main street. He counted ten but wasn't certain how many others were threaded on foot around the village. On the cart, Will twisted round to watch him, his eyes understandably round with terror, but he managed to present at least some measure of calm. Good lad, Flynt thought, never let them see the fear, for in that they can sense victory. The noose draped about his neck was loose, not tightened, so that was something. He gave the lad what he hoped was a reassuring smile as he had Horse walk at an easy pace towards the inn.

Fitzgerald emerged, placing his hat upon his head and carrying his cane, followed by Moncrieff and the man Gabriel said had many names.

'Jonas Flynt,' said Fitzgerald, squinting up at him against the sun, 'you have been something of an inconvenience.'

Flynt came to a halt. 'My apologies, for it was my intention to be considerably more than a mere inconvenience.'

'It would take better than a Scotch gutter rat with ideas above his station in life to discommode me in any serious way.' He rested the cane on his shoulder as if it were musket while making a show of looking back along the road. 'And where is the one named Gabriel Cain?'

'Gone,' Flynt said.

Fitzgerald's eyebrows shot up. 'He has deserted you?'

Flynt shrugged. 'The quality of friendship these days is not what it was. He decided this was not his fight and so he left.'

'After all he has done for you? Broken you free from my custody, helped you burn my barn, ambush my men?'

'When we came upon your men's handiwork at the lady's farm, he decided this struggle was not for him.'

Fitzgerald considered Flynt's words. 'If you lie and he interferes it will not go well for the boy, you do understand that?'

The man with Moncrieff had amended his stance slightly, his eyes roaming to the hill beyond the village, a tiny frown striping his brow for a moment then vanishing. His hand drifted towards one of the pistols in his belt. The movement was marginal, little more than a flinch, but Flynt caught it and knew he must move the conversation away from Gabriel.

He ignored Fitzgerald and addressed his next words to Moncrieff. 'What occurred on that farm was unnecessary.'

Moncrieff had the good grace to look away for a moment, his jaw tightening, and when his gaze returned to Flynt, he saw something that might have been regret.

'My man Cooper thought it most necessary,' Fitzgerald said. 'Where is he, by the way?'

'He won't be joining us, nor will his friend.'

'You killed them?'

'Let's say they will not trouble ladies further with their unwanted attentions.'

'And the, eh, *lady*?'

Flynt allowed a long moment to stretch. 'She won't be joining us either.'

Fitzgerald feigned sorrow and he stared across the green to the boy on the back of the cart. 'Such a pity, the poor lad be orphan now. That is a circumstance we share.'

'You share something else. You were the prime mover in the death of both your mother and his.'

Fitzgerald's mournful expression vanished to be replaced with what might have been a fond smile, as if he was momentarily reliving the moment of his mother's death. 'We all have skills, Flynt. Now, I would have you step down from that fine steed, for we have business to which we must attend. I have not eaten since breakfast and am extreme gutfoundered.'

Flynt climbed down and tied Horse to the hitching post.

'I forget my manners, however,' Fitzgerald said. 'Be you two acquainted? This handsome fellow is Lord James Moncrieff, the man who sent you to my domain.' He made a show of looking from Flynt to Moncrieff. 'By God, there be a strong resemblance, I think. Both dark-haired, both of similar height and build. You might be brothers.'

'We do not share blood,' Moncrieff said, flatly. Flynt couldn't tell if it was because he was weary of making such a denial or due to antagonism between he and Fitzgerald, for he sensed something brittle in the air not explained simply by his own presence.

'Of course not, such a notion be unthinkable,' said Fitzgerald.

'I do not know this other gentleman,' Flynt said, nodding towards the bespectacled man at Moncrieff's side.

'You may call me Mr Lester,' he said in a curiously high voice.

They studied one another as if each were predator and the other prey as Fitzgerald crooked a finger at one of his men. 'Henry, be so good as to relieve Mr Flynt of his weapons. We wouldn't want him to consider any form of aggression, would we? That would be most unpleasant and ill-advised, for if he did, it would be my pleasure to choose three random villagers and have them shot.' His stare was level as he said to Flynt, 'You do know I am capable of that, don't you?'

Flynt handed the man Henry his pistols, then raised his arms to allow him to check his pockets, stealing a glance towards the watching villagers. His eyes locked with Old Ralph, who had emerged from his doorway, and the old man gave him a nod. Henry's hands emerged from his pockets with Flynt's tinderbox and dub, and then ran his fingers under his coat and down his legs, where he found Gabriel's dagger thrust into his boot.

'My,' Fitzgerald said, 'you do not travel light, do you?'

'It's a dangerous world.'

Fitzgerald lowered the cane from his shoulder. 'This fine piece was, until recently, yours too.' He examined it closely then twisted the handle to free the blade within. 'A cunning device, to be sure.'

Flynt amended his position so he could look towards the elderly dyke builder who was now taking a casual walk away, exchanging a word or two here and there. 'As I said, it's a dangerous world.'

'It is indeed, but that is something that will not concern you much longer.' The blade was hidden once more and he tapped the cane against his neck.

'I shall wish that returned,' Flynt said.

Fitzgerald smiled. 'Where you are going you will have no need for it.'

Flynt's lips tightened. 'Wherever I'm going, Lord Gallowmire, I'm confident you'll be there ahead of me.'

Fitzgerald laughed, genuinely amused. 'By God, I almost regret having to hang you. But hang you I will and right smartly.'

'I thought I was to be tried,' Flynt said, noting that Ralph had said something to Martha Harland as he passed and she and her husband were easing back towards the door of their home. Ralph disappeared behind a clutch of villagers in the direction of the church. Flynt looked for him no further. He knew where he was going.

'You have tried my patience, sir, and that is sufficient for sentence to be passed.'

'So, due process is to be ignored?'

A sigh, then Fitzgerald turned to a rotund little man who kept himself to the twilight between the sunlight and the inn's exterior. 'Justice Black has heard the evidence and sentenced you in absentia. Is that not so?'

The little man hesitated but then nodded and retreated immediately back to the darkness of the inn.

'As you see, all proprieties have been observed.' Fitzgerald waved to his man. 'Bind him well for he is a tricky customer, then take him to the gallows pole.'

Pulling a length of rope from his pocket, Henry moved to do his master's bidding, as Moncrieff asked, 'And what of the boy? Where will he go, for he has no family now?'

'That is not my concern, nor will it be the boy's much longer. For it is my intention that he watch this man dangle and then he will follow. I want that half-blood whelp to witness his fate before he suffers it.'

Flynt fought the urge to lunge at Fitzgerald, knowing he wouldn't get far before he was brought down and couldn't risk being in any way incapacitated. He was gratified to see Moncrieff's look of horror as he stepped forward. 'You said you would set him free.'

'I said I do not make empty threats.'

'But Flynt has presented himself...'

Fitzgerald's good humour vanished in an instant. 'God's teeth, Moncrieff, I have warned you before about questioning my authority on my own land. I will not allow the boy to live so that he may become a menace towards me in a few years. He is gypsy and the blood feud runs deep with his kind. Now, if you have no stomach for what has to be done then feel free to leave this place and allow me to bring this interlude to its belated conclusion.'

Moncrieff's fury was clear in the tight set of his mouth and the continuing tension in his jaw but his eyes, when he dragged them from Fitzgerald to meet Flynt's, were deeply troubled. It was obvious that he was unhappy with the turn of events. Had he not been the one who had set this entire plan in motion, Flynt would have felt sorry for him.

'Blood feud also runs deep with my race,' Flynt said, observing other villagers almost casually melt away to their homes. 'As you shall see presently.'

Fitzgerald laughed. 'By God, such braggadocio is impressive. I hope you die as well as you talk, sir.'

His arms now secured behind his back, Flynt was propelled across the green towards the gallows pole. The boy watched them approach, still scared but his eyes questioning as to what was occurring.

'Fear not, boy,' Fitzgerald strode ahead of them waving Flynt's cane like a banner, 'your saviour is here!'

Flynt craned his neck to address Moncrieff walking behind. 'I trust you are pleased with your handiwork. Fitzgerald is not of right mind, so he at least has some form of excuse, not that it will assist him when the time comes, but you are motivated only by self-interest and hatred. Whatever happens in the next few minutes, you should pray that it is sufficient salve to your conscience for the evil you have wrought.'

Moncrieff blinked a few times but couldn't meet Flynt's gaze. Beside him, Lester remained alert, his head turning this way and that as if expecting attack. Ahead of them all, Fitzgerald seemed to be enjoying himself.

The man holding the cart horse's bridle jumped up beside Will, slipped the noose from around his neck and carried him from the cart. Flynt glanced to his left to where the bulk of Fitzgerald's forces had ranged themselves, seeing a new rider emerge from a small passageway between two houses to join them, but keeping a distance, his hat down low, his shoulders hunched. Flynt hid a smile, then gave the pale, solemn-faced boy a wink.

'Keep the faith, Will,' Flynt said. 'All is not lost yet.'

That provoked a laugh from Fitzgerald but Lester caught something in Flynt's tone that made him come to a halt, one hand resting on Moncrieff's arm to hold him back, the other finding the butt of a pistol as he continued to cautiously take close note of all around them. His presence and reaction proved three things to Flynt: that he was a professional, and that he was employed by Moncrieff and not Fitzgerald.

The third was that, if what Jonathan Wild had told him was true, he was not the Wraith.

Henry pushed him onto the back of the cart then climbed up to take the noose in his hand. The skin of Flynt's neck began to itch, an unpleasant sensation, and for the first time he grew anxious, even though he knew this was the way it was to be. Even though Henry had not yet draped it around his neck, he had never before been this close to the hemp, had always feared its touch, believing that one day it would take him, and here he was, gambling that this was not that moment.

Fitzgerald himself took hold of the bridle of the horse and rested the cane on its flank. 'As you be a stickler for the proprieties, Flynt, it is customary for the condemned to say some final words. Do you have any?'

Flynt looked away, as if taking a moment to consider, but searching for the black rider he had seen before. He had left the line of horsemen and was ambling towards them, his hat still low. The villagers' numbers had depleted considerably, as if they had an urgent appointment to attend. Old Ralph would have reached his destination by now. It was time, he thought.

'Well, Flynt? What final utterance do you have?'

Flynt settled on the nobleman. 'Hell's fury, Fitzgerald.'

'You promised that before and yet, there you are, staring into the abyss,' he raised the cane slightly, 'and here I am with the means of plunging you into that abyss in my hand.'

Flynt forced a smile. 'Are you acquainted with the words of the poet John Donne, Lord Gallowmire?'

Fitzgerald was puzzled. 'Poetry, Flynt, is that what fills your mind at this moment?'

'All life is poetry, Fitzgerald...'

And that was when the church bell rang out, causing Fitzgerald to whirl in shock in shock.

'Send not for whom the bell tolls, you mad bastard,' Flynt said, 'it tolls for thee...'

36

'Who tolls that bell?' Fitzgerald yelled, then repeated in a higher register, 'Who tolls that bell?! I ordered it never to peal.' He peered over the cart horse's back and shouted to the rider approaching at a faster pace. 'You there – stop that damned bell!'

The rider ignored him.

'Damn you,' Fitzgerald screamed, 'do you not hear me? Do as I order, still that bell.'

Gabriel swept his hat from his head and grinned. 'I hear you, but I like its sound.'

Everyone moved and all at once. Events merged, actions were taken simultaneously, each step part of a whole in a frenzy of motion, a blur of concerted effort to escape, to attack.

The bell tolling...

Drummond and Masilda erupting from Ralph's home. Drummond, without hesitation, firing his pistol at a Fitzgerald man running towards him, missing his mark but swinging a cudgel in his left hand at the man's jaw, sending him sprawling...

Lester moving, his pistol in his hand, deciding Gabriel posed the greater threat, aiming, spinning away when a musket ball buried itself in his shoulder...

Masilda dropping her musket, reaching behind her to produce two knives...

A roar rising, villagers bursting from their homes, carrying whatever weapons they could lay their hands on...

Fitzgerald stunned, shouting, 'Get back to your homes! Cease this now! I order you...'

The bell tolling...

Everyone moving...

Firearms popping, blades unsheathing, villagers hauling black riders from saddles, beating them with clubs, brooms, iron pots, even chairs...

Fitzgerald's screaming grew shrill. 'Stop this now! I am your lord...'

The bell tolling...

...and all at once...

Flynt slamming his shoulder forcefully against Henry, sending him flying from the cart to land heavily on his back...

Moncrieff dragging Will to the ground, covering him with his body...

Flynt jumping from the cart, swinging his boot into Henry's face, repeating the action when the man seemed to come at him, rendering him insensate...

Gabriel whirling to face a rider heading his way, firing, dropping him from the saddle...

The bell tolling...

Everyone moving...

Lester raising himself to his feet, his right arm dangling uselessly but another pistol already in his left...

Gabriel tackling another black rider, ducking under a sword swing and firing his second pistol...

Lester focusing on Flynt, drawing a bead, his eyes hard behind his spectacles...

Flynt, his hands still bound, ducking behind the cart as the ball buried itself in the wood...

The bell tolling...

...and all at once...

Lester searching the ground for the pistol that had fallen when he was wounded. Finding it. Stepping towards it...

Flynt lunging from behind the cart, head down, throwing his shoulder into him, pitching him backwards but also losing his own footing, landing on his knees, his arms still pinioned, the pistol a few feet away from them both...

The bell tolling...

Everyone...

Fitzgerald still foaming, men and women screaming and yelling...

...moving...

Masilda calling out to her son while running across the green towards Moncrieff, still shielding him...

...all at...

Samson surging ahead, all four paws leaving the ground to leap at a black-clad man trying to intercept Masilda, his teeth clamping around his wrist, the man wrenching his arm away and running off...

...once...

The riders in disarray, having no expertise in quelling such a rebellion, and their leader, still screaming for a halt to the rising, of little use. There were few of them still standing, the others lying immobile or groaning on the earth or fleeing. Fitzgerald swearing with considerable fluency, taking to his heels...

Moncrieff seeing him go, shooting to his feet, barely glancing around him as he took off in pursuit...

Lester springing to his feet, the bullet wound hardly bothering him as he lunged forward to snatch up the pistol. Flynt could do nothing to stop him...

'Don't do it...'

Gabriel standing on the far side of the cart, his arm steadied on its sides, a pistol held in a steady hand...

The bell ceased tolling.

Lester had frozen, his hand only inches away from the butt of his weapon, his eyes fixed on Flynt. 'You are not my target, Cain.'

'If you come for one, you come for both. Such is friendship but then, you never had a friend in your life, did you?'

The man remained hunched, his eyes narrowed behind his spectacles as he made a swift calculation. 'You expelled both pistols,' he said.

'I relieved one of Fitzgerald's men of his.'

'I didn't see that.'

'Not my concern.' Gabriel spoke as if they were having coffee at Nando's.

Lester's hand still stretched to the pistol. 'I thought you had given up the way of the sword for hire.'

'I had.'

On hearing this, Flynt glanced towards his friend, whose focus was intent upon the man standing so still with his hand hovering inches from the pistol butt, his expression colder than he had ever seen. Masilda watched as she squatted on her knees, holding her son close, one hand stroking his hair, his face, Samson circling them, ready to spring to their defence. The gunfire and angry cries had subsided and although activity around them remained, this conversation between two men seemed to be the only sound.

'Submit, Lester, and you can walk away,' Gabriel offered. 'You have my word.'

'You know the rules, Cain,' Lester said.

Gabriel's reply was businesslike. 'I do.'

'You know once a commission is accepted then it must be pursued to its conclusion.'

'Yes.'

'And even if I walk away this day, I will, must, return on another to complete the transaction.'

'I know that, too.'

'Then all you do is delay the inevitable.'

Gabriel did not respond at first. Then…

'Not if I kill you.'

'I believe that to be a pretence. Your pistol is empty.'

'There is only one way to find out.'

Lester thought about it, his eyes darting towards Gabriel. 'Your proposal is hardly sporting.'

'Killing is not a sport,' said Gabriel. 'It's sometimes a necessity, but it should never be a pleasurable pursuit.'

'I agree. But you would at least grant me leave of a fair opportunity of defence?'

'If I truly do practise some form of subterfuge, if this pistol be in fact empty, then you have more than a fair chance.'

There was some humour in Lester's smile. 'That's true.' His eye flicked to where Flynt still knelt, then to the pistol so near to his fingers. A split second would be all it would take for him to snatch it up. 'I did what I could to keep you away from this, Gabriel, to separate you from this man. It was not my wish to have you involved.'

'Yet involved I am, and...'

That was when Lester moved, his fingers wrapping themselves around the pistol and raising it in a move so quick, so precise, so fluid that Flynt barely saw it.

But Gabriel did. And he was quicker.

Lester didn't fall when Gabriel's ball took him. He straightened, swayed for a moment, the barrel continuing to lift, his mouth a tight line with the effort. Gabriel ran around the cart, his pistol wielded like a club. Lester, his eyes burning with an intensity Flynt had never before seen in a man, saw him move but did not amend his aim. The weapon settled on Flynt and there was nothing to be done, he was determined to fulfil his contract.

Then he coughed and his head drooped to his chest, where blood seeped through his waistcoat, like red wine spilled on a table covering. He blinked as if surprised, staggered back a few unsteady paces, his mouth opening but no words leaving his lips, just blood, dark blood, viscous blood, that streamed down his chin. His legs buckled and he fell first to his knees, his pistol arm now dangling at his side but still maintaining hold of the weapon as if it were somehow adhered to his hand. He tried to speak again but managed only a strangled croak before he pitched forward face first onto the ground.

Gabriel kicked the pistol away and stared down at the man for a moment as if saying a silent prayer.

Flynt gave him that moment even though he was aware the struggle was not yet over. Finally, he said softly, 'I need you to free me, Gabriel.'

With a final look at Lester, Gabriel said, 'Where is my knife?'

Flynt jerked his head towards Henry, lying unconscious behind him. 'In his pocket.'

Gabriel found the blade and sliced the bonds at Flynt's wrists.

'You were late,' Flynt said.

'I took a moment to enjoy the show.' He cut through the last bond. 'That's the second time I've had to do this. I think you must enjoy it.'

Flynt retrieved Tact and Diplomacy as well as his other goods from the unconscious Henry's pockets. 'Which way did Fitzgerald go?'

'Heading home, I shouldn't wonder,' said Gabriel. 'Your friend Moncrieff too.'

'Remain here, help the villagers control what's left of Fitzgerald's men,' Flynt said as he thrust Tact and Diplomacy into his belt and began to stride towards Horse, pausing to ensure Masilda and the boy were unharmed.

'Kill him, Jonas,' she said. 'He does not deserve to live.'

Flynt didn't reply as he surveyed wounded and the dead laying upon the green, villagers lying among the riders. There had already been a considerable amount of blood spilled on this land. A little more wouldn't make any difference.

'You don't want me to come?' Gabriel shouted after him. 'They are two to your one.'

'This part of the fight is mine alone,' Flynt said over his shoulder. 'Anyway, the bastard still has my cane...'

37

Fitzgerald had pulled one of his own men from a horse and leaped on its back to bolt from the village as though the devils of hell were on his tail, his body bent low over the animal's neck, his terrified glances backwards showing him to be the coward he was. By the time Moncrieff ran to where he had tethered his own mount outside the inn and galloped after him he was gone from sight. That was of no concern, for he knew where he would go.

The lord of Gallowmire had to die, of that he was certain. If the Fellowship was to progress further then it required not just competence in the extreme and an excess of ruthlessness but also trustworthiness to a consistent degree. Philip Fitzgerald had proved he was lacking in the first, possessed an overabundance of the second and absolutely none off the third. He didn't deserve to be part of the Fellowship.

He had also demeaned Moncrieff, defied him, disrespected him and so doubly deserved what was to come.

He found him in the courtyard of the hall, calling out to staff though none seemed to answer.

'Damn you lazy curs,' Fitzgerald screamed, 'where in hell's name are you all?'

'I believe word has reached them of your fall from grace, my lord,' Moncrieff said as he walked his horse into the courtyard. Fitzgerald spun around, a pistol raised in an unsteady grip. His eyes were wild, not just with the madness that afflicted him but also terror. Part of him knew that in a matter of minutes, the world he had killed to create had collapsed upon itself. Such worlds were built upon sand and all it took was the tolling of a bell and a wave of insurrection for everything to be swept away and all at once.

'Moncrieff,' Fitzgerald said, his relief obvious.

'You expected Flynt, perhaps?'

'Lester will see to him, I have no doubt.'

'Lester was otherwise engaged when I left.'

'Then I will give that dog Flynt what he deserves if he does come, mark me,' Fitzgerald said, the tension in his voice and the trembling of his hand making mockery of his words.

Moncrieff eased himself from the saddle, his back to Fitzgerald as if loosening straps on the horse. 'He will not be far behind, I would suggest.'

'Let him come, for he shall see that I am ready for him. He may have confounded me thanks to the rebellious scum in the village – and they shall pay dearly for this day, of that I assure you – but he will learn that a Fitzgerald is not easily vanquished. I will...'

'You will do nothing, my lord,' Moncrieff said softly, turning from his horse and raising the pistol he had taken from his saddlebag.

Fitzgerald instantly hefted his own weapon. 'You dare to threaten me, sir?'

'I do not threaten, I promise,' Moncrieff said.

Hearing his own words used against him, Fitzgerald sneered. 'You would turn on your own kind?'

'You forget, my lord, that I am not of your kind, as you yourself pointed out. My blood is from scurvy Scots while yours carries that of the Plantagenets.'

Fitzgerald blinked at his own words being cast back at him twice. 'I am Fellowship. You are Fellowship.'

'I hereby negate your membership.'

'High Council you may be but you do not have the power to do so. You cannot kill a Fellowship member without approval. Your own life would be forfeit.'

Moncrieff knew this was true but he was determined to see this through. He forced his voice to remain calm, even though every nerve fluttered like a frightened bird. 'You were killed during the revolt. A villager you had wronged, the woman perhaps whose son you threatened and who you left to be raped and murdered by your man. I am not even present.'

Fitzgerald's old confidence seemed to return and his hand ceased to quiver. 'I do not believe you have the stomach for the killing, sir. Otherwise why do we stand here and converse.'

Moncrieff swallowed, knowing that the man had sensed his nervousness. 'I wouldn't stake my life on that.'

'But you are staking your life, my Lord Moncrieff. You are one who has others do his bloody work, men like Lester. You are most careful not to get blood on your hands.' Fitzgerald smiled. 'I, on the other hand, have killed. I know the thrill of it and seek it out. I have watched the life fade from men's eyes and listened as the last breath left their body. And I will do so again. I live for the kill, sir, I thrive upon it.'

Moncrieff had intended to kill Fitzgerald. He wanted to kill him.

'Come then, sir, pull that trigger,' Fitzgerald taunted.

Moncrieff willed his finger to tighten but it would not.

'It is an action most simple,' Fitzgerald said.

In the name of God, why couldn't he pull that trigger?

'You fire, I fire, and if our aim is true one of us will live, one will die,' Fitzgerald said, his eyes dancing. In that moment, he had obviously cast the events in the village from his mind. In that moment, he was enjoying himself. 'Or perhaps both of us will die.'

Taking a life required a certain type of man, Moncrieff realised that now. A man who was born to it or trained for it, like Flynt. He was neither. He could order a death but could not cause it directly. If that was a form of cowardice then so be it.

The issue now was, how to extricate himself from this predicament with his life, for he was certain Fitzgerald would not allow him to simply walk away.

And so they stood in the summer sunshine, two men regarding each other across an empty courtyard, each waiting for the other to make a move.

And then Flynt made it three.

–

He had decided not to announce his approach so had brought Horse to a halt a little distance down the track and entered the courtyard on foot. He was glad he had done so because the scene he found – Moncrieff and Fitzgerald presenting pistols at one another – was not what he had expected. He had no firm idea what had led to this singular scene, although the look of disdain his half-brother had earlier shown towards the nobleman had suggested all was not well in their alliance.

'Gentlemen,' he said, 'it's a lovely day for a rebellion, is it not?'

They each turned, their weapons swiping in his direction. Naturally, he already had Tact and Diplomacy at the ready.

'Please,' he said, 'don't let me interrupt. Carry on with whatever you were doing.'

'Flynt,' Fitzgerald snarled.

'Thank you, Lord Fitzgerald, but I already know my name.'

'You are a damned menace.'

'That's better than an inconvenience.'

The grimace and familiar look creeping into Fitzgerald's eye told Flynt that he was prepared to fire. 'Think carefully before you pull that trigger. I witnessed your handiwork when you murdered Templeton, but he was but two feet from you. I am considerably further away and that pistol of yours is reasonably sturdy at close quarters but damnably erratic at distance. My own weapons, as you so correctly divined when you examined them, are finely wrought and the gunsmith rifled the barrels for greater accuracy. Also, I am most proficient in their use. You may fire first but I am confident the odds remain in my favour.'

Flynt's easy manner caused doubt to flick across Fitzgerald's face and he licked his lips. 'Moncrieff, you are the closer. Put a ball in him.'

Moncrieff was extremely pale and distinctly uncomfortable.

'Damn you, man, this is what you wished,' Fitzgerald said through clenched teeth. 'Shoot the fellow and be done with it.'

Moncrieff hesitated, his eyes dropping briefly to the weapon in his hand as if wondering what to do with it.

Flynt fixed his attention again on Fitzgerald. 'I know this was all a ruse to bring me here, Moncrieff, but I suspect you didn't anticipate that being in league with this madman meant you were shaking hands with the devil. Don't compound it by doing his bidding.'

Moncrieff took a deep breath as his mind worked and Flynt said nothing further. He had to let the man reach his own decision. As in the stand-off in that cramped room in the Rookery, as in Fitzgerald a few seconds before, he would see the trigger being pulled in Moncrieff's eyes before the finger tightened. He had Tact centred solidly upon him, Diplomacy on Fitzgerald, and he wouldn't hesitate to discharge either of them.

Fitzgerald's desperation grew. 'Damn you, Moncrieff, what delays you? In the name of Christ, shoot!'

Moncrieff's head rose, his eyes harder now. He had found something within to steel his resolve and he straightened his arm in Fitzgerald's direction. Fitzgerald realised too late what was about to happen, fell to a crouch, bringing his own pistol round.

Moncrieff's aim was faulty.

The ball flew harmlessly across the courtyard, Fitzgerald took aim.

Flynt fired.

348

His aim was better.

Fitzgerald's free hand shot to his throat and he emitted a grotesque gurgling sound as blood cascaded between his fingers like water through a fissure. He wheeled away, managed a few steps, a spasm of the finger triggering his pistol into the ground before his body folded and he toppled forward, his legs continuing to twitch as if he was attempting to rise like Lazarus. But he was already dead.

Moncrieff observed the agitation of the man's limbs in horror. By the time he tore his eyes away from it he saw Flynt with his second weapon still locked upon him.

'Death isn't pretty, is it?' Flynt said. 'Even in someone as deserving of it as he.'

Moncrieff shook his head, swallowed. 'I didn't know the stripe of the man when I engaged him in this enterprise,' he said, as though he felt some explanation, some plea, was required.

'I expect you didn't even try,' Flynt said, his voice flat.

Moncrieff's nod conveyed that was a truth he already accepted. He looked once more at the body, which had now ceased its exertions, then stared at the weapon in Flynt's hand. 'So now you will kill me.'

'I haven't decided,' Flynt replied, truthfully.

Moncrieff seemed to find some vestige of his old arrogance. 'It is what you do, is it not? Kill people?'

'On occasion, when circumstance requires it.'

'Then why hesitate? You hate me enough…'

'I don't hate you. The hate is on your side.'

'You hated my father.'

'He was a hateful man.'

'His blood runs in my veins.'

'And in mine.'

Moncrieff blinked. 'That I will never accept publicly.'

'Nor will I.'

Moncrieff was puzzled. 'You do not claim position? Even as bastard you would have some claim.'

'I care nothing for the Moncrieff name, title or fortune. In truth I abhor the very thought of sharing any blood with you or your father. I am content being the son of Gideon Flynt, a good man, and Jenny Flynt, a fine woman who was wronged. I am content in knowing I delivered justice for that wrong, even though she never saw it. You were not to blame for what happened so there is no justice in killing you.'

'I have tried to have you killed.'

'There is that,' Flynt conceded.

'I may do so again.'

'You have been most unsuccessful thus far and this latest, I would say inadvisable, escapade has taken a most tragic turn. I would, if I were you, put the past where it belongs and be satisfied that I have no interest in the family name.'

'But you have an interest in the Fellowship.'

'My interest in that body is fleeting and only when our paths transect.'

'They will do so most frequent, I believe. Your Colonel Charters is most fascinated by our work.'

'Killing you will not prevent that. The Fellowship will continue.'

'And it will prevail. We are the future.'

'Then the future looks bleak for us all.'

'We are interested only in commerce.'

'You are interested only in lining your own pockets, like most men of power. You will say that what is good for your pockets is good for the people but that is never the way of it. There will be those lower down who will feed from your table but it will be the crumbs you and your like throw them and make it seem like largesse.' Flynt lowered his pistol and sighed. 'Go, Moncrieff, and go now. You were seen with Fitzgerald and I suspect there will be villagers on their way who will not take kindly to your involvement.'

Moncrieff, clearly relieved, needed no further encouragement. He backed towards his horse, swung into the saddle and pulled the reins towards the archway leading from the courtyard. He held the horse steady as he looked down at Flynt. 'You are a curious individual.'

'Such has been said before.'

'We will always be enemies, you know that, do you not? When you cross the Fellowship in the future, what has occurred here will not prevent me from doing what I must.'

'I would expect nothing else of you,' Flynt said. 'And perhaps, when that moment comes, I will not be as merciful.'

Their eyes locked, each uncertain of their position in a world that had temporarily shifted, neither of them understanding why matters had ended with both of them still living.

'There is one thing more,' Flynt said, taking hold of the reins. 'Questions may well be asked regarding what has occurred this day. If they are, I would wish that you speak up for the people and instruct those who query regarding the kind of man Fitzgerald was. What was done here was done because the authorities didn't act in the past. A word from a peer of the realm would bear more weight than mine.'

Moncrieff stared around at the walls of the manor, the stables, the archway. 'The responsibility of what occurred here falls on my shoulders. I acted rashly and chose my accomplices poorly. You must believe me when I say that I have no desire to wage war upon women and children. I will do as you say. You have my word.'

Fleetingly, Flynt weighed up the chances that Moncrieff was simply saying what he needed to in order to save his own life. He knew not fully the why of his mercy, only that in that moment he could not bring himself to pull the trigger. He had already committed patricide, he could not add fratricide to his list of sins. Moncrieff had shown regret over the manner in which events had played out, had protected Will and had pursued Fitzgerald. Old Lord Moncrieff would never have displayed such repentance, would never have taken such action, so it proved that though the son carried the father's blood, they were not completely alike. Their father. With a nod, he relinquished the reins and Moncrieff prodded his horse into motion. Flynt watched as his half-brother disappeared from view beyond the archway without a second look back.

Only time would tell if he might come to regret his mercy.

38

The following morning Flynt and Gabriel watched from their mounts as the gallows pole was dismantled and prepared to be burned on the green.

'There will be no more of that in Gallowmire,' Drummond said.

'There may be investigation made,' said Flynt.

'Of what?' Drummond said, smiling. 'Lord Philip Fitzgerald has taken himself away somewhere, we know not where. He has no kin, no issue that we know of.'

'What did you do with his remains?'

'Buried, high on the fells, where he planned to put you to rest. He will never be found. Justice Black is a concern, however.'

They had found the man cowering in the inn when the action was over. When he returned from the hall, Flynt and Gabriel had taken the man aside and with a few forceful words had made it clear that he was up to his neck in the murderous deeds in Gallowmire and that neck was forfeit if he did not support the people. The terrified judge assured them he had seen nothing, knew nothing and, in fact, wasn't even in Gallowmire when that nothing occurred.

'I don't think you have anything to fear from him,' Flynt said. 'Do you trust all to remain silent regarding the true events?'

Drummond was confident. 'We all be in this together. Philip Fitzgerald had no friends here, of that you can be assured.'

'Nevertheless, if questions be asked, you send word to me at the Golden Cross in London. I will have powerful people speak on behalf of the village.'

Whether Moncrieff would keep his word was a test for the future but perhaps Charters could provide support if needed. He watched Masilda hand Will a torch and point to the pile of timber that had once been the gallows. The boy stepped forward and set light to the kindling on which it lay. The wood was dry and ready for the flame, which took hold immediately. The assembled villagers cheered.

'How many of them died?' Flynt asked, facing Drummond again. 'Yesterday.'

Drummond sighed. 'Three, another five wounded. But it had to be done. Casualties among the riders were greater. The rest were set free with a warning never to return. I think that is a warning they will heed.'

Flynt noted the pride in the man's voice. 'And you, Andrew, you'll remain here? You'll no return to Scotland?'

'I said this was my home and I meant it. I'll end my days here. There's nothing for me back there.' He looked to the north, where beyond the moorland and the hills lay Scotland. 'I was married, once. We grew up in Kelso, had known each other all our lives. Sometimes it felt we had never spent a day apart.' He paused, his hand reaching out to stroke Horse's mane in an absent manner. 'She died in childbirth. The bairn too. I couldn't remain in a place where everywhere I went, every person I met, reminded me of her in some way. So I came here, took over the inn. And here I will stay.'

Any words that came to Flynt's mind sounded hollow, so he merely nodded and held out his hand. 'It's been an honour, Andrew Drummond.'

The innkeeper managed a smile. 'It's been an experience, Jonas Flynt.'

As Drummond moved round Horse to shake hands with Gabriel, Masilda led Will by the hand towards them, the flames of the burning gallows leaping high. Samson, as ever, was at their heels.

'You leave now?' she asked.

'Aye,' said Flynt.

'You know you are welcome to remain here,' Drummond said.

A slight smile teased Masilda's lips as she glanced at Gabriel. 'The other one, too.'

Gabriel laughed and ruffled Will's hair. 'Farewell, lad. Watch out for those geese.'

Masilda recognised that this was goodbye. 'Then we thank you for all that you have done and wish you God speed, and know that, should you ever need to find that peace, there is a place here for you.'

Flynt leaned down to Will. 'You must look after your mother, young man. You are the man of the house and you have responsibilities.' The dog watched him with wary eyes. 'You and Samson.'

The boy nodded and his hand rested on Samson's head. With a final nod to Masilda and Drummond, they urged their horses into motion, trotting round the green, watching the flames consume the hated gallows pole, accepting the grateful thanks of villagers who lined the route, including Old Ralph and even Martha, her face still hard as granite. They were almost at the bridge when they heard a little voice shout, 'God speed to you both. And thank you for all you have done.'

They halted and looked back to see a grinning Masilda standing behind her son, one hand on his shoulder, the other fingering his hair. The vision of another woman embracing her son sprang into his mind and Flynt felt something catch in his throat and burn behind his eyes as he touched the brim of his hat. Will smiled and waved. Even Samson wagged his tail.

They left the village, but paused at the top of the same hill from which Flynt had first surveyed it. Masilda and Will remained where they had left them, outside the inn. They heard his little voice drift towards them. 'Goodbye, Jonas and Gabriel. We'll never forget you.'

They flourished their hats in return before trotting over the brow of the hill.

–

They rode east for a few miles until, at a crossroads, one road heading north and south, the other east and west, they stopped.

'I think this must be where we part, Jonas,' Gabriel said. Flynt was not surprised, for his friend had been unusually silent between the village and this spot and he had suspected something troubled him. 'I do not relish returning to London only to work further for Charters. I do not have your nobility.'

Flynt had still not decided what he would do with the information Gabriel had provided regarding the robbery that Charters wielded against them both. 'It isn't nobility, it's self-preservation.'

Gabriel's smile was tinged with sadness. 'No, my friend, you do it because you believe you might do some good. There's something within you that I don't possess. A need, perhaps, to do the right thing.'

'And does the Wraith not have that need on occasion?'

To Flynt's eye Gabriel's smile seemed a little suspended, as though it could fall at any time. 'Do we return to that, Jonas?'

'Lester was not the Wraith.'

'There is no Wraith.'

'I think perhaps there is, or was.'

'Very well, I shall play this hand with you. Deal your cards.'

'Jonathan Wild informed me that the individual who used the soubriquet kept distance between himself and whoever engaged his services. Lester was in plain view alongside Moncrieff and even Fitzgerald. He was too open. The Wraith, as his name suggests, keeps himself hid.'

'And yet he was fixed upon ending your existence to the very end, just as the Wraith would have done. If he existed.'

'A code of professionalism that they shared, and one of which you were aware, Gabriel.'

Gabriel took a breath, recalling the conversation at gunpoint. 'I asked you before that if I were he, then why do you still breathe? I have had ample opportunity to fulfil any contract.'

'I don't believe there was a contract, apart from the one Lester had with Moncrieff. He himself supplied the final part of the riddle when he told you that he'd made efforts to separate us, to ensure you were kept away from what was to follow. I think it was he who leaked the rumour that the Wraith was in London and linked my name to it, knowing that it would reach me, then trusting that circumstance would make me suspect that all was not as it seemed.'

'Which you did.'

'Which I did.'

Gabriel's smile still dangled precariously but there was a hard glitter in his eyes. 'And so, here we are.'

'Indeed,' Flynt said, 'here we are.'

Gabriel sighed, his hand casually moving to rest on his lap, near to the butt of a pistol. Flynt noted the movement but didn't match it. He didn't believe he needed to.

'I will say this then,' Gabriel said, looking away for a moment. 'If you are faulty in your reasoning, and Lester was the Wraith, then you're safe from him.'

'And if my reasoning is not faulty?'

There was a silence for a moment as Gabriel turned his eyes back to him, the smile gone completely and only the sadness remained. 'Then you're still safe, for he never posed a threat to you.'

The words lay between them for a few moments until a breeze carried them away.

'I have many questions, Gabriel.'

'I know,' said Gabriel.

'You will not answer, I take it?'

Gabriel's smile returned but was tinged with melancholy. 'A man takes a wrong turn, Jonas, and cannot find his way back.'

'Then perhaps he should stay in one place for a period. Somewhere he is welcome.'

Gabriel looked along the trail they had followed, knowing Flynt did not refer to London.

'I think there might be a life for a man there, with Masilda,' said Flynt.

'No,' Gabriel said. 'It is tempting, I will admit, but men like us do not belong here. Our pasts never allow us to find peace.'

'We all have pasts. We all deserve peace.'

'Some pasts deserve peace,' Gabriel said. 'Others don't. The past cannot be changed. It's something we carry with us wherever we go. Some of us can make amends for it, those of us with a streak of altruism. Others cannot.'

'The future is in our control, though.'

'Not for men like me. My past is a burden, it weighs upon me and I cannot set it aside.'

Flynt understood that this was as close to an admission as he would get. He had further questions but he sensed none would be answered. 'Very well,' he said. 'Where are you headed?'

The cocky smile returned. 'Where we are all headed, a lonely death, a cold grave and a warm welcome in another place.'

'It needn't be such.'

Gabriel's eyes were soft again. 'It's the path we choose that dictates the end we deserve.' He blinked away the regret. 'And you, Jonas. What path will you choose now? That way,' he indicated to their left, 'is to Scotland and that childhood sweetheart, t'other is to London and the beautiful Ms St Clair. You must decide in which direction your heart lies. Don't take the wrong turn.' Gabriel held out his hand. 'Good times and bad times, Jonas.'

Flynt took the hand in his. 'And those in between.'

With a final smile, banishing the sadness from his eyes, Gabriel rode across the intersection. 'We'll meet again, Jonas,' he said as he moved. 'Here or in hell.'

Flynt laughed. 'Let's hope it's the former.'

Gabriel laughed and had his horse pick up the pace to a gallop. The last Flynt saw of him was as he disappeared behind a stand of trees and only the sound of the hooves on the dry ground remained. Soon, that too was gone.

Flynt sat alone in the silence and looked from north to south, unsure where his heart truly lay.

Historical Notes

The previous two titles in this series were each based on actual events but this one is all fiction. However, as before, I have threaded real London locations through the narrative. The taverns, inns and – yes – Nando's all existed, as did Lintot's Bookshop.

Jonathan Wild, Jack Sheppard, Blueskin Blake, Edgeworth Bess were living, breathing individuals in 1716 but the versions presented here are my invention.

Sir Isaac Newton, obviously, also was a real-life historical figure but again the character here is my personal take, as is John Duck, who did at one time have a fencing school in Little White's Alley. His sister, as far as I am aware, is my invention. As a side note, he had a daughter, Ann, who ran with a criminal gang and was later executed for robbery and murder at Tyburn. From the condemned cell at Newgate she wrote:

> I acknowledge I have been in almost all the gaols in London, viz. Wood-street and the Poultry Compters; New-Prison, Clerkenwell Bridewell, three times in the London Work-House, once in Bridewell Hospital, and several times in Newgate. I hope none will reflect on my poor mother, for if I had taken her advice, I had not brought myself to such an unhappy end. I hope my sister will take warning by me, and take care what company she keeps, for ill company has been the ruin of me. So the Lord have Mercy on my poor soul.

Gallowmire, its river and lord of the manor, are a complete invention, so please don't go looking for it on any map, old or new.

Acknowledgements

As usual, my thanks go to many people, because although an author's life is solitary in the conception of the child that is a book, it takes a village to raise it.

So I am grateful to my agent Jo Bell for being in my corner, to my editors Kit Nevile and Miranda Ward for their keen eye and to all at Canelo for their hard work in bringing the adventures to a wider audience.

Also to my author friends Caro Ramsay, Theresa Talbot, Gordon Brown, Michael J Malone and Denzil Meyrick who are always available for support and advice. Gratitude also goes to those authors who read and commented on the previous books, including Ian Rankin, Ambrose Parry, SG MacLean, James Oswald, Marion Todd, DV Bishop, Craig Russell, the aforementioned Denzil Meyrick (he gets everywhere), David Gilman, Alison Belsham, Paul Doherty, Neil Broadfoot, Laura Shepherd-Robinson, Anna Mazzola, Chris Lloyd, Mark Ellis, Candace Robb, Michael Jecks, Alis Hawkins.

And huge thanks to the festival organisers, bloggers, reviewers, librarians, booksellers and, of course, the readers, without whom these words would be little more than fading shadows on a page, unread, unloved, unlived.

Finally, my thanks to Sarah Frame, who has made life so much better.

More from the Author

Blood City
Crow Bait
Devil's Knock
Open Wounds
The Dead Don't Boogie
Tag – You're Dead
The Janus Run
Thunder Bay
The Blood is Still
Death Insurance with Morgan Cry
A Rattle of Bones
Where Demons Hide
Children of the Mist
Tigers in the Dark